Praise for Nicholas Luard

GONDAR

"Exotic, imaginative, and gorgeously readable – exciting enough to take me back to childhood nights of reading Rider Haggard by torchlight under the blankets"

Sunday Times

"Sex, violence, horror, beauty and love in a well written and very readable mix"

Publishers Weekly

"Authenticity, drama, adventure and excitement . . . I defy any reader to skip a single page"

Gary Jennings, author of Aztec *and* Spangle

KALA

"Adventure and romance on a lavish scale . . . a fascinating feat of storytelling"

New York Times Review of Books

THE ORION LINE

"Sensitive, exciting, and brilliant"

Daily Telegraph

About the Author

Nicholas Luard, novelist and explorer, is the author of fifteen books including the international bestseller *Gondar*. A passionate conservationist, he has lived and worked in Africa, and now divides his time between Wales and London. He is married to the writer Elisabeth Luard.

Sanctuary

Nicholas Luard

CORONET BOOKS
Hodder and Stoughton

Copyright © 1995 by Nicholas Luard

First published in Great Britain in 1994
by Hodder and Stoughton

First published in paperback in 1995
by Hodder and Stoughton
A division of Hodder Headline PLC
A Coronet paperback

The right of Nicholas Luard to be identified as the author
of this work has been asserted by him in accordance with the
Copyright, Designs and Patents Act 1988.

10 9 8 7 6 5 4 3 2 1

All rights reserved. No part of this publication may be
reproduced, stored in a retrieval system, or transmitted,
in any form or by any means without the prior written
permission of the publisher, nor be otherwise circulated
in any form of binding or cover other than that in which
it is published and without a similar condition being
imposed on the subsequent purchaser.

All characters in this publication are fictitious
and any resemblance to real persons, living or dead,
is purely coincidental.

A CIP catalogue record for this book is available
from the British Library

ISBN 0 340 62588 0

Typeset by Hewer Text Composition Services, Edinburgh
Printed and bound in Great Britain by
Cox & Wyman Ltd, Reading, Berks

Hodder and Stoughton
A division of Hodder Headline PLC
338 Euston Road
London NW1 3BH

For Honey Luard

1

'How about there by the big pool?'

Shouting to make himself heard above the roar of the helicopter blades, the stocky young man beside the pilot pointed downwards into the gorge. The pilot shook his head.

'Too narrow,' he called back. 'The up-draughts from those walls would give them kittens.'

The pilot glanced over his shoulder. The two passengers in the seats immediately behind wouldn't have heard him, but he smiled reassuringly all the same.

'We'll try downriver,' he directed. 'If it opens out, there'll be less turbulence.'

The tempo of the blades increased and the helicopter surged forward. Through the plexiglass canopy the pilot's gaze swept from side to side, quartering the river's winding path.

He'd been flying charter helicopters out of Nairobi for almost twenty years, but he'd never before been this far north-west into the back country beyond the Aberdare Mountains. It was the loneliest, most desolate part of Africa he'd ever seen. No scenery, no hunting concession camps, no tourist lodges, not even a native village.

Nothing – except wilderness.

Still, if this was where they wanted to go, he was happy to fly them in – more than happy with Boy Cameron as the charterer. The pilot raised his head and studied his passengers again in the mirror above the control console.

Boy Cameron he knew well. Not personally, of course, but in the way that everyone knew of the multi-millionaire businessman. Cameron was the best-known tycoon in Africa.

His interests ranged across the continent. In several countries, it was rumoured, his companies dominated and manipulated the entire national economy.

Cameron was reputedly seventy-nine, but could easily have been fifteen years younger. He was tall and powerfully built with a mane of white hair, a florid strong-jawed face, and a dynamic domineering manner which was punctuated by flashes of captivating grace and charm.

The woman with him was an enigma.

Cameron had introduced her as his wife. The pilot was surprised. As far as he knew Cameron had never married, although over the years his many female companions had been regularly photographed by the press. The pilot had never seen or read anything about this one.

If the woman really was his wife, Cameron must have married her very recently.

She was in her forties, the pilot guessed. Although pale and tense – a legacy of some illness perhaps – she was still one of the most beautiful women he had ever seen. Her figure was like a girl's, firm and supple and graceful. Her legs seemed to go on and on for ever. Her face was flawless, and her hair shone a deep dusty-gold in the early-morning sun.

More than anything, it was her eyes which struck him. Huge and direct beneath sleepy eyelids, they had the deep luminous blue of African violets.

'This should do.'

The pilot nudged the young man, a hunter-guide Cameron had hired to set up camp and oversee the five African boys huddled together at the rear of the helicopter behind the third European passenger, a thin middle-aged man in glasses. Cameron had introduced him as what sounded like a palaeontologist – whatever that was.

He pointed and the young man peered down again.

A plume of smoke was rising from a small fire on a broad shelf of earth at a curve in the bank of the river. The guide nodded. The place looked an ideal set-down point and camp site. The pilot circled lower. He banked to make a final check, then they both frowned.

The fire, they'd assumed, had been made by a group of

the nomadic hunter-gatherers who sometimes roamed the region. It hadn't. Standing beside the flames and gazing up was a solitary white man. Puzzled, the pilot feathered the blades, and put the helicopter down.

A few moments later his passengers were disembarking.

The man walked towards them from the fire. He was about fifty with a hard muscular body, a flat high-cheekboned face, and narrow penetrating eyes, slate-grey and ridged above the eyelids with scar tissue. He was obviously as surprised by their arrival as they were to find him there.

When he was twenty yards away he saw the woman and checked in mid-stride. At the same instant she saw him. She froze at Cameron's side, and the two stared at each other. Aware that something strange was happening, everyone else stopped too. Even the African boys' chatter died away and they stood still.

For several long minutes the two gazed at each other in silence.

The smell of wood-smoke drifted through the hot African morning, and the sound of water cascading over the rocks echoed up the gorge. Then, hesitantly, they approached each other. They stopped again with only a few feet between them.

'Billy?' the woman said hesitantly.

The man nodded.

The woman stared at him in disbelief, and a tremor ran through her. She tried to speak. Her mouth opened and closed, but no words came out.

Eventually she managed to say, 'This is the same place, isn't it, where the elephants came?' Her voice was barely a whisper.

'Yes.'

She tore her eyes from his face and glanced round. Of course it was here. Now she looked at the gorge she remembered every detail of the way the glittering sandstone cliffs folded round the river.

She closed her eyes for an instant, shivering with a mixture of weakness from her breakdown and the sharpness of the memories that were surging through her. She began to stumble and thought she would faint.

The man stepped forward and caught her arm.

'You're tired,' he said anxiously.

His voice had the same nasal rasp, the rasp of the South London slums, that she remembered even more vividly than the gorge. She recovered and smiled.

'No, I'm fine,' she said. She paused and frowned. 'Is it really you, Billy?'

'It's me—'

He smiled back.

It was the tight wary smile she remembered just as vividly and painfully as his voice. Nothing had changed, not even the aggressive way he'd placed his feet four-square in the sand before her like a prizefighter challenging contenders to move him.

She swayed again and he put his hand under her elbow. 'Come and sit down.'

He led her away out of the sight of the others, and sat her down on a rock above the water.

'Why have you come back, Violet?'

'Why have you— ?'

They both spoke almost at once. They broke off and laughed awkwardly. Then, haltingly and uncertainly, they started to talk.

After more than forty years apart, they had the unfinished stories of two separate lifetimes to exchange.

The Garden of Eden

The Valley

Green as a garden, the valley drowsed under the searing
midday heat.

The great grey creatures moved slowly through the broken
sunlight and shade at the river's edge as they had done almost
from the dawn of time. Many other animals came to the river
to drink, but the elephants were the oldest of all.

The river and the valley had a far-off beginning, just as one
remote day they would have an end.

The beginning came when the weight of the sky bore down
on the earth. The clouds had rolled out of the west, bringing
rain in their wake. Where the earth felt the weight of the
sky, a crack formed. Through the crack a spring bubbled up.
The spring became a river which spread out and watered the
plain beyond, so that its fertile red soil blossomed with trees,
fruits, and grasses.

Herds and packs and clans of other creatures were drawn
to the place, but they came in the wake of the elephants which
found it first.

Neither the river nor the valley had a name.

Two million years ago, as it was that morning, nothing
had a name. There was no one to name anything. The
nameless place existed for itself alone, as a tiny physical
feature in the planet's time and space, and a source of
food and water in the consciousness of the animals of the
African plains.

In two million years' time, those who gave names to things
would describe the protein the valley produced as the building
blocks of life. That day the valley was simply a shallow bowl

of extraordinary natural richness, a cornucopia of nutriment unmatched anywhere on the planet's surface.

Over the millennia that followed the rains would gnaw away at the sandstone and bedrock until they had carved out a deep gorge for the river to flow through. That morning the water had not yet made a bed for itself, still less defined and enclosed the valley.

The plain the river irrigated was a mosaic of forest, copse, thorn scrub, and grass savannah.

Some of the creatures who fed off it were destined to be lost as the millennia passed, unable to adapt to changes in the climate or the pressures of competition from more skilful and versatile animals. Others, better equipped, outlasted the changes and the challenges.

That particular day, the drowsy innocent day of the world's morning, a dozen lion prides were sleeping out the heat within a mile of the river. Herds of antelope were grazing the sun-dried grasses. Leopards, dozing too, lay on the branches of the trees in the patches of forest. Rhino lumbered along the game tracks, looking like relics from an even remoter past, from the age of the dinosaurs.

The pounding feet of buffalo herds raised clouds of dust as they streamed across the landscape. Zebras neighed and whinnied and jostled in packs of dazzling black and white stripes. Wild cats, servals, civets, and genets, mewed and battled for territory. Wheeling vultures patrolled the skies, interacting with the hyenas and jackals prowling below in their common search for carrion.

They were all survivors. None of them was as well-equipped for survival as the elephants.

The elephants had no predators. They were simply too large and powerful. Very occasionally a new-born elephant calf might be killed by a particularly hungry and daring group of hunting lionesses, but almost always the prides knew better – they left even the calves alone. The elephants weren't only vast and strong. They were well-organised.

They functioned not just as herds but as tightly knit groups within the herds. A young elephant not only had a mother. It was surrounded, taught, and protected by a whole extended family of aunts, sisters, and female cousins. By the time it broke away from them at the age of sixteen or seventeen, it not only had its own awesome maturing strength but an entire range of skills and knowledge that had been passed on to it.

From then on nothing except the infernos of the savannah fires could harm it. It could effortlessly travel immense distances. It could browse or graze with equal facility. It could count on the support and companionship of the herd, on the accumulated wisdom of generations of the herd's ancestors. Its only need was for water.

An adult elephant requires up to eighty gallons of water a day. To the elephants of the valley, the river at its centre was literally the river of life.

The herd's wisdom was entrusted to the females.

It was impossible to know why the females rather than the males had been chosen. Perhaps millions of years earlier still, the dynamics of the species' breeding had demanded that the cow elephants, who carried the embryos, gave birth to the young, nurtured, educated, and reared them, should also assume ultimate responsibility for the herd's survival.

It was always the herd's dominant matriarch who led them down to drink.

The day passed.

The heat lifted. The light poured away from the darkening sky and evening approached. On the branches the leopards opened their eyes, and blinked. In the tall trimedra grasses of the plain, red-gold and rustling in the sunset, the lionesses yawned and uncoiled their limbs. There was a sharp hollow of hunger in their bellies.

They stood up, sniffed the air, and readied themselves to hunt.

On the bank of the river a towering grey shape emerged from the bush. She raised her trunk, spread her nostrils, and tested the air. She explored it carefully, sifting through every scent spore carried to her on the evening breeze. Usually she trumpeted and moved down to the water, the signal that it was safe for them all to drink.

Today was different.

She tensed and stood immobile, analysing the information brought to her on the breeze. Her senses told her there was a new creature in the valley. A scavenger, two-legged, tuskless, weak-limbed, and as hairless as a snake. She had occasionally encountered the creatures before on the distant plains and forests where the herd sometimes roamed.

It was part of her accumulated knowledge that they had no power to harm her, but she was wary and uncertain. The creatures might be harmless, but none of them had ever entered the valley before.

She scanned the breeze again. There was only one and from its palpitations – its movements were transmitted in pressure waves across the air – it was weak, perhaps dying. Its presence was strange, but the creature posed no threat.

Secure in what she knew, the matriarch raised her trunk and gave the signal. Her ancestors had done the same for millions of years before. Her descendants would do it for millions of years to come.

A moment later the bank was lined by the rest of the herd.

The matriarch's knowledge was ancient and trustworthy. It was, however, only ancestral wisdom, not understanding. Had it been understanding, her brain might have taken the first step towards realizing the weak fork-legged interloper was the most dangerous animal which had ever entered the valley.

The elephant's mind was incapable of ordering and assessing the possible consequences of the creature's intrusion. All she could do was dismiss it as an immediate threat and lead the herd to water.

Silent in the shadows, the scavenger watched and waited until the great grey animals had drunk their fill. The scavenger wasn't yet lord of the earth. Those who later gave names to things would have said the sixth day of creation hadn't yet dawned.

Not yet but soon, very soon.

There are certain conjunctions of time and place which act as a catalyst, a fusing together of elements which create something new and different from anything that has gone before. Then the world and maybe the universe changes.

The arrival of the hairless two-legged scavenger in the valley was perhaps the most momentous incident in the planet's history.

Only the matriarchal elephant registered the creature's presence – and she was utterly unaware of its significance.

PART ONE

Africa: 1944

2

'Do you know how many games of racing demon I've played this morning? Eleven! And now she's bored and it's still an hour to lunch. She's driving me to distraction!'

Mrs Somerset tossed her head in despair.

'For heaven's sake, Nanny, there must be *something* we can do!' she wailed.

Nanny Mackenzie was sitting in the armchair by the porthole. She lowered her knitting to her lap, and gazed at Margaret Somerset over the top of her gold-rimmed glasses.

Nanny had been with the tall imperious young woman in front of her for thirty years. She'd looked after her as a child, stayed on to take care of her clothes when she grew up, and then when Margaret married and gave birth to her own daughter, Nanny had remained to look after the baby.

The child, Violet, was five now. At the same age Mrs Somerset had often been, in Nanny's words, 'more trouble than a barrel-load of monkeys'. Violet more than matched her.

'She needs a playmate,' Nanny Mackenzie said crisply.

'Well, there aren't any other children on board.'

'There's one,' Nanny reminded her.

Margaret Somerset stared at her. 'You don't mean that filthy little creature in the army jacket who's always swinging on the rails by the galley? He looks like a cross between a scarecrow and a rat. God knows what diseases he's riddled with.'

She shuddered. Nanny went back to her knitting.

'He may be a poor wee scrap of a thing but he looks healthy enough to me,' she replied.

13

'You can't be serious, Nanny?' Margaret protested

'Children need other children. He's here, he's the only one, and he's nae doubt as bored as Violet. Anyway, it'll only be for a week—'

The clicking needles paused for a moment. 'Of course we could go on with the racing demon until we reach Mombasa,' she added innocently.

Margaret Somerset clenched her hands in frustration. She hesitated. Then she said angrily, 'I know it's going to end in tears, but I suppose I might as well speak to the captain. At least we'll find out who he is.'

She stormed out of the cabin. Nanny smiled and reached for a new ball of wool.

Captain Williamson walked across the bridge and stopped behind the helmsman's shoulder.

He checked the compass, and gave a grudging sniff of approval. They were exactly on course, as every ship under his command had always been. Williamson stood looking out at the flat lead-coloured sea and the school of dolphins planing across the foam at the ship's bows.

The P&O cargo ship the *Star of Russia* was midway across the Indian Ocean.

As well as its load of baled jute and leather, the ship's cramped cabins carried a number of British passengers who'd embarked at various ports as it made its way from Bombay to Kenya. All of them had been trapped overseas since the outbreak of the Second World War. Now with the allied victory close, they were at last able to head for home.

With the exception of one group, the passengers were a motley collection – three petroleum engineers and their families, five nuns, an assortment of retired colonial officials, and a few military casualties from the Far Eastern campaigns. The exception was a Mrs Margaret Somerset and her party – her lady's maid, her child's nurse, and the child herself, a five-year-old named Violet.

They had joined the ship at the Iranian port of Abadan. Mrs Somerset was the wife of the second secretary at the British Embassy in Tehran, and the god-daughter of the under-secretary of state at the Foreign Office. Captain Williamson had learned that in a telegraph from Whitehall to the P&O office in Bombay. The message requested P&O to see that she and her party were very carefully looked after.

Mrs Somerset was clearly a VIP indeed. Judging by her entourage, she was very rich.

She was also, Williamson had discovered – he had naturally invited her to eat at the captain's table – an outstandingly beautiful and intelligent woman. In fact, he had never met any woman like her. If she ever had any competition, he reflected quizzically, it was only likely to come from her daughter. He had five daughters of his own but Violet was the boldest and brightest child he'd ever encountered.

Williamson chuckled. God help the man who set his cap at little Violet when she began to blossom into womanhood.

He was still chuckling when the door to the bridge opened. He swung round.

'Captain, I do hope I'm not disturbing you?'

It was Mrs Somerset herself. She was the only passenger he'd ever invited to visit the bridge whenever she wanted. Now he came forward to greet her.

'Of course not, dear lady. How can I help you?'

'It's Violet,' Margaret said. 'She's an active little girl, and she's getting rather restless. Nanny suggested she needs a playmate. I gather there's another child on board, a small boy. I wonder if you could tell me something about him?'

'Do you mean young Billy?'

'I haven't the slightest idea what he's called. I think I may have seen him once or twice near the galley.'

'That'll be him, Billy Ramsden.' Williamson swallowed awkwardly. 'He's not a bad lad in my view, but whether you'd consider him a suitable friend for your daughter, I'm not so sure.'

The captain described the boy's background.

Billy Ramsden was eight, illegitimate, and an orphan. His mother had died at his birth, and he'd been brought up in the military barracks at Lucknow by his father, a bugler with the Anglo-Indian regiment, Rattray's Sikhs. The regiment had been sent to Burma where Billy's father had been killed fighting the Japanese.

15

Nicholas Luard

The regimental colonel had a soft spot for his bugler, and he'd arranged for young Billy to be sent back to Britain, where the boy had an aunt living in Brixton in South London. Williamson had been asked to keep an eye on him during the voyage.

As she listened Margaret Somerset's heart sank.

The child sounded as bad, if not worse, than she'd thought. She remembered her first glimpse of him when they'd boarded. He'd been lurking by the gang-plank picking his nose, a scrawny hollow-cheeked child with a surly face and fierce scowling eyes. She'd shivered in distaste as she passed.

'Also, I fear, the lad's without much schooling,' Williamson finished. 'I doubt he can read or write.'

Margaret was silent for a moment. She thought of the seven days ahead and the endless tedious games of cards.

'Thank you, Captain,' she said. 'You've been very helpful. I'm not sure he's what I'd have chosen, but don't they say "needs must when the devil rides" – and, my goodness, I sometimes feel the devil has saddled up my daughter!'

She smiled brightly and walked out on the bewildered Williamson. Five minutes later she was back in Nanny Mackenzie's cabin.

'The boy's a little monster, Nanny,' she said. 'He comes from the slums, he's illegitimate, and totally illiterate. I just don't know.' She paused. Then added plaintively, 'Do you think he knows how to play racing demon?'

Nanny glanced up.

The little 'madam', as she privately called her employer, using the name she'd given her as a child, could fret as much as she liked. Her daughter was just as wilful. If anything Violet's resolve was even more steely. Nanny had already seen her eyeing the raggedly dressed boy. If Margaret decided against him and Violet chose to take him as a friend, there would be a battle royal between mother and daughter.

Nanny had no doubt who would win – and it wouldn't be 'madam'.

'If he doesn't, dear,' Nanny answered, 'I'll teach him.'

* * *

16

Billy spotted her approaching him along the deck.

He'd seen her often before, of course. Usually she was with her mum or one of the other women. Her mum was unmistakable – tall and elegant and wearing a long skirt like the colonel's wife. He wasn't quite sure about the other women. One of them, the dumpy one with the dark hair, was probably a maid. The other, much older and grey-haired, looked somewhere between an aunt and a servant.

The girl called the older woman 'Nanny'. Nanny, in Billy's world, meant a grandmother. This one clearly wasn't a gran, not that Billy had one. She was more like a nurse, like the ayahs the wives of the regimental officers employed to look after their children.

The girl came closer.

Billy did a tentative roll round the bottom rail, stretching out his legs and pointing his feet as he completed it. He looked up to see if she'd noticed. The girl was looking the other way – deliberately, Billy thought.

'Bitch!' he said to himself. 'Stuck-up little bitch!'

He lay on his stomach on the iron bar. The girl came closer still. She stopped opposite him and looked at the rail.

'Bet you can't do all three,' she said.

''Course I can,' Billy answered scornfully, realising she had been watching him after all. 'It's easy.'

'Do it then.'

The railing was three-tiered. Billy scrambled to the top and flipped himself forward. He swung round the first rail and dropped to the second. He swung round that one too but when he lowered himself to the third, he slithered off and fell to the deck.

The girl gave a peal of derisive laughter. Billy flushed. He gritted his teeth and tried again. The same thing happened. He tried once more with the same result. This time he collided painfully with the deck. He stood up, rubbing his bruised elbow.

'It's only because it's wet and slippery,' he said sullenly.

The girl wasn't even listening to him. She kicked off her shoes, pulled up her blue velvet lace-trimmed dress, and tucked it into her knickers. Then she climbed up.

17

She balanced herself on the top rail and launched herself forward.

Spinning like an acrobat, she came down through all three bars and landed neatly on her feet.

'Bloody sissy!' she said.

Billy could think of only one reply. He drew back his leg and kicked at her knee. She was too fast for him. She jumped back, made claws of her hands, and steadied herself to leap for his face.

'Violet, where are you? Violet!'

The two children froze. Violet knew the voice echoing down from the fore-deck. It was her mother's lady's maid, Bobbity – Nanny was too old and arthritic to be sent out to find her. She glanced anxiously at Billy.

'Where can we hide?'

'Here, where they keep the swill,' he said. 'Fernando, he's the cook, he is a mate of mine. He won't say even if he sees us.'

Billy pulled Violet across the deck and into a narrow shed tacked on to the back of the galley. He slammed the door and the children crouched down between the bins of foul-smelling garbage.

Bobbity's voice, still shouting 'Violet', came closer. It rang out shrilly as she passed the shed, and then faded away as she went down on to the after-deck. After a while Billy stood up. He pushed the door open and peered out.

'Safe now,' he said.

Violet climbed to her feet. She pulled her dress out of her knickers and brushed off the cabbage and potato peelings clinging to the velvet. Then she looked at the boy.

'What's your name?' she asked.

'Billy. What's yours?'

'Violet.' She paused. 'Do you want to be my friend?'

Billy stared back at her.

She was younger than he, but just as tall. She had a bold fine-boned face, deceptively sleepy blue eyes – the same colour as her name – and tangled fair hair which still smelled of a sewer in spite of her efforts to clean herself up.

Billy shrugged. 'Maybe.'

He desperately wanted to be her friend, but he had his pride, she was a girl, and the memory of her spinning through the three rails rankled like an open sore.

'I can show you how to do the rails—'

Violet knew she'd made a mistake as soon as she'd spoken. Before Billy had a chance to bristle and react, she changed tack.

'I know lots of swear words. "Bloody", that's a good one. I bet you know others that are better.'

'"Course I do,' he replied, half-mollified.

'You could tell me.'

'Well, there's "bugger". Bet you don't know that, do you?'

'No. What's it mean?'

'*Violet!*'

The call came again before he could explain. Bobbity must have circled the after-deck and be making her way back.

'I've got to go—'

Violet paused.

Then for the first time in her life she impetuously did something that, equally impetuously, she was to do with many men across the years that followed – although never with the same passion and conviction. She put her arms round Billy and kissed him.

'I don't care if you don't want to be my friend,' she said. 'You *are* my friend.'

She slipped out of the shed door and vanished as Bobbity's cries came closer.

Billy stood quite still in the darkness.

He was a boy, well, a man really – at least that's what his father had always taught him to believe. Billy didn't like girls. He bitterly resented the stupid little cow's acrobatics on the railing. Anyone could have done the same if they'd dried off the bars first – and he knew she must have done.

She was a vain silly stuck-up little bitch, like all of the daughters of all of the colonels.

And then he remembered the steadfast gaze in her eyes and the touch of her lips on his cheek.

Billy lashed out at the door-jamb.

3

A week later as Captain Williamson guided the *Star of Russia* into its berth in the Mombasa docks, the British consul standing on the quay rubbed his moustache apprehensively.

The consul was no stranger to dealing with war-time refugees. This group had been due to disembark, travel north by train to Alexandria, and take another boat to Britain from there. Unfortunately, barely hours before the ship arrived, Hitler had launched a last offensive in the Mediterranean. German U-boats were prowling the sea from Istanbul to Gibraltar, attacking every allied ship they spotted. There were reports, too, that the Luftwaffe had been ordered to strike at the allied airbases round Cairo and Alexandria.

For the immediate future there was no question of the passengers continuing to Egypt – let alone crossing the Mediterranean. Until the fighting ended, they would have to stay in Kenya.

Normally the consul would have billeted them all in one of Mombasa's hotels until it was safe to go on. He could do that for most of them – but not for one group

Mrs Margaret Somerset and her party.

Like the P&O office in Bombay, the consul had also received a telegram from Whitehall. It was even more forthright than Captain Williamson's. Under no circumstances, the cable read, was Mrs Somerset to be stranded in Mombasa – a hot and humid breeding ground, as the consul knew well, for all manner of African fevers. Instead she was to be accommodated somewhere comfortable and healthy until she could travel on.

The consul racked his brains.

Then he had an inspiration. Using Kenya's primitive telephone service, he managed to persuade the owner of the Laager game lodge, high up in the cool clear air of the Aberdare Mountains to the north, to reopen – it had been closed since the start of the war – and take in Mrs Somerset's party.

He had no idea what she would make of the Laager. It was set in the mountain forest with the plains sweeping out below. On every side the landscape teemed with game. Many visitors to Kenya were frightened by the African wilderness and its animals. On the other hand that crusty old lecher Finlay Hampton, the Laager's owner and a former white hunter, provided good clean rondavels, acceptable food, and the best service in East Africa – his Kikuyu and Samburu staff were second to none.

At the very least, the consul reflected, Mrs Somerset wouldn't be able to complain he'd exposed her daughter to the stench, squalor and diseases of the port.

The ship slid into its berth, the gang-plank was lowered, and the consul adjusted his hat. He tugged nervously at his moustache again and stepped forward to greet the arrivals.

Finlay Hampton looked at Margaret Somerset across the dinner table.

'To your beauty, your wit, but most of all to your health, my dear,' he said.

He raised his glass and drained the champagne. Then in one of the flamboyant gestures for which he was famous, he tossed the glass over his shoulder. It shattered against the wall behind. One of the Kikuyu servants shuffled forward and began to brush up the broken fragments.

Margaret laughed happily. 'Finlay, you're completely mad! Give me some more champagne, please.'

'For you, anything.'

He snapped his fingers and pointed. Another of the Kikuyu, dressed like the first in a spotless white gown and a red turban, opened a second bottle and filled her glass.

Margaret sipped it and gazed at him over the bubbling straw-coloured wine.

He was a rogue, she had little doubt of that, and old enough

21

to be her father. On the other hand he was tall, vigorous, and entertaining, and it was years since anyone had courted her so assiduously – the almost constant presence of her husband, Michael, had been enough to put any suitors off.

She hadn't seen Michael for a year.

Now four months into her enforced stay in Kenya – she'd been bed-ridden for the past three weeks with a bout of malaria and Finlay had been a wonderfully attentive companion – she was restless.

Margaret looked at him again. She wondered.

'I'll tell you what,' Hampton might almost have been reading her mind, 'I've got a little hut in the trees over a salt-lick. Treetops, it's called, lovely place. The animals go there to drink. Why don't we pay it a visit for a few days?'

'What about the children?'

She'd reluctantly become used to thinking of them in the plural. Since she'd allowed Violet to play with Billy Ramsden on board the *Star of Russia*, they'd become inseparable. There was no question of Billy's being left behind in Mombasa with the other passengers. Violet had insisted he come with them, and Nanny had supported her.

Much as Margaret still disliked the gaunt and sullen little boy, she had to admit he'd made all the difference to their time at the lodge. She hadn't had to play racing demon for months.

'Well, they'd be fine here, of course,' Hampton said. 'But I've planned a treat for them too. A day's drive west there's a gorge and a river. You can see elephant there better than anywhere else I know. Years ago I made a track to it and cleared a camp-site for visitors. I'll send them out with old Ngoro and some of the boys. They'll have a whale of a time – it'll be a real adventure.'

An expression of alarm crossed Margaret's face. 'Alone with just some blacks?'

Hampton shook with laughter. 'Ngoro's been with me for forty years. He was my gun-bearer when I hunted. He's a Masai and the best, bravest, and wisest man I've ever known. They'll be far safer with him than they would with me.'

'Are you really sure?' she said doubtfully.

'Margaret, my dear,' he leant forward and took her hand, 'after you, the most beautiful and valued lady I know is your daughter. I'd no more put her at risk than I would you.'

Margaret hesitated. Nanny and Bobbity might click their tongues in disapproval at her going off alone with a man who wasn't her husband, but they were only servants. They could think what they liked. And if Finlay said Violet would be safe, Margaret was sure she would be.

'It sounds wonderful,' she said, smiling.

'This is Ngoro,' said Hampton. 'He's going to take you on an adventure.'

The two children blinked sleepily in the light of the oil lantern swinging from Hampton's hand.

It was 5.00 am and the African night was still impenetrably dark. Hampton had woken them ten minutes earlier with steaming mugs of tea. Now wrapped in blankets against the chill highland air, they were standing on the front porch of the lodge. Dimly Violet could see the outline of an African at the foot of the steps.

'Ngoro, this is Missy Violet,' Hampton went on. 'And this is young Billy.'

The African inclined his head.

He was immensely tall. Even though he was standing on the ground beneath her, Violet had to peer up to see his face. He had tightly curled grey hair, hollowed cheeks, and ancient mahogany-coloured eyes, ringed with strange green and white circles.

'Missy. Young bwana.'

Ngoro's voice was deep and slow.

He touched his right elbow with the cupped palm of his left hand, and stretched out his arm. Violet took his hand. It felt as hard and old as stone. He was wearing a Masai leather apron, and planted in the earth beside him was a spear almost as tall as he was. Behind him were three younger Africans, one of them with a rifle and a shotgun slung over his shoulders. A fourth African was sitting behind the wheel of one of the lodge's open-roofed safari trucks.

The children stared at Ngoro transfixed. All their sleepiness had vanished. In the darkness the Masai looked like an enormous ebony-coloured stork. Violet tore her gaze away and glanced back.

'Where are we going?' she demanded. 'And what's the adventure?'

'You're going to the valley of the elephants,' Hampton answered. 'Ngoro knows more about them than anyone in Africa. He'll show you the secret place where they live, and tell you all about them.'

In turn Hampton picked up the children and swung them up on to the raised viewing bench behind the driver. Ngoro climbed into the passenger seat. The other three Africans scrambled up at the rear.

'Is it really secret?' Violet asked, hardly able to speak for excitement.

From the ground below Hampton nodded.

'Very soon it'll be one of the last secrets left in Africa. You and Billy will know it, but almost no one else. You must do everything Ngoro says, and he'll look after you. Listen very carefully to him. Before long there may be no elephants left, only ghosts.'

He said something in Swahili to the driver. The engine started and then they drove out through the gates of the lodge's compound. Rocking and swaying, the two children clung to the safety bar as the truck bucketed away down the winding cratered track.

It was still over an hour before dawn.

Banners of whirling grey mist threaded the forest on either side. Occasionally through the gaps in the leaf canopy they glimpsed the dazzling constellations in the night sky above. Ahead the truck's headlamps picked out the ghostly swooping shapes of hunting owls, and the glittering amber eyes of nightjars. Once a lion called so close that the great grunting roar briefly drowned out the sound of the engine.

Violet glanced at Billy. Like hers his eyes were watering and the cold rushing wind had tugged his hair flat against his head.

'It's a real adventure!' she shouted rapturously. 'A *secret* adventure!'

Billy didn't reply.

Violet didn't know whether her words had been plucked away and lost in the noise of the wind and the truck. But he turned to look at her and a fleeting smile crossed his sallow, shuttered face.

They drove all day.

The sun rose, the wind died away, the heat grew stronger hour by hour as the morning passed. At midday they paused briefly to eat. Then they headed on again. They were still travelling north-west, but they were coming down now towards the lowlands and the forest was beginning to thin out. The children were no longer standing and clinging to the safety bar, but curled up and sleeping fitfully on the bench.

Once or twice Violet woke and raised her head.

Ngoro sat upright and motionless in front with the spear between his knees. Flares of light flickered from its razor-sharp metal tip. When she slept again her dreams were filled with pacing water birds and haloes of blue-white radiance.

She woke again in the late afternoon to find Billy shaking her shoulder. Violet sat up. The light had begun to fade and the truck's pace had slowed to a crawl.

'Look!' Billy pointed forward.

The track had vanished and in front of them was a wall of scrub. The three Africans at the back had climbed out and were hacking a path through it with long broad-bladed knives.

'Pangas, that's what they are,' Billy said. 'Ngoro told me. I'd have known anyway. The little brown buggers at the barracks had them. Gurkhas, they were, and they called them khukris. Bet you didn't know that.'

He looked at her challengingly. Violet shook her head.

'Where are we?'

'Not far from camp. Ngoro says the boys and me, we're going to pitch the tent. You can watch if you want,' he added generously.

Violet was silent.

There was boys' work and there was girls' work, her mother had taught her that. Making camp was obviously

25

boys' work. She didn't mind. There were more important matters than pitching tents. She wanted to know about the secret. That, she sensed, was held by the gaunt towering figure she was already beginning to think of as more a bird than a man.

It took the Africans with the pangas two more hours to clear the overgrown track far enough for Ngoro to be satisfied. Finally he stamped the spear on the truck's floor and the driver switched off the engine.

Ngoro climbed out.

Although by then darkness had closed in again, the Masai stood gazing round with his eyes narrowed and his nostrils flared as if he could see and smell every inch of the hidden landscape. At last, satisfied, he grunted. He planted the spear's shaft in the earth and raised his hand to the other Africans.

An hour later the children's tent was pitched. A fire was blazing, and a metal cauldron was bubbling over the flames. They ate in three groups; Billy and Violet seated on stools closest to the fire, Ngoro squatting on his haunches beyond them, and the others further back still. Afterwards both the children tried to question him.

'Where are we?' Violet said.

'What are we going to do tomorrow?' Billy asked.

Ngoro shook his head. 'Missy, little bwana, we wait for the night to end. If the sun rises again, then we choose where we will go. But we must wait for the sun.'

He used the spear to heave himself to his feet. For an instant he stood above them smiling, the same huge and angular silhouette they had seen at dawn.

'I sleep now, so should you.'

He stalked away. Beyond the rim of the fire's flames he wrapped himself in a thick kaross of jackal and genet hides, settled himself on the ground, and lay still.

The children crawled into their sleeping-bags inside the tent. Within minutes Billy was breathing deeply and slowly. Violet lay on her back listening to the quiet murmurs and the occasional laughter of the other Africans by the fire.

'Billy,' she whispered.

He didn't answer. She reached out and twisted his ear. Billy turned over, protesting.

'What is it?' he asked drowsily.

'I think Ngoro's magic.' Violet was still whispering. 'I mean, real magic like Merlin in the story. The place is magic, too. What do you think, Billy?'

He muttered something which Violet couldn't hear. She tweaked his ear again, but he kicked out and rolled away from her.

She turned on to her back again and lay waiting wide-eyed for the morning. She was determined to stay awake all night, but exhausted by the journey, in moments she too was asleep.

4

It was still dark when Ngoro woke them.

The boys had already rekindled the fire. Yawning and rubbing their eyes, the children breakfasted on mealy-meal warmed over the embers. Then Ngoro picked up his spear and beckoned them to follow him. They walked for an hour under the stars along a path that threaded its way between thorn bush and copses of acacia. When they stopped the sky was just beginning to pale with morning.

Ngoro inclined the spear, and Violet and Billy peered down where the tip pointed.

They were standing on the edge of a cliff above a winding valley with a river running through its centre. The valley was deep in shadow and the river's surface was covered in mist, but the children could just make out broad shelving banks of earth with heavily trodden paths leading down to the water's edge.

The three of them waited, the children shivering in the chill dawn air. Finally the sun lifted over the horizon.

At the same instant two things happened so extraordinary and unexpected that Violet gasped and Billy stiffened in astonishment. The first was that the valley was transformed. The dark and shadowy cavern suddenly burst into colour. The cliffs on either side blazed in glittering bands of pink and crimson, orange and scarlet, and the tawny-ochre of a lion's hide. It was as if a golden rainbow had been painted across the dusky walls.

Violet blinked. Then she remembered what Hampton had taught them about the African landscape.

He'd told the children how the wild had come into being – how the distant past had shaped and formed it. The valley was made up of layers of Africa's differently coloured sand and earth speckled with crystals, piling up and silting on top of each other over the course of hundreds of thousands, even millions, of years. The layers of sand had created the effect of the rainbow, the specks of quartz and mica the diamond-like glitter.

The second revelation of the sunrise was almost more astonishing.

Silently, and without anything to signal their approach, out of the mist below them there emerged columns of great grey shapes. For an instant they looked like an endless army of gigantic ghosts. Then the two children realised they were elephants coming down to the river to drink. Violet and Billy had seen elephants before round the Laager but never in these numbers, never in this seemingly infinite procession of bulls and mothers and calves.

It was minutes before Violet could speak. Finally she managed to pull her eyes away from the scene below. She glanced up at Ngoro.

'Is this the secret place?' she asked.

A slow smile crossed the face of the old Masai.

'That is how the bwana names it. In the tongue of my people it is the valley of the drinking-place of the great ones. This is where the elephants come to seed each other, to give birth, to die. Most of all it is where they come to drink. Without water there is no life for anything. Here is where they find life—'

In a gesture Violet was becoming familiar with, Ngoro raised his spear and plunged its shaft in the earth. He squatted beside it, folding himself over his haunches like a bird settling down to roost.

'Sit.'

His arm swept out and indicated a fallen tree trunk. The two children scuttled to sit down.

'The bwana said that I must tell you of the valley and the elephants,' Ngoro went on. 'I shall do so. I am Ngoro, I am Masai, listen well!'

His voice was commanding, almost hypnotic.

Violet and Billy hunched themselves forward, hardly even daring to breathe. They both sensed they were in the presence of something unlike anything they had never known. They waited in silence.

'When time began there was only water,' Ngoro said. 'All the spirits drank from it, and were at peace. The water made their hearts free and generous, so generous that one day they went to the great black-maned lion of the spirits and said: "We should share the water with others". The lion of the spirits answered: "There is no other". The spirits said: "Then make another just as you made us."

'The lion thought long about what the spirits wished. At the end he reached down and took the red clay and shaped it. He baked the clay in an oven and when he opened the oven, he saw he had made the Masai. The first Masai he made was a warrior. The lion of the spirits parted the water and let the Masai walk on land. The warrior walked and drank and was at peace like the spirits. But soon the warrior became lonely. He called to the lion: "I am not one of the spirits. They do not speak to me, they do not lie with me to keep me warm, they do not prepare my food. Make me a companion that I shall not be alone."'

Ngoro gripped the spear with one of his bony hands. His green and brown-ringed eyes seemed to glaze as he stared out over the valley.

'The lion of the spirits took clay again. This time when he opened the oven, he found he had made a Masai woman. He gave her to the man. The warrior and the woman were the first of all people. They lay together and seeded more Masai. They had water to drink but because they were not spirits – they were made of red clay – they needed also to eat. That is when the lion went to the oven again. He made the elephant.'

Violet had been biting her tongue to stop herself asking questions since Ngoro started. She couldn't restrain herself any longer.

'Why?' she demanded. 'Why an elephant?'

Billy kicked her on the ankle, but the old Masai didn't seem to mind.

'When the lion parted the water, trees came and covered the land,' he replied. 'Beneath the trees there was no sun.

Neither crops nor grass grew and the cattle could not graze, for the lion had made cattle for the Masai too. The lion made the elephant to clear the forest and let in the light. Look!'

Ngoro pointed. The children followed his outstretched arm.

The sun was clear of the horizon and the mist had lifted.

On the far side of the gorge the land rolled away towards the west. Once, according to Ngoro, it had been unbroken forest. Now it was a tapestry of scrub, trees, open grass plain, and meandering streams.

Several groups of elephant had finished drinking and moved away from the river. As the children watched, one young bull elephant rested his head against a tree trunk and began to push. For several minutes the tree rocked backwards and forwards. Then it toppled and fell with a crash that echoed through the still morning air. Moments later the young bull was using his trunk to tear off and eat the leafy branches that had been out of reach before.

'So when they push over the trees to feed themselves, they let people eat too?' Violet said.

Ngoro nodded. 'The grass grows, the cattle can feed, so can the Masai, so too all the other animals the lion made later.'

Billy had said nothing until then. Now he wrinkled his face and spoke. With the clear observant eye of a child he had noticed something.

'Why have they got longer legs and bigger feet?' he asked.

Violet peered down into the gorge again. Billy was right. The elephants still drinking were subtly different from the ones they'd seen round the Outspan.

Ngoro smiled in approval. 'The little bwana sees clearly. These are the children of the first elephant that the lion of the spirits made. He made them with long legs and large feet so they could move easily in the water that was round the forest. These are the oldest elephants in all the world. They are different from all others.'

As he spoke one of the elephants lifted its trunk, spread out the tip like a dark tulip, and gave a sudden trumpeting

31

scream. It was a huge female with a dusty grey-brown hide, streaked with shining bands of wetness, and a young calf at its side.

'What was that?'

Startled, Violet shivered. Long after the scream ended and the elephant had lowered its trunk, the sound was still vibrating through her like a call from the beginning of time.

'The bwana has named her Uhuru,' Ngoro said. 'It is a name for "Freedom". The lion made a female elephant first and said they should always lead the herds. Uhuru is the oldest and wisest of the females. One day her daughter, the calf beside her, will take her place. Uhuru is saying the morning's drinking is finished, and it is time to eat.'

The great cow elephant turned and moved away into the bush with her calf behind her. Within minutes all the other elephants had followed.

'Ngoro,' Violet turned to the Masai, 'Finlay said soon there may not be any elephants left, only ghosts. Why's that?'

She was frightened of ghosts, and Hampton's remark had plucked disturbingly at her mind ever since they'd left the Laager in the darkness.

'I think the bwana talks of the hunting and the killing for ivory and the taking of the land for farms,' Ngoro replied. 'The bwana knows much more than I. You must ask him.'

'But if the elephants go,' she insisted, 'what will happen?'

Ngoro was silent for a long time. Then he raised his shoulders and shrugged.

'Maybe the lion of the spirits will take back the red clay of the people and the animals, and bake it to dust in the oven. Then he will throw the dust away and let the waters return.'

'But then there'd be nothing!' she protested, appalled.

'If the lion decides, so it will be.'

Ngoro heaved himself to his feet. He pulled the spear from the earth and headed for the truck, beckoning the children to follow him.

Violet didn't move for a moment. She sat on the log, frightened as she'd never been before. She was right. Ngoro was magic and so was the valley and the elephants. They all shone with magic. Only now the old Masai had said the lion of the spirits might take everything back, turn it into dust again, and toss it away.

With a sudden chilling flash of insight, Violet realised what that would mean. If the lion put them all back in his oven, the world would end.

She reached out, gripped Billy's hand, and clung to it. His fingers felt as cold as her own.

5

Hitler's final U-boat offensive ended within a week of the children's return from the valley.

In a telephone call to the Laager the consul in Mombasa said the Mediterranean was considered relatively safe again, and Mrs Somerset's party should prepare to continue their journey. They would be on their way to Alexandria in a matter of days.

The call was taken by Finlay Hampton. As he put the receiver down, he shrugged ruefully.

His trip to Treetops with Margaret had been a success – he'd never seen so many animals visit the salt-lick – but he hadn't made his planned conquest of his elegant guest. Now he knew he never would. Margaret, he was sure, had been intrigued and attracted by his advances but she'd gracefully sidestepped them. With a little more time it might have been different. Herr Hitler's naval incompetence had removed the possibility.

He gave a good-humoured private smile and went off to warn her to get ready to leave.

Forty-eight hours later he was standing once more on the lodge's porch in the pre-dawn darkness. Two cars were waiting to take the party down to Nairobi, where they'd board the train to Cairo. Nanny Mackenzie and the lady's maid, Bobbity, were already installed in the first. Margaret and the two children, wrapped again in coats and blankets for the journey, were standing with him.

Hampton had said good-bye to Margaret over dinner and champagne the night before. He looked down at the children.

'Will you come back and see me one day, young lady?' he said to Violet.

Wide-eyed but silent, she nodded. She was clutching her favourite toy, a threadbare and moth-eaten teddy. Hampton chuckled and ruffled the bear's ears.

'Well, I've shown you quite a few animals, even if not one of these.'

'We saw the elephants,' Violet said.

'So you did and in their secret place too,' Hampton turned to Billy. 'And what about you, you young rascal?'

'I saw 'em,' Billy said in his flat voice, his pinched face as expressionless as always.

'And you both liked them?'

'They were the best, the most beautiful thing in all the whole world,' Violet burst out. 'I don't want them to be ghosts – I just want them to go on being elephants like the lion of the spirits baked them.'

Tears welled up in her eyes, and she flung herself against him. Hampton picked her up and held her to him while she sobbed. Then he got out his handkerchief, dried her eyes, and gently put her down.

'Ngoro!' he called.

The old Masai must have been waiting somewhere out of sight. He came forward, moving with slow stately steps like a heron pacing across a lagoon. His spear was in his hand and the lantern light glowed like a halo round its tip.

'When Missy Violet comes back, will we still have elephants to greet her?' Hampton said.

Ngoro hammered the spear into the earth.

'There will be elephants,' he answered. 'We will keep them for her. And when you and I are gone, bwana, it will be for her and the little bwana to see the elephants remain still.'

He paused and looked at the two children. His eyes with their green and white rings of age were steady and thoughtful. Then he withdrew the spear from the ground, and raised it in the night air.

'I am Ngoro, I am Masai, I have spoken,' he finished.

He stalked back into the darkness.

'There,' Finlay Hampton said, 'you have Ngoro's word.'

He kissed Violet, patted Billy on the head, and embraced Margaret. She started to say something, but he cut her off.

'There's no need to remind me. I'll go down to Nairobi myself later today. The paperwork will only take a couple of hours, the ministry's next door to my lawyer. It should be with you before you leave Alexandria.'

He smiled. 'It's a pretty rum idea, but I suppose by your standards the investment's tiny. And if it's going to bring Violet back here, not to mention you, then I'd walk the whole bloody way to my damn' lawyer's office.'

Margaret gave him a last kiss.

'I love you, Finlay, quite a little bit and quite a large bit, but mostly the large bit.'

A moment later the two cars, their headlamps bright in the waning African night, were on their way.

'Look after the bold young lady,' Hampton shouted after them. 'And look after that little tyke, the bugler's son, too!'

He waved. A hand came out through the window of the leading car and waved back.

Two days after his visitors left, Finlay Hampton was sitting on the rear verandah of the Laager drinking his first whisky and soda of the evening as the sun began to set, when one of the house-boys padded out of the hotel.

'There is a bwana at the door, sir,' he said.

Hampton looked at him in surprise. 'A bwana? I didn't hear a car, Mtumbi.'

'No, sir. This bwana, he come walking. He has bad leg and cuts on him. I think he is hurt, sir.'

Hampton stood up, astonished.

Bwana meant a white man. No other Europeans lived in Nyeri, the nearest village to the lodge, and the closest white-owned farm, the Crombies', was miles away. If Jack Crombie or one of his sons had had an accident, Sue Crombie would have driven them straight down to the hospital in Nairobi. No one would have climbed on foot up to the Laager, particularly if they were hurt.

Hampton hurried through the lodge to the porch.

The man was leaning against the hardwood railing. He was about thirty, a tall strongly built young man with fair hair, striking pale blue eyes, and a deeply tanned face. Two crutches, improvised from tree branches, were propped beside him. One of his ankles was heavily swollen and bandaged with what looked like strips torn from a khaki shirt, and there was crusted blood on his face and arms.

'Good day, sir.' The young man held out his hand. 'The name's Cameron. I'm afraid I've had a spot of bother. I wonder if you could help?'

He spoke fluent English but with a thick guttural accent that could have been either Afrikaans or German – there were enough of either in southern Africa with Scottish names.

Hampton shook the man's hand.

'What the hell's happened?'

'Kite crashed,' replied Cameron. 'I'm South African RAF. We were flying a mission Jo'burg to Nairobi. Two days back we got double engine failure and wheel-lock somewhere west of here over the river. It was one of the pre-war Herc amphibians. We tried to put down on an ox-bow, but every goddam' system died on us and we turned arse over tit. The bloke with me, Heini, my co-pilot, bought it, but I got out—'

His breathing was laboured and under the tan Hampton could see his skin was pallid. The man was holding himself together by an immense effort of will.

'I swam ashore, then I started to walk. Last night I saw the lights up here and headed for them. I wasn't sure I'd make it, but I did. Lady Luck's an old mate.'

He tried to smile. The effort or the pain or the exhaustion from what he'd been through was too much for him. His knees sagged and he crumpled unconscious on the porch.

'Mtumbi!' called Hampton.

'Sir!'

He had been waiting inside the hall. 'Get another couple of the boys,' Hampton instructed. 'Take the bwana into one of the bedrooms. Strip him down and wash him. Put a pair of my pyjamas on him. Then put him to bed. I'm going to telephone Dr Robbins.'

'Yes, bwana.'

Hampton went back inside.

As he walked towards the telephone he paused. The young

South African's story, not to mention his injuries, was entirely convincing. He believed every word of it. In Africa, above all in wartime, events that would have been bizarre elsewhere – strange accidents, plane crashes, agonising limping walks to safety – were commonplace.

The dark continent was, after all, the stage on which Anthony and Cleopatra, Dr Livingstone, and Chaka, the psychopathic Zulu king, had all lived out their strange tormented fantasies and lives.

What momentarily puzzled Finlay Hampton was why Cameron, on a mission from Johannesberg to Nairobi, had been flying over the Aberdare Mountains.

He dismissed the riddle from his mind, picked up the bakelite handset and dialled Dr Robbins.

6

It took Margaret Somerset and her party five days to travel from Nairobi to Cairo.

There they were stranded again for three weeks. They spent the time at the Mena House Hotel almost in the shadow of the pyramids. Then the British Embassy told them they had been allocated berths on a ship leaving Alexandria for Britain in twelve hours.

With Nanny Mackenzie fussing and clucking and Bobbity fretting that she hadn't had time to finish ironing 'Madam's' underwear, they set off in two Embassy-hired taxis for Alexandria. Sometime after midnight they left port and began the voyage towards Britain as part of an armed convoy.

Only one incident marred the trip.

Midway between Egypt and Gibraltar a rogue German U-boat, a wandering relic of the last German offensive, surfaced to attack the convoy. The ship they were on happened to be the U-boat's target. Briefly, before the guarding destroyers circled back and chased the attacker away, there was an exchange of fire. The passengers were herded up to the lifeboat mustering stations as the ship engaged the U-boat with its own guns. The destroyers appeared, the U-boat vanished, the decks were left wreathed with the lingering smoke of gunfire.

As Violet stood surrounded by her mother, Nanny, and Bobbity waiting for the all-clear siren, Billy appeared.

He was staggering under the weight of a large spent brass shell which he must have picked up from one of the gun batteries. The brass was still hot and Billy's hands were blistered and bleeding. He stopped in front of Violet and put the shell on the deck at her feet. For a moment the two

39

children stared at each other, Violet with her extraordinarily vivid eyes, Billy with his pale inscrutable face.

Then he turned and ran away.

'Well, whatever next!' Nanny exclaimed as the siren finally sounded. 'Red roses and chocolates are one thing, but I hope your admirer's not going to bring you a cannon, my wee hen.'

She and Bobbity laughed. Mrs Somerset looked bewildered and disapproving.

The arrangements on the ship were quite different from those on the earlier part of the journey. The Somerset party was quartered high up on the fore-deck. Billy was billetted with the returning service personnel, the other ranks, who slept in the cramped rear cabins by the hold.

He and Violet still saw each other every day, but they no longer slept or ate together. The world of class, wealth, and privilege was inexorably separating them. Meal times, bath times, recreational times, all were different. Innocently and unaware, they tried to bridge the growing distance thrust between the two.

They were constantly frustrated.

When Billy's tinned baked beans and isinglass-preserved eggs were ready for his 'tea' in the armed forces quarters, Violet's 'supper' was still an hour away. Long before Billy's daily shower was hot, Violet had been summoned to her bath. When Billy was called to the nightly sing-song in the lower-deck mess-hall, Violet was being forced to accompany her mother to a drinks party in the captain's cabin.

The safe comfortable patterns of the daily lives they'd shared – the clear and simple rhythms they'd settled into and trustingly had never questioned in the months they'd been together – became dislocated. Deliberately or by chance, they were being made strangers to each other.

And then, one evening, something happened.

It was 21 April, Violet's sixth birthday. The ship had passed through the Strait of Gibraltar, crossed the Bay of Biscay, and was heading north-west for Liverpool. To celebrate her daughter's birthday, Margaret Somerset gave her a party which Nanny and Bobbity organised. There was a treasure hunt with a basket of presents at the end of it, a tea to which the captain, the ship's officers and Billy were invited, and a cake with candles.

Afterwards, when everyone had gone and Violet had changed for bed, Margaret closed the cabin door and swung her daughter up on to her knee.

'I hoped you liked it, darling?'

'It was lovely, Mummy,' answered Violet, although she'd have been much happier if Billy was still there with her.

'The presents weren't much, I'm afraid,' her mother went on. 'They were the best Nanny and I could find in Cairo before we sailed. But I have something else for you, something rather strange and a bit grown-up.'

'What's that?' Violet asked eagerly.

'You really liked the valley where you saw the elephants, didn't you?'

Violet nodded. 'I told Uncle Finlay. It's the best place in the whole world.'

'Darling, I've bought it for you – the valley and all the land beyond. It was Uncle Finlay's suggestion. I thought it was an enchanting idea. He saw how much you loved the place and so suggested it. Then he organised everything. He got the papers to me just before we left Egypt. He said it could be a good investment. With the war on and so much uncertainty, it was very cheap. Even if things change in Africa and everything goes to the blacks, it won't really matter. We'll have lost very little.'

Violet stared at her mother dumb-founded.

She hadn't taken in the last part of what Margaret had said. All she was thinking about were the glittering cliffs, the pools where she'd seen Uhuru and her calf drink, and the wild patchwork of the landscape that lay beyond.

'You mean it's really mine?' she whispered.

'Yes, darling,' Margaret laughed. She hugged and kissed the child.

'Does Ngoro know?'

'Who's Ngoro?'

'He took us there.'

'The old black man with the spear and the funny eyes? Yes, I remember. Well, I imagine Uncle Finlay's told him.'

Violet was silent. Stupefied, she sat numbly on her mother's knee.

'Aren't you pleased, little one?' Margaret asked her teasingly.

Still unable to speak, Violet nodded in frantic agreement.

'And just to make sure you believe me, look at this.'

Margaret Somerset produced an envelope. She pulled out a sheaf of densely type-written pages stapled together with a brass clip. She handed the pages to Violet.

'These are what are called the deeds to the land. Look, there's your name.'

Violet glanced down. Halfway down the first page she saw her name spelt out in bold lettering.

She took the document from her mother. 'Can I keep it?'

Margaret frowned. 'I think it would be safer with me. I'll look after it for you, I promise.'

'Please, Mummy. Just for tonight. I want—'

Violet stopped. What she wanted to do, what she'd been on the point of saying, she suddenly realised was impossible – at least as far as her mother was concerned.

'I just want to sleep with it under my pillow,' she finished.

'Of course, darling,' her mother smiled. 'Sleep very well and happy birthday again.'

Violet gave her mother the biggest tightest hug she'd ever given her. She left the cabin and went back to her own sandwiched between Nanny's and Bobbity's and lay awake in her bunk until she heard the night steward switch off all but the safety lights outside.

She listened to his footsteps fading then slid out of the sheets and put on her slippers and dressing-gown. Then she stepped into the corridor and closed the door silently behind her.

The day they boarded at Alexandria Billy had shown her where he'd been billeted. That was two weeks ago. Violet had never been to his quarters since. All she remembered was a large steel dormitory, thudding with the vibrations of the ship's propellers and buried somewhere next to the cargo holds in the depths of the stern. Billy's bunk was high up and close to the door.

She made her way towards the back of the ship.

Twice she heard sailors approaching her. She hid in the shadows until they passed. Once she found herself lost and had to climb a long metal staircase to the deck. The sea was calm but the night was bitterly cold and the stars gleamed through a frost-laden mist. Her teeth chattering, Violet headed on, weaving her way between coils of rope and stanchions coated with ice.

She found another staircase and climbed down again. The metal floor she reached looked identical to all the others, but she was certain of where she was. She leant on a brass handle, struggled against the weight of its spring, and pushed the door open into the dormitory.

'Billy!' she whispered.

She reached up on tiptoe and tugged at the shoulder of a sleeping figure in the bunk above her. It wasn't Billy but a burly unknown man who rolled over, grunted, and cursed her.

Violet shrank back. She was terrified, but she'd committed herself. She reached up again and tried the next bunk.

'Violet?'

This time it was Billy. For a moment her knees buckled and she closed her eyes in relief. Billy rolled off the bunk and dropped down beside her.

'What is it?'

Violet didn't answer. Instead she took his arm and pulled him outside. Under one of the weak bulkhead lights she fumbled in the pocket of her dressing-gown.

'My mother,' said Violet, 'she's a bit batty. But where we were, where the elephants were, the valley – well, she says she's bought it and given it to me. She says Uncle Finlay arranged it all and now it's mine. Here are the papers.'

She pushed the stiff stapled sheets into Billy's hand.

He stared at them bewildered and uncomprehending. He wasn't illiterate as Mrs Somerset still believed, he'd been taught how to read English in the Lucknow army school, but the stilted archaic language of the document might have been Chinese.

'What's it mean, then?'

'It means it's mine, doesn't it?' Violet paused. 'Except it's not really mine. It's yours too.'

'Mine?'

'Yes, you were there with me. It belongs to us both.'

'It doesn't. It's got your bloody name on top. Look!'

He pointed at the only part of the inscription they could both understand, 'Miss Violet Somerset' at the head of the deeds.

'You're just stupid! Bugger you!' Violet stormed at him.

'Bugger you, too!' Billy shouted back.

He dropped his voice. Someone was muttering angrily behind the dormitory door. He was tired and wanted to get back to bed.

'Fuck off, Vi! I'm going to sleep.'

'Billy—'

Violet caught his arm as he turned.

She reached into the other pocket in her dressing-gown and pulled out the pair of scissors – the ones Nanny used to trim her hair – which she'd brought with her from the cabin.

She let go of Billy. Slicing away with a furious intensity by the dim bulkhead light, she cut the sheaf of papers in half.

'Here.' She thrust one half of the jaggedly cut bundle into his hand. 'Keep it safe. Keep it safe for ever and ever.'

Violet didn't wait to see Billy's reaction. She turned and ran.

Back in her cabin she slipped her half of the papers into the envelope her mother had given her, and sealed it. She put the envelope under her pillow. With any luck her mother wouldn't open it and discover what she'd done for ages. By then, Violet thought, she'd have worked out a way to explain it.

For a long time she lay awake on her back, her arms crossed behind her head.

Billy was her friend, the only real friend she'd ever had. He couldn't spin round the three rails – she hadn't dried them, he just couldn't do it, although she'd never brought that up again

– but he'd taught her wonderful swear-words and he'd come to the valley with her.

Violet loved him.

She loved him so passionately and deeply she couldn't find words for it. She could only feel it deep inside herself. She hugged teddy so tightly she was suddenly frightened she was going to squeeze the stuffing out of the ragged little bear. She knew she was luckiest person in the world. She had Billy and the secret valley and the elephants, real live elephants – and now they were all hers.

The only shadow over her life had been the terrifying possibility that the lion of the spirits might take it all away, and bake it into dust again. Now the valley belonged to her, that couldn't happen. She wouldn't let anyone *ever* take the elephants from her.

She turned over, snuggled down between the sheets, and slept.

Two days later the ship docked at Liverpool.

'Shake hands with wee Billy, hen,' Nanny said as they stood on the quay. 'Lord knows when ye'll be meeting up again.'

The two children gravely shook hands as the disembarking passengers swirled round them.

A large military policeman appeared through the throng calling out Billy's name. He saluted Mrs Somerset, took Billy by the arm, and led him away. Tearfully, Violet watched him disappear into the chill soot-laden Liverpool mist as the tugs hooted mournfully in the harbour behind her. He didn't even glance back.

It was over forty years before they saw each other again.

The Garden of Eden

The Man

The man was small and apricot-skinned.

He was naked apart from a leather thong circling his waist – the emblem of the hunter and the scavenger. Hanging from the thong was a pouch containing an obsidian cutting blade. The blade's edges had been whitted away until they were razor-sharp.

The man had waited patiently for the elephants to drink their fill. Now it was his turn. Cautiously, his alert eyes darting quickly from side to side, he padded on soft feet down the river bank. His body was wasted from lack of food almost to the point of starvation, but the water was more important than any nourishment.

First he must drink, then if he could find anything, he would eat.

He lay down in the shallows among the tall grasses, feeling the water caress his parched skin, its pores crusted with salt from the long journey to reach the nameless place which was not yet even a valley.

The man drank thirstily and deeply.

As he raised his head, he caught a flicker of movement on the bank to his left. His survival depended on detecting the presence of predators, and his nostrils instantly recognised the rank smell of a lion pride on a kill. He made a window in the trimedra grass by parting the tall amber-coloured stems, and looked through.

As he did he noticed that some unfamiliar creature had made a large nest in the reeds on the river's edge.

For a moment he couldn't see the lions, although the pride

would know he was there – they'd have caught his scent in the light swirling wind. They were obviously unconcerned. They were equally unworried by the two black-backed jackals to his left, the solitary hyena in the mopane copse behind, and the vultures dropping from the dawn-streaked sky to perch awkwardly and hungrily on the branches.

The man stared keenly ahead until he picked out the almost-hidden silhouettes of the pride.

There were six lions round the kill. A mature female. Her three almost fully grown cubs. An accompanying unmated female – it was the two females and the cubs who'd made the kill. And finally a big male with a greying mane who'd arrogantly prowled in to shoulder the others aside long after the prey animal had been pulled down. The prey was a magnificent eland bull. Limping from a broken fetlock, the great antelope had been defenceless against the pride's attack.

Darts of ravenous hunger pricked the man's sunken stomach, and he licked his swollen lips.

The very size of the prize allowed the lions to ignore the other predators round it. There was enough protein to satisfy every animal there, even down to the beetles and insects who'd eventually cleanse the carcass.

The lions gorged themselves throughout the morning. At midday they retired to sleep in the shade of the mopane trees. They would return to the carcase when the heat lifted, but this was his chance.

Cautiously the man raised himself to his feet.

As he crept forward, he reached down and plucked out the obsidian blade from its pouch. He was hefting it in his hand when the two jackals raced past him. They too had spotted the opportunity to plunder the kill.

'Crarrk!'

His voice rasped out in a fierce hoarse call like the alarm cry of a pied crow.

The jackals swerved and hesitated. Behind him the vultures launched themselves into the air and beat like a dark cloud towards the eland. The man began to run. He reached the eland's body, and stooped over it. Swiftly and expertly he cut a crescent of flesh from the antelope's haunch. As he heaved the meat on to his shoulder, he froze.

Behind him the lioness had stood up. Her tail twitched from side to side. Her ears pricked, she lowered her head, and charged.

All the man could see through the cloud of spiralling sand were twin blazing agate eyes, full of rage. He hurled the blade at her face. He heard her snarl and saw her shake her head. Then he ran again.

He ran faster than he'd ever run in his life.

The man had never hunted the valley before.

He had been driven there far from his native hunting grounds by necessity – by hunger.

He came from a clan of the people who had deserted the trees to live on the edges of the primeval forest which had once covered the entire African continent. For thousands of years the forest had been shrinking, the trees pushed back by drought and lightning-ignited blazes. As the forest retreated the open savannah rippled forward, its tenacious grasses overrunning the glades where the trees had once stood.

The swelling antelope herds, cropping everything in their path, stopped the forest from growing back. The man's clan had had to adapt. In the past they had gathered and foraged among the trees. Now, driven down on to the advancing open plain, they were forced to scavenge off the leavings of the great predators which fed on the herds.

Soon, copying the lions and leopards, they learnt to hunt too.

The great fire came at the end of a time when the rains had failed for seven years in succession. The antelope had scattered and drawn back to the few permanent sources of water, the great rivers that threaded the heart of the land. The predators retreated with them, and the clan's protein supply dwindled to the point where daily some member died of starvation.

He and his five companions had been scouring the plains for food for weeks. Parched, exhausted, and close to starvation themselves, when they found the waterhole they were further away from their home territory than his people had ever travelled.

At first they thought the waterhole was a trick of the light – a mirage in the sand that covered the stone plateau of what much later was named the Kalahari Desert. Hardly daring to hope, they ran towards it. The water gleamed dark and glutinous like wax from the honeycomb of a wild bees' nest, and a faint stench of putrefaction rose from the surface.

The man's five companions plunged into the pool and drank in a frenzy of thirst. For some reason the man never knew, some instinct, some warning from the guardian spirits in the stars, he didn't join them. Dehydrated as he was, he refused to drink.

The other five lay down while the man kept watch. He knew the water was treacherous, he knew it would take revenge. He was right. When morning came the faces of the five were black and their bodies were jerking in spasms of fever. By midday they were dead, and he was alone.

The man turned and began to retrace his steps. He knew he would die before he got back to the clan, but there was nothing else left for him to do.

That afternoon he smelled the smoke.

By evening he could see a cordon of flame on the horizon, and hear the crackle of burning grass and thorn. Like an antelope cornered by lions, he turned again and broke into a stumbling run back in the direction he'd been following with the hunters.

He was dizzy and reeling when he found the tracks of the great grey creatures who were neither prey nor predator. Even in his delirium he knew they could be trusted to lead him to water. They were the oldest and truest, the surest guides of all.

Sometime that night, at the very limit of what was left of his powers, he tripped and pitched forward.

His face plunged into a stream. He gasped and lifted his head. He licked his lips as the drops sluiced down his face. It wasn't the foul water of the hole. It was sweet and fresh. He had fallen into a tributary that fed one of the great rivers.

He drank until his stomach was bloated. Then he lay still, his heart pounding and his limbs aching.

In the morning, with the smoke still billowing across the horizon behind, he headed on, tracing the stream's path, now bubbling clear, now vanishing underground, towards the river it flowed into. His luck had changed. He surprised and killed a porcupine. He gutted and ate every part of the animal apart from its quills.

Afterwards he drove himself on again.

The savage red tide was still pursuing him and the wind-borne stench of smoke constantly filled his nostrils, but he had the measure of it now. He was keeping in front of it. Behind him, he knew, everything had been destroyed. All of his people, all of the tree and savannah-dwelling clans, were lost. Nothing could have survived the savage intensity of what the skies had hurled down and sent raging across the earth.

Sometimes, as he followed the elephant tracks, his eyes always scanning the bush ahead for danger, he felt an unbearable sense of loneliness. He knew he was the last of his kind. When he died – and he would surely die soon – his line would end.

He had a memory, a consciousness of the world, of the past and the future, of dreams and stars and spirits and portents, which no other creature possessed.

For the moment on the river bank with the eland meat in his hand – the lioness had broken from its charge and he was briefly safe – it was enough that he had food. He ate ravenously, tearing at the raw flesh with his teeth until he was satiated. Then he lay down in the nest he had found in the reeds. As he drifted into sleep a strange scent drifted up from the bed of grass beneath him, and coiled mystifyingly round his face.

Later that night, for the second time in millions of years, the weight of the sky bore down on the place, the miraculous life-giving place which was still not yet a valley but a teeming luxuriant garden.

Crackling and hissing, the clouds advanced from the west as if pushed by a giant hand, drawing the rains in their wake until earth and sky and water were joined in a thunderous fusion.

The thunder and lightning became one with the man's troubled dreams. Raindrops drummed like voices in his ears. The voices became a single voice, soft as the dawn wind through the reeds but strong and terrible. Harsh and scorching like the churning flames, but gentle and caressing too. He listened to the voice and wept, and in his dreams the man's tears blended with the rain. His heart ached and his bones were cold.

The voice spoke to him not of the past or the future. Not of the terror and darkness, but of sweetness and laughter, of warmth and light. The voice spoke of women – not the females of his vanished clan, but of one woman.

His woman.

Afterwards, as the tumult of the storm passed, loneliness swept over him again. It was a loneliness for which there could be only one healing.

PART TWO

Billy's Story

8

'So this is him?'

'Yes, ma'am.'

'Don't you go calling me "ma'am". I'm not one of your bleeding officers' wives. Or was it me fancy frock and me elegant manners as mixed you up?'

The woman's cackle of laughter echoed through the narrow little hallway.

She was stocky and dark-haired with a massive bosom, sharp shrewd eyes and great mutton-coloured hands. A hand-rolled cigarette was slanted down between her lips, and she was wearing a filthy foul-smelling pinafore over a gaudy cotton dress that flapped round her ankles in the draught from the door.

'Doris, that's me name,' she added, coughing.

The man laughed back. 'Well, that's him, Doris.'

'Let's have a look at him.'

The hallway was almost dark, but halfway along the passage a pool of light spilled out from an open doorway. Billy Ramsden felt a hand grip him by the shoulder and propel him forward. He came to a stop, blinking in the brightness.

In the silence that followed, he sensed he was being inspected.

'Right little darkie, isn't he?' It was the woman's voice again.

'That's just the sun,' the man replied. 'India, Africa, them sort of places where he's grown up, you get a lot of it out there. A couple of months back here and he'll come up all normal.'

'I hope you're right,' the woman said doubtfully. 'Wouldn't

want the street thinking Charlie's lad had a drop of the nigger in him. We'd better let my Alf have a look.'

The woman paused. 'Blow me down, would you believe it – his name's gone clean out of me head! What's the little tyke called?'

'Billy,' the man said.

'Billy, of course! I'll be forgetting me own name next. Hullo there, young Billy.'

They were the first words his aunt had addressed to him. She removed the cigarette from her mouth and bellowed upstairs.

'Alf, come on down! It's Charlie's lad, Billy!'

There was a clatter on the landing and a man stumped down the stairs in a pair of unlaced boots. He was dressed in a grey shirt, a thick felt waistcoat smeared with coal-dust and oil, and serge army trousers bound below the knees with twine.

He stared at Billy.

'Good God, sonny. So you're Charlie's boy?'

Billy shrugged awkwardly and nodded.

He glanced furtively at the man. His Uncle Alf, as Billy came to know him, had a shining bald head, a worn kindly face, and tired eyes. He had descended the stairs with a heavy limp, dragging a twisted foot behind him. For some reason Billy decided he liked him better than his raucous wheezing Aunt Doris.

'Been out in the sun, have you, lad?'

'We've gone into that, haven't we—?'

Doris paused and looked at the other man in the hall. He was a tall smart young corporal in the uniform of the military police. He'd met Billy off the train from the Liverpool docks, and brought the boy to the Brixton house.

'Jeff,' the corporal said.

'Jeff, is it?' Doris turned back to her husband. 'Jeff and me, we've been into all that. Young Billy, he's been in Africa and such. That darkie look, it'll go when he's been back with his own kind for a few weeks.'

'That's true, sir,' the corporal said.

'"Sir"?' Doris cackled. '"Ma'am" and now "Sir", if you

please. Christ, Jeff, what do we call you – Your Majesty or what?'

The corporal laughed again. 'Regulations, Doris.'

Uncle Alf seemed to notice him for the first time. His eyes swept over the uniform and the red band round the hat the young man was holding in his hand.

'Your mob, they sorted us out when we came off the boats from Dunkirk. That's where I got this,' he lifted his leg and shook his crippled foot. 'There was one sergeant I remember, Dave he was called. Got me on the last ambulance from Dover to London. You probably know him. Come and have a cup of tea, and I'll tell you about it.'

He limped away towards the kitchen. The corporal and Aunt Doris followed him.

Billy was left in the hall. He felt more alone than he'd ever felt before.

All his life Billy would remember his first few weeks in London. Not for the strangeness or the loneliness, but the cold.

It was late-November when the ship docked and winter had already set in. It proved to be one of the longest and hardest winters of the century. Billy had never known cold before. Now it dominated everything. His bones ached, his face was chapped with sores, his breath came in raw painful clouds of steam.

At night, unable to sleep, he lay huddled in a shivering ball. Whenever he was sent outside, which happened twice a day, the wind on the street stung his skin, and left a bitter stoney taste in his mouth. If he tried to crouch by the coal-fired kitchen range, the only source of heat in the little house, the other children who'd gathered there kicked him away.

Billy was too numb and dispirited to fight back.

He slunk to the edge of the room and lay down with the household cats and dogs who'd been kicked there too. He didn't even know who the children were. Their faces and the faces of the adults in the house were nothing more than a blur. So were the rest of his surroundings.

Billy's entire concentration and energies were spent on

surviving the freezing draughts and the icy air. To everyone else in the house he might as well have been a ghost.

And then, one Friday evening, Billy heard a new voice.

'So you're Uncle Charlie's lad, are you, sonny boy?'

Billy was passing through the hall. The voice was unmistakably addressing him. It didn't belong to one of the children, and it wasn't hostile. He glanced back warily.

The front door had just opened, letting in a tall young man in a heavy military greatcoat, its brass buttons gleaming in the dusk.

'Yes, mister.' Billy's teeth began to chatter in the wind howling in off the street.

The young man closed the door. He took off his peaked khaki cap, and Billy saw his face. It was open and friendly with dark eyes under wiry black hair.

'Billy, isn't it?'

'Yes, mister.'

'Don't you call me mister, lad. My name's Jack. I'm your cousin.'

'Yes, mister. I mean, yes, Jack.'

Billy's teeth were chattering so badly now he could hardly speak.

'Is that you, Jack?' Aunt Doris' voice bellowed from the kitchen.

'Yes, Mum. I got a weekend pass,' Jack shouted back.

'I'll put your tea on, son,' Doris went on. 'But be a love and do the usual, would you? Feed Bonnie and Bess first. Dad's in bed with the flu, and no one's seen to them since yesterday.'

Jack was struggling out of his coat. He paused and swore. Then he put the coat back on.

'All right, Mum,' he called again.

He glanced at Billy. 'Just my bleeding luck! Well, you can give me a hand, sonny boy.'

Jack opened the door. Billy seized his own coat and hurried out on to the street after him.

The wind was stronger than ever. It screamed in Billy's face, making his eyes stream and his ears feel like chips of ice, but for the first time since he'd arrived he had something more important than the cold to think about.

Someone had taken notice of him.

Billy had no idea where they were going or how long they walked for. The neighbourhood was still a mystery to him. Until then he hadn't ventured farther than the street where the house stood. Apart from a thin bowl of light round the occasional street lamp, the darkness was so intense he wouldn't have known where they were heading anyway.

Tripping and stumbling over the broken flagstones, he tried to keep up as Jack strode confidently ahead.

Finally his cousin stopped before a towering black wall. Billy heard a key rattling in a lock and then another sound, farther away and somewhere above them. The sound grew closer and louder, and turned into a roar as something pounded by overhead. Scarlet sparks showered down, and Billy's nostrils were filled with the acrid stench of smoke.

Billy cowered back. Then he realised what it was. The Lucknow barracks were close to the railway station, and he'd grown up with the sound and stench of trains. The railway here obviously ran above their heads along an embankment.

A door creaked open, there was the fizz of a striking match, and a kerosene lamp flared. Billy blinked. He just had time to see he was peering into a large arched vault, when Jack shouted at him.

'For Christ's sake, Billy, are you trying to freeze us both to death? Shut the bloody door!'

As Billy scuttled inside, another smell swirled over his face.

Utterly unlike the harsh fumes that had billowed down outside, this one was warm and rich and damp. He stood quite still. Billy knew the smell even better than the coal and sulphur of the train.

'Horses!' he whispered to himself.

In front of him, dividing the vault in two, was a heavy wooden partition. From the far side, still out of Billy's sight, came a deep-throated whinny, the jangle of a harness, and the clop of iron-shod hooves on a brick floor.

Jack hung the lantern from a nail and opened the door to the stable. Billy followed him through. Two huge dray horses, the biggest and most beautiful horses Billy had ever seen, were standing side by side in the gloom beyond. Their coats shone with a silky mahogany glow, and long feathers of steam coiled in the air as they turned their heads.

'Are they yours, mister?' Billy's voice was almost a whisper.

'Call me mister again and I'll leather your arse, you little twerp,' said Jack. 'No, they're not mine. They're my dad's. Know about horses, do you, lad?'

'Course I know about horses,' Billy answered. 'Rattray's Sikhs, that's me dad's mob, they ride horses, don't they? I been working with horses long as I know. Rambahadur Singh, I used to help him. We even did the colonel's polo ponies, didn't we?'

He drew himself up confidently. 'Nothing I don't know about horses, Jack. You want any help with your dad's?'

Jack looked down at the pinch-faced little urchin standing eagerly in front of him. Jack smiled. Then he dipped a metal bucket into a sack, scooped it out full of oats, and handed it to the boy.

'They're called Bonnie and Bess. Let's see you feed them.'

Billy staggered under the bucket's weight. He pushed his way between the two animals, speaking to them softly in the phrases he'd learned from Rambahadur Singh, the regiment's oldest groom, and heaved the oats up into their feeding troughs.

Then, without prompting from Jack, he looked round for a spade. He shovelled the horses' droppings into a pile by the stable door, tugged some armfuls of straw from a bale, and scattered it over the floor. Finally he filled the water basin from a barrel.

Billy wiped the dirt from his hands on his coat, and stood with his hands on his hips. In spite of the cold, he was sweating.

'All right, Jack?'

Jack chuckled. 'Not bad at all, young Billy.'

'Next time we'll have a look at their hooves. Old Singh taught me a few tricks about looking after them. I'll show you if you want.'

Jack started to laugh but managed to restrain himself. 'Like animals, do you?'

Billy shrugged. 'Elephants, that's what I really want to do.'

'Elephants?' Jack couldn't stop his laughter now. 'You won't find many of them in Brixton. Where the hell did you learn to fancy elephants?'

'Ngoro told us—'

Billy stopped abruptly.

He glanced at Jack. There was nothing unkind in his laughter, but for some reason Billy didn't want to talk about the valley and the old Masai. He changed the subject, looking back at the horses.

'What does your dad use them for?'

'Dad's a totter. Didn't you know that?'

Billy shook his head. 'No one's told me nothing. What's a totter?'

'Christ, what a lot you've got to learn, Billy boy!'

Jack explained.

A totter, he said, drove a horse and cart round the streets collecting and sometimes buying the odds and ends – unwanted furniture, scrap metal, discarded clothing – that people wanted to get rid of. He then sold them to the traders in London's street markets. Some people derisively called totters rag-and-bone men, but in Jack's view it was a skilled and demanding profession, needing a shrewd eye to separate the rubbish from what still had use and value.

As a child Jack had often accompanied his father on his rounds, and he was proud of him. Uncle Alf's brother had been a totter, too. When he'd died a couple of years ago, Alf had taken in his horse, Bess. That was why there were two horses in the stable.

'So now you know,' Jack finished as they walked home. 'And I'll tell you something else for free. You just talked yourself into a job back there.'

'What do you mean?'

'Bonnie and Bess, you made a fair hand with them. I usually see to them weekends when I'm back, whether Dad's ill or not. From now on you can.'

Billy stared up at him. 'I can look after them?'

'That's what I said. Here.'

They'd reached the front door. Jack paused and fumbled in his pocket. He pulled out the key to the stable and gave it to Billy.

'Don't lose it or I'll give you a right bloody tanning.'

He went into the house. Billy stood outside for a moment in the darkness with the rain streaming down his face.

The key, warm from Jack's pocket, felt hard and heavy in his hand. At least someone had accepted him. Billy gripped it tightly as if it was the most valuable thing he'd ever been given.

9

Jack went back to barracks on Sunday evening.

He was a Coldstream Guardsman and was stationed at Chelsea, where his battalion had just taken up ceremonial duties again after returning from the war. Before he left he showed Billy a photograph of himself in a bearskin and tunic, mounting guard at Buckingham Palace.

'Oldest regiment in the whole bloody army and still the best, we are,' Jack said. '"Second to None", that's the Lilywhites' motto, and no one even comes close. More battle honours than all of the rest of the buggers put together. The other mobs, they're just a bunch of tossers. Don't even talk to me about the Grenadiers. They couldn't fight their way out of a paper-bag with fixed bayonets.'

Billy looked entranced at the marching line of giants with the royal standard waving above them.

'Think they'd have me, Jack?'

Jack chuckled. 'You'll need to eat an awful lot of Mum's dinners first, Billy boy.'

Billy made a private resolution never again to refuse a second helping of Aunt Doris' cabbage and turnip stew. It was the most revolting dish he'd ever eaten, but if that was the price he had to pay, he'd cheerfully pay it. His loyalty to Rattray's Sikhs would never waver, but all he wanted now was to be like Jack.

Jack had changed his life.

The Monday morning after Jack's departure it was colder than ever. When Billy went down to the kitchen, the usual group of children were squatting shoulder to shoulder round the stove. Billy hesitated for a moment. There was no sign of his aunt. He breathed in deeply. His stomach felt even icier than the air in the hall. He stepped forward and butted his way into the circle of figures.

'Christ, what the bleeding hell do you think you're doing?'

The shout came from the only child whose name Billy knew. He was a hulking boy called Steve, three years older than Billy and half a head taller. Billy's shoulder had sent him sprawling on to his back.

'I can get warm, can't I?' Billy answered. 'Got as much right as you.'

Steve heaved himself upright. He stared at Billy, his eyes narrow and furious.

'We don't want no niggers here. Fuck off, you little bastard!'

To Billy the insults were unimportant. They were just hollow noises lost in the air. What was important were the other watching children, the place by the fire, and Steve's malevolent, threatening presence.

Billy didn't stop to think. His father had told him once never to get into a fight unless he was going to win it. Billy knew he briefly had the initiative and he took it. He hurled himself at Steve while the boy was still unbalanced.

Blindly and single-mindedly, Billy fought to win.

He savaged Steve with the ferocity of a wounded leopard. He kicked and stamped and gouged, he spat and bit, he tore out tufts of Steve's hair and clawed at his eyes. Astounded and unnerved, Steve reeled back and collapsed. He rolled on to his stomach and began to scream.

Billy wasn't satisfied.

Anger at the humiliation he'd been forced to endure – and the shame he felt at allowing it to happen – goaded him on in a rising red tide of fury. He grasped Steve's head and began to batter it against the bottom rim of the range. Steve squirmed and moaned with pain. Blood trickled out between Billy's fingers, and he could smell the harsh smell of burning hair.

'Billy!'

The shout stopped him. His chest heaving, he looked at the door. It was Aunt Doris. She had come into the kitchen and was gazing down at the scene appalled.

'What the hell's going on?'

Billy glanced at Steve lying on the floor between his legs.

Although his anger had started to cool at Aunt Doris' appearance, it hadn't faded enough for him to accept responsibility for what had happened. That was Steve's fault and he was going to face up to it.

He kicked Steve hard in the ribs. 'Tell her!'

'Billy wanted to sit by the stove.' Steve's voice was weak and tears mingled with blood were streaming down his face. 'We had a bit of a quarrel. It was nothing really, Auntie. He can sit there if he wants to.'

'Well, I never! You young hooligans!'

Billy stood up.

His aunt's scolding went on. He took no notice. He stared at the other children still crouched by the fire. One by one their eyes slid away as they confronted his gaze. Billy went out.

When he came down for breakfast next day the circle of kneeling figures shuffled hastily aside and left a large empty space before the centre of the fire. Billy squatted down.

Before he held his hands out to the flames, he called to the cats and dogs lurking by the wall to share the warmth with him.

They weren't really as bad as he'd thought, the other children in the house.

Billy realised it partly at that time, but mainly much later. Until the fight with Steve they'd just been anonymous faces. Afterwards as they cautiously started to talk to him, accepting his authority as the unexpected new leader of the pack round the kitchen stove, Billy began to put names and identities to them.

There were seven in all. Sally, Val, and Bert were the orphaned children of Uncle Alf's brother, the former owner of Bonnie, whose wife had died long ago. Di, Daisy, and Frank were Alf and Doris' own children, the younger sisters and brother of Billy's new hero, Jack. The vanquished Steve was another orphan, the only son of Doris' sister who had been killed with her husband in the German blitz on London.

Billy wasn't sure Steve ever really forgave him for the fight, but afterwards he must have decided Billy was better as an ally than an enemy. It was the bigger and older boy – pasty-faced, cunning, and sly – who first took Billy out and taught him about Brixton.

The street where they lived was called Malplaquet Road, although no one ever called it that. To its inhabitants it was either the 'street' or more often just 'Mally'.

Half a mile south of the Thames, Mally was one of dozens of roads built in the London borough of Lambeth in the middle of Queen Victoria's reign. Named after one of Marlborough's famous victories – the two neighbouring roads were called Blenheim and Oudenaard – its little red-brick houses must once have looked trim and attractive, at least compared to the decaying tenements where most of the city's poor then lived.

By 1945, blackened and crumbling from a century of smoke and pollution, shadowed by the towers of the gas storage plant, choked intermittently for six months of the year by lung-corroding fogs even thicker than the famous Victorian pea-soupers, riddled with pot-holes and gaping with blind cavities where the Nazi bombers had blasted away not just houses but entire generations of their inhabitants too, Malplaquet Road when Billy first saw it looked on the surface as desolate, derelict and sad as the slums it had been meant to replace.

'Doesn't look like much, Mally, does it, I mean not to a world traveller like you, Billy?' his big cousin Jack said teasingly.

It was the following spring.

Jack had returned on one of his weekend passes from Chelsea barracks, and he'd been to visit the horses with Billy, now firmly ensconced as their keeper. They were walking back together in the thin March sun.

'There's more to Mally than meets the eye,' Jack went on. 'See that house over there.'

He pointed at a house at the end of the street.

'Kid Hawkins, he was born and lived there.'

'Who was Kid Hawkins?' Billy asked.

'Jesus, you've got a way to go, haven't you, Billy boy? Kid Hawkins was the best fighter to come out of London in the last twenty-five years, that's all. Only a blown-up middleweight but he went the distance with Tommy Farr, and we all know who Farr almost beat, don't we?'

Billy shook his head.

'Joe bloody Louis, that's who,' Jack said in exasperation. 'The brown bomber himself. Him that's still world champ today.'

Billy nodded. At least he'd heard of Joe Louis. He remembered the troopers in Lucknow talking with awe about the great American boxer.

'I remember the Kid coming home after he won his first title,' Jack went on. 'Everyone turned out to see him. He'd bought himself a car, the first in Lambeth except for the big villains'. He used to give us nippers rides. Forget about the Coldstream, Billy. If you want to make yourself real money – and I don't mean a totter's tanners – you become a scrapper.'

He paused and looked at the boy speculatively. 'You're on the skinny side, but I heard you gave young Steve a right spanking.'

Billy shrugged and didn't reply.

'Met Father Geoffrey yet?'

Billy shook his head again.

'Just see it from here, you can.'

Jack's arm reached out again. In the distance at the far end of Malplaquet Road was a church spire framed by a group of trees, their leaves just starting to break out into fragile yellow-green.

'St Barnabas, that's his church. Lives in the little old rectory next door. Father Geoffrey, he was the one who started the Kid off. Well, he's started dozens of them, hasn't he, him and Len? I reckon he should take a butcher's at you.'

Jack chuckled. 'Wait till you meet him, Billy. I'll tell you something for free. Father Geoffrey'll make your bloody elephants look tame!'

Jack headed on with his long guardsman's stride.

'No, I can't, Father. I can't remember the bleeding words, can I?'

'Course you can, darling.'

'It's me mind, Father. It's been on the slippery slope for years. One foot in the grave and the other on a banana skin, that's me.'

'Nonsense. Give it a go.'

On the landing Billy hesitated.

One of the two voices coming up to him from the hall below was Aunt Doris'. He'd never heard the other before. It belonged to a man, it was hoarse and rasping, and it clearly didn't come from Lambeth. Its accent was what the street called 'educated' – or it would have been if it hadn't been so slurred the words were almost incomprehensible.

'And if you do forget,' the man went on, 'flash the old leg, Doris. That'll give them something to think about while you fish around for the lines.'

'Dirty old bugger!'

Doris hooted with laughter.

A moment later her voice lifted in a rendering of the First World War song 'Goodbye, Dolly Grey'. Billy waited until she'd finished. Then he continued downstairs.

'Perfection!' It was the man again. 'It'll be the triumph of the concert as it always is – as you bloody well know, you old baggage. If I'd closed my eyes, I might have been listening to Nelly Melba. What are you going to do for an encore?'

Doris giggled, her face pink with pleasure. Then both she and the man noticed Billy at the foot of the stairs. Doris swung round.

'Talk of the devil, so to speak,' she exclaimed. 'Here he is, Father, just as I was about to fetch him down. Billy, say hullo to Father Geoffrey. He's come specially to see you.'

She caught Billy's arm and tugged him forward so violently he tripped, fell, and slid across the worn linoleum to the man's feet. Flushing scarlet, Billy scrambled to his feet and held out his hand.

'Pleased to meet you, sir,' he said.

Father Geoffrey shook his hand vaguely. He was one of the strangest figures Billy had ever seen.

Very short, barely taller than Billy himself, he was thickset and dressed in black and white clerical robes. He had a bald head, a jowled unshaven face, and dark pouches under his eyes. The eyes themselves looked out myopically from behind pebble-glass spectacles like little black stones framed by scarlet veins. A hand-rolled cigarette slanted down from his mouth, and a yellow nicotine stain ran from his lips to his chin.

Smoke from the cigarette wound up into the air, and the smell of whisky came off him in waves of sour-smelling fumes.

He let go of Billy and heaved up the skirts of his robes. He tucked his hands into the pockets beneath, rocked back on his heels, and tilted his head to one side, studying Billy for a long time.

'Like his balance,' the priest said eventually. 'Protein and carbohydrates, and we'll give him a try. And don't say you don't know what I mean, Doris.'

'We can't afford that stuff, Father,' she complained.

'Balls!' Father Geoffrey snapped back. 'Look what it did for Jack. Would you've had a guardsman as a son without it? Of course you wouldn't, you mean old trollop! You found it for him, you can find it for this one too.'

He broke off and his little black eyes turned back to Billy.

'I've forgotten your name, young man.'

'Billy.'

'Of course. Jack told me about you, back in the spring I think it was. I should have been here much sooner, but I was busy. Never mind. October's a good time to start. Here.'

He felt in his pocket and pulled out five silver florins.

'That's for the bus for the next month. Don't thank me, thank the trust. You pick up the number 9 in the Brixton Road. Your aunt Doris will tell you where to get on and where to get off. Only two rules: be just like me. Don't drink and don't smoke.'

He inhaled on the cigarette. Billy could still smell the whisky fumes coming out of his pores.

'You'll have learnt the first principle of life: grown-ups lie. You don't have to be like them. You can be yourself. That's an even more important lesson.'

Father Geoffrey stopped talking and glanced at Doris.

'I want him there, Doris. If he's not, no "Goodbye Dollie Grey" at the concert. Bargain?'

'Yes, Father,' she said meekly. Not for anything in the world was she about to jeopardise her role as the star of St Barnabas' Christmas fund-raising concert.

Father Geoffrey turned.

As he went out his black and white robes swept round his legs like the wing-beats, Billy thought, of a heron taking off from the Kenyan swamps. Not a huge one, a goliath heron like Ngoro. A little one. A night heron, hunched and stocky and combative.

10

'Now!' the voice said.

Billy's hands were encased in sparring gloves. He speared out his left arm.

Barely moving his hips, Len swayed and Billy's punch swung harmlessly away through the air. He blinked.

'And again,' Len instructed.

Billy tried again. The same thing happened. Then again and again, and it was always the same. One moment the battered old face was immediately in front of him: the next, as he tried to hit it, the face had gone.

Billy dropped his arms in frustration.

Instantly Len's own gloved hand snapped forward and caught Billy square on his nose. It was only a light blow but Billy's head jerked back and his eyes watered with pain.

'Don't you ever bleeding listen? Never drop your guard, lad!'

Wearily Billy raised his gloves to his face and began to circle round Len once more.

'How's he making out, Len?' a voice called out a few minutes later.

Len pushed Billy away.

Both of them looked down from the raised floor of the boxing ring to see Father Geoffrey. He was standing below them leaning over the canvas-covered platform with his arms folded beneath the ropes, and the inevitable cigarette drooping from his mouth.

Len walked over. 'If he left his mouth open as often as his guard, it'd be so full of flies he couldn't ask his way to the bleeding toilet.

'All right, that's enough for today,' he said to Billy. Then he added grudgingly to the priest, 'Bit of faith, hope, and charity from you, Father, and he'll probably do.'

Billy climbed down from the ring, watching the two of them talking as he unlaced his gloves.

It was three and a half years since Billy had first visited the gym of the Crown and Garter Boys' Club in the docks of East London. All round him boys from the East End or across the Thames were sparring in pairs, working out on punch bags, or exercising with weights and skipping-ropes. The club was owned by a trust founded earlier in the century by a millionaire Jewish philanthropist, who'd grown up in the nearby streets before making his fortune.

The gym smelled of dried sweat, rosin, sawdust, and oily green muscle embrocation. In the years since he'd been going there it had become a second home to Billy, and Len, the boxing coach, his new hero. Len was a former professional fighter. He was harsh, short-tempered, authoritarian, white-haired, and built, it seemed to Billy when he occasionally managed to hit him, out of brick and ironwood.

Len had been born while Queen Victoria was on the throne.

He'd fought in the fields of Flanders in the First World War, he'd lived through the savage depression of the thirties, when his fists had supported three generations of his family, he'd survived Hitler's pattern-bombing raids on London in the second great war. He believed there was only one way out of the ghettoes of the East End: boxing.

That required, in Len's view, skill, discipline, and what he called 'bottle'. Once a week he'd gather the club's boys round him and lecture them on his philosophy.

'Skill, I can teach you,' he'd say. 'Discipline, I can belt into you. Bottle's all your own. You've got it or you haven't. And if you haven't, there's always the other way up. You can go whoring.'

He'd pause then and glance slowly round the circle of listening youngsters.

'Hands up who wants to be a whore!'

The question was always greeted by silence. None of the crouching boys even laughed. To them all, like Billy, Len offered a bold masculine future threaded through with money and girls and cars. That was something they could understand. That was something to be yearned after and battled for.

'I'll run you back to your auntie's, Billy.'

Father Geoffrey had finished his conversation with Len. Wheezing and coughing, he'd come up to Billy.

'If she hasn't done a bunk, we should find Esmerelda outside.'

'Esmerelda' was Father Geoffrey's ancient black open-topped MG. Billy followed him out and climbed into the passenger seat.

He knew little about cars, but Father Geoffrey clashed the gears with a metallic grinding sound that made even Billy wince. The priest set off, weaving, slamming on the brakes, and then suddenly and wildly accelerating through the traffic as if he'd been a racing driver. Whenever other drivers hooted in anger or alarm, he simply waved his hand and smiled benignly.

'Don't blame the poor creatures,' he beamed at Billy. 'The internal combustion engine's still new to most of them. It's as unfamiliar as a camel. By the time you've reached man's state, they'll be handling it as skilfully as I do.'

Billy gripped the sides of his seat and stared fixedly ahead.

Twenty minutes later they came into Malplaquet Road. The car mounted the pavement, slewed across it, and came to a stop with one of the rear wheels in the air and the other buried in the sunken storm drain. Father Geoffrey switched off the engine.

'You're making progress, Billy. Len's quite pleased with you, did you know that?'

Billy shook his head.

With the dour and taciturn Len, it was impossible to tell. He also remembered the fugitive target of Len's head and how that day, as so often before, he hadn't been able to catch it. Bleakly, he wondered if he ever would.

'He doesn't want to rush you, but he's thinking of putting you in for the London Boys' next year. Know what they are?'

'Yes, Father.'

The London Boys' Championships were the first major step on the ladder that for some – Kid Hawkins was just one of them – had led on to Olympic selection, a medal, a professional career, and a national, even an international, title.

'So that's good,' Father Geoffrey went on. 'What isn't so good is I haven't seen you at St Barnabas since the last Christmas concert, where your auntie did her famous party-piece.'

'No, Father.'

'Why not?'

Billy didn't answer. None of his new family, he'd discovered, went to church except for occasions like the concert. There'd been no reason for him to go either.

'Skill, discipline, and bottle,' the priest said thoughtfully. 'Len's giving you the skill. Bottle he says you've got. Leaves discipline, doesn't it? Doesn't come easily, Billy. Needs practice until it's a habit of mind. But without it, neither of the others are any use. And once you have discipline, it's with you forever.'

He broke off, rolled and lit another cigarette, coughing as he inhaled.

'We've got a service at St Barnabas next Sunday. I want you there. I want you there once every month from now on. You don't have to do anything. You don't have to pray or sing or even listen. But I want you there. It's called discipline. Understand?'

'Yes, Father.'

Father Geoffrey hadn't made any threats.

He didn't need to. Billy was beginning to understand how the priest worked. He, Billy, was in the same position as Aunt Doris. If she, redoubtable as she was, hadn't done what Father Geoffrey wanted, she wouldn't have sung at the Christmas concert.

If Billy wasn't in church once a month, he knew his visits to the Crown and Garter would end.

'Besides, I think it'll interest you,' Father Geoffrey added. 'It's a special service. We're making an appeal for the Church Missionary Society in Africa. They're trying to help a group

74

of villages whose crops have been attacked by a plague of marauding elephants.'

He leant across and opened the door. 'Hop out, young man. I'll see you on Sunday.'

He started the engine and the car lurched away, the bottom of its chassis throwing out sparks as it scraped along the pavement's edge.

Billy stood quite still. Africa and elephants. The hairs prickled on the back of his neck.

It was 1949 and Billy was almost fourteen.

Until the previous winter he'd shared a bedroom in the Mally house with four of the other children. Then, watching Billy one day as he took his weekly bath in a tin tub in front of the kitchen range – she always supervised the children as they bathed to make sure they scrubbed themselves almost raw – Aunt Doris noticed a fringe of hair, emerging at his groin.

Billy was approaching puberty.

Puberty, in Doris' long experience, meant the start of another cycle of trouble. She couldn't control its rampaging urges, but it was certainly time to move young Billy away from the girls. A week later he was given a tiny space of his own in a garret under the eaves.

This evening after supper he lay on the truckle bed which occupied most of the floor, with his arms crossed behind his head.

Africa and elephants meant the valley and Ngoro. Most of all they meant Violet.

During the first lonely bitter winter in Brixton, Billy had thought of Africa every night. Rolled up in a ball unable to sleep because of the icy cold, he had drawn it to him for comfort and warmth. If he concentrated hard enough, he could even persuade himself he was back in the valley with Violet at his side, old Ngoro's spear-tip flaring blue-gold in the sunlight, and the elephants moving through the mist to drink at the river below.

Sometimes, if he *really* tried, Billy could even stop his teeth chattering and his body shivering.

He wasn't any longer in the cramped and noisy dormitory

in the Mally house, with the other children's breath hanging in the cold air as they tossed and shifted restlessly in the dark. He was sitting on the tree-trunk above the gorge. Ngoro was speaking about the lion of the spirits and Violet was gripping his hand and the sun was cascading down over them both.

Often, in the depths of his worst misery over those first months, Billy had thought of running away from Mally and trying to find her.

He knew, even as the yearning came to him, it was hopeless. He had no idea where Violet was and, anyway, she belonged to a different world – a world as alien and impenetrable to him as the world of Mally would have been to her. Yet Billy never let go of her or Ngoro or the valley or the elephants.

Together they remained a talisman, they were safety, they were his refuge.

And then Jack entered his life and gave him charge of the horses. That had changed almost everything. He was no longer an outcast. He had a function and an identity – and he'd proved it when he beat Steve for a place at the fire. Then he'd started to box. He was good, Billy had no doubt about that, very good. Even at thirteen he believed he was good enough to go, as Father Geoffrey and Len reluctantly agreed, 'all the way'.

Which meant out from Brixton to anywhere he wanted.

Skill, discipline and bottle. Billy knew he had all three. He no longer needed to gather Violet, the valley, and the elephants round him like a cloak at night for comfort. They belonged to the past. Billy would join the Coldstream Guards like Jack – they were 'hot' on good scrappers, Jack had told him – and hone his skills and his fists while he was paid as a soldier.

Billy could make his own warmth now.

And yet . . .

He frowned, sat upright and swung his legs off the bed. There was barely enough space between the bed's edge and the door to accommodate his knees. His hand explored the dusty cobwebbed floor-boards beneath the lumpy mattress. He found what he was looking for and pulled it out.

It was a yellow oilskin army ammunition pouch Jack had

given him as a reward for feeding Bonnie and Bess. Billy opened it and pulled out what he'd stored inside. There were only two objects, both of them dirt-stained and worn. One was the passport he'd been issued with in Lucknow before his journey back to Britain.

The other, a grubby jagged bundle of papers roughly scissored down one side, was his half of the deeds to the valley that Violet had thrust at him with implacable determination as they both stood, sleepy and shivering in their pyjamas, on one of the ship's metal-floored corridors.

Billy sat with the shared deeds in his hand gazing up through the grimed pane of glass in the roof at the stars in the night sky.

For a while he had let go of Violet. She had never, he sensed, let go of him. The elephants bound them together. They always would.

11

It was Aunt Doris who made Steve accompany Billy when she learnt he was going to Sunday's service at St Barnabas.

'Be bloody good for you, you young tearaway,' she said. 'Make it a habit and maybe you'll learn a little respect for your elders and betters. Don't you even think of bunking off. I'll ask Father Geoffrey if he saw you there. And brush your bleeding hair, the pair of you!'

Their hair brushed and flattened with water, the two boys walked out of the house.

'Bitch!' Steve said sulkily. 'You, too, Billy. You fucking got me into this.'

Billy glanced at him as they trudged up the road in the Sunday morning sunshine.

At seventeen and over six foot tall, Steve had ballooned out until he was almost grotesquely fat. He waddled beside Billy like a giant penguin, his threadbare suit straining over his swollen and bulging body, his little darting eyes, furtive and sharp as a ferret's, almost buried in mounds of soft pink flesh.

Billy knew that if he himself was an outsider in the household, Steve was one too. He shouldn't have been. He had just the same blood relationship with Aunt Doris and Uncle Alf, and he'd been there even longer than his orphaned cousins – let alone Billy.

Something about Steve put people's backs up. It wasn't just that he was awkward and graceless – there'd never been any question of his going to the Crown and Garter gym – there was something untrustworthy about him too. He was a bully, using his size and weight to terrorise the younger children. He was lazy, he lied, and he was

78

constantly fomenting trouble, not just among the children but the adults too.

If any quarrel arose – Alf returning home drunk or Doris being too exhausted to cook a hot dinner – Steve could be counted on slyly to prolong it and make it worse. Billy knew that. In spite of it, he'd come to tolerate Steve, almost to like him.

Steve was bright, he was cunning, he was devious and informed. He knew things Billy would never have found out without his help. He also had imagination, a wild soaring imagination that Billy somehow found seductive. It had made Steve into an ally.

'It's not my fault and I'm not a bitch,' Billy answered. 'Say that again and I'll bust your fucking face.'

'Give over, Billy,' Steve protested. 'I didn't mean you. It's just a bleeding great yawn, isn't it?'

As always Steve backed down. Billy might be smaller and younger, but he was a real frightener when his blood was up. Steve had seen it once and he wasn't ever going to provoke the fury again.

Billy didn't answer.

He would have thought it a waste of time too if it hadn't have been for Father Geoffrey's mention of Africa and the elephants. He'd tried to tell Steve about them, but Steve simply slouched along beside him shuffling his feet, uninterested.

They reached the end of the road, circled Ramillies Crescent, and went into the church. They were late and the service had already started. They took their seats at the back as the first hymn ended.

Father Geoffrey read out the order of the day and the service continued. From time to time Steve nudged Billy and yawned ostentatiously, patting his mouth with his hand and winking. Billy kicked him and stared angrily at the candle-lit altar. He knew Steve blamed him for them being there. Guiltily he felt just as bored as his cousin.

Then Father Geoffrey stood up and crossed to the centre of the raised aisle in front of the altar. Billy sat forward.

The priest staggered slightly. He was wheezing as usual,

his voice was as hoarse and throaty as ever, and Billy could almost smell the alcohol coming off his skin.

'Rat-arsed!' Steve whispered, giggling.

'Normally, as you know,' Father Geoffrey said, 'this is the moment when I deliver my sermon. Today is different. Today I hand over the pulpit to one of my brothers-in-Christ from what we have been taught to think of as the dark continent of Africa. Its darkness is for you to consider. But not before, I suggest, you have listened to Father Thomas Moffat Akhashi.'

Father Geoffrey swept out his arm, and his robes fluttered wildly in the wind gusting in from below the west door.

Billy stiffened.

A man was climbing up into the pulpit. He was wearing the same robes as Father Geoffry and the same clerical dog-collar. He was the same height, he was also portly and, to Billy's eye, he was slightly unsteady on his feet, too.

There was one difference. The preacher was black.

The man opened the Bible on the lectern in front of him, and searched through it for his text. He found it, straightened the wobbling spectacles on his nose, and began to speak.

'Brothers and sisters in God . . .'

Beside Billy, Steve gave a low involuntary whistle. 'Shit, Billy, look at him, for Christ's sake. He's a bloody nigger!'

Billy kicked him again. He tried to listen to what the man was saying.

It was very difficult. The black man spoke in a high excitable voice that was unmistakably African, although it lacked Ngoro's clarity and slow sonorous cadences, and his words were often almost unintelligible. He was sponsored by the Church Missionary Society, Billy managed to gather that, and his parish was in somewhere called Uganda – a country Billy had never heard of.

There were many villages in the parish and the fields on which the people depended for their food were being ravaged by elephants. He was appealing for money first to pay for a hunter to shoot the elephants, and second to buy rifles for the villagers so that in future they could kill the animals themselves.

'My people are the children of God!' The black preacher hammered the pulpit as he finished, his voice rising in a frenzy. 'They are being savaged by the beasts of the field. Help us, o my brothers and sisters, I beseech you, help us so that the Almighty's work may continue. Praise be the Lord!'

He stopped suddenly. He gave a great beaming smile and stumbled down to the foot of the pulpit where Father Geoffrey caught and embraced him.

'Shit!' Steve said in awe. He looked astounded. 'Would you believe it, Billy? The monkey's rat-arsed too.'

They were filing out of the church a few minutes later when the service had ended.

Billy didn't reply. For some reason he felt acutely embarrassed. He was used to Father Geoffrey's drinking and eccentric behaviour, everyone in Brixton was and no one thought any the less of him for it – people like his Uncle Alf chuckled admiringly about it, it justified their own nightly visits to the pub.

That the black preacher was drunk too shocked him. It was so totally unexpected. So was the preacher's plea for money to kill the elephants. That was even more shocking and surprising. It was contrary to everything he'd been trying to explain to Steve. Somehow he felt both betrayed and responsible.

They reached the door where Father Geoffrey and the black man were shaking hands with the congregation – a few old women, a few even older men, and a handful of babies who'd been brought there as part of their grandmothers' babysitting duties.

Billy tried to slip out without the priest seeing him, but he was spotted.

'Billy!' Father Geoffrey scuttled across the porch and seized him. 'I want you to come back to the rectory and have a talk with Father Thomas. There aren't many children in Brixton who've been to Africa. And you can bring your cousin Steve, too.'

Five minutes later the two boys were perched uncomfortably on stools in Father Geoffrey's study.

It was the first time Billy had been there.

He glanced round. The room was shadowy and dusty, and cluttered with mounds of yellowing newspapers, piles of leather-bound books, vases of dead flowers, overflowing ashtrays, and inevitably a scattering of empty whisky bottles. A newly-opened bottle already two-thirds empty was standing on the desk. That, Billy guessed, explained the African's condition. Father Geoffrey must have been fortifying him from it before the service.

'So, young people, out of the goodness of your hearts will you help us?' the African priest asked.

'How?' Billy stammered.

The African had been expanding on what he'd said in his sermon – about how the elephants were destroying the villagers' crops and in some cases killing the villagers themselves.

'I bring them God's message,' the priest said. 'I say He will help and save them. How are they to believe me if I cannot show how He will do this? We must have money for a hunter and rifles. Later we build churches and schools and hospitals. But how shall this be if His children cannot feed themselves? Father Geoffrey said you would assist us.'

Billy stared at him. He glanced at Steve, who gave him a quick knowing grin. Then he looked in silent appeal at Father Geoffrey.

Whether it was due to the whisky or a conviction that all white people had money, Billy had no idea. All he knew was that there had been a terrible misunderstanding. Brixton children were penniless – surely even an African knew that?

'A project,' Father Geoffrey said. 'That's what Father Thomas has in mind – well, it's certainly what I have. St Barnabas is launching an appeal for funds. Everyone can find ways to contribute. You and Steve, for instance, you could do weekend jobs. Window-cleaning, filling coal cellars, sweeping out back yards. You'll have lots of ideas of your own. And every farthing you earn will count.'

'To help kill elephants?' Billy asked.

'As a start, yes.'

Billy was silent. 'I don't want to kill elephants,' he said

defiantly. 'I want to look after them. They're – well, they're beautiful.'

He flushed and stopped. He hadn't meant to say it, but there was no other word he could think of. He'd been going to add that was the message he and Violet had learned from Nogoro, but he didn't. No one in the room would have understood.

Billy was wrong.

Steve was still grinning smugly and the African had sunk back into his chair in a haze of alcohol, the whites of his eyes rolling upwards and his wrists falling limply towards the floor, but Father Geoffrey walked thoughtfully to the window.

He drew on his cigarette and his chest heaved as he coughed.

'Idiosyncratic, but it's a point of view, Billy,' he said thoughtfully. 'Maybe there's a place for both – people and elephants. Perhaps we should have two funds. One for the villagers and one for the animals. If we can make space for each, perhaps they could live together. People need sanctuary. Maybe animals do too. I have a feeling St Francis advocated it. Don't they have places called parks or reserves or something in Africa?'

Billy shook his head. He didn't know – he didn't even know what a park or reserve was. Father Geoffrey looked at the black priest but the man had fallen asleep.

'I'm sure they do,' Father Geoffrey went on. 'I think you and Steve could raise money for that. Now bugger off home for your dinner while I think about it.'

He broke off in another spasm of coughing and reached for his glass. The two boys left the room with the African snoring in his chair behind them.

'Jesus Christ!' Steve said as they walked home. 'Stupid old sod! He may be half-cut, but does he really think anyone's going to raise money for fucking elephants? What does he think we are – nutters?'

Billy trudged frowning beside him, his hands thrust deep into his pockets.

'You haven't seen them, Steve,' he answered. 'I have. I'd give it a go.'

'You're not bleeding serious?' Steve looked at him amazed.

'What, you'd do "window-cleaning, filling coal-cellars, sweeping out back yards"?'

He mimicked Father Geoffrey's voice which always became more patrician the more he'd drunk.

'And all for a bunch of darkies, a sozzled monkey in a dog collar, and a few stupid animals?' He hooted with laughter. 'Grow up and give us a break, Billy boy.'

Billy caught him by the elbow. He whirled Steve round and stood in front of him, his fists clenched and his knuckles white.

'They're elephants, not stupid animals,' he spat out between his teeth. 'Just watch it, Steve.'

Billy's anger flared across his face, almost incandescent in its intensity. It frightened the bigger boy more than it had ever done before. He stepped back and raised his pudgy hands pacifyingly.

'You like elephants, fine, Billy, fine,' he said. 'I go along with that. But do you really want to spend the weekends sweeping and shovelling coal?'

Billy didn't answer. He shrugged his shoulders in a gesture of dismissal and headed along the pavement again. Steve hurried to catch up with him. He plucked at Billy's sleeve to slow him down.

'There's much easier ways to pick up a few bob. I'll tell you. Just listen, old pal.'

Steve started to talk. Reluctantly and in spite of himself, his head still lowered angrily on his chest, Billy listened.

12

The figure in front of him swayed tantalisingly from side to side on the square of white canvas.

Billy tracked him across the ring, stalking him, keeping exactly the same distance between them – the range from where he could hit with either hand – as if he was measuring it with a slide-rule.

The young man danced away.

'Out of Bristol, he is,' Len had said before the bout. 'Sharp and fancy. That's how they learn them there, but he's got a mule-kick if he settles. Don't let him, Billy! He'll take your bleeding head off. Just keep chasing. Sooner or later you'll catch up. Then nail the bugger.'

Billy's opponent backed into the ropes.

He side-stepped and skipped away again, rocking on the balls of his feet. There was a taunting half-smile on his face. Billy turned and followed. His own face was pale and expressionless and his eyes were hooded in concentration. He could smell rosin and sweat, the old familiar smells of the gym. Now there were other new sounds and smells round him – a crowd baying and roaring and the hot metallic stench from the arclights.

The young man stopped.

He jabbed out his hand and caught Billy hard above the eye. Then he dropped his arms, challenging Billy to hit back. Billy shook his head. The blow had rocked him and he could feel blood trickling down his face. He gathered himself and came forward again.

This time the young man didn't give ground. He saw the cut and the flowing blood and he waited – waited to chop Billy down with his swift tormenting fists.

Billy licked the blood from his lips, and snapped out his left arm. He'd done it time and again at Len in the past, and the result had always been the same. Not now. Billy had learned. The young man swayed, Billy pulled his punch, at the same moment he pivoted and unleashed his right hand.

The young man stepped straight into the blow. Billy felt the shock of the collision travel up his arm and ripple in shivers across his shoulder. He spun round ready to hit him again, but there wasn't any need. His opponent was lying on his stomach with his arms spread-eagled on the canvas.

The referee was already counting him out.

'Jesus, Billy, don't you ever do that to me again!'

Len was muttering and swearing as he pushed Billy down on to the corner stool and unlaced his gloves.

'Forty seconds more and he'd have taken it on points. Let's have a butcher's.'

He took Billy's head in his hands and inspected his face. Billy's cheeks and eyelids were bruised and blood was still trickling from the cut, but there was no serious damage.

'You'll live.' Len's face cracked into a smile and he gave Billy a quick embrace. 'Not bad, son. National finals next. In the gym six tomorrow on the dot. National's where you'll stop if we don't sort out your sodding defence.'

Billy ducked through the ropes and climbed down the steps as the boxer in the next bout waited to climb up.

As he made his way through the crowd, people stood up and cheered and clapped him on the back. Billy grinned awkwardly. He was exhausted, his eye was puffy and closing, and he knew he'd made bad mistakes – Len would mercilessly make him pay for them tomorrow.

It was also one of the proudest and happiest moments in his life.

It was 1954 and Billy was just eighteen. 1954 was midway between Olympic years. He'd fought his way through the local, district, area, and regional tournaments. Now only the national championships lay ahead. With Len at his side, Billy knew he'd get through the nationals too. Eighteen months on and he'd be fighting for an Olympic berth. Nothing on earth was going to stop him winning that.

For the moment even the Olympics didn't matter.

Billy had arrived in Brixton as a foreign-born, brown-skinned alien, the skinny tongue-tied bastard child of the dead Rattray's Sikhs bugler. The African tan had faded quickly, but it had taken him all the long ten years between to win acceptance from the people who crowded round him tonight. They had crossed the river, from Mally and the surrounding streets – some of them had come from as far as Camberwell and even Peckham – to cheer him on.

Billy hadn't let them down. He'd won and they were celebrating him almost, it flashed across his mind, as if they'd been celebrating Kid Hawkins or the long-haired Jew, Daniel Mendoza, or any other of South London's fighting heroes that his cousin Jack had told him about while walking back after feeding the horses.

Suddenly he was one of them. It was too much for Billy to take in. In a daze he shouldered his way through the last rank in the throng, and walked down the passage to the dressing-room. Len had taken off his gloves but he hadn't cut away the bandages taped round Billy's hands. Wally, Len's assistant, would do that.

Billy stepped through the door and stopped.

There were three men inside. Wally was one, of course. Billy didn't know the other two. They were wearing grey serge suits and the older of the two, a big raw-boned man with pepper-and-salt coloured hair and a pock-marked face, was holding a black Homburg hat.

Billy didn't need to ask who they were. They were plain clothes police – the 'Old Bill' to the older generation in Brixton or 'rozzers' to the young. He thought he knew all of the police in the manor, but he'd never seen these two before.

'Good scrap, Billy,' the older one said. 'Watched it from the back. Left it late, you did, son, but you could go all the way.'

Billy said nothing.

He stood with his bandaged hands hanging down by his sides. The wound above his forehead had opened again and blood was seeping down one side of his cheek.

'Trouble is, my son,' the man went on, 'There's a few things you need to explain first.'

He paused.

Dimly through his swollen eye, and the other seemed to be closing too, Billy could see Wally's head lowered thoughtfully, and his face – older and even more battered than Len's – frowning and unhappy.

'That's why I'm here, Billy,' the voice continued. 'The stuff's turning up all over the place. Coventry Street market, that was the last. But they've been offering it as far away as bleeding Glasgow. Glasgow! Would you believe it? But it's so, isn't it, Jock – and, Christ, you should know, you bloody celt!'

He glanced at his colleague.

'Aye,' the younger policeman agreed in a Scottish accent. 'We're getting reports from Dumfries and Galloway, too.'

There was silence for several moments. The older man turned his gaze back to Billy.

'We've picked up Charlie and Steve.'

He waited to let the information sink in. Then quietly and bleakly he added, 'They've talked, Billy. My God, have they talked!'

Billy's stomach went cold.

It had started four years earlier within a few weeks of the African preacher's visit to St Barnabas.

'Listen, Billy, there's much easier ways to pick up a few bob,' Steve had said on the way home.

Billy knew of course what Steve meant even before the elder boy started to explain.

Thieving – nicking or brickering as it was more often known in the manor. Every child in Mally, every child in Brixton, did it. Billy did it himself. A handful of sweets from a shop counter when the shop-owner wasn't looking, fruit or biscuits from the market stalls, money hidden in supposedly secret cavities for the talley-man to collect, even raids on a kitchen if a rear window was carelessly left open.

Aunt Doris walloped anyone she caught at it. Once she even called in the local constable to give them all a grim reminder of the consequences if the law caught them. The children listened in silence with solemn penitent faces, and went straight out to go on as before.

The children's thieving, like Billy's until then, was random and opportune – small-scale pilfering for themselves. What Steve proposed to Billy that day was different.

'The street markets, Billy boy, where do they get their stuff from? Legit? You must be joking! How could they flog it off at those prices? No, Billy, they need suppliers. They need people like us, and they pay cash on the nail. Without us they'd go out of bleeding business.'

Steve was seventeen then.

Parrot-like he used the phrases he'd learned from his dead father, a war-time street trader who dealt in the nylon stockings and American cigarettes that somehow slipped through the security net surrounding the commissariats of the US air-force bases.

Steve's father had worn wide-shouldered suits with trousers that tapered to the ankles. His hair was thick and glossy, his shoes were two-tone tan and white, and whenever Steve had seen him there'd always been a young blonde with wide blue eyes on his arm.

To Steve he was a god. Steve even copied what he remembered of his voice, confident and wheedling as he launched another scheme or proposed another deal.

'You and I, Billy,' Steve said. 'We could supply them.'

'How?' Billy demanded.

'The warehouses down the river. Bloody Aladdin's caves, they are.'

Billy knew about the warehouses that lined the south bank of the Thames. They stocked the merchandise sold in the famous stores of Knightsbridge, Piccadilly, Regent Street, and Oxford Street.

'Come off it, Steve,' Billy said. 'For Christ's sake, they got guards and watchmen.'

Steve sniffed contemptuously. 'Those warehouses, they're warrens, that's what they are. There's a thousand ways into them. My cousin Charlie, he knows them all.'

'Who's Charlie?' Billy asked suspiciously.

After six years he thought he knew all the members of the

extended family who lived in or visited the Mally house. He'd never heard of Charlie.

'Charlie done a stretch, didn't he? Uncle Alf and Aunt Doris, they told him to stay away when he came out, stupid old prats!'

Steve tapped his nose. 'I tell you, Billy, Charlie knows what's what, no one like him. He's got a job doing deliveries to the stores. Been at it a year now. He knows every bloody inch of the warehouses. He'll show us. We nick the stuff, we pile it up, then he shifts it Saturdays to the markets in his van and we all divvy up equal. Easy!'

Billy said nothing.

He strode ahead of Steve kicking moodily at the beer bottles that always littered the Brixton streets after a Saturday night. Steve caught up with him and clutched his arm.

'Come on, Billy! You want to give Father Geoffrey something for your bleeding elephants. Fine, you do that. But there's going to be a lot more left over, and all the rest's for you. Think what you could do with it.'

He stopped Billy and pulled him round. Steve gave him the expansive smile he'd seen so often on his father's face.

'How about it, chum?'

'Chum' was something else he'd learned from his father, who in turn had learned the word from the war-time Americans.

Steve waited. Billy hesitated. He frowned, he chewed on his tongue, he studied the pink blossom on the grime-smeared cherry trees that studded Mally's worn and pot-holed pavements.

'I'll give it a go once,' he said. 'Just once.'

Steve laughed. 'You're a soldier!'

He tried to clap Billy on the shoulders. Billy shrugged and walked on.

He was thinking of Hampton and Ngoro and the gorge in the morning mist and the great matriarchal elephant, Uhuru. He was not thinking of Violet. She stood at the centre of everything, but deliberately Billy put her out of his mind.

He was into thieving now. It was not something she could be part of.

13

'Easy!' Steve had said.

He was right. It was easy. That was largely due to Steve's cousin, Charlie.

Charlie, Billy thought after he'd first met him, might have been Steve's elder brother. In his early twenties, he had the same big, bulky, and awkward build. The same pale pasty face. The same dark button-bright eyes filled with the same cunning and shrewdness. Even the same American mannerisms of speech.

'Okay, fellows—?'

He'd just told them how to break into one of the depositories by manipulating a faulty lock at the top of a second floor fire-escape staircase.

'The ladies' winter coats are in racks on the left, gents' on the right. The electrical stuff, the toasters and so on, right below them on the floor beneath. Just take a few of each from the back. They won't show up till the next stock take and even then no one's going to be sure. And remember . . .' Charlie paused. 'Anything goes wrong – it won't – you've never heard of me from God Almighty himself. Understand?'

The two boys nodded.

A week later they slipped out of the house as soon as everyone was in bed and asleep. Charlie was waiting in his van in Ramallies Crescent. He drove them south along the river and dropped them off half a mile from the warehouse.

The whole job took barely two hours.

Billy, the agile and athletic one, made the break-in and brought the goods outside. Steve carried them away and hid them in a disused coal bunker. When they'd finished they rejoined Charlie in the van and by 4.00 am they were both back in their beds.

The following week Billy rang the rectory bell after school. He had to ring several times, but eventually Father Geoffrey came to the door. He must have been asleep. He was yawning, and his little owlish eyes blinked blearily behind the pebble glasses.

He peered at Billy before he recognised him.

'Ah, Billy. What can I do for you, young man?'

The whisky fumes were so strong they seemed to frame him in a pale amber halo. Billy fumbled in his pocket and held out two bright newly minted sixpenny coins.

He didn't know why but he'd asked the corner tobacconist to put aside any new coins that came into the shop. Billy had exchanged these two for a handful of old coppers.

'It's for the elephants, Father,' he answered.

'Excellent. Follow me, Billy.'

Father Geoffrey turned and Billy followed him inside. The priest stopped by the table in the hall.

On it were two large glass jars, sweet jars like they had in confectionery shops, Billy thought, which hadn't been there before. Both of them were labelled in Father Geoffrey's bold haphazard handwriting. The first read: Uganda CMS Project – Elephants (killing). On the other it said: Uganda Billy Ramsden Project Elephants (living).

Billy stared at them. 'That's got my name on it, Father.' The words burst out of him in surprise.

'Of course it has. It was your idea, wasn't it?'

Billy flushed with pride. He'd never seen his name written on anything like that before.

The priest looked at the two sixpences and then glanced at Billy.

'A whole shilling. You must have been working hard, lad.'

'Yes, Father,' Billy answered. 'Weekends me and Steve, we've been doing jobs all over the place, right down to Camberwell and that. There'll be more to come, too.'

Father Geoffrey was silent. He tossed the coins up and down in his palm, and gazed steadily at Billy. Then he dropped the sixpences into the jar.

'That's good, Billy, but not too much more, I trust,' he said. 'Just a sensible amount that an honest hardworking boy like you can earn.'

Billy's eyes slid away from the priest's face. He knew exactly what Father Geoffrey meant.

'Yes, Father.'

Billy went out.

Through the window Father Geoffrey watched the boy disappear up the street, skipping and running.

He was a strange one, young Billy Ramsden. Something violent, passionate, and even dangerous was hidden behind that flat shuttered face. He lied glibly but then all of the South London children did that. The sixpences didn't come from the jobs he claimed to have done. The money was stolen.

The priest was unconcerned about that. Theft was a matter for the Almighty to adjudicate on, not him. Father Geoffrey dealt with people, flawed, complicated, wayward people. They were always interesting and sometimes exceptionally so.

The bugler's illegitimate son came into the second category.

Len said he had the makings of a fine boxer, even a great one. Perhaps that would be Billy's way out of the Brixton slums. Only time, discipline, and Billy's own talent would tell. What was intriguing was what he'd done with the money he'd thieved. Billy hadn't kept it for himself, he'd brought it to the rectory.

For some reason the child really did love elephants.

As Billy vanished round the corner Father Geoffrey turned from the window and walked through to his study. He'd given Billy an oblique warning. The boy was shrewd enough to understand it – his furtive glance away showed that – but it didn't mean he'd rein himself in. The trouble with the brightest and the best was that often they didn't know where to stop.

Father Geoffrey poured himself a whisky and sat staring thoughtfully into the gathering twilight.

'Charlie's talked, Steve's talked, now it's your turn, Billy,' the slate-faced man said. 'When did it all start?'

Billy didn't answer.

He was sitting on a hard upright chair in one of the interrogation rooms in Savile Row police station. He'd been there for two hours.

He'd been driven to the station straight from the hall, sandwiched in the back of the car between the two policemen. The older one, the one who was questioning him, was called Detective Inspector Simons. The young one, Detective Constable McMurray, had left the room to get them all mugs of tea.

They'd allowed Wally to cut off the tapes round his hands, and let Billy put on a sweater and trousers over his singlet and shorts. Otherwise he was dressed as he had been when he left the ring. He was still even wearing the lightweight black boxing boots Uncle Alf had bought him when he won the district finals.

'Billy boy, it's finished, it's all over, lad,' Simons said. 'We don't even need you. I just like to be tidy, cross the T's and dot the I's, know what I mean? Help me do that and it'll look good in court, I'll personally see it does. Difference between probation and custodial sentence, if I know the wigs.'

Simons paused and bent over him. 'And I *do* know the wigs, Billy, I know how they think. With me on your side you've got a chance. Just tell me how it started.'

Billy remained silent. His head ached. The cut over his eye had closed as the blood dried, but now in the cold of the interrogation room the dry tissue was cracking open and fresh blood was dripping down his face.

He shook his head, trying to toss it away. He set his mouth in bitter stubborn defiance. He knew all about the police. They were the common enemy, they always had been. Even at Lucknow the troopers had regarded the military red-caps with hatred and contempt, spitting in the dust as their horses trotted by.

Nothing in the world was going to make him talk to these bastards.

'All right, Billy.' Simons stood up. 'You don't want to talk, but perhaps some of your friends will. There's Father

Geoffrey, for instance, isn't there? Haven't you been giving him money?'

Simons broke off and and consulted a notebook. He looked at McMurray and chuckled disbelievingly.

'It says here for elephants, Constable. Is that right?'

McMurray laughed back. 'Aye, sir. It appears so.'

'What a strange and wonderful world we live in!' Simons heaved with laughter. 'Here we have a little South London thief and he's stealing for elephants, God help us—'

Billy didn't let him finish.

He pushed back his chair and stood up, splaying out his hands on the table as he tried to control his fury. His cheeks were white and his eyes blazed between his narrowed eyelids.

'Don't ever mention Father Geoffrey, nor elephants neither! Just you fuck off!'

His gaze switched between the two policemen, willing them, scorching them, into cinders. Then, drained, he dropped back into his seat.

'What do you want to know?' Billy whispered after a while.

'Everything, Billy,' Simons said mildly.

He winked at McMurray. Simons straddled a chair opposite Billy, while the detective constable got out his notebook and started to write.

It had gone on for four years. Billy had never intended it to last that long. He'd just meant to raise some money to help the elephants and keep his promise to Father Geoffrey. Then somehow the whole business seemed to acquire a momentum of its own.

It was so easy.

After the long and painful depression of the post-war years, the economy was starting to pick up. The London street markets were thriving as never before. They were hungry for goods, and the merchandise that reached them was being recycled all over the country.

Billy, Steve, and Charlie only went out every few weeks. They moved around between the many warehouses – Charlie knew them all – and they stole little enough for the losses not to be questioned when the stores checked their stock. Every month Billy went to the rectory and gave the priest a couple of sixpences or the occasional shilling, and watched him place them in the jar.

In the end it was Charlie who ruined it.

Charlie had never owned a car. Now, his appetite whetted by his years of driving the Smith and Nicholls' van, he decided he had to have one.

'We'll do a last month,' he told the two boys. 'One job a night every three days. Take everything you can find, Billy. They're shouting for stuff far away as Scotland. Then we'll knock it off.'

Charlie paused and put his arms round both of their shoulders.

'Know what, my sons? You're going to be rich.'

'That's all?' asked Inspector Simons.

Billy nodded.

Simons rocked back in his chair and crossed his arms behind his head. On the other side of the room McMurray scrawled a few last lines and snapped his notebook shut.

Billy glanced at the elder policeman, his eyes staring out warily from behind his half-lowered head.

'Got nothing to do with Father Geoffrey, has it? Nor elephants neither. I mean, it's just Charlie and Steve and me, isn't it?'

'"Touch anything in the universe and you'll find it's hitched to everything else",' Simons replied. He looked at McMurray. 'Know who wrote that, Constable?'

'No, sir,' McMurray answered.

'You should, you bloody celt. Your fellow countryman, the philosopher John Muir, that's who.'

Simons looked back at Billy.

'You're a thief, Billy. Everything you thieve you touch, and everything you touch touches someone else. You'll be charged, arraigned, and tried. Father Geoffrey will be called to give evidence. Charlie and Steve, they'll be up in the box explaining themselves too. The only witnesses who won't be called are your elephants.'

Simons stopped and stared at Billy. The expression on his face was half-sorrowful and half-infuriated.

'I don't know much about elephants, lad. I just get paid to keep the peace. Elephants don't wander much into my patch, but I'm told they sometimes trample people to death. When I look at scum like you, I think we could do with some of them in the manor.'

He swung away and barked at McMurray: 'That's off the record, Constable. Don't write it down. Just take him away and bang him up.'

'Yes, sir,' McMurray got to his feet.

Bewildered, Billy stood too.

'I've told you everything, Inspector,' he said. 'Just like I said. I've got to be in the gym tomorrow. I promised Len, he wants me there. There's only two weeks to the finals.'

'The finals are going to have to do without you, Billy boy,' Simons replied. 'As far as you're concerned, everything's over. You're a thief, you've been nicked, you're going to pay. Just be glad we haven't got any elephants to ram the message home.'

He chuckled.

McMurray took Billy's arm. He pulled him out of the room and led him down to the cells.

14

'In view of your youth, and the eloquent arguments advanced by your counsel that you may well have been led on by your older companions, I have decided to err perhaps on the side of leniency.'

The recorder paused.

He was a small stout man with a nervous fussy manner and constantly agitated hands. In his grey wig and scarlet robes he reminded Billy of one of the shy woodland animals dressed in human clothing pictured in the children's books Violet's nanny used to read to them in Africa.

Billy gazed at him expressionlessly across the courtroom. The man wasn't shy at all. He was powerful and ruthless and he held Billy's future in his hands.

'It's been suggested you were initially motivated by a desire to protect elephants. I always take careful account of character witnesses of the standing of parish priests, but it is a bizarre claim and to employ a colloquialism, I was not born yesterday. I fear you deluded the good father, as you have attempted to delude the court.'

The recorder fiddled with his glasses. 'We do not live in Africa. Elephants are neither here nor there. Be in no doubt, theft is a despicable crime. If you are convicted again on similar charges, you can expect to receive the approbrium of the law. I am going to give you a short sharp shock. Let it be a lesson you never forget.'

He raised his gavel and hammered it down on the bench.

'Nine months' custody in an appropriate borstal.'

He peered down at the clerk of the court. The clerk nodded and entered the sentence in his ledger. Detective Constable McMurray gripped Billy's arm and led him out of the dock.

On the way down to the detention cells, Billy stopped. He frowned, then looked at McMurray and grinned.

'Ever seen an elephant, copper?'

Unsettled for an instant, McMurray shook his head.

'Haven't bloody well lived, have you?'

Billy hurled away McMurray's hand, and continued down the stairs. McMurray caught up with him. He reached out to seize Billy again, and decided against it.

They tramped down together side by side.

With remission Billy served six months of his nine-month sentence.

He spent the time at a young offenders' prison, a borstal as the recorder referred to it, on the outskirts of Maidstone in Kent. The months passed quickly. In a sense Billy had lived in institutions all his life. The Lucknow barracks was certainly one, in a different way so was the house in Mally – chill and crowded and ruled either by Aunt Doris' stinging hand or the blows dealt out by Uncle Alf when he reeled back from the pub.

Outwardly Billy soon adjusted to the new regime.

He came in with two advantages; he'd been a successful villain and he'd fought his way through to the national finals. The prison grapevine ensured everyone knew that within twenty-four hours of his arrival. It didn't prevent a ritual testing by a group of the few boys there who were older than him.

Among the information that had been circulated about him was the story of the elephants.

'Got a bleeding trunk down there, have you, then?'

Five of them cornered him at the end of his first week as he left the tiled shower room.

Billy had a towel knotted round his waist. They pulled it off, soaked it, and snapped it at him like a whip, making stinging assaults on his skin. He stood naked and silent as they cavorted jeering and laughing round him. All he did was memorise their faces. When he spotted a gap in the wall of figures, he burst through it and ran.

Billy fled to howls of derisive laughter.

Back in the dormitory he shared with a dozen others, he made a list and tucked it behind his iron bedhead. Two nights later he waited on the landing. The first name on his list appeared, a gangling raw-boned boy named Neil. Billy leapt at him and beat him unmercifully, hammering his head against the wall until he was almost unconscious.

Three days afterwards Billy caught up with the second name on the list in the corridor behind the prison laundry. He gave this one an even more brutal battering. The following morning the remaining three shuffled up to him as they all stood in line to rinse their plates at the end of the midday meal.

'Fair's fair, Billy,' said their leader, Duncan. 'It was only a joke, mate. Enough's enough, right?'

Billy looked at the three faces. There was a patina of anxiety, almost of fear, on all of them.

'Ever seen an elephant?' he asked. It was the identical question he'd put to McMurray.

Duncan shook his head, so did the other two.

'And with any fucking luck – for the elephants, that is – you never will,' Billy went on. 'But you can pay for them. Five bob a month into my hand.'

Duncan dipped his plate into the sluice basin. He and his two cronies ran the prison's tobacco market.

'Don't be daft, Billy,' he protested. 'That's more than we all clear together. I've said we're sorry. We are. Just a mistake, pal. But five bob . . .'

Billy cut him off. 'I'll see you on the landing, then. Two of us each time, face to fucking face. Or if you want the whole gang together, fine. I've dealt with more.'

He scraped the left-overs on his plate into the bucket, and walked away. No one came forward to fight him on the landing. Instead every month he was given five shillings from the tobacco ring's profits.

Billy passed on the money to Aunt Doris on her monthly visits to the prison.

He hadn't expected her to come and was surprised when the warder first summoned him to the visiting room. In the Mally house Doris had been a remote domineering figure who ruled the household like a tyrant. She had never, it seemed to Billy, paid any attention to him at all except to bellow angrily when he did something wrong.

During his stay in prison Billy saw an entirely different side to her. The first time she came she scolded him for getting involved with Steve and Charlie in the first place, and then for his stupidity in being caught. After that she never mentioned it again. She would bring him a cake or some biscuits, and keep him up to date with what was happening in Mally.

Prison-visiting was part of Doris' life. She'd been doing it since she was a child, to her father, to her elder brothers, to her cousins. She'd be doing it too, she knew fatalistically, to her grandchildren. Crime, its rewards and its consequences, was an inescapable strand of what it meant to be born and grow up in South London.

The family was much more real and important than anything authority could do to it. When things were going well, the family didn't really need her except as a provider of meals, bandages, discipline, and instruction. But when things went wrong, Doris came into her own. She had her duty to do and part of her duty was to visit Billy.

Billy was Charlie's lad, Charlie was family, and so was his son.

'Sally's been taken on at the new Boots down Nine Elms way,' Doris said on her last visit before Billy's release. 'Little Val, she's coming out of a bad patch. Just starting to bleed, that's what I put it down to. Miss Robinson, the teacher, she's lifted the suspension and let her back into class. Frank, he's been put on West Ham's list. A month's free coaching this summer and pocket money, too.'

Billy nodded.

All of them – Sally, Val, and Frank – were his cousins, three of the once blurred and unknown faces round the Mally stove that first bitter winter, who'd since taken on names and identities.

A warder, a 'screw' in the prison's private language, shouted that visiting time was over.

Doris collected the bags strewn round her feet. As she

lowered her head, Billy noticed with a shock that her hair was greying. He'd never thought of her growing old.

'You and Uncle Alf, you're all right, aren't you, auntie?' Billy asked, not quite sure what he was saying.

Doris looked up at him.

'Right now I could do with a drag and I'll have one soon as I get out of this shit-house. Apart from that we're fine, Billy boy. Don't you worry about us.'

She smiled reassuringly. Then she paused. Her expression changed.

'Something I meant to tell you. Wasn't quite sure how to do it. I know you love the horses.' Doris hesitated again. 'Bess died. Your Uncle Alf, well, he sort of gave up on Bonnie then. Broke his heart in a way when Bess went. Alf's close to sixty-five now, near his pension. He's sold Bonnie to a bloke who come up from the west, down Dorset way. Alf's closed the stable and the totting's over.'

'That's it!' the warder shouted. He began to shepherd people out of the visiting hall. Doris stood up.

'Don't fret over it, Billy,' she said. 'She's gone to a good home has Bonnie. Your cousin Jack, he helped load her into the van. He said the bloke that's got her, he'll look after her good.'

She blew him a kiss and left.

That night Billy crossed his arms behind his head and lay awake on his bed for a long time after he normally slept.

Sally getting a job at Boots and Val, she was just a child surely, starting to bleed. His aunt's hair greying, Bess dying and Bonnie being sold, his uncle giving up totting. It seemed impossible, unbelievable. It was still less than six months since his conviction, and yet the entire world appeared to have changed.

Perhaps the world always did that, perhaps he'd simply never noticed before how fast it happened. Life in Mally had never been particularly secure, but after nine years the house, the street, the neighbourhood and the people who thronged it, had come to represent some form of safety. Everything about it was familiar and reliable, from

the clop of Bonnie's hoofs in the early morning to Uncle
Alf cursing and stumbling as he tried to climb the stairs on
Friday nights.

Not any longer. The safety had gone. Somehow it had
malignly been plucked away from him while his back was
turned. Billy turned onto his stomach and buried his face in
the bulky horse-hair pillow.

For the first time in months he thought of Violet.

'Hullo, Father.'

It was a warm June evening only a few days after his
release.

Billy had walked down to the rectory with the last contri-
bution from the prison's youthful tobacco barons in his pocket.
His hair was cropped short and he was wearing the cheap fawn
suit he'd been issued with on his release.

Father Geoffrey peered at him. 'God Almighty, it's Billy!'

He kicked the door wide open behind him, stepped forward,
and embraced him. Billy flushed, mostly from embarassment
but also with pleasure.

'Thanks for what you tried to do, Father. I really appreci-
ated that.'

Billy didn't add that when he was told Father Geoffrey
would be giving evidence, his first bewildered thought was
it would be against him. Only when the priest appeared in
court did he realise Father Geoffrey was trying to help.

Father Geoffrey ignored his thanks. 'How old are you now?'
the priest said as he beckoned him inside.

'Almost eighteen, Father.'

'Then it's long, long overdue.'

They crossed the hall.

As they passed the table Billy noticed the sweet jar labelled
with his name still standing on the top. Aunt Doris had dutifully
passed on the money he'd given her in prison, but apart from
those contributions no one had added anything to it. Billy
pulled out the coins from his pocket and dropped them in.
The other jar had vanished.

Father Geoffrey glanced back. He saw what Billy was doing
but didn't comment. He scurried ahead into the study, his

robes billowing round him, and reached for the bottle of whisky. He filled two glasses almost to the brim.

'Your health, young man.' He emptied half his glass in a single gulp. 'I see you noticed your jar is still there.'

Billy drank. The undiluted spirit burnt his throat and made him cough. He recovered his breath and put the glass down.

'Yes, Father.'

'The other one, I have to say, the one to buy rifles, was filled within a month of your leaving. Worthy souls left it overflowing. We could indeed have filled many more.'

'People, they're just ignorant,' Billy said angrily. 'They don't know nothing about elephants.'

'And you do?'

Billy was silent. He *did* know about elephants, but not in a way he could put into words.

He knew about them like Violet did, partly because Finlay Hampton and Ngoro had taught them, but mostly because of the valley. He and Violet had watched the sun rise and the mist clear from the water, they'd seen the cliffs dazzle as if they were embedded with the night's stars, they'd crouched breathless as Uhuru led the great grey columns of the herd down to drink while the fish eagles screamed above.

It wasn't something you could explain. It was something you could only feel, and Billy couldn't say why or how.

The silence went on. Then Father Geoffrey spoke.

'It could be said, Billy, that you're just some young crook fresh out of prison, back on your home patch, and ready for more villainy. It could be said, it will be said, but in my view it won't be true.'

Father Geoffrey removed his spectacles and polished them, his plump little hands quivering like a well-fed squirrel's as they circled the lenses.

'I have no window into your soul, Billy, and I know nothing about elephants. I do know that a few people, the fortunate few, have dreams. I think you have a dream and it's about elephants and you should pursue it. How and where you do that, I have no idea. I doubt you'll ever be worthy, Billy, but then—'

Father Geoffrey coughed out one of his hoarse croaking laughs. 'I've never found the worthy very interesting. My impression is the Lord doesn't either. He and I, I've found, tend to think alike.'

He laughed again. Then he dismissed the subject. He drained his glass and glanced reproachfully at Billy.

'Good God, lad! What's the matter with you? I detest drinking on my own.'

Spluttering, Billy managed to empty his glass and hold it out to be filled again.

When he left the rectory he felt dazed and light-headed. He placed his feet carefully one after the other on the pavement and occasionally steadied himself against a lamp-post or one of the Brixton cherry trees.

As he walked he tried to grapple with what Father Geoffrey had said. A dream? Certainly he'd dreamt about Violet and the valley and the elephants, but not in the way he guessed the priest meant. To Father Geoffrey, Billy sensed, a dream was entirely different.

It was something to be pursued and battled for, something that controlled and shaped his life. In the end its realisation was his destiny. It was all he had been born to achieve.

Billy reached the start of Malplaquet Road. Laughing and still slightly giddy, he swung round the iron pillar at the entrance to the street.

The pillar had been placed there a century ago as a tethering post for horses using a watering-trough that had long since been removed. The pillar remained and all the Mally children used it as a focus for their street games. Billy made a final whirl round it, and headed for Aunt Doris' house.

Father Geoffrey was right. Billy did have a dream and it was a dream of elephants. The trouble was he was almost eighteen and at eighteen there was another more urgent demand on his life than fulfilling the dream.

The following week Billy presented himself for enlistment in the army.

15

The Guards' depot stood on top of Caterham Hill twenty-five miles to the south of London.

Billy arrived there late on a chill November afternoon. He stood between the great iron gates holding his cheap suitcase, a present from Doris and Alf. Through the lighted guardhouse window he could see the duty sergeant was on the telephone.

Billy glanced round.

Ahead of him was the drill square, a great expanse of damp black tarmac, gleaming from the day's rain. Banners of grey mist were swirling across it and drifts of fallen leaves rustled in the wind. In the distance lights gleamed from a towering row of brick-built Victorian barrack blocks. Somewhere a bugle sounded and he could hear the tramp of hidden marching feet.

Billy shivered. The whole place was harsh and mournful and intimidating.

'Who the hell are you?' The sergeant had come out of the guardhouse.

'Billy Ramsden.'

'Billy Ramsden, *Sergeant*!' The man shouted at him.

'Yes, sir.'

'Not bloody sir, *Sergeant*, I said. Sir's what you call officers. Me, you call Sergeant or God fucking Almighty, because that's what I am. Understand?'

'Yes, Sergeant.'

The sergeant consulted a list on a clip-board.

He was tall and ramrod straight with a black moustache and a khaki hat slanted so tightly down over his face its peak almost touched his nose. From the bronze grenade symbol on the hat, Billy knew he was in the Grenadiers – his cousin Jack had taught him how to recognise the five different regiments of foot-guards.

'Ramsden, W. Assigned to Trained Soldier Davis, 13 Company, Coldstream Guards. Barrack block D.'

He paused and looked at Billy again, his face wrinkled in contempt.

'Jesus Christ, if the Lilywhites have come down to the likes of you, they soon won't have any barrels left to scrape. Black monkeys, it'll be next.'

The sergeant's voice suddenly rose to a roar. 'Block D! It's on the right! Move, you little toe-rag, move!'

Billy gripped his case and ran through the mist and gathering darkness towards the flickering lights.

'The shortest verse in the Bible is "Jesus wept".'

There was a long and ominous pause.

Billy stood stiffly in the front row of the squad, his rifle at his side. The words had come from behind him. They'd been spoken in a thick Irish brogue.

'If He saw ye now, He'd stand on his fucking head.'

There was a hiss as the wooden brass-tipped paystick lashed through the air and slammed against his legs. Billy's knees buckled. Tears of pain filled his eyes and he almost fell. Somehow, using the rifle as a support, he managed to stay upright.

'March them away, Trained Soldier, before I vomit to death in despair.'

'Yes, Sergeant-major.'

Trained Soldier Davis barked out an order. The squad swung round and set off with Davis prowling beside them like an angry old sheep-dog.

It was 8.00 am, on a bitterly cold January morning – plumes of steam rose from the squad's mouths as their boots hammered the concrete and ice rimmed the iron railings round the barracks.

He'd been at the depot for almost two months. From the moment Jack put him in charge of the horses there'd never been any doubt in Billy's mind that one day he too would join the Coldstream Guards. Jack was Billy's first hero in Brixton. In Billy's eyes he could do no wrong. If Jack was a guardsman, then Billy would become one too.

Of course if Billy's father had lived and he'd still been in India, it would have been different. Then he'd have joined Rattray's Sikhs. Either way Billy knew he was destined to become a soldier. In a way being a guardsman was even better than being a cavalryman. The Coldstream, as Jack had taught him, were the finest soldiers in the world. They were even the personal bodyguards of the young Queen.

Billy fitted in quickly to life at depot. Caterham, like the Lucknow barracks, the Mally house, and the Maidstone borstal, was just another institution, and within days his initial bewilderment vanished. Once he'd picked up the depot's rhythms, its language, and its hierarchy, he felt safe.

The 'Lilywhites' was one of several nicknames given to the Coldstream Guards after the white band round their forage caps. Sergeants, as the duty sergeant at the gate told him the evening he arrived, were God Almighty. Trained soldiers, skilled and veteran guardsmen, ranked only slightly below them. Sergeant-majors, like the one in the Irish Guards who'd slashed him with his paystick, were above the gods and only just below the stars.

Officers were a breed apart. They came from another universe.

'What the hell do they do?' Billy asked Trained Soldier Davis one evening as Davis walked round the barrack room, checking on how they were polishing their boots.

'Officers?' Davis rubbed his chin. 'Mainly, fuck all.'

He smiled reflectively.

He'd fought in the Italian campaigns of the Second World War from the Anzio landings up through the Monte Casino siege to the battles in the Alps.

'Except when the shooting starts. Then they go up front and take it first. With any luck they'll stop the bullet with your fucking name on it. Some of them can read maps too. That comes in handy if you're looking for a cat-house when you've liberated some God-fucking-forsaken bit of Tuscany.

I've a great fucking liking for officers. Sometimes I almost love the wankers.'

Davis moved on.

Billy spat on his boot and rubbed in the wax.

Billy left the depot at Caterham in March as a trained and qualified guardsman.

He was given ten days' home leave. Then he was sent to join the first battalion of the Coldstream Guards in Germany. He arrived with a good report from the commanding officer of 13 Training Company, and an even better recommendation for his success as a boxer. Billy had won the depot tournament and gone on to lose a hotly disputed decision in the inter-services championships.

'Handy with your fists, I see, Guardsman Ramsden.'

'Sir. Well, yes, sir, sort of.'

Lieutenant-colonel the Hon. Richard Willoughby DSO, MC – 'Old Willow Tree' as he was known to his men – didn't usually call newly arrived guardsmen in front of him.

Ramsden was an exception. He was clearly close to winning international selection as a boxer. That would reflect well on the battalion in any event. He would also strengthen the battalion team at next winter's NATO tournament in Berlin. Meanwhile he was interesting to Willoughby for another reason.

Willoughby had served with his old school-friend, David Stirling, the founder of the SAS, in the West African desert. Like Stirling he'd been captured and imprisoned in Germany. Rejoining his regiment on his release, he'd worked his way back up the hierarchy to the position he held now – commanding officer of the elite first battalion.

At a recent meeting of senior NATO field officers, he'd suggested forming a multi-national NATO equivalent of the SAS. The idea was accepted, and Willoughby was detailed to launch a pilot scheme to explore how it might work. He was looking for men of the calibre and skills he and Stirling had recruited in West Africa.

Ramsden was not only an accomplished athlete. He was a first-class marksman – he'd been ranked first in his squad when they were sent to the Pirbright ranges for weapons training. Almost more important, his background suggested the mental toughness and self-sufficiency Willoughby was looking for.

There was one problem.

Ramsden clearly had an awkward streak. There was the prison sentence, of course. More than that, there was the prison governor's report of his behaviour there. Ramsden, it seemed, wasn't averse to using his fists to impose his authority outside the ring.

'You've got a bit of what I believe is called "form", Guardsman.' Colonel Willoughby leant back. He rested the stump of his arm – the rest had been shot off in the Arno valley – on the desk. 'No doubt a misunderstanding?'

'Sir!'

Officers were always addressed as 'sir'. The word needed no explanation. Its meaning – and there were endless shades of meaning – was expressed in the tone in which it was delivered.

Billy knew, and Colonel Willoughby knew, that here it meant first, yes, he had a criminal conviction, and second, well, those were the sort of things that happened in life.

Colonel Willoughby picked up his gold pencil and revolved it thoughtfully between the fingers of his good hand.

'I'm seconding you from normal battalion duties,' he said. 'You're going to our tented base in the woods on Luneberg Heath to train for long-range patrol operations. By the time the Berlin championships come round, you should be fitter than you've ever been in your life.'

Willoughby paused. 'Make damn sure you don't get into trouble again, Ramsden, and you could be at the start of a useful career in the brigade. Just watch the short fuse. Short fuses blow up more friends than they ever do the enemy.'

'Sir!'

Billy stamped his foot. He saluted and went out.

16

The months Billy spent on Luneberg Heath were the happiest since he'd left Africa.

He was one of fewer than thirty soldiers there. A few had been drawn like him from his own battalion. The rest came from more specialized units – signals, engineering, and intelligence. They were divided into teams of four, each under the command of a young officer, and they trained not just from dawn to dusk but often through the night as well.

The life suited Billy perfectly.

Instead of regulation khaki and heavy army boots, they were allowed to wear tracksuits and lightweight field shoes. They practised daily with a whole range of weapons from the old Lee Enfield to the new Sterling submachine gun. They were taught how to use explosives, and tutored in radio communications. Best of all were the long hours they spent roaming great swathes of the heath, learning to live off the land and sleeping out under the stars.

Only one thing marred it – the officer in overall command of the camp.

He was called Major Forbes and had come to Germany from a desk job in London. Forbes was middle-aged, old-fashioned, arrogant, quick-tempered, and a stickler for military rules and discipline. How and why he'd been put in charge of a young and individualistic combat group, where officers and men used first names to each other, was a mystery. He was detested by everyone, and he in turn lost no chance of showing his contempt for the men under him.

For some reason the particular focus of his dislike was Billy. Billy had no idea why. All he knew was that Forbes constantly picked on him, constantly sneered at him, constantly gave

111

him extra duties and assigned him the worst of the tasks in camp.

'I'm going to kill that bastard,' he said venomously one August evening as he lay on the ground smoking a cigarette with the other members of his patrol.

It was Friday. The patrol had just returned after completing a thirty-mile cross-country exercise. They were all due for a weekend pass but Major Forbes had met them as they came in, and told Billy he was to stay in camp on guard duty.

'Don't let him get to you, Billy boy,' one of the other members of the patrol said. 'Don't give him the satisfaction. Two months and you'll never have to see the sod again.'

Billy drew on his cigarette and swore.

The man was right. The training programme finished at the end of October. After that they'd disperse and return to their units. In Billy's case that meant back to the battalion at Krefeld with the Berlin championships to concentrate on. And Old Willow Tree was right too, Billy would be fitter than he'd ever been. A month of sparring in the ring to sharpen up, and he knew he could take the title.

In fact, Major fucking Forbes apart, the spring and summer had gone so well, he'd enjoyed the time so much, Billy had sent in an application to extend his National Service term into a full seven-year enlistment.

'*Honi soit qui mal y pense*, Billy,' his cousin Jack had said to him once as they fed the horses. 'Regiment's motto, on the cap badge, it is. If you ever get to polish that silver star, you won't be in no hurry to let go of it.'

Jack was right, too. Billy had polished the star every night at the depot. He still polished it every Friday here – even if Major Forbes did spitefully withdraw his pass. He could live with Forbes for another eight weeks.

Both Jack and Billy's fellow patrol member were right. It was Billy who turned out to be wrong.

October came and so did the culmination of the task force's six-month training. The programme ended with six successive all-night patrols across the heath. Every patrol was required to cover thirty miles a night. On the way they had to carry out a number of tasks, from gathering intelligence to attacking enemy transport concentrations to blowing up bridges and severing communications.

The targets were guarded by 'hostile' forces, and the whole exercise was watched by a group of senior NATO observers. Billy's patrol performed outstandingly until the final night. Then, as they approached their check-in point in the hour before dawn, a light suddenly dazzled in the face of the patrol commander.

'Stop!' a voice called out.

Billy knew the voice well, as did all the others. It belonged to Major Forbes. As well as the NATO observers, the exercise was being monitored by 'umpires'. Forbes was one of them.

'I heard you almost half a mile away,' he went on. 'Report to the debriefing centre. You will do the course again tomorrow.'

He swung the powerful torch across them. 'Guardsman Ramsden, I particularly heard you.'

He strode away into the darkness, the beam lighting up the undergrowth in front of him.

The patrol stood up.

There was no need for silence or stealth any longer. Exhausted and dispirited they tramped towards the glowing windows of the field caravans where the debriefing took place. As they walked, one of the patrol, the same man who'd told Billy to disregard Forbes a couple of months earlier, tapped him on the shoulder.

'He's nuts, Billy,' he said. 'The bastard couldn't have heard any of us. He knew we'd be coming in that way because he's seen us doing it for months now. He just wanted to shovel us in it deep. Don't even ignore him, son. We'll go back tomorrow. Maybe we'll trip over him and bounce him around a little.'

He grinned.

Billy said nothing, but briefly he checked his stride. Anger, hot raging anger, had coursed through him ever since Forbes had turned the beam on his face and accused him of being principally responsible for the noise. Now it cooled. Instead it turned to cold purposeful rage.

Under the rules of the exercise the patrols were allowed to use 'reasonable force' in dealing with members of the 'enemy' they encountered in trying to achieve their objectives. In the darkness it was impossible to distinguish between the enemy and the umpires.

Billy signed himself in at the debriefing caravan. Then as the other members of the patrol gathered round the monitoring officer to go through the night's events, he slipped out and back into the darkness.

He stalked and caught up with Forbes – his intermittently flashing torch was a beacon in the scrub on the heath – half an hour later. Billy came up to his shoulder.

His eyes misted with rage and tiredness, Billy jumped on him.

'You've buggered me up, Guardsman Ramsden,' Colonel Willoughby said.

'Sir!' Billy shouted back at him.

This time he wasn't alone in front of the colonel. There was an escort of a sergeant on one side of him and a corporal on the other.

'You assaulted an officer,' Willoughby went on. 'You broke several of his ribs, broke his arm, broke his jaw and his nose, and fractured one of his legs.'

'Sir!' Billy shouted in agreement again.

Willoughby studied him for a moment. Then he dismissed the escort.

'Leave me alone with the guardsman.'

'Sir!' they bellowed. The two heavily-built men saluted and left the room, glowering at Billy as they went out.

Willoughby gestured at a chair. Billy reached for it uncertainly. Willoughby nodded, and Billy pulled it up and sat down.

'I believe you know Father Geoffrey?'

Billy started. He looked at the colonel in astonishment. He couldn't think of any possible connection between Colonel Willoughby and the Brixton priest.

'Sir!' he answered.

'When you're alone with me, just "yes, sir" will do,'

Willoughby said. 'Father Geoffrey was my battalion's padre when we landed at Normandy. Padres are meant to stay behind and minister. Not Father Geoffrey. He went ashore on one of the first boats. When one of my men was cut down, he picked up his Bren and ran forward firing. He knew we needed all the help we could get. Highly unorthodox for a priest, but he's one of the bravest men I've ever known,'

Willoughby paused. 'He wrote and put in a good word for you when he heard you were joining the battalion. It was largely because of what he said that I seconded you to special forces. You've haven't just buggered me up, you've done the same to him.'

Billy closed his eyes for an instant in anguish. Both men had trusted him and he'd let them both down.

'I'm sorry, sir.'

'Too late for that, Ramsden,' Willoughby said crisply. 'You'll face a court martial and the charges will be serious. There's no question of your staying in the regiment. A dishonourable discharge will be the least of it. The only issue is how long you'll get in the glasshouse. Never say I didn't give you fair warning.'

Billy nodded bleakly.

'There's just one other thing.' Colonel Willoughby was playing with his gold pencil again. 'The padre said you were interested in elephants. Why's that?'

Haltingly Billy told him about Ngoro and the gorge and the great matriarch, Uhuru.

Willoughby was silent for several moments.

'Funnily enough, Ramsden,' he said finally, 'I was born in Kenya. My father was one of the first settlers, the Happy Valley set as they're now idiotically known. He was a great hunter in his time, particularly of elephants. Then he gave it all up. He said they were disappearing and he wanted no part of it. Made a considerable impression on me.'

He looked down.

The light flashed off the slim golden tube as he revolved the pencil between his fingers. For an instant his mind was no longer on Billy but his own childhood. Then his head lifted again.

'I'll do my best for you, Ramsden,' he said. 'I fear it won't cut much ice. In future use your fists in the ring or on behalf of your elephants. That's all.'

'Sir!' Billy stood up and saluted. He turned to leave.

'Oh, just one last point, Guardsman.'

Colonel Willoughby called him back. 'Major Forbes is a lamentably poor soldier and an unutterable swine to boot.' His voice was icy. 'I don't believe for one moment he heard your patrol come in. I'll do my level best to see he never commands combat troops again. And don't forget I never said that.'

'Sir!' Billy shouted.

He went out. The escort stepped in on either side of him and marched him away.

For the first time since his arrest Billy was smiling.

17

Colonel Willoughby kept his word.

He appeared at the court martial along with Billy's patrol commander, the three other members of the patrol, and Billy's company commander in the battalion. There was no doubt about the facts. Billy had attacked and seriously wounded a senior officer. If he hadn't signed in with the other patrol members, he could have claimed it was a misunderstanding in the darkness at the end of a long and demanding night exercise.

As it was, the only possible explanation was that he'd deliberately returned to the heath after the exercise was over, and ambushed Major Forbes. Forbes, humiliated and enraged, with his leg still in plaster and his ribs bandaged, made it quite clear to the adjudicating panel it had been a potentially murderous assault.

All that those who appeared on Billy's behalf could do was give character references. They were all good but the most effective came from Colonel Willoughby. Without his statement, Billy could have been sentenced to five years. Willoughby was a distinguished and much-decorated soldier. His crisp eloquent appeal resulted in the panel giving Billy only eighteen months.

He was also, inevitably, given a dishonourable discharge from the army.

Billy served his time in a military prison outside Colchester. A few months after his arrival he was told he had a visitor. He went through to the visiting room expecting to see Aunt Doris, Uncle Alf, or even perhaps Father Geoffrey.

To his amazement it was Steve.

'Hullo, Billy boy. Greetings, my son!'

Steve winked at him. He was sitting across one of the small bare tables that lined the centre of the room.

Billy hadn't seen him for over two years. Steve was just as he remembered, swollen and pasty-faced with quick furtive eyes and black slicked-back hair that gleamed with oil. The only difference was that he'd grown grotesquely. He was barely Billy's height but he must have weighed close to twenty stone.

He looked, in one of the Mally children's favourite phrases, like a huge great barrel of lard.

'Steve, for Christ's sake! What are you doing here?'

Billy sat down on the other side of the table.

'Keeping up with the family, that's all. Blood's thicker than water, right?'

'But they banged you up for three years,' Billy said.

'Remission, good behaviour, keep your nose clean.' Steve winked again. 'I've been out for six months now. Charlie, he got five, and he'll be out March. Been minding his manners, Charlie has, just like I did. Come the summer, all us three musketeers will be back in the manor.'

He grinned. Billy said nothing. Steve leant forward across the table.

'Listen, Billy, things have changed since they sent us down and you tossed off into the army. Night clubs and gambling, that's what's happening now. We've got families getting organised down on the manor, I mean real serious operations. You heard of the Krays, the Richardsons, and the Clarks?'

Billy shook his head.

'Wave of the future, Billy, believe me. They're all getting set to push up West. I've got connections with all of them. Real close to the Clarks, I am. Joe, Doug, and Benjie, them and me, we're like that.'

Steve crossed his fingers and tilted his head confidentially.

'Why are you telling me?' Billy asked.

'Opportunities, Billy boy. I heard you learned to drive in the army, right?'

Still Billy said nothing.

He didn't know how Steve had discovered that – perhaps

Billy himself had mentioned it in one of his rare postcards to Aunt Doris – but Steve was right. It was one of the skills Billy had been taught on Luneberg Heath.

'Very useful, Billy. Good drivers who are hard cases too – and I don't have to ask you about that, do I? – they can earn these days. What about sixty quid a week regular plus bonuses – and I mean real bonuses?'

Billy stared at him.

In Brixton you were lucky to earn ten or twelve pounds a week, and that was only when work was available. Sixty pounds was unheard of. There had to be a reason, of course, and Billy knew what it was.

'Villainy,' he said.

'Nuts, Billy. Business, that's all it is.' Steve gave a sly smile. Then his face hardened. 'What else are you going to do, my son? Out of here by June and then what? Back with Auntie Doris, if she'll have you. If you're lucky humping sodding bricks for a few bob until the winter. After that, nothing.'

He leant forward intently. 'This is a chance, Billy, a big one. Money in your pocket, your own place. Christ, before long even your own car. And the Clarks, they look after their own. You think about it carefully, son. It won't come round again.'

'Nice to meet you, Billy.'

Joe Clark held out his hand. His two cousins, Doug and Benjie, were standing behind him. Billy's glance flashed across their faces.

Joe Clark was a short compact man of about forty with pale eyes and a trim black moustache. Doug and Benjie were younger, taller, and heavier. Doug's face was solemn and jowelled and thoughtful, and the scent of cologne came off his skin in thick cloying waves. Benjie had a cast in his eye which gave him a strange wild look. He also had great club-like hands and the thickest wrists Billy had ever seen.

All three of them were wearing dark suits and glossy brown shoes. They were all hard and violent, Billy thought, and in Benjie's case possibly mad too.

'Me too, Joe,' Billy replied as he shook hands.

'It's Mr Clark to you, Billy,' Joe said mildly. He paused. 'We've heard good things of you from Steve.'

He gestured at Steve who was standing to one side. An expression of pain had crossed his face when Billy addressed Clark as 'Joe'. Now he was smirking again.

'We trust Steve, we trust his judgement, but we make up our own minds. Benjie, he saw you fight in the regionals. He reckoned you could have taken the national title. Doug, well, you know about that. Satisfied, weren't you, Doug?'

Doug nodded. 'He can handle wheels.'

Billy had spent an hour that morning driving one of Joe Clark's cars, a new Austin A40. Doug had been in the passenger seat telling him what to do and watching how Billy performed. They'd started with a short run through the morning traffic. Then they'd driven across the Thames to a huge empty expanse of concrete behind the dock warehouses.

There Doug had made him race the car at close to its top speed, weave it between the old freight marker bollards, spin it in four-point turns, halt at a shouted command, and an instant later roar away again. Party tricks, Billy's instructor in Germany had scornfully called the manoeuvres, and Billy had carried them out effortlessly.

'So you've got three voices for you, Billy,' Joe went on. 'That's very good, good enough for me. Except now there's my voice and it says this. You're in the firm. I run the firm. I only employ the disabled – people with a speech impediment. Medically it's called a permanently closed mouth. Understand?'

'Yes, Mr Clark,' Billy said flatly.

'That's good, Billy. Because anyone who turns out not to have the impediment, I make them a present of it. Benjie here does the surgery. He cuts their fucking mouths off and just to prevent infection, most of their fucking faces too.'

Joe Clark smoothed his moustache and smiled. Doug frowned gravely. Benjie lifted his head. The light from the window caught his grotesqely slanted eye, and made its pupil glow for an instant like the misshapen body of a plump white spider in a web of black and red veins.

'See you later, Mr Clark,' said Steve.

He caught Billy's arm and led him out.

Billy sat behind the wheel of the car in the darkness.

It was almost 2.00 am and he was parked on a side road near the Elephant and Castle. Through the window a grimy flickering neon light spelled out in a crimson scroll Caribbean Paradise Club. Below it another smaller light said Members Only.

Billy breathed out in a cloud of steam and shivered.

He reached out and pushed up the heating control lever. The car's engine was running – Joe Clark insisted that every car on the Thursday evening collection rounds always had its engine running – and a small ripple of warmth filtered up from beneath the instrument panel.

Benjie was inside picking up the weekly 'insurance' premium. The Caribbean Paradise, a late-night drinking club for black immigrants, was a tiny operation and its payment for protection – against fire-bombs or razor attacks on its owners – was proportionately small. Yet as Joe Clark was fond of saying: 'Remember the motto carved above Rothschild's Bank – "A profit is never a loss". Also it helps spread the word.'

As soon as Benjie came out they'd cross the river and head up West. That's where the serious collections were made.

Billy rubbed his hands together and waited.

It was five years since his release from the military prison. He'd joined the Clarks only weeks after he came out. Billy hadn't wanted to. He'd learned enough about them in those few weeks to know before he met them that even by the standards of South London villains, the Clarks were monsters. But there hadn't really been any choice.

Aunt Doris had taken him back, but as a grown man now he was expected to contribute to the household expenses. Money had always been tight in the house on Mally. Uncle Alf had died while Billy was in prison, and then it had become far tighter still. The trouble was there wasn't any work in Brixton. When Steve arrived one evening and took him down to the pub, Billy knew exactly what he was going to say.

This time Billy accepted.

'Right, Billy.' Benjie came out of the club. He stuffed an envelope into his pocket and climbed inside. 'Three more down in the manor here, then let's see what they've got for us at The Pink Elephant. Seeing as it's the last one tonight, they might even give us a bottle of champagne to celebrate.'

Benjie chuckled.

Benjie, Billy had quickly discovered, had violent and irrational mood swings. At times he'd make Billy stop so he could give money to some vagrant sleeping out on the streets. When they drove on his eyes would brim with sentimental tears. More often he'd erupt in fearsome rages, brutally and sadistically beating one of the firm's protected 'clients' for some imagined insult.

Billy had guessed at the start that Benjie was mad. He was right. The man was a psychopath. Tonight he was in a good humour. When they got to The Pink Elephant, a new and expensive West End night club, Billy knew he'd be invited in to share the champagne.

He put the car into gear and headed West. As he drove he thought about the past five years.

The Clarks ran what the Sunday newspapers, without ever naming them, were already beginning to refer to as 'the fastest-growing kingdom in London's empire of crime'. They were less well-known, shadowier and more secretive than either the Richardsons or the Krays. They were also, the papers hinted, becoming richer and more powerful. Joe Clark, as he'd said, ran the firm. Doug handled the money. Benjie was the chief enforcer, the muscle, the razor, and the threat.

They were allied by blood. They complemented each other. They trusted each other unquestioningly. Together they formed, Billy realised, a ruthlessly efficient team.

They'd started with a small protection operation among the shops, pubs and clubs in Lambeth. Protection was still the firm's main business, but now they were expanding everywhere and into everything. Property dealing, gambling, prostitution, soft drinks and dry cleaning – if any activity could be manipulated and exploited by intimidation, Joe Clark attacked it with a ferocity and cunning few could stand up against.

The lights turned red as they crossed Westminster Bridge into Parliament Square, and Billy braked to a halt.

Beside him Benjie used his palm to force the lid off a Coca-Cola bottle. Benjie never touched alcohol but he was a compulsive Coca-Cola drinker. He drained the bottle and tossed it over the seat. It rattled against the half-dozen empty bottles already there.

As Big Ben sounded the quarter hour, the lights changed to green. They'd done the three other pick-ups south of the river. Now it was time for the The Pink Elephant.

Billy headed on.

For once Steve had been telling the truth when he'd visited Billy in prison and said he was offering him the chance of a lifetime. Billy had done well out of the five years. The Clarks employed only two drivers when he started. There were seven now, several of them older than him, but Billy was considered the best. He always took Benjie on the collection runs and Joe Clark invariably called for him when he needed a driver.

The sixty pounds a week at the start had doubled. Billy rented a small flat of his own not far from Aunt Doris' house. He'd bought a car, a second-hand Morris. By the standards of Mally he was rich. Almost more important, he'd won back the neighbourhood's respect. He was no longer the bugler's illegitimate 'foreign' child who'd been dumped on Doris and Alf, got himself into trouble, thrown away a career as a boxer, and then ended up in prison again.

Billy was the confident and successful young man who wore sharp suits, bought the local children bags of liquorice All Sorts, and took them out for rides in his motor. Like every good South London lad he also looked after his aunt – everyone knew he gave Doris expensive presents and, it was rumoured, money too.

For a twenty-five-year-old from the back streets of Brixton, Billy had everything. And if he worked for the Clarks, what the hell? It took all sorts, didn't it? Billy had deep pockets but not the short arms that usually went with them. He was generous with what he earned from those swine.

'Hey, Billy, I said champagne. Coming in – or not good enough for you?'

Billy glanced round.

Benjie was staring at him in amusement. Billy had automatically pulled up in front of the club and switched off the engine. Lost in his thoughts, he realised he must have been sitting gazing through the windscreen.

'Sure, Benjie. Right with you,' he said awkwardly.

Billy opened the door and got out. He followed Benjie inside behind a group of chattering young men in dinner jackets.

Billy didn't have everything he wanted. In fact, he wasn't sure what it was he did want until much later that night when he was back in his flat lying awake on his bed. The champagne was still tingling in his veins and he couldn't sleep. Something was teasing and tormenting him, some puzzle he couldn't unravel which had nothing to do with the champagne.

Suddenly it came to him.

The neon signs on the clubs. The Caribbean Paradise first, then the three dives on the Old Kent Road, finally The Pink Elephant. Whoever made the first four signs was a journeyman. The man who'd made The Pink Elephant emblem was an artist, an artist in line and light. Half-close your eyes and view it through the filter of the winter rain, as Billy had done, and the neon turned grey.

The sign could have been the head of a real elephant silhouetted against the rising sun. It could almost have been the head of Uhuru.

Billy realised then what had been troubling him. He remembered Father Geoffrey speaking of the few people who were lucky enough to have dreams, and how they had to realise them. He remembered the jar on the hall table with its inscription: 'Uganda Billy Ramsden Project – Elephants (living)'.

Suddenly and irresistibly he knew he had to go back to Africa.

18

'So you want out, Billy,' Joe Clark said. 'You want to broaden your mind through travel. That it?'

'Yes, Mr Clark.'

Joe studied him.

Billy's face was blank and expressionless, and his eyes above the high cheekbones were hooded. His physical presence gave nothing away, but then it never had.

Joe stroked his moustache.

After five years Billy knew a great deal about the firm's operations. If anyone else who worked for him had come with the same request, Joe would have been instantly suspicious. Somehow not with Billy. What Billy had told him he intended to do – to go to Africa, where the hell was Africa, for Christ's sake? – sounded mad, but true.

Joe worked on his instincts. He knew he didn't even need repeat the warning he'd given Billy five years earlier. He was rock solid.

'What are you going to use for money?' he asked.

'I've put some by.'

'Enough?'

Billy hesitated. 'Well, almost.'

'Almost?' Joe picked on it quickly. 'Almost?'

Billy hesitated again. He didn't know how it had happened, but when he checked his savings he'd found virtually everything he'd earned from the firm seemed to have gone. He still had the car and a few odds and ends, but everything else had mysteriously drained away.

'I can manage,' he answered.

Joe didn't speak for several moments. Then he said, 'You can go, Billy. I won't stop you. But you've chosen the wrong moment. There's something I want you to do first. A driving job. I could use one of the others but they're not as good. It's you I want for this.'

Joe paused. He gazed at Billy. Then he added, 'It's worth five thousand, my son. That could change the "almost", couldn't it?'

Billy stared at him.

The job was a raid on a van delivering the weekly wages to a large motor components factory at Chelmsford in Essex.

Armed robbery wasn't a normal part of the firm's activities. This one was different. This one, according to Joe, didn't just warrant the risk – provided it was properly organised, there was no risk. The reason was the wages van's driver.

The driver was Billy and Steve's accomplice in the warehouse thefts, Charlie.

Charlie had never worked for the firm. When he came out after being banged up, he stayed away from Steve for a couple of years. Steve was in with the Clarks, Charlie had his own interests to look after. Then he got the job with J&L Motor Parts. He waited eighteen months until he knew every detail of the weekly wages run, and then he went to Steve.

Steve took the proposition to Joe Clark.

The van carried almost £250,000 folding money in packets, Steve said. Most of the notes were used and untraceable. No record was kept of the new ones – Charlie knew that because he'd got to know the bank cashier and chatted her up over a few drinks. The van took a different route to the factory each week, but Charlie was given it forty-eight hours ahead.

Two guards travelled in the van's cab with Charlie, and there was one more in the back. None of them, in Charlie's opinion, had much bottle. Dummy diversion signs on the road somewhere beyond Basildon, he suggested, on to one of the country lanes, and he'd pull up in a suitable lay-by with alternator or dynamo trouble – Charlie could rig the engine for that. Or the lane could simply be blocked.

Either way all that was needed then was a bit of serious muscle coming out of the bushes and hitting them like the

Normandy landings going in. Three minutes and they'd be away.

'Charlie will need a bit of a spanking,' Steve said to Joe, 'Cuts and bruises and blood and that. And he'll be roped up hard like the other bastards. When the police get there, they won't know the fucking difference.'

'What does he want?' Joe asked.

Steve hesitated. 'Twenty-five per cent, he said to me.'

'Twenty-five?' Joe hooted with laughter. 'Is he mad or insane or bananas or just your fucking cousin, Steve? Ten, that's what he gets. And each time he bitches, it goes down a point. Tell him that from me. Right?'

Steve swallowed. 'Yes, Mr Clark.'

Joe Clark prowled across the room to the window. He stood for a while with his back to Steve gazing outside. Then he turned. As always he was plucking at his moustache.

'We'll go with this one, Steve. And just to be sure we'll take shooters.'

There were three cars in all.

Billy was at the wheel of the first with Benjie in the passenger seat. Behind them in the second car was the rest of the muscle, four men whose job was to surround the van when it pulled up, threaten Charlie and the guards, and seize the wages bags. The third car contained the two who would put out the diversion signs on the Basildon road.

The three cars drove away in the bright sunlight of a May morning.

Billy glanced at Benjie as they threaded their way through the London traffic. He was contentedly sucking at a bottle of Coca-Cola. His wandering eye looked even wilder than ever, but his face was tranquil. For Benjie it was just another job for the firm or rather for Joe who, Billy had come to realise, he idolised.

Benjie had never carried a gun before as far as Billy knew. Billy wasn't even sure Benjie really knew how to handle it. Benjie dealt out violence – 'spanking' it was called in the firm – either with his great mallet-like hands or with a razor. This time Joe had insisted he took a shooter. It wasn't meant to be used, Joe said, but its very presence should snuff out any resistance from the wages' guards.

They drove east along the Mile End Road and headed out into the Essex countryside.

Half an hour later Billy turned off the A4 on to a side road. He knew the way well. He and the other two drivers had driven it several times since Charlie telephoned in with the details of the van's route. Somewhere out of sight the third car had already stopped on the main road, ready to put out the diversion signs.

Billy rounded a corner and pulled into the side. The second car drew in behind. Benjie glanced at his watch.

'Seven minutes, give or take the traffic,' Benjie said. He opened the door. 'No problems, Billy?'

He shook his head.

They'd gone over it again and again.

One of the men – he was already running to his position a hundred yards back – would signal the van's approach with a wave. The second car would swing out and block the road, forcing Charlie to brake to a halt as he came round the corner. Benjie and the others would leap out from the hedge and take over the van.

They'd tie up Charlie and the guards, and throw the wages bags into the two cars. Then they'd drive off. All Billy had to do was sit waiting with the engine running until Benjie climbed in beside him and shouted at him to leave.

Billy watched in the driving mirror as Benjie spoke to the others. They stood for a moment, four tall and burly silhouettes against the sun. As they split up Billy saw Benjie reach under his jacket for the shooter. Then they melted away into the hedgerow.

Billy gunned the engine lightly to make sure all the cylinders were firing. There was a reassuring surge of sound. He took his foot off the accelerator and sat back. He felt utterly calm, almost cold in spite of the warmth of the morning.

He might have been back on Luneberg Heath again in one of the mock ambushes they'd staged so often in training. He knew exactly what would happen. The long still minutes of waiting would be followed by a sudden explosion of sound and movement. There would be shouting, confusion, and probably the violent struggle of men fighting.

Moments later it would end as abruptly as it started.

Benjie would throw himself into the car, Billy would swing back on to the road, and they'd be heading back for London. On the rear seat would be at least half of the wages bags.

Five thousand pounds belonged to him. Charlie was getting five times as much for taking almost less risk than he was. Steve was probably getting the same as Billy for no risk at all. Billy wasn't interested in the others. Five thousand pounds wasn't only going to change his life – it was going to take him back to Africa.

Billy checked the rear mirror again.

There was nothing, only the last of the blossom on the blackthorn of the hedge, the clouds drifting across a bird's egg blue sky, and the driver of the second car sitting hunched over the wheel. Billy glanced at his watch.

If the van wasn't held up, there was less than a minute to go. He tested the motor again. It was still firing perfectly. He sat with his hands on the wheel.

Billy heard the sound of the van even before it rounded the corner. The driver of the ambush car had received the signal of its approach seconds earlier. As he pulled out to block the road, the noise of the two engines blended into one. The van swerved, plunged into the ditch, and came to a halt with its offside wheels spinning.

Darts of adrenalin pumped across Billy's stomach as he watched through the driving mirror.

He saw Benjie break from his hiding-place in the hedge and race forward. Two of the firm's men were at his shoulder wielding pick handles and a third was closing on them from the other side. They reached the front cabin of the van and began to tug at the doors. They were swearing and shouting, and Benjie was brandishing the gun.

For an instant they were on their own – four men battering and kicking at the van. Then, suddenly, they weren't alone. Out of the same hedges and bushes where they'd been hiding erupted another wave of men. Billy stiffened. Some were in uniform, others were in civilian clothes.

They were police.

'Drop that gun!'

The shout came from the policeman who'd burst out first.

He had grey hair and Billy glimpsed the silver stars of a superintendent on his epaulettes. Benjie whirled round and lifted the revolver. He hesitated. Then as the police raced forward, Billy saw his jaw clench as his finger tightened on the trigger.

There was a sharp metallic detonation. Dimly Billy was aware of a cracking sound behind him. Something whined past his head. The mirror shattered and Billy's face was showered with lacerating slivers of glass. Frantically he brushed the glass away. There seemed to be blood everywhere, on his face, on his hands, all over the wheel.

Billy fumbled for the door handle and tumbled out.

As he staggered to his feet he realised what had happened. The bullet from Benjie's gun had gone through the rear windscreen, sliced past his head, and hit the driving mirror. It had missed his brain by little more than an inch. Billy turned. He peered back through the blood that was already cascading down into his eyes.

'Police, put it down!'

The superintendent had dropped to his knees at the shot. Now he was upright and running forward again. Surrounding him in a wedge were five or six other policemen.

Benjie's gaze flickered over them.

His slanted eye swivelled crazily upwards, leaving only a blank white oval in the eye-socket. The police were almost on him when he fired again. The superintendent's legs seemed to be kicked backwards from under him. He clutched his stomach and crashed down on his face. Through the smoke curling up from the gun's barrel Billy could see him writhing on the ground.

Benjie hurled the gun away and broke for the hedge.

He'd barely taken two steps when the other police-men overwhelmed him. The blood was sheeting Billy's face so heavily now he barely saw what happened next. Five of the policemen were kicking Benjie and hammering him with their fists. The gun spun away and lay glittering on the roadway. Then two of the group turned and ran at Billy.

He tried to duck away from them. It was useless. His eyes were blinded by blood and·he careered sightlessly into the car. He heard their feet and then their breath and then their curses. A steel-tipped boot drove into the back of his leg and his knees buckled. He clutched blindly at the car's wing and held himself half-upright. Something crashed down on his arm and he fell to the road.

'Fucking little swine! Give it to him, Johnnie!'

As the booted feet smashed into his ribs, Billy lost consciousness.

He was small, dapper, and silver-haired.

He sat across the interview table from Billy, slowly swinging his gold watch from side to side on the chain that normally anchored the watch to his waistcoat. To his fellow barristers it was known as 'Mischley's Magical Mannerism'. For some reason it was supposed to have a hypnotic effect on the juries he addressed with such consistently successful effect.

Billy didn't know that.

He'd never even heard of Mischley until a few weeks ago. All he knew was that Joe Clark had promised that he, Benjie, and the others would have the best brief money could buy – and Mischley was the best.

'You haven't given me much to work with, Mr Ramsden.'

'I'm called Billy,' he said bleakly.

'Yes, of course.' Mischley drew the words out. 'What about Charlie? Can we suggest some sort of coercion? Mind you, we'd have to find him first.'

Billy shrugged.

Charlie was the only one who'd got away. He'd bolted from the van as soon as the police appeared and somehow had managed to evade them. He was still missing. It was Charlie of course who'd been responsible. He liked his beer and he had a notoriously loose tongue. He'd probably boasted of something big about to happen to one of his fancy ladies.

As likely as not, knowing Charlie, the lady was also

keeping company, in the Brixton phrase, with one of the coppers.

'Or if not Charlie, what about pressure on you from the Clarks?'

Billy shook his head. 'I'm not saying a word against them. Never.'

Mischley was silent. It didn't surprise him. He'd acted often enough for members of the South London gangs. Whether it was fear or loyalty, he'd long since discovered it was almost impossible to persuade them to speak against each other.

The barrister put away his watch and stood up. 'Then all I can do is go for mitigation on the grounds of relative youth,' he said. 'It's a bit of an old chestnut and with your record it's not going to carry much weight, but I'll do the best I can.'

He paused while the warder opened the door.

'In a way you're lucky, Billy,' Mischley added just before he went out. 'If that superintendent had died you'd be on a murder charge along with the rest. That would probably have meant life. As it is I'm afraid it's going to be heavy. Judges don't like guns one little bit. They like the idea of shot and wounded policemen even less.'

The door slammed.

Billy waited for the warder to return and escort him back to his cell. As they walked together down the echoing corridor, the warder looked at him with a mixture of pity and contempt.

'They put the lists up this morning,' the warder said. 'You've got Mr Justice Instone, you poor sod. Wicked he is, Mr Instone, a real hard one. If I was a betting man, I'd say fifteen years for boss-eye and nine for the rest of you.'

The warder was right about Benjie and the others, and only a year out for Billy. In his plea for leniency Mischley made great play of the fact that Billy was the youngest member of the gang, and he'd been sitting in the car when the shots were fired.

Mr Justice Instone grunted. More as a tribute to Mischley's advocacy than anything else, he sentenced Billy to eight years.

19

'You've got five! Move it! Move it!'

The shouts of the warders echoed along the metal landings outside.

It was five minutes to lights out. Billy squatted down in the corner. The three other prisoners he shared the cell with were already lying down in the cramped and rusting two-tier bunks. Billy slid out the nail which served as a communal pencil from its hiding-place in a crack between the floor tiles, and cut another line on the space of wall he'd been allocated by the cell boss for his private calendar.

Every prisoner in Wormwood Scrubs marked the day-by-day passing of their sentence. It was one of the traditional prison rituals, as invariable as the morning slopping-out, and Billy had adopted it within his first week. That evening marked the end of another month, and he scored a longer line diagonally through the scratches to indicate it.

He put the nail away, tugged the slop bucket over the crack, and began to climb up to his own bunk.

'For Christ's sake, you bastard, watch your bleeding feet!'

It was Dusty Miller on the bunk below. White-haired, watery-eyed and constantly complaining, Dusty had spent most of his life in prison. He cursed Billy in the same words every night, although Billy never came near to treading on him.

'Stuff it, you old moaner!'

Billy swung his legs over the bunk's guard-rail. He lay down on the lumpy straw-filled mattress.

A moment later the cover of the inspection hatch in the door rattled open, and an eye appeared in the hole. The

133

eye belonged to the floor's duty screw, a taciturn Northern Irishman named McVey. He surveyed the cell, and slid the cover back again. The overhead light went out, the cell was plunged into darkness, and McVey's footsteps continued along the landing.

Billy crossed his hands behind his head and waited.

For a while the cavernous hall beyond the cell door echoed with cries and curses, and the clatter of the warders' boots on the flights of iron stairs. Gradually the noise faded and silence descended on the prison. For the rest of the night it would be broken only by the sound of snoring and the occasional scream of some prisoner tossing in a nightmare.

Billy lay on his back with his eyes open. He would sleep when he was ready, but not yet. The nights were when he did his thinking.

Three years and seven months exactly.

That was what the wall calendar recorded, but Billy would have known it anyway. The accumulating total of weeks, days, almost of hours, was burnt into his mind. Some prisoners welcomed prison life as in many ways better than life outside. Some sank under it with a numb despairing fatalism. Some, like the tobacco barons and workshop trusties, saw it as simply another arena in which to build careers and businesses.

Not Billy. He'd observed them all and he despised them. To Billy prison was death.

He propped himself up on the bunk and thumped the lumps in the mattress flat, prodding and teasing them out over the supporting slats. Beneath him Dusty Miller groaned in his sleep. Billy lay back.

He'd tried to explain it to Aunt Doris once on one of her visits. Technically all prisoners were allowed one visit a month. In practice it seldom worked out like that. The Scrubs housed long-term hard-core prisoners. For the first year or two, wives and family members came with reasonable regularity. Afterwards their visits tailed away. Wives acquired other men-friends to look after them, families drifted apart, the prisoners were left on their own.

Aunt Doris was much better than most. To begin with she came every month. Then arthritis started to invade her. By the start of his third year, it was as much as she could do to make the wearisome journey by tube and bus once every quarter. Billy could see she was in increasing pain, but still she battled on.

'You shouldn't be doing this, Auntie.' Billy had tried to be stern the last time she'd arrived at the start of the winter.

She smiled at him through the glass partition that separated them.

'How are you going to stop me? Fly through the glass, Superman?'

Billy grinned back. 'What's going on in Mally?'

She told him the news from the street. 'And you, Billy boy, how are you bearing up, son?' she asked.

He thought for a moment.

'Like being in the ring when you're looking at the other bloke before the bell goes,' he said. 'You've got to stare him down. I'll stare these sods down, but it's not living. It's a fucking grave.'

Aunt Doris shrugged. 'Your bleeding elephants, Billy, it was them that got you here.'

'Keeping bad company with elephants?' He laughed. 'That's a new one. I'll try it on the parole board. Trouble is that's two years down the road.'

Doris sniffed. 'You get out, Billy, you pick your mates more carefully.'

'All right, Auntie. There won't be an elephant among them – promise!'

Aunt Doris screwed up her face and gave him a withering look. Then she returned to the subject of Mally.

Billy was still chuckling when she left.

As he returned to his cell he thought that, strangely, in a way Aunt Doris was right. If it hadn't been for Ngoro and the valley and the great matriarch Uhuru, he might indeed not have been there with the iron doors slamming on every side and the warders' shouts ringing off the tiled floors.

He shook his head.

Life wasn't like that. Anyway he wouldn't have traded the elephants for anything in the world, even to escape this. Billy didn't fancy his chances with the parole board, not with his record, but in three years' time, given remission, they'd have to let him go.

Billy didn't have to wait three years.

'How you doing then, Billy, me old mate?'

The voice was soft and lisping, and the words were delivered with an ingratiating chuckle. Billy recognized it instantly.

He glanced at the speaker with a mixture of distaste and surprise.

It was the daily exercise break. Each morning the prisoners from the various blocks were escorted in rotation to the open central yard, and made to tramp in circles two-by-two for exactly an hour under the eyes of four screws standing at the corners. Most of the prisoners welcomed it, not so much for the exercise as the chance to talk to someone other than their cell-mates.

Billy was the exception. He enjoyed the exercise, but he was indifferent to the company. The rules required that someone walk with him. Billy either picked another silent loner like himself, or if he got stuck with someone who insisted on talking, he simply ignored them.

Lenny Goldstone was different.

Lenny was a lifer. An orthodox Jewish accountant, he'd fallen in love with a gentile show-girl from the London production of *Oklahoma*. His appalled family told him that if he married her, he'd come home within six months to find her in bed with the milkman. It was what all the goyim girls did.

Lenny ignored his family. Three years later he came home to find his wife in bed not with the milkman, but with his partner and best friend in the accountancy firm. For the first and only time in his life, something in Lenny flared up. In a frenzy of humiliation and betrayal, he killed them both. When the police arrived he was kneeling weeping over the bodies.

His death sentence was commuted on appeal to the House of Lords to life. With twenty or more years of prison in front of him, Lenny decided to work with the system. He was a merchant and a Jew, and it was his role in life. He became a trusty, then a fixer and arbitrator of prison employment, then a bargainer between the prisoners and the screws. Even the governor consulted him.

'What the hell do you want, Lenny?' Billy replied.

'It's not what I want, Billy boy, but it could be what you want.'

Lenny shuffled closer to him. He lowered his voice. 'You're being moved, sonny. Tuesday week, Chelmsford. You and three others from A block. Four more from B. Benjie's one of them.'

Billy checked for an instant as he absorbed the news.

Rotating long-term inmates between prisons was part of the system. The authorities believed it helped break down the hierarchies that developed in penal institutions. Billy had always known it was a possibility for him, but after more than three years in Wormwood Scrubs he'd put it to the back of his mind.

Billy strode on. 'How do you know, Lenny?'

'My business to know, isn't it?' Lenny caught up with him. 'Except that's not all. The firm, your firm, they're going to spring Benjie from the van that's taking you all there.' Lenny's voice had fallen to a whisper. 'They want to know if you want out too?'

Astonished, Billy was about to stop again. He forced himself to walk on. He felt dizzy.

He hadn't seen Benjie since the trial. Most of the members of the gang had been sent to Durham gaol. Only he and Benjie had been sent to the Scrubs, but as they'd been put in different blocks there'd been almost no contact between them. Now they were both being transferred to Chelmsford – ironically the place where the raid had taken place – and he was being offered the chance to escape.

'What do you say, Billy?' Lenny pressed him.

He tried to sort out the thoughts tumbling through his mind.

If the attempt failed it would certainly add another three years to his sentence. Six and a half more years of Dusty Miller's complaints, the cramped little cell, the shouts and screams at night, the echoing tramp of feet on the metal staircases, the terrible suffocating enclosure of the Victorian brick walls.

Billy hesitated.

This time he stopped walking. He planted his feet apart on the worn tarmac of the exercise yard and put his hands on his hips. Lenny was staring anxiously up at him. Behind them the circle of prisoners shuffled to a halt.

'In a word, Lenny,' he said, 'yes!'

Billy laughed.

One of the screws at the corner of the yard removed his cigarette from his mouth and bellowed, 'Keep fucking moving, Ramsden!'

Billy looked at him.

On his face was an expression of triumphant scorn. The screw would go home that night to his neat little council house, eat his neat little meal, and creep into bed with his neat little wife. He would never in his life see elephants drinking at the hidden river. Billy had done so once and he'd do it again.

Billy raised his hand in a V-gesture of defiance. Alarmed, Lenny caught his arm and pulled it down. Then they tramped on. The column of prisoners behind rippled into movement.

Billy was still laughing.

Billy and Benjie barely glanced at each other as they climbed into the van.

They sat down, one at the front and the other at the back, with the six other transferred prisoners round them and the three escort screws placed at random among them. All of the prisoners were handcuffed in pairs – in Billy's case to a bald pot-bellied man he'd never seen before.

The van headed north.

They crossed the river, wound through the city, and drove out into East Anglia. Once Billy turned and looked back. One of the screws was gazing through the window and the other two were dozing. Billy caught Benjie's glance and winked at him. Because of Benjie's wandering eye it was impossible to be sure, but he thought Benjie winked back.

Billy had no idea what was going to happen, where it would happen, or even whether it would happen at all.

All he knew was that he had to be ready. As they came closer to Chelmsford he sat forward on his seat and flexed his hands.

'Watch out!' The shout came from the driver.

It was an almost identical replay of the raid. They'd turned a corner less than ten miles from the prison to find a truck blocking the road. There wasn't time to stop and the van crashed into the truck's side. With everyone else, Billy was hurled forward.

As he scrambled upright he heard shouts and the shattering of glass. He gazed out. Four or five men in grey balaclavas were battering at the van with axes and pick-handles. One of them forced open the door and leapt inside. A screw ran towards him from the back, but the man clubbed him down.

'Benjie!' the man called.

Benjie was already on his feet. He lunged forward, pulling the prisoner he was handcuffed to with him. The man in the balaclava dropped his pick, pulled out a pair of heavy bolt-cutters, and sheared through the handcuff chain. He pushed Benjie out.

'Where's Billy?' the man bellowed again.

'Here!' he shouted back.

They were almost side by side. The man rounded on him and the cutters snapped again, slicing through the metal as if it had been butter. The man propelled Billy down the van's steps, and backed out after him.

'Stay where you are, all of you, or you'll get your fucking heads blown off!'

'Over here, Benjie, quick!'

'Get down, you bastard!'

There was a confused tangle of voices cursing and shouting. Then Billy heard a new voice close to his shoulder.

'Are you Billy?'

He whirled round. 'Yes.'

'I'm Frankie. You're with me. We're over here. Run, for Christ's sake!'

Billy sprinted after him. They rounded the rear of the

truck and scrambled into a battered Ford parked a hundred yards away.

Frankie slammed it into gear and they whip-lashed away along the road, the tyres screaming on the metalled surface.

20

'Listen, Billy—'

It was twenty minutes later.

They were somewhere in the built-up beginnings of London's East End. Frankie, a stocky bull-necked figure Billy hadn't met before – he must have joined the firm after Billy was sent down – had slowed the car by then until they were travelling well within the speed limit. He turned off the Southend Road into the customer car-park behind a discount carpet store, and switched off the engine.

'Here's where we split,' Frankie said. 'Round the corner's Epping tube station. It's on the Central line, it'll take you to Liverpool Street. From there you can go anywhere you bloody well like.'

Billy nodded. He knew every route on the London underground.

'Except you'll need a ticket.'

Frankie felt inside his dark blue duffle jacket, and handed Billy an envelope.

'There's a monkey in ones inside there, Billy boy.'

Briefly Billy's eyes widened. A monkey was five hundred pounds. It was a huge sum of money.

'Joe said you'd done good, Billy,' Frankie explained. 'You never said nothing from the nick to the Bailey to the sentencing.'

Frankie paused. 'Joe's way of saying thank you. 'Course, what he also means is he knows you'll never say anything about anything ever again, not even when you're dead. Right, Billy?'

Billy lifted his head.

Unblinking he gazed at Frankie through his cold and

flint grey eyes. He didn't say anything. He had no need to.

"Course, not. Just a joke, Billy.' Frankie must have been fifteen years older but his laugh was nervous. 'Anyway, that's for you. There's also this stuff from your Auntie Doris.'

He fumbled in his pocket and passed over the yellow oilskin pouch Jack had given Billy years ago.

'Lenny said you wanted your passport. It's there, Billy. I checked to be sure. There's a bundle of other papers inside too. I didn't look at them, private business, I reckoned, but someone seems to have taken a pair of scissors to them. Is it all right or do you want me to check back with Doris?'

Billy took the pouch. He ran his fingers over the oilskin. He could feel the inset window that framed his name on his passport. He could also feel the jagged wad of papers Frankie had mentioned.

'No need, Frankie, it's fine,' he said.

'Thinking of foreign travel, are we?'

'Maybe.'

'You go where you want to, Billy boy, but take some advice.' Frankie's voice hardened. 'Stay away from the manor, stay away from your auntie's, stay away from anywhere you've ever been. That's where they'll be looking for you. You did good by the firm, the firm's looked after you. That's all over. You're on your own now.'

Billy swung himself out of the car. He wound down the window and slammed the door. Then he bent down and looked back inside.

'I've always been on my own, sunshine. What's so fucking different?'

Billy didn't wait for an answer. He walked away towards the underground station.

Billy came cautiously up the stairs into the main concourse at Victoria station. He stopped into a well of shadow, and glanced round.

A moment later he relaxed.

Mid-afternoon was normally one of the quietest times of day at Victoria, but that Thursday marked the start of the schools' half-term summer break. Frankie had warned him the police would have a full alert out within an hour, and they'd obviously target the railway stations. Even if the warning had reached the duty constables – Billy could spot three pairs of them, their uniforms and helmets conspicuous in the crowds – it was unlikely they'd notice him in the holiday bustle.

He pushed his way through the throng until he could see the departures board.

He wanted Eastbourne, the south coast resort and fishing port. There was a direct train in forty minutes. He bought a one-way ticket and filled in the time in the station bar, reading his first newspaper and having his first pint of beer in almost four years.

Only seconds before departure time Billy showed his ticket to the inspector at the gate, sprinted down the platform, and swung himself up onto the train. An hour and twenty minutes later he got out at Eastbourne.

Five minutes afterwards he was dialling from one of the public call-boxes opposite the taxi-rank in the station forecourt.

'Hullo,' a voice said.

'Is that Debbie?'

Billy had hoped Kevin would have answered, but Debbie would do almost as well.

Kevin and Debbie were the children of one of Aunt Doris' sisters. They'd lived in Mally for a time while their parents were stationed abroad with the army. Kevin had become a friend of Billy's, and Billy had sometimes visited him when the family moved to Eastbourne.

'Yes. Who's that?' asked Debbie.

'Hullo, darling,' said Billy. 'Get ready for a lovely surprise. It's me, Billy.'

'Billy?' There was a long uncertain pause. 'I thought you was away.'

'I was, darling. Now I'm back.'

'Already?'

Debbie stopped again. When she went on there was more than uncertainty in her voice, there was fear.

'Shirley's dad, he brings me and Shirl back from sixth form, he keeps the radio on. On the news they said there was a break-out today, from Chelmsford in a van or something. Billy, is that . . .'

'Listen to me, Debs.'

Billy cut her off.

'I'm in a hurry, darling. I need to find Kev. Does he still sail your dad's boat?'

'Well, yes, only it's his now. Dad retired and gave it to him. But Billy—'

'Debbie,' Billy interrupted her again. 'Just tell me where I can find him.'

'You shouldn't have brought the kid in, Billy, that was out of order.'

Billy and Kevin were standing in the upper car-park of the Silver Oak on the Lewes Road. It was approaching 9.00 pm and the light was fading.

'Right out of order,' Kevin repeated.

He was a big powerful young man wearing jeans. His face was creased by a worried scowl. He kept irritably pushing his hands into his trouser pockets, pulling them out to inspect them, and them jamming them back again.

'She's my kid sister, Billy.'

'I'm sorry, Kev. I didn't have any choice.'

'She's going for college, know that? This could bugger it all up.'

'For Christ's sake, I've said I'm sorry,' Billy protested. 'What else do you want? I thought we were mates from way back. I thought we was all family. Are you going to help me or not?'

Kevin frowned.

'Okay, Billy,' he nodded reluctantly. 'There's a bloke called Bret. We've got a small deal going in brandy. He comes out from Boulogne and I meet him beyond the three-mile limit. I'm picking up from him tomorrow. He'll take you across. Be down at the boat by 4.00 in the morning.'

He paused. 'And, Billy, stay away from the house tonight. I don't want Debbie knowing nothing more from this. I tell you, it's all out of order.'

'Don't worry, Kev,' Billy snapped. 'I won't come near anyone with a fucking barge-pole. Fucking leper, that's me, isn't it?'

Kevin didn't answer. He turned and walked unhappily away.

Billy spent the night in a carelessly unlocked sail-loft on the harbour front. Well before 4.00 am he was standing by the boat, a 25-foot motor cruiser whose berth he remembered well. Kevin appeared and they set off in the darkness.

An hour later when they were beyond the three-mile limit and the sky was starting to pale with dawn, they spotted another slightly larger boat. Kevin pulled alongside.

'Right, Bret?' he called out.

Their engines idling, the two boats nudged each other in the light swell. A man put his head out of the wheelhouse and gave a quick wave. Billy caught a glimpse of a pale and ferrety face under a faded beret. Then the head ducked back out of sight.

Kevin looked at Billy.

'The frogs call him Johnnie the Breton,' Kevin said. 'It's a sort of a joke. His dad's from Brittany and his ma, she's English. She works as a maid in Brighton in the hotels. Brittany-Brighton, get it?'

Billy nodded.

'We just call him Bret. He speaks English perfect from his ma. He may be a frog but he's not bad. He'll get you across. If you've any idea about trying to stitch him on the money, forget it. He carries a blade. Believe me, he can use it.'

'I'm not stitching anyone,' Billy said.

'Here!' Bret reappeared.

He was carrying a crate of brandy. He heaved over a dozen of them, and Billy helped Kevin stow them under the forehatch. Then at a call from Bret, Billy scrambled across into the other boat. He shook hands with the Frenchman and glanced back.

Kevin had already engaged the diesel engine and was pulling away. As Billy lifted his hand in a gesture of farewell, Kevin's voice drifted back to him.

'Good luck, Billy,' he was shouting. 'But for Christ's

sake, don't try that on me again. That was right out of order, mate.'

'Wait until you get done for smuggling, son,' he bellowed back. 'You'll be needing me and wheels then. I'll send a card from Africa.'

Billy chuckled.

Bret had also started his engine. As the boat's bows rose and began to plane across the sea, Billy walked back to join the Frenchman by the wheel at the stern. Bret pointed at the locker at his feet. Billy opened it. Inside was a bottle of brandy.

'Your cousin, is he?' Bret asked.

Billy nodded.

'One two, buckle my shoe!' Bret laughed mischievously. 'You rosbifs, you never can count, can you? Open it, my friend. Kevin won't even notice it's gone.'

Billy frowned. Then he realised what the Frenchman meant. Bret had purloined the bottle from one of the crates he'd sold Kevin.

Billy started to laugh too. There were two chipped pottery mugs in the locker. He pulled them out, unscrewed the bottle top, and poured some brandy into the mugs.

He propped himself on the rail beside Bret and leant there drinking as the sun rose and the coast of France came into sight through the dawn mist.

21

'*Votre nom* – your name?'

The sergeant spoke English awkwardly in quick clipped phrases with a heavy American accent.

He sat behind the desk in a short-sleeved olive shirt, a wiry crop-haired man with a face the colour of dry birch bark. His white peaked cap, the uniform equivalent of the French Foreign Legion's famous *képis blanc*, hung from a peg on the wall behind his head.

'Ramsden,' Billy said, 'Billy Ramsden.'

The sergeant licked his finger and flicked through the pages of a dog-eared dictionary.

'Billy is Guillaume, William, no?'

Billy nodded.

'Is on your passport?'

'Yes.'

'Give!'

Billy reached into his pocket and handed over his passport. The sergeant studied it.

'Is no entry stamp to France.' The sergeant looked up. 'Is stolen or legal this passport?'

'It's legal,' Billy said. 'It's not stamped because I came in on a small boat. I didn't go through customs.'

The sergeant stared at him. He yawned. Then he picked up the telephone and dialled. There was a flurry of French and he put the receiver down. He gestured at Billy to be patient.

Billy crossed his hands behind his back and waited.

He'd been in France for twenty-four hours. Bret had landed him at a private jetty in a bay eight miles west of Boulogne. Billy had walked inland to the main road and hitched a lift on a fish truck into the town. From there he caught a train to

Paris. It was Sunday. Almost everything was closed, and he spent the night in a cheap hotel near the station.

That morning he got up early and took another train out to the suburb of Cergy-Pontoise. It took him an hour to find the address he was looking for – he'd written it out on a card so he could ask directions from people in the streets – but he was still early enough to have time for a coffee before the building opened.

When the bolts slid back on the great brass-studded door, Billy walked in beneath the tricolor hanging above the entrance and presented himself at the reception desk of the Paris recruiting office of the Legion.

From the moment he'd said yes to Lenny Goldstone, Billy knew exactly what he'd do if the prison breakout was successful. It was the only thing he could do. He couldn't stay in Britain. Sooner or later he'd be arrested again. He had to go abroad, he had to practise a trade and earn money, he had to obliterate his past and start again.

Billy's trade was soldiering and he'd known about the Legion all his life. One of his earliest memories was of a group of legionnaires at Lucknow, sent there to train for the jungle warfare in Indo-China. He remembered the big burly men striding round the barracks, wearing the white *képi* and talking in a welter of incomprehensible languages.

Billy's father had spoken of them.

'Considering they're foreigners' he'd said, 'not a bad lot. Hard with it, too, bullet hard.' Billy's cousin Jack had also talked of them in Brixton; so had the soldiers Billy served with in Germany. 'Never mind, Billy,' one of his patrol companions remarked chuckling after another of Billy's furious collisions with Major Forbes. 'If the Lilywhites toss you out, there's always the frogs – they go for the awkward squad. Always pick up a shilling with their mob.'

The Legion not only offered men like Billy a second start and a new life, they policed and defended what was left of France's empire. By the time Billy presented himself in Cergy-Pontoise, the remnants of that empire mainly lay in Africa.

'So, you are Ramsden.'

Another man had come into the room. From the gleaming brass stars on his epaulettes he was obviously an officer. The sergeant got to his feet and Billy instinctively drew his heels together. He stood rigidly with his arms pressed down against his sides.

The officer noticed and looked at him curiously. 'You are a soldier, Ramsden, no?'

'I was, sir.'

'Which regiment?'

'Coldstream Guards, sir.'

'Ah.' A smile crossed the officer's face. 'Last year I went on a course with your "lot" at Pirbright camp. "Lot" is right, no?'

'Sir!'

The officer's English was much more fluent than the sergeant's. He said something and the sergeant left the room. The officer sat down behind the desk and studied the sergeant's notes.

'A soldier with a passport but no entry stamp.' He paused. 'You know of course the Legion cannot accept anyone who faces criminal charges or is wanted in their own country?'

'Sir!'

'Also,' the officer went on, 'that if we suspect this, we are bound by law to *faire les enquêtes*, to make enquiries. This naturally can take a long time. At the end, if our suspicions our correct, the person is sent home to face justice.'

'Yes, sir.'

'And yet still you come here, still you want to join the Legion. Why is this, Ramsden?'

Billy looked at him.

The officer was much younger than the sergeant. His face was open and unlined, but his eyes were acute and penetrating. The French regular army, Billy knew, tested out their best officers by sending them to command posts in the Legion. This man was clearly one of them.

'A bit of bother, sir.'

Billy knew there was no point in lying. He described the events of the past eight years in a few sentences.

'And Colonel Willoughby,' the officer said as Billy finished –

149

the officer was referring back to the court-martial – 'he really talked for you, *non?*'

'Yes, sir.'

The officer was silent for several minutes.

'French law says I must make studies and maybe at the end send you back to Britain,' he said eventually. 'Sometimes the Legion makes its own laws. I know your Colonel Willoughby. He was the *co-ordinateur* on my course. He is a fine brave man. He landed with the Guards Armoured Brigade on Juno beach. You will know that, of course?'

Billy said nothing.

He knew Willoughby had been wounded in the Italian campaign. He didn't know he'd also taken part in the Normandy landings. The officer didn't seem to notice his silence.

'For Colonel Willoughby I make the exception. I say this.'

He took Billy's passport and suddenly tore it two. He threw the pieces into the wastepaper basket.

Billy stood utterly still. He felt cold. A part of his life, of his very existence, seemed to have been taken away from him. Something unexpected and irrevocable had happened.

'You are no longer British, Ramsden. You have no nationality. You are not even named Ramsden.' He thought for a moment. 'You keep your initials, of course, it is the custom. But from now your name is Bernard Roget.'

He sat forward and began writing as he continued to speak.

'The sergeant will give you a *carte d'identité provisoire* in your new name. Also a rail warrant to Toulouse and money for the *car* from there to the training depot at Castelnaudary. You will sign on for seven years. At the end of that time, providing you have served well and there is nothing against you, you will be given French citizenship and a French passport. You may also then extend your service for a further seven years and so on until the age of *retraite* – retirement.'

The officer pushed a form and a pen across the table.

'Sign here as Bernard Roget. I have printed it above so you know how it is written.'

Dazed, Billy took the pen and signed. He straightened up.

'Thank you, sir.'

The officer shook his head. 'Do not thank me. Thank your Colonel Willoughby and the great regiment he commands. I would bend the rules – is that correct, no? – for no one else. But for the colonel and the Coldstream, I take a gamble.'

He stood and held out his hand. 'Welcome to *La Légion étrangère*, Roget.'

Billy shook hands. Then, instinctively, he saluted. The officer left the room.

As Billy waited for the sergeant to return he stared at the *képi blanc* hanging on the wall. The white band round the cap, perhaps the most famous military symbol in the world, gleamed in the sunlight streaming in through the window. Billy knew he was committed to wearing the *képi* for seven years.

He had no idea as he stood there that morning it would be twenty-eight years before he finally put it aside.

Billy took the train south across France to Toulouse, and the bus onwards to Castelnaudary.

There in the grim barracks outside the little medieval town, barracks that Billy recognised with a shock were almost identical to those at the guards' depot at Caterham, and in the lonely Languedoc countryside reaching up into the foothills of the Pyrennees, he became a member of the strange, often brutal, and almost hermetically private world of the French Foreign Legion.

Like the British army's Gurkha regiments, the Legion was an entirely mercenary force. Unlike the Gurkhas who all came from the tiny state of Nepal in the shadow of the Himalayas, the Legion drew its recruits from all over the world. At Castelnaudary Billy found himself in the company of Brazilians, Spaniards, Yugoslavs, Turks, Hungarians, Australians, and twenty or thirty other races.

The legion offered them all a new identity, a new nationality, and a new name. In return it demanded their unquestioning allegiance – not to France, although French was the Legion's language and France was the nation they served, but to the Legion itself. It was a nation of its own. It had its own history, its own traditions, its hierarchy, its customs and songs and laws.

To belong to the Legion was to belong to a huge but tightly knit family, which ruthlessly punished anyone who betrayed it. Few ever did.

'To dump *merde*, to shit on *la Légion*,' the recruit reception sergeant at Castelnaudary said, 'that's like fucking your mother. *Degardando en tu madre*.'

He repeated the coarse phrase in Spanish and again in German.

'*Verstehen sie, me comprendes*, understand, *mes petits bonhommes*?'

The circle of recruits, Billy sitting at the centre, nodded.

'*Bon*! Because if you shit, the Legion will follow you *jusque au bout du monde*, to the end of the earth. And there, my friends, we will cut off your balls, barbecue them, and stuff them down your *gorges*.'

The sergeant used the French word for throat. He grinned malevolently. Then he suddenly shouted, '*J'adore ma mère*! *J'adore la Légion*! *Les deux sont inséparables*.'

He raised his arms like the conductor of an orchestra and made them chant the words with him. One by one they all joined in.

Your mother and the Legion. There was no difference. The two were one. They gave you life, they nourished, guided, and supported you from the cradle to the grave.

Billy learnt French.

He learnt it in the same way the reception sergeant had taught it that first night, chanting out the words and phrases shouted by the Legion's language instructors round camp fires in the Languedoc hills. He learnt the Legion's marching songs – '*Auprès de ma blonde*', '*Milord*', which they'd borrowed from Piaf, and many more.

He learnt the Legion's folklore – the story of Cameroun in the Mexican wars, the battles among the forts in the North African deserts, and the siege of the Dienbienphu valley where a lowly major called Marcel Bigeard and a handful of Legion paras had fought the entire North Vietnamese army to a standstill in a defiance even greater than at Cameroun.

Billy was absorbed by the Legion and he in turn pulled it round him like a warm protective cloak.

He discarded the past – Brixton, the house in Mally, Aunt Doris, Father Geoffrey, the Crown and Garter Club, his employment by the Clarks, the years in prison – like the clothes that had been stripped off him when he arrived at Castelnaudary. They were taken away to be burned. So, in Billy's mind, was everything that had happened to him until then.

The slate on which his history was scrawled had been sluiced down and scrubbed clean. Billy Ramsden no longer existed except as a name which stubbornly clung like a burr to his memory. In every other way he'd been born again as Bernard Roget. Only the initials were the same.

To Billy the seal on his new life came after eight months at Castelnaudary when he was awarded his *képi blanc*.

Far from all those who'd enlisted with him did the same. Billy's earlier experience as a soldier gave him a major advantage. It wasn't everything. Two out of three of his fellow recruits, including several who'd been soldiers too, were discharged for one reason or another along the course.

By chance on the day of Billy's passing out ceremony, the young officer from the Paris recruiting office happened to be visiting Castelnaudary. He accompanied the camp commandant as he inspected the ranks of the Legion's new intake.

The officer passed Billy, hesitated, and turned back.

Légionnaire Roget?' he asked.

'*Oui, mon capitaine,*' Billy replied in French.

The officer smiled quizzically and switched to English.

'Colonel Willoughby asked me to your country for the Easter *fête,*' he said. 'I stayed with him near the barracks of Windsor. We spoke of you. He sent you a message if I might see you . . .'

The man wrinkled his face, trying to recollect it.

'Yes.' It came back to him. 'He said there was an officer you had some *bagarre* with. That officer, he said for me to tell you, no longer serves. He is *foutu* – dismissed. Colonel Willoughby also said he wished you served with the Coldstream still.'

'Sir!' Billy smiled back.

He came to attention, slammed his heel into the parade ground concrete, and saluted.

The officer acknowledged the salute and walked on.

That night in celebration Billy drank a large quantity of calvados mixed with *vin-gel* – the gelatine-based red wine which had been parachuted into the Dienbienphu valley, and which along with calvados had been adopted by the Legion as its ceremonial drink.

In the early hours of the following morning he tumbled drunkenly into a gutter outside one of Castelnaudary's bars. He was hauled out by a Legion military police patrol.

'Who the hell are you?' one of the military policemen said.

'Bernard Roget,' replied Billy. '*Légionnaire* Bernard Roget,' he added proudly.

Billy beamed. His white *képi* had fallen off. He managed to retrieve it from the gutter and clamp it back on his head.

Then he vomited and lost consciousness.

22

From Castelnaudary Billy was sent to Corsica.

He spent two years at the Legion's base near Ajaccio. Then he was posted to the barracks outside Marseille. Two years later still he was moved on again, this time to North Africa.

It was the start of an odyssey that was to last for almost a quarter of a century.

'You'll come in here on runway two.'

The briefing officer tapped the map with his long ebony-tipped pointer stick.

'Intelligence from local sources in Fort Lamy say there may be a few pockets of monkeys with heavy automatics round the perimeter. There may be, there may not. Assume there are. Hit the ground firing. Anything that moves, a dog or a fucking kid, cut it down.'

He paused. 'This is Africa, my friends. Animals and children, they could be wired for explosives. Never forget it. We want both those runways secured, and we don't mind how you do it.'

Six hours later Billy tumbled out of an old Dassault troop transporter on to the chipped and cratered concrete of Chad's Fort Lamy airport.

Local intelligence was right. Even before the plane touched down the assault group could hear tracer fire from heavy machine-guns patterning the runway. On the ground Billy rolled over and pulled himself upright. Following his platoon sergeant, he raced to the right firing blindly from the hip with his own automatic as he ran.

Beside him Jean-Jacques, one of his fellow legionnaires, suddenly staggered and dropped. Billy checked and glanced back. The man was lying on his face clutching his stomach.

A great red pool was already spreading out from between his thighs, and Billy could hear his screams above the sound of the gunfire.

'Move, for Christ's sake, move!' the sergeant bellowed. 'We'll get him later!'

Billy ran on.

They reached the edge of the airfield and crouched under the bank that supported the perimeter fence.

The machine-gun emplacement that was still pouring out its lacerating fire was sited above them and just to their left. Typically *les singes* – black Africans were always known to the Legion as 'monkeys' – hadn't protected themselves from a counter-attack from below.

'Grenades!' the sergeant snapped. He pointed quickly. 'Roget, you this side. Lecanouet, you on the other. When I signal, throw! The rest of us will go in over the top to tidy up.'

The platoon spread out, crawling along the bank's foot.

Billy unclipped two grenades from his belt. He plucked out their pins with his teeth and held them in either hand, his fingers clamped over the levers that held down the springs to the detonators. He watched the sergeant. He saw him raise his arm and sweep it down.

Billy stood up and released the levers. The grenades had a seven-second fuse. Billy counted slowly to four and hurled them upwards. Almost instantly out of his sight there was a deafening double-explosion followed by another – Lecanouet had thrown his two grenades at the same moment.

Billy grasped his automatic carbine and scrambled up the bank, his feet sinking deep into the sand as he climbed.

He reached the top and gazed down.

The scene inside the fortified machine-gun nest was carnage. The position had been manned by about thirty Chad rebels. Half of them had been killed by the grenades, or by the raking fire the sergeant and the rest of the platoon had rained down on them at point-blank range after the explosions.

The rest were still alive although several were badly wounded. None of them was capable of offering any resistance. The sun was high now and the legionnaires stood in a ring round the dug-out, silhouetted against the morning sky like vultures.

'Bernard,' the sergeant snapped to Billy, 'See to Jean-Jacques. He fell beside you. Pierre, you go with him. Here, take my radio so you can call the support *médécins*.'

Billy took the transceiver and ran back down the bank on to the runway with Pierre behind him. Five minutes later they returned.

'Jean-Jacques is dead, *mon sergeant*,' he said. 'We have signalled command assault mobile HQ. They will collect him.'

He gave the transceiver back.

The pool of blood round Jean-Jacques' body was already turning dark and hardening in the heat of the Chad morning when he and Pierre reached it. Billy was almost sure the man was dying the moment he saw the legionnaire rock back and fall. The sergeant, he sensed, knew it too.

'So.'

The sergeant pulled out the .99mm Mauser at his waist. He stepped down into the warren of trenches and short tunnels that had made up the machine-gun post. The Chad natives who were still alive gazed up at him in terror.

He caught one of the wounded by the throat, and wrenched the man to his knees.

'How many, *mon petit bonhomme*, for a legionnaire?'

The sergeant spoke in French.

It was the universal language of Chad, and the man must have understood what the sergeant was saying. The man was too terrified to reply. His eyes rolled in terror and he stared vacantly upwards as the sergeant's hand tightened on his neck.

'More than you can count, *mon petit*, more than there are stars in the sky. That's the price of a legionnaire. Today it'll be paid in *monnaie*, small change, because it's all you've fucking got. But next time it'll be the whole country.'

He put the barrel of the pistol against the man's head and pulled the trigger.

Billy swayed back as the explosion rocked the dug-out bowl. He looked down again as the smoke cleared. Filaments of the man's brain tissue, milky-brown and stippled like a fish's roe, were trickling down the ochre banks of sand. Before Billy had a chance to react, the sergeant fired again.

He walked round the dug-out killing everyone who was left alive. Three times he had to stop and reload his pistol from the clips of amunition in his belt. None of the Chad tried to escape or stop him. They simply lay, stood or squatted there with dilated eyes and shuddering limbs as one by one he executed them.

When there was only one left the sergeant paused. He glanced up and beckoned to Billy. Billy jumped down beside him.

'Jean-Jacques, he was your *copain*, no?'

Billy nodded. Jean-Jacques had been his closest friend in the platoon.

'Then you can have this one for him.'

He handed Billy the pistol. Billy raised it and fired.

It was the first time he had killed.

That night the legionnaires camped above the runway close to the shattered rebel machine-gun post. The rebels had stockpiled wood and the platoon used it to fuel their own fire. Billy was assigned the dawn watch. After he'd eaten he slept for a while. He was woken by the outgoing guard as the sky started to pale, and crawled out of his bivouac.

Billy settled himself down on the bank with his rifle on his knees. He gazed across the cratered airfield and then glanced up. It was still dark enough for the stars to shine out against the approaching morning. He couldn't see the Southern Cross – he was too far north for that – but he could make out the Plough, Orion's belt, and Sirius.

The slender sickle of a crescent moon dipped towards the horizon. Owls were calling, somewhere a jackal barked fretfully, the dawn breeze was fresh and clean and moist on his face. It was exactly as it had been when Ngoro had woken him, and led him and Violet forward to the rim of the gorge above the river.

Billy thought of the elephants and the valley. Most of all he thought of Violet. It was over twenty years since he'd seen her. The child, as she was then, would be a woman now.

He cradled the rifle in his arms.

As the sun rose, as the jackal howled again, and dust began to stir in coils over the runway, Billy tried to imagine what might have happened to her.

The Garden of Eden

The Woman

The woman was small and dark-skinned.

She was naked apart from a thong circling her neck – the emblem of the gatherer. Hanging from the thong was a pouch containing a piece of blade-bone. The bone had been smoothed and polished to make a digging tool.

When the rains came the previous night, the woman had abandoned her nest in the reeds and taken refuge in the trees which overhung the river. She feared the storm and the rushing waters it brought which would carve out the river's gorge over the millennia ahead, although she had no means of knowing that.

Now, in the bright morning sunlight, she stepped into the calm waters of the pool in the river which gave life to the valley and all its animals.

For a moment she gazed at her own reflection in the water.

The mirrored surface showed her many things. It showed her that her figure was muscular and strong. That her skin was the colour of a ripe walnut. That her breasts stood out firm and proud. That her eyes were dark and almond-shaped, so dark they were almost black. That her lips were full, the cheekbones high, the forehead broad.

What it did not tell her was that she was beautiful. There was no one in all the world to admire her beauty, even though the dark wedge of hair at the groin told her that her body was ready for childbearing.

The woman slipped beneath the waters of the pool. It was a tiny oxbow lake at a bend in the winding river. She gripped a clump of papyrus and lay floating on her back, staring up at the sky. A pied kingfisher hovered overhead before plunging down near her feet. The bird rose again in a glitter of spray with a fish in its beak.

The woman closed her eyes and let the water ripple round her.

It was very warm, but she was shivering, regretting for a moment she had not returned to her nest in the reeds to sleep out the hours of daylight after the storm.

For some reason the plunging kingfisher – it was as black as her eyes as it soared away against the light – had brought the past surging back to her. Memories of the past, of the terrible things that had happened, still chilled her.

She wasn't sure when the badness had started.

Perhaps it was as early as the eleventh summer of her life. Until then her people, she had no idea how many there were in the clan, perhaps thirty or forty, had lived in the forest. At night they slept high up in the trees on platforms of loosely-woven branches like great untidy birds' nests. By day they came down to the forest floor to gather. They did not hunt – there was no need to expend the energy hunting required. They simply took what came most easily to hand.

They gathered roots and fruits and tubers. They searched for birds' eggs, grubs, insects, fungi, lizards, and the few small animals which fell into their simple traps, spider's webs of woven grasses to catch the unwary.

It was a hard but not normally a hazardous existence. For those first years the trees framed the boundaries of her world. Then the fire came.

The fire changed everything.

The forest had known fires before. This one was different. Although she had no way of knowing the cause, the flames had been ignited by the incandescent heat created by a rogue meteorite colliding with the desert floor. Fanned by freak gale-force winds from the distant western ocean, it raged across the land in a blood-red wave of destruction that incinerated everything in its path. Hundreds of thousands and then millions of square miles of the primeval African forest were reduced to a bed of ash.

Along with every other living thing in the forest, the woman's clan and the other tree-dwelling clans near them were exterminated in the furnace of the conflagration.

The woman alone survived.

She owed her life to her mother. Somehow the older woman managed to pluck her little daughter from the tree nest before the flames engulfed it. For days she carried the child to the north-east. She didn't chose the direction. It was chosen for her by the Atlantic wind blowing from behind her back and carrying the gnawing flames with it. There was nowhere else to go except to run before the blaze that snarled constantly at their heels.

She did not choose the path itself.

That had been hewn from the savannah by the passage of a great herd of elephants whose annual migrations in search of sustenance had created a broad corridor of highway. The corridors regenerated from year to year, but the elephant matriarchs always knew where they were, knowing too that the new grasses would be tender and sweet for their soft-mouthed calves on the endless journeys from forest to plain to river.

The highways which criss-crossed the savannah served as natural firebreaks against the conflagrations of summer. This was no summer fire – the flames leapt the open corridors with scarcely a pause. There was no highway broad enough to contain the fireball which dropped out of the sky – all the elephant lanes could do was offer the brief sanctuary of passage through the blaze.

The fires raged to the left and right of the two females as they fled, but in the centre they were temporarily safe.

Two months later they stopped. Although a great pall of smoke still hung in the sky behind them, the wind had dropped and the fire had almost burnt itself out.

By then they'd travelled over six hundred miles. They'd managed to survive on the insects and the other small creatures which scuttled across the highway to escape the flames. Now, their skins blistered from the unrelenting heat, they were both emaciated and exhausted.

The child's mother climbed up into a camel-thorn acacia

tree, and tied her daughter with vines to a split branch for safety against the predators that roamed the ground. Then she dropped back to the earth and set out to scavenge once more. She was returning to the tree with a nest-full of birds eggs and a hollowed log containing honey and caterpillars when a pack of hyenas scented her.

She screamed – a high curving wail of noise and anger which was as much a weapon of defence as an expression of fear.

Her cries woke the child. She peered down through the leaves, her arms and legs tethered to the branches. Her mother reached the trunk as the hyenas caught up with her. She tried to climb, but the heavy-shouldered animals leapt up and dragged her down, tearing at the dangling body with their massive jaws.

The child watched as they killed and ate her, grunts and squeals of hunger punctuating their meal.

Later she fell asleep. She woke before dawn to find the tree thronged with roosting vultures. They were waiting for the light so they could flap down and claim the bones below. They had already been at work on the flesh, and the stench from the fragments of carrion clinging to their claws and bills was overpowering.

The child shook her head. She felt loss. She felt fear. Above all she felt ravenously, achingly hungry.

She gnawed through the vine ties and scrambled down the trunk. She paused for a moment, listening and searching the early light. The hyenas had gone. They had eaten the spilled birds' eggs, but they had ignored the honey and the caterpillers. She stuffed handfuls of them into her mouth and chewed greedily. Then she began to cast round the tree.

In the frenzy of the hyenas' attack, a rib from her mother's body had been hurled away into the bush. A cluster of buzzing flies marked its resting place. She reached into the thorn and dragged it out. There was flesh clinging to bone – enough to sustain her for several days, or at least until the meat rotted in the heat.

She licked it experimentally, tasting the sweetness. She had no sentiment about the flesh itself, no guilt. It was not her mother's flesh and blood which stained her lips. Dead meat was carrion, carrion was food. Her mother's spirit could not be harmed by what she had done – her mother's spirit lived on in her, and it was right that her flesh should fuel that spirit.

She heaved the bone on to her shoulders and set off. She headed north-east in the same direction her mother had taken. There were no smouldering flames behind her now to propel her that way. She took the path instinctively and with utter certainty.

She was just as much the child of a female mammal as was the calf of an elephant. She followed the course the wisdom of her mother had taught her she should follow.

What separated her from the elephants was not what she knew but what she understood. She understood she had no herd to support her. She understood she was alone, utterly alone. She was eleven years old and she sensed – with the terrible haunting memories of the fire behind her – she was the last of her kind left in the world.

She carried within her, although again she had no means of knowing it, the genetic rootstock of all humanity. What she did know in the loneliness that enveloped her was that after her there would be nothing. The carrion – her mother's final gift – lasted her for a week.

By then she had learned she could survive on her own.

A month later she found the river. Close to the river's banks were fat waxy grains, succulent tsama melons, and in the overhanging trees the hives of honey bees – it was a bird, a honey-guide, that led her there. There was both food and water. She tore out armfuls of reeds and made a nest on the ground like the nests her clan had made in the trees. She settled down to live for as long as the predators allowed her life.

Four years passed until the rains came. The morning after the storm, on her return from the oxbow pool she found him. She found him curled in her nest in the reeds, asleep and as helpless as a new born baby.

As soon as she saw him, she knew he was hers.

PART THREE

Violet's Story

24

Violet reached through the railings and picked up one of the
bamboos the gardener used for staking his plants.

'Race you, Angie!' she shouted. 'And you've got to touch
every one!'

Angie, Violet's new best friend from the expensive day-
school her mother had chosen for her, was trailing a few
steps behind.

'Not fair!' she cried. 'Wait till I've got a stick too!'

Angie seized another bamboo and the two little girls, black
coats flaring out behind them and white socks flashing in the
sunlight, set off round the square drumming the sticks on the
ironwork as they ran.

It was early-April.

Two and a half years had passed since the boat bringing
Violet and her mother home docked at Liverpool at the start
of the winter of 1945. Like Billy, Violet had never known cold
before, but her experience of that first London winter was
very different from his.

Three miles north-west of Lambeth on the other side of
the Thames, the Somersets' London home was a large and
elegant Georgian house in Kensington, which a combination of
central heating and open coal fires kept warm throughout the
worst of the bitter weather. Nanny and Violet had their own
suite of rooms at the top of the house where the rest of the
staff – a cook, a butler, a parlour maid, and Mrs Somerset's
lady's maid – also slept.

Violet and Nanny's suite included a large nursery where
Violet's friends like Angie often came back for tea after school.
Not today. Angie was going out to a party to which, to Violet's
irritation, she hadn't been invited. It didn't really matter.

At least today she had something exciting to tell her mother.

The two children reached Violet's front door, and Angie waved and ran on. Violet clattered up the steps and went inside.

'Mummy, Mummy!' Violet came bounding into the room and threw her arms round her mother. 'Guess what!'

'Darling, please!' Margaret Somerset drew back and tried to push Violet away. 'I've just had my hair done. You're going to absolutely ruin it. And where's Nanny, anyway?'

'Oh, somewhere behind. Angie and I had a race. I won.'

'Violet, I keep telling you, when Nanny brings you back, you're not to run ahead and leave her. She's too old to keep up and she worries terribly about something happening you while you're out of her sight.'

Violet wrinkled her nose. 'I'm big now, Mummy. Nothing's going to happen to me.'

'You do as I say, young lady,' Mrs Somerset's voice was stern. 'Or I'll speak to Angie's mother. We'll see what she has to say.'

She paused. Then her tone brightened. 'So, what am I meant to guess?'

'We've all done so well this term, we're getting a special treat. Miss Palmer's taking the whole class to the zoo.'

'Darling, how lovely! When?'

'Tomorrow, Mummy. And Miss Archer said to tell you I've got to bring sandwiches for a picnic.'

'My goodness, aren't you lucky?'

She paused and looked at her daughter. Violet's hair was tousled from the wind outside, her cheeks glowed from the April sun, and her eyes were shining with excitement at the thought of the trip. Even at nine she was one of the most beautiful children Margaret Somerset had ever seen.

Guiltily she thought she might have been a little hard on the child. Nanny was getting on and at almost ten it would have been frustrating for any child to stay by her side as the old woman limped home.

'Give me another kiss – very carefully this time – then you

can go and tell Mrs Benson to make you whatever you'd like for tomorrow.'

'Really anything I want?'

'Yes, darling.'

'Even if Nanny says no?'

'Don't tell her, you little goose. Just go to Mrs Benson and ask her.'

'Goodee!'

Mrs Somerset tilted her head so her daughter could kiss her on the cheek. Then Violet ran downstairs to the kitchen to find Mrs Benson, the cook.

Violet knew exactly what she'd ask Mrs Benson for: marmite sandwiches, fried chip potatoes she'd keep warm in the thermos flask her uncle had given her, and a big slab of chocolate. Angie loved chocolate, so did all her school-friends, but it was 1948, rationing was still in force, and most of them only had the chance to eat it very occasionally.

For some reason rationing didn't seem to apply to the Somerset household. There was always chocolate available; so was almost everything else that was meant to be in short supply. One day Violet asked her mother why.

'You know how it is, darling.' Margaret Somerset waved her hand vaguely. 'Daddy's job – diplomats have to keep up appearances. And then we have so many kind friends in America.'

Violet chewed her lip thoughtfully.

She didn't quite see how appearances and chocolate were joined together. Kind friends in America was easier – her father was often away on trips, and she supposed he must have made friends then. There seemed to a several different varieties of friendship in the grown-up world. As far as her mother was concerned, there were friends, girl friends and good friends.

'For heaven's sake, Michael, we're just good friends, that's all,' Violet had heard her mother say once when her father asked about a man who had taken her out to dinner.

Lots of people seemed to be eager to take her mother out to dinner. Whenever Violet's father was abroad, her mother didn't stay quietly at home like her friends' mothers when their husbands were away. If anything, Mrs Somerset's trips to the hairdressers were more frequent and her taffeta petticoats rustled even louder when she left to go out in the evenings.

It was one of her mother's men friends who prompted a question Violet had decided to ask Angie. It wasn't a question she could ask her at school, or when Nanny might be within earshot. It was private and it had to wait for the right moment.

That might be tomorrow at the zoo.

Angie could be relied on to know things. Her father was a society portrait-painter and her mother had been quite a famous actress. They were 'Good value but rather racy', Mrs Somerset had said once with an edge of disapproval in her voice. It was true. Angie's father often painted naked models – women and men too – and Violet and Angie sometimes hid behind the big screen in his studio and watched.

Afterwards they discussed the curious differences between grown-up bodies and their own, the hairy bits and the dangling and sticking out bits. That was when Violet discovered Angie knew things she didn't. Artistic parents told you things ordinary parents wouldn't dream of talking about. Angie knew all about sex.

The answer to her question, Violet was sure, almost certainly involved sex.

Next day Violet took her battered teddy bear with her on the school outing, partly because she thought teddy would enjoy the company of other animals, and partly to give her courage when she spoke to Angie. When they reached the zoo the teachers divided the children into groups, and shepherded them round the enclosures.

'Now keep together, everyone,' Miss Palmer said. 'I want you to pay particular attention in the small mammal house.'

As Miss Palmer led them inside, Violet tugged at Angie's sleeve and put her lips close to her ear

'Boring,' she whispered. 'Let's bunk off.'

'All right,' Angie whispered back. 'But how?'

'I'll do it.' Violet ran up to the teacher. 'Please, Miss Palmer, Angie and I want to go to the lavatory.'

'Oh, my goodness, Violet!' Miss Palmer gazed down at

her in exasperation. 'Why is it always you two? We'll be starting biology next term. I do so want you all to have some background first.'

'We'll be really quick, and catch you up,' said Violet eagerly.

The teacher sighed. She always found it difficult to argue with Violet Somerset. It was something about the child's extraordinary and utterly unselfconscious beauty, the dreaming turquoise eyes, the rosebud mouth, and the tumbling tangle of golden hair, which made it almost impossible to deny her.

'Then just be quick!'

'Yes, Miss Palmer.'

Violet and Angie scampered away. Out of Miss Palmer's sight, they slowed down. Violet glanced round. She spotted what she was searching for and beckoned for Angie to follow her. They ducked into the tunnel leading to the great concrete enclosure which housed the animals from Africa.

'Here,' said Violet

The sign above the entrance said: The Elephant House.

It was dark and quiet inside. The cavernous shelter was huge and smelt of dung and new hay. The towering grey animals rustled in the gloom, pacing slowly and restlessly backwards and forwards through a forest of stone pillars. It was almost as if they were imprisoned in a dream world, as if at any moment they would waken, push down the walls, and wander out to uproot the trees in Regent's Park.

'Is it safe?' Angie asked anxiously.

'Of course it's safe,' said Violet scornfully. 'I know all about elephants. Ngoro taught me. They'd never harm me even if they did get out.'

Violet closed her eyes for a moment and filled her nostrils with the animals' scent.

She remembered the herd in the valley with Uhuru leading them down to drink. Her valley and Billy's, but which really belonged to neither of them, only to the elephants. The valley they would reclaim together when she was grown and she too could be free.

The presence of the enormous animals somehow made her

feel bold and brave. She knew it would. That was why she'd come there. It made her even bold enough to ask Angie her question.

She pulled at teddy's balding fur just to be absolutely sure. She looked round to see if anyone else was there who might hear her. There was no one.

'Angie, what's a mistress?'

Angie stared at her, startled. 'A miss what?'

Violet knew that in her anxiety she must have mumbled the word. She tried again. 'Not a miss anything. A mis-tress.'

'Oh, a *mistress*.' Angie giggled. 'Why do you want to know, Vi?'

Violet hesitated. She gave teddy a reassuring squeeze. 'My mum's a mistress.'

'Are you sure?' Angie's eyes widened.

'I heard her say it on the telephone,' Violet said. 'It was a little while ago when Daddy was away on one of his trips. The telephone rang and Mummy was upstairs dressing for dinner. Bobbity, Mummy's maid, picked it up and came upstairs to say it was for Mummy. "It's that Lord Cranleigh," Bobbity said. I thought it might be Daddy, so I came down the stairs to listen. Then I heard Mummy shouting. She sounded really angry.'

'What did she say?'

'"I may be your mistress, Johnnie, but that's no reason to treat me like a whore."'

Angie stiffened. Then she whistled. She'd learned to whistle from the butcher's boy. Violet's nanny said it was vulgar but news like that deserved a whistle.

The two girls looked at each other.

'What did Mummy mean?' Violet said.

'Whore or mistress?' Angie asked. 'Which one don't you know?'

'Whore's a swear word, I know that,' Violet frowned. 'Bobbity calls Mummy her mistress, but I know Mummy didn't mean it like that. What do they both mean, Angie?'

She took a deep breath.

Violet had always been the leader since the two of them became best friends. Now it was Angie's turn. It was her moment of triumph. She could tell Violet things she didn't know.

'Mistress is what you do when you kiss and cuddle, you know, all the rest of it. Taking your clothes off and pushing your legs together and things like that. It's making babies with someone who isn't your husband.'

'Then what's a whore?'

Angie racked her brains.

'It's the same really,' she ventured. 'Except my dad says they make you pay through the nose for it. Grown-ups call it all fucking.'

Violet stared at Angie in silence.

'Fucking's easy,' she said crossly.

She spoke with much more confidence that she felt. Until then she'd only known that 'fucking' and 'whore' were bad words. Grown-ups smacked you if they heard you saying 'fuck'. She'd used it all the time with Billy Ramsden in Africa. It had been a badge of freedom, of solidarity with what her mother called the 'common people', those who were not, like Violet, 'properly educated'.

Billy Ramsden was common. Even nanny, who wasn't a lady, had considered him very common indeed.

Violet hadn't realised 'fuck' meant pushing your legs together and making babies. She didn't much mind who her mother chose to push her legs together with or even if that made her a whore. It didn't seem to be any business of hers. But she did mind very much if her mother made a baby. That was absolutely Violet's business.

'Bugger!' she said.

Angie gave a nervous laugh. 'What'll you do, Vi?'

Violet's eyes blazed. 'You'll see.'

'You won't tell on me, I mean for telling you?'

'Don't be silly.'

Violet shook her head fiercely. She had much more important fish to fry than Angie. She had a job to do.

She took a last look at the elephants. One of them had a young calf sheltering under her wrinkled grey belly. The mother nudged the baby gently with her trunk until the calf clumsily began to suckle.

Violet had once asked her mother if she had been breast-fed as a baby. The question had come after Violet and Angie had peeped out through the screen at one of Angie's father's female models, a plump young woman with round full breasts he'd been using for a painting of a madonna with child. The child in the picture was clamped to the woman's breast.

Mrs Somerset had looked quite shocked by the question.

'Of course not, darling. Nobody does that nowadays. It's terribly bad for the figure. Whatever made you ask?'

Violet explained about the painting. Her mother laughed and patted her cheek. Later Violet heard her telling the story to one of her friends, a girl friend this time.

'Can you imagine?' Mrs Somerset finished.

The two women laughed loudly together, as if they knew something Violet didn't. She had felt humiliated. Humiliated and angry.

All of a sudden, watching the great grey creature stroking her child with her trunk, Violet was angry again. She turned her back on the mother elephant with her calf. Suddenly she didn't want to watch the elephants any more.

'We'd better find the others, Angie,' she snapped.

The school bus dropped Violet at the side of the square where she lived.

She walked the last hundred yards home. She was still angry and frightened now too. She no longer felt secure. Perhaps her mother didn't want her, perhaps she'd never wanted her. Maybe that was why she didn't want to lose her figure. It even might be why she wanted to make a new baby to replace Violet.

She kicked the broken bits of pavement, punctuating each stab of her toe with a muttered swearword. She'd made up her mind.

Violet was an only child. Whether her mother liked it or not, she was going to stay that way.

25

'May I speak to Lord Cranleigh, please?' said Violet.

'Who shall I say is calling, miss?'

It was the maid who had answered the telephone. Violet hadn't expected a female voice. For a moment she was unsettled.

She hesitated.

It was two days after her visit to the zoo. She'd had to wait until then to be sure her mother was out of the house for long enough. Violet's chance came when her mother told her she was going out to the opening of an exhibition and wouldn't be back until dinner.

Violet knew the name and it was easy to look up the telephone number in her mother's leather-bound address book – the one she kept in her bureau and was always careful to hide away in the secret drawer. Violet had always made it her business to know about secret drawers. She waited until Nanny and Bobbity were having their afternoon rests. Then she crept down to her mother's bedroom, pulled out the book, found the number, and dialled.

Now her heart was beating so loud she was sure it could be heard down the telephone.

Miss, the maid said. Violet wrinkled her face in anguish. She was certain she'd made her voice so deep she could only have been taken for an adult.

'A friend,' she stammered.

'Hold on, please. I'll see if he's in.'

To her relief the maid didn't ask her name again. Shoes clicked away across a polished floor. Violet almost changed her mind and decided to ring off. No. It was too important to give up now. Her knuckles white, she forced herself to hold on to the receiver.

'Hullo. Cranleigh speaking. Who's that?'

Violet shivered.

'Hullo?' The man said again. 'Anyone there?'

'Lord Cranleigh?' Violet asked.

'That's me.' The voice was jaunty. 'Who are you and what can I do for you?'

She took a deep breath.

'You don't know me, but my name is Miss Violet Somerset.' She knew she was sounding breathless but there was nothing she could do about it, and she was committed now. 'I believe you are acquainted with my mother.'

'Of course.' There was a moment of hesitation. 'How I can help, my dear?'

'It's about my mother being your mistress.'

There was silence at the other end of the telephone.

Violet pressed on frantically. 'It's not that I mind my mother being a whore or anything. I don't mind a bit, even if *she* does. It's just about not fucking my mother so that she makes another baby. You see—'

Violet was halfway through what she'd carefully planned to say when she felt the hairs prickle on the back of her neck. Someone else had come into the room.

She stopped and turned her head.

Her mother was standing in the doorway. Her face was completely white even under the makeup, and Violet could see she was shaking. Her mother came forward. She removed the telephone from Violet's hand, and replaced it on the receiver.

'Violet,' her voice was icy, 'I think you owe me an explanation.'

Ten days later Violet was on her way to a girls' boarding school in the Malvern Hills.

She had been in disgrace ever since the episode of the telephone call. Neither Nanny nor Bobbity knew exactly what Violet had done, only that in her mother's words she had been 'unforgivably rude' to a friend of hers, but Nanny had barely spoken to her since and even beloved Bobbity had looked at her as if she had somehow betrayed her name, her family, and the entire household.

Nanny had taken her silently to Debenham and Freebody's to be equipped with an ugly brown school uniform. In her hand was a list of clothes which referred to strange and unknown activities, and which had to be stitched with a name tag and ticked off as they were packed into a big trunk.

In those ten days Violet was stripped of everything which made her Violet Somerset. Her pretty clothes, the company of her friends, the refuge which had been her little bedroom under the eaves, Nanny, Bobbity, and Mrs Benson, all of them were being taken from her. She realised with a terrible sickening finality that nothing would ever be the same again when Nanny wouldn't let her pack her teddy bear.

'Better not,' Nanny said. The kindly old woman had just started to talk to her again. 'Teddy can wait for ye here. He won't run away.'

'*I* will,' Violet said furiously and defiantly.

'That's as may be. But teddy stays here,' Nanny replied. Then she went on more gently: 'They'll laugh at ye, hen. Young girls can be terrible hard on each other.'

Violet soon learned the truth of Nanny's words when she saw the mob of brown-uniformed schoolgirls milling around on Paddington station.

The train journey was bewildering. Violet knew she didn't belong, that she would never belong. Even though the other girls were dressed in the same drab uniform, there were subtle differences in the tilt of the brim of the pudding-basin hats, the knotting of the yellow-striped tie which went round the collar of the Viyella shirt, even in the way their scratchy Harris tweed coats were buttoned.

Violet had arrived at the wrong time of year.

She was like a young animal who had been born when winter was just closing in. It was the spring term, and the start of the school year was in the autumn. All the other girls already belonged. They seemed to know each other's names and have best friends they greeted with squeals of delight. They bagged the best seats by the window for each other. Even the youngest girls seemed to have formed alliances.

They had clubs and teams and secret societies. She was a stranger, an outcast, a pariah. She was alone.

No one knew Violet's name or seemed interested in asking her for it. Violet was simply called 'squib'. One of the other girls told her, not particularly unkindly but in a matter-of-fact way, that all the new girls were known as squibs.

'Damp, you know. As in damp squibs,' she said. Then she added by way of explanation, 'Always blubbing.'

Violet surreptitiously rubbed away a small salty drop which already threatened to run down her cheek. She had no desire to earn her name so obviously.

There were only two new girls who arrived that term – Violet and a graceful Indian girl who, although Violet discovered later was three years older than her, looked even more bewildered. The Indian girl didn't even have a uniform and she was shivering in her silk sari under a heavy overcoat which reached unfashionably down to her ankles.

The two squibs sat together on the five-hour journey through the bare ploughed fields of the garden of England. As squibs – the underclass – they had no option. No one else would demean themselves by joining them.

Somewhere around Cheltenham, after three hours of the journey, Violet plucked up courage to speak to her fellow-sufferer.

'My name's Violet. What's yours?' she asked.

The big brown eyes looked at her solemnly. The older girl made a salaam, nodding her neat dark head towards the little temple of brown fingers loaded with tinkling rings.

'Mahadur, if you please,' she said.

Violet gazed with interest at the little red blob on the girl's forehead. It looked very exotic. As if the Indian girl belonged to a secret society, but a more interesting and important one than their raucous fellow pupils belonged to.

'I am Indian,' Mahadur offered unnecessarily.

'I don't mind a bit,' Violet said. Then, anxious not to offend the person who might be her only ally in the hell-hole to which she knew she was being delivered, she added, 'your being Indian, I mean. I'm a bit foreign myself.'

Mahadur smiled, white teeth shining against her smooth chestnut skin. Violet noticed that right in the middle of the smile, the Indian girl had a magnificent gold tooth with a little diamond twinkling in it.

From that moment on, Mahadur and Violet were friends.

Once at school, it was difficult to be together. Mahadur was a sixth former. She had been sent by her parents, who seemed to be extraordinarily rich and important in their own country, to acquire a smattering of English education before settling down to marriage. In spite of the school's attempts to separate them – relationships between older and younger girls were regarded as distinctly undesirable, even dangerous – Violet and Mahadur took every opportunity to seek out each other's company whenever their free time coincided.

At all other times, the school was undiluted misery.

Violet hated everything about it – from the ugly uniform, to the monotonously disgusting food, to the unbending teachers, to the rigid conformity of her contemporaries, to the all-embracing discipline of the time-table. Violet loathed Miss Prescott's College for the Daughters of Gentlefolk with all the force of her being.

All she could do was endure as best she could and wait for release.

In common with twenty-five other girls, she was in Form 2B. Her private world was limited to a locker with her name on it and an iron bedstead with a lumpy mattress in a cold dormitory in the sprawling Victorian building which housed some hundred and fifty privileged young ladies.

Finally the term ended and she went home.

In London Violet discovered that everything had changed, above all her relationship with her mother. Violet's telephone call to Lord Cranleigh was never going to be forgotten or forgiven. Sometimes, she began to feel, her mother actively disliked her. Certainly whatever love she'd ever felt had evaporated. All she felt now, Violet sensed, was pride in the way her daughter looked.

Violet never thought of herself as beautiful. It was impossible to think of oneself as beautiful. But she came to realise everyone else did, and that her mother was proud of it. It was the last bond between the two of them, and Violet clung desperately to it.

If her mother wanted her as an adornment to her life, an accessory she could flaunt almost like a piece of jewellery, then Violet would go along with it. It was better, far better, than having no mother at all. And at least she showed no sign of producing the baby which had provoked the whole disastrous rupture in the relationship between them.

Violet went back to school.

Apart from the moments with Mahadur, it was as lonely and desolate as ever. Even the holidays were joyless. Angie had acquired a new best friend, and anyway Mrs Somerset had rightly judged Angie's upbringing was to some extent responsible for Violet's fall from grace. She made it as difficult as possible for the two girls to see each other.

The misery really became unbearable in the third year, when Mahadur left to return to India. Violet knew from now on she would really be alone. All her pleas to her mother not to be sent back after the summer break met with a stony refusal.

'You're fourteen, Violet. It's only sensible for you to stay at school until you're sixteen. Then we'll see.'

'But Mummy—'

'No buts, darling, please. You must accept your father and I know best.'

'I never see Daddy,' burst out Violet. 'He's never here. Sod him as a father!'

'Violet! That's shocking! Where *do* you learn such language? Your father's a very busy and important man. He works to support the three of us.'

Violet glowered at her mother.

'I'm not a fool, Mummy,' she said. 'Dad may work, but you're the one who pays for everything. You're the one who's rich. You decide everything. Sometimes I think you despise Daddy. That's why you have all your "good friends".'

Violet knew she'd caught her mother on the raw.

Mrs Somerset sat upright and rigid in her chair. Violet could see her hands were shaking with anger and what, Violet guessed, was guilt. She managed to control herself.

'You can be a deeply thoughtless, misguided, and wicked child,' she spat out. 'There are things you simply don't understand. What you need to learn is common manners. I hope your school will teach them to you.'

They gazed at each other in mutual fury. Violet refused to back down.

'School's horrible. I hate it!' she shouted.

'So I gather. I read your report to your father in Washington over the telephone. "Violet," your form mistress wrote, "although a remarkable child in many ways, has developed a protective shell which makes her extremely difficult to teach. None of us can do more than attempt to penetrate it – with a dispiriting lack of success."'

'I did well in biology,' she countered bitterly. 'Really well. I thought you and Daddy would be pleased.'

'It also said you'd been rude and impertinent to your geography teacher,' Mrs Somerset added, ignoring her.

'She's a silly cow and ignorant too,' Violet said fiercely. 'She said all black people are savages. You know that's not true, Mummy. I told her about Ngoro and the elephants and the valley. I just told her she was wrong.'

Mrs Somerset narrowed her eyes at her stubborn and recalcitrant daughter.

'Ngoro? Was he that old man with fleas and rickets who took you out into the bush? When you came back with those bizarre stories about people and elephants being baked in ovens? Oh, Vi, my darling . . .'

Mrs Somerset shook her head sorrowfully. 'You must try and forget about Africa. You're back in Britain now. You've got to grow up and become a proper person.'

Violet looked at her mother with fierce hot rage. Tears filled her eyes.

'I don't want to forget,' she screamed. 'I loved Africa, I loved Ngoro, I loved Billy. And I bet you fucked Uncle Finlay Hampton, too!'

She stormed from the room before her mother could reply.

26

At the end of the summer holidays, when she stood once again
on the platform of Paddington station in her brown uniform
and scanned the faces, searching in vain for the miracle which
would tell her that Mahadur had returned, Violet had made up
her mind to run away.

She saved up her week's allowance, which was doled out
each Saturday in miserly pennies to be spent in the school's
tuckshop, and began to make discreet enquiries about bus
routes and train timetables.

Violet had no idea where she was going to go.

All she knew was that she had to escape. Once she'd
managed to get away, she was certain the future would open
before her and she'd know what to do. Until she did she was a
slave. All that mattered was throwing off her chains. Freedom
needed no planning – in her gulf of misery and despair, it was
its own answer.

And then before her ideas crystallised, a letter came which
changed everything.

The headmistress opened and read all correspondence
which didn't come from the pupils' parents or grandparents. Authorised letter-writers were provided with
a special stamp for their envelopes. Envelopes without
a stamp went to the headmistress for scrutiny. If the
letter inside was considered acceptable, the girl it was
addressed to was summoned to the headmistress' study
and given it.

Letters from girl friends or brothers were usually permit-
ted. Letters from boy friends weren't. All the girls' boy friends
knew how to get round the system. It wasn't so difficult as
most of the boy friends were brothers of girls at the school.

Violet had no brother to trade and no boy friend whose letters needed smuggling in.

It was during the second week of the autumn term that the headmistress sent for Violet.

'Press-button's after you, Vi,' the hockey captain told her as they walked back to the pavilion.

'What for?' Violet looked scared. For a terrible moment she thought her plans to escape might have been discovered.

'Don't have a heart attack,' the older girl smiled. 'Maybe it's just a letter.'

Violet went to the headmistress's study and knocked nervously on the door.

'Ah, Violet,' Miss Prescott's voice was unusually cheerful. 'I've got something for you.'

It *was* a letter. Violet glanced down at the thick cream-laid envelope lined with dark green tissue-paper, the flap neatly slit open with a paper-knife. It was postmarked India.

'No doubt you've guessed, my dear. It's from Princess Mahadur,' Miss Prescott smiled.

'Princess?' Violet was surprised. She'd had no idea Mahadur was a princess.

The headmistress nodded. 'We didn't make it public, of course. Her father the Maharajah was determined his daughter shouldn't receive any special treatment.'

Miss Prescott leant back in her chair.

'It's an invitation to Mahadur's wedding. I've discussed it with your mother. We both agree it could be a fascinating experience for you. It would also be deeply discourteous to the Maharanee to refuse. However, you must make up your own mind. Let me know what you decide when you've read it.'

Violet didn't read the letter immediately. It was much too important for that. She saved it until after supper, when she was alone in the cupboard under the stairs where she hid herself when she needed to be private.

'Most beloved and esteemed little sister,' Mahadur had written in her long sloping hand.

Violet read the words again and smiled. Sister. She liked being a little sister.

'With great trepidation and in the hope of your favourable decision, I write with the permission of my beloved parents to invite you to honour with your gracious presence the celebration of your devoted friend's nuptials to His Highness the Prince of Bhandapur.'

Violet's heart leapt as she read on.

The Prince of Bhandapur sounded fantastically exotic, although Violet vaguely remembered Mahadur showing her a photograph of a round-faced earnestly bespectacled young man in cricketing flannels who didn't look much like a prince of anything.

She turned the page.

The celebrations were to last for a whole month. There was to be a specially chartered aeroplane to carry the English guests – all of them, apart from Violet, elderly friends of the Maharajah and Maharanee. Everyone would be accommodated in the Summer Palace, or the Winter Palace, or the Spring Palace, or even the River Palace – Violet could choose which one she preferred.

Mahadur had never said her family had so many palaces. Once she had admitted to one.

'But only a little one, mind,' she'd giggled, putting her fingertips to her lips in the Indian gesture of disparagement.

Even though it was written in language which didn't sound much like the Mahadur Violet knew, it was the most exciting letter she'd ever had. Mahadur had often described what happened at Indian weddings: the lengthy preparations, the jewels and the clothes, the banquets and the processions on the ceremonial elephants. It was the elephants above all, painted and bejewelled, Mahadur said, like dancing girls, which had fascinated Violet.

Mahadur had shown Violet a photograph of herself as a small child sitting in a little tasselled castle – it was called a howdah, Mahadur said – perched on top of one of the great grey animals. Violet had just been able to make out Mahadur, dressed in a pink sari embroidered with gold.

Violet read the letter one more time.

The River Palace, she decided, sounded the most romantic of the four, but any of them would do. The invitation was the most wonderful thing that had ever happened to her.

To crown it the wedding was in the middle of the spring term – just after her sixteenth birthday. With any luck it would mean a whole term out of school. With O-level exams approaching, she'd no doubt have to work all through the Christmas holidays. She could handle that. Violet knew she could handle anything if it meant escaping from her prison. Not that her mother believed exams were important for girls.

'Education's all very well, Vi,' Margaret Somerset was fond of saying. 'You should certainly work hard and apply yourself to it. But it won't find you the right husband. Men simply don't like clever girls.'

Violet wondered irritably why on earth, if that was so, she had to go to school at all. Now her mother's views seemed to have worked in her favour. Her mother, according to Miss Prescott, had enthusiastically agreed to her going to India.

Margaret Somerset was still just as enthusiastic when Violet returned home at the end of the term.

'It's a delightful opportunity,' she said. 'You must make the most of it. The grand Indians – and the Maharajah and his wife are very grand – have such beautiful manners. You could learn a lot from them in the way of social graces.'

Violet glanced at her mother slyly. 'I think they're brown, Mummy, like Mahadur. I thought all blacks and browns were savages.'

Mrs Somerset looked at her sharply. 'Don't be cheeky and vulgar, Violet. Any more remarks like that and you won't go.'

'Sorry,' she said hastily.

'I can't believe it, Mahadur!'

As Violet gazed round the gilded ballroom of the Winter Palace in Kashrimi she pirouetted slowly on her feet.

Her voice was breathless and her eyes wide and shining. Her gown, a confection of lilac, peach and white panels ribbed with endless whorls of pearls like a ball dress of the young Virgin Queen, stirred and whispered round her.

'It's like fairyland!'

Mahadur, in a pale emerald sari embroidered with torquoise beads over which had been tied a large white apron, was sitting on a low stool at the far end of the vast room.

Mahadur smiled.

Her hands were being patterned with henna by two pretty young Indian girls. Violet and her two large trunks had arrived at Kashrimi the day before.

One of Violet's first impressions of India was that there seemed to be a great many women of all ages everywhere – from the Maharanee herself down to the most humble servant girl.

The women appeared to organise everything, leaving the men to smoke pipes and gossip. There had been no less than six girls to help Violet and Mahadur unpack her luggage. Mrs Somerset had thrown herself into providing a suitable wardrobe for her daughter with astonishing energy.

'Such fun!' she'd beamed radiantly in one of the many couture houses they'd visited. 'It's going to be a month of parties and we can't have you traipsing around in rags. The Office would be scandalised. Anyway, I do so adore shopping, don't you, darling?'

'Yes, Mummy.'

The 'Office' was what her father worked for, the Foreign Office. Quite what they had to do with Mahadur's wedding, Violet wasn't sure. What she did share with her mother was an intense desire that her clothes didn't let her beloved Mahadur down.

From the time they started until the moment she left, Violet felt there was hardly a minute when someone wasn't adjusting a seam or measuring her narrow waist or sticking pins in her shoulder to make sure a sleeve was set neatly and properly. For the first time in her life she had her mother's entire attention.

It was strange and comforting, but more than once Violet wondered uneasily if she didn't have more to offer her mother as a tailor's dummy than she had ever had as a daughter.

From Hardy Amies, her mother bought her a primrose linen coat and skirt with matching hat which Mrs Somerset said was essential for tea-parties.

'Tiffin, they call it. My great-aunt was married to a colonial and she was always telling me about tiffin,' Mrs Somerset laughed happily.

For riding, there were elegant cavalry twill jodhpurs and a smart tweed jacket with a nipped in waist from Rowes in Bond Street.

'Everyone will know where it came from and therefore who you are. We can't let the side down.'

Violet struggled into the jacket. Buttoned, it was tight and painful across her breast but glancing in the fitting-room mirror she saw it looked superbly elegant. She gritted her teeth. She would wear it. She had no intention of letting any side down.

'The evenings, well, heaven only knows. Two cocktail dresses at least, and one long for the wedding.'

The cocktail dresses came from Victor Stiebel. They were ballerina length, thick jewel-coloured satins with full net underskirts – one pink and one blue – both with a matching tailored bolero.

'The Indians are terribly formal,' Mrs Somerset observed. 'Great-Aunt Winifred said it was all a fearful palaver. I can't think what she was complaining about. I'm sure I'd have enjoyed it hugely.'

The dress for the wedding was the greatest triumph. It was ordered from Norman Hartnell's spring collection – stitched and pinned on Violet herself from the first toile to the last petticoat – and it was the most beautiful thing Violet had ever seen, let alone owned.

Mahadur thought so too. It was the very first of Violet's possessions she unpacked. She dived into the suitcase, pulled out the clouds of silk, and squealed with delight.

'Put it on *immediately*, Violet. I absolutely insist on seeing it *now*!'

'Honestly, Mahadur!' Violet protested. She blushed with a mixture of embarrassment and pleasure.

Mahadur watched her enraptured as Violet took off the clothes she was wearing and pulled the gown on.

'Darling Vi, it's gorgeous! All the princes will fall at your feet. You're so lucky you can wear all those wonderful western clothes and nobody will think you are a wicked woman – or anything at all but how marvellously glamorous you look!'

Violet laughed. She spun round on her toes, watching her reflection in the mirrored pillars as she moved.

'You're crazy, Mahadur,' she said. 'Your saris are so much more romantic than anything I've got. You've got to show me how to wear them, promise!'

Mahadur waved back servant girls and stood up. She began to move slowly and sensuously in the gossamer thin silk wrap that sheathed her, profiling her arms and angling her head in the ancient ritual movements of the Indian courtesan dance.

'Dance, Violet! Dance with me!'

'Mahadur, you idiot!'

Laughing, Violet began to dance, her feet bare under the rippling petticoats, her arms outstretched to embrace the tall pillars, her body floating over the pale floor.

The two young girls, alone in the great empty ballroom with only the servant girls for audience, danced – each holding in their arms a phantom lover. Neither, for different reasons, had any choice in the man they embraced.

Mahadur's arms enfolded the prince she had never seen except in the faded photograph she'd once shown Violet in the icy Malvern Hills. He was none of her finding, but she was betrothed to him and soon he would own her body and soul.

Violet, for want of any other lover, held in her arms the memory of a wiry foul-mouthed urchin with a shuttered face and cold and angry grey-green eyes – angry except when he was with her. Violet knew she could always still his anger. She was stronger than him. She'd spun through the three rails on the ship, when he could only manage two.

He'd be grown tall and strong now. He'd never want to own anyone body and soul. It didn't matter if he did.

Violet loved him.

27

'It's the most beautiful thing I've ever seen, Mahadur,' breathed Violet.

The two girls hung over the balcony gazing down at the glittering throng below.

It was the last day of the celebrations before the bridegroom's arrival. The mahouts had been grooming and painting the elephants since before dawn. By the time the sun rose the whole troupe was parading in all its finery round the square in front of the Summer Palace. Astride their mounts the mahouts were tunicked and turbaned, and the howdahs on the elephants' backs were shaded with fringed canopies, the interiors plumped up with cushions and draped with jewelled silks.

The wedding party was to go on a picnic into the hills, with all the guests carried in the howdahs. Somehow Violet sensed it was going to be the best day of all.

In their different ways all the days of her month in India had been wonderful. They'd passed so quickly it seemed only yesterday when she'd arrived, put on her dress for the wedding at Mahadur's insistence, and danced with her in the ballroom. She'd been happy that night. She'd been happy ever since. In fact she'd never been so happy since her time in Africa with Billy.

India was very different from Africa. It wasn't a land of raw lonely beauty like the forests, plains, and valleys round the Laager, but a continent shaped by an ancient and sophisticated culture. Even the jungle seemed to have been polished and honed by centuries of human presence.

The palaces, with their vast gardens filled with exotic birds and butterflies, were magnificent. The entertainments were sumptuous. Each day brought a new programme of amusements. The men, many of them the Maharajah's contemporaries from Eton, played the games of the Raj – cricket, croquet, bowls and polo. The ladies gossiped, went on excursions in carriages, and took tea in the rose gardens.

At dusk both groups, the men and the women, gathered for cocktails in the orangerie before the evening's round of banquets and receptions began.

Violet and Mahadur found every excuse they could to avoid the formal gatherings. Instead they escaped on furtive forays into the sprawling town to visit Mahadur's childhood playmates, or wander round the markets, or simply sit at little cafes, watching the teeming life of the streets.

For Violet, the Rose Palace – the Maharanee's quarters where men were forbidden – with its chiming fountains, scented arbours and graceful arched patios, held the most magic of all. Mahadur's mother had taken to Violet instantly, captivated by the young girl's beauty and her boyish exuberance. Each day as the wedding grew closer the Maharanee, a stately white-haired matron who ruled her household with an iron hand, drew the young visitor closer into her fold.

The Maharanee spoke fluent English with a soft and lilting Scots accent.

'I had a Scottish ayah,' she explained in answer to Violet's question. 'When I was young, it was quite the thing. All over the world they were known to be the best.'

The Maharanee was intrigued by an adolescent girl who seemed quite unaware of her incandescent beauty and the effect it had on men. Violet also clearly hadn't the slightest idea of how to order a household. Her own daughter, Mahadur, had been schooled in the arts of pleasing a man and taking charge of a domestic empire since she was a small child – to a high-born Indian girl the skills were as natural as breathing.

The Maharanee saw the young foreigner, with her ripening willowy figure, her unruly waterfall of blonde hair and her brilliant blue eyes, as a kind of noble savage – lacking any of the polish of civilisation.

Mrs Somerset might have been outraged by the Maharanee's view of her daughter, but Violet settled into her role of pupil with a bemused and yearning curiosity. In Mahadur's mother she found a concerned affection she'd never known in her own. Practically, she discovered something else.

For the first time Violet began to understand what neither biology lessons at school, nor her mother's evasive replies to her questions, had ever taught her about. Sex. There was sex, Violet learnt, and there was love-making. The two were very closely linked.

The ancient civilisation of India approved of both. It was more interested in the second.

'Little savage, come and sit by me,' the Maharanee would call across the glittering Hall of the Women, beckoning Violet to a stool by her feet so she might explain the movements of a particular dance or the significance of a theatrical performance.

The performances, given by the younger women of the palace, were an education in themselves. It seemed there was no activity in which a man and woman could take part together which couldn't be graphically demonstrated in the ancient rituals. They covered every preoccupation of a woman from birth to death with almost all the possibilities in between.

Even better, from Violet's point of view, the Maharanee had a way of delivering what Mrs Somerset would consider the most indelicate anatomical information without the slightest embarrassment.

'This is the dance of the lotus bud – what you would know as the clitoris. The lotus bud is like a musical instrument, it must be carefully tuned and played with subtlety. Pay attention and I will explain what you are seeing.'

At other times, the Maharanee would question Violet about western customs. And here, too, Violet, accustomed to the oblique social communication of her own culture, found the Maharanee disconcertingly direct.

'You are betrothed, my little savage?'

Violet shook her head. 'I'm only sixteen, Your Highness.'

'What does that mean?'

'Sixteen is too young for marriage.'

'It's not at all too young.' The Maharanee was indignant. 'I was betrothed to His Highness at six, and the marriage was celebrated when I was twelve. From that moment his family became my own. I never returned to the land of my birth. Naturally the union was not consummated until three years later, when the Maharanee my mother-in-law judged me ready. Mahadur was born when I was seventeen – a year older than you, my dear. Are you certain your parents have made no plans for a suitable alliance?'

Violet was flustered. 'I don't think so.'

The Maharanee frowned. 'Unusual in my view. I don't know your country well, but my husband was educated there. You are of good family. You are certainly ripe. Your parents should take care the apple does not fall from the tree.'

The Maharanee shook her head disapprovingly. 'I imagine at least you have a suitable dowry?'

Violet hesitated. 'Mummy and I, well, we don't really talk about things like that. I don't really know about money,' she finished lamely.

The Maharanee made a click of disapproval.

'I knew my bridal value from as far back as I can remember. I can still tell you the value of my dowry – the name of each village I brought, the value of each forest, how many oxen for the plough, how many elephants to crop the timber. That was my responsiblity – my duty to the people as much as to those of us who own the land. It's the same for Mahadur. Her inheritance is a holy obligation as well as a privilege. What else is as important as a daughter's dowry? How will you make a suitable match if you have no knowledge of such things from your earliest years? Perhaps I should write to your mother.'

Violet shook her head frantically.

'No, Your Highness, please.' She hesitated, knowing she had to be immensely careful not to offend Mahadur's mother. 'My mother wouldn't understand.'

'She would not? How strange. What does Mrs Somerset think of then?'

Violet paused again. 'She has fun. She's very glamorous, everybody says so. Daddy's not with us very much because of his work. Mummy doesn't like the places he gets sent to, so she doesn't go with him. I suppose she just enjoys herself on her own.'

'On her own? How dull!'

'Well, not really on her own,' Violet corrected herself hurriedly. 'She goes to dinner parties all the time.'

'Alone?'

'With friends.'

Violet waved her hand vaguely but she hoped convincingly. She knew it was impossible to try to explain to the Maharanee the differences between the various categories of her mother's friends.

The Maharanee studied Violet with serious questioning eyes. At last she nodded and her face settled into its habitual expression of tranquillity.

'I think I understand, my little savage.'

With a rustle of silk, she reached out her slender jewelled fingers and stroked Violet's cheek. When she spoke again, there was such pity in her voice that Violet could only gaze back in bewilderment.

'Poor child,' she said. 'Poor little orphan child!'

The two, woman and girl, stared at each other for a long time without speaking. Then, as abruptly as she had begun, the Maharanee broke the silence.

'We shall not speak of it again,' she said. 'I consider you my daughter. All daughters dislike their mother's questions. So enough of them. I'm sure Mahadur is anxious for your company.'

The Maharanee smiled. She laid her hand on the arm of her serving woman, and stood up.

The conversation was over.

Violet went to find Mahadur. Her mind was in turmoil. Until that moment she hadn't envied Mahadur anything – apart of course from the palaces and the elephants. Marriage in India was like a business arrangement, as dull and unromantic as a transaction in a banking hall.

When Violet married she was going to do it passionately

for love. She was going to follow the dictates of her heart as it said in the photo-romances Bobbity bought, and which even old Nanny surreptitiously glanced at.

But in that moment of silence as the Maharanee studied her, Violet had seen herself as the Indian woman did – a little orphan, no better than a savage, without a history or responsibilities, a child whose family didn't value her enough to calculate her dowry or make arrangements for her future.

She ran weeping to her room.

It was the day before the elephant picnic. That was so marvellous it chased everything else from her mind.

28

The ride on the painted elephants, with their attendants on their necks and the howdahs full of chattering guests, was unforgettable. Even more wonderful to Violet was where she found herself now a few hours later – standing alone with Mahadur in the darkened elephant stable.

Violet held her breath, waiting for her eyes to accustom themselves to the gloom.

'Don't make a sound!' Mahadur put her fingers to her lips and glanced round nervously.

The two girls had been forbidden to visit the elephants in the stable before the animals were painted and dressed in their finery again for tomorrow's wedding procession.

'It's supposed to be bad luck,' Mahadur had explained. 'Like a bridegroom seeing his bride's gown before the marriage.'

Mahadur had decided to disobey the instruction. She'd chosen her time carefully. The mahouts were all at their evening meal. The stolen visit was partly a present to Violet for coming to her wedding, and partly a present to herself – her last treat before she took on the responsibilities of being a wife.

Violet had ridden on the elephants several times in the past month. Until today, the last day of Mahadur's freedom, they'd seemed more like beasts of burden than the great wild creatures she remembered from Africa. Now, standing among them in the dusk, she saw them for the first time without their scrolls of paint, their howdahs, and their jewelled hangings.

Now they too were wild.

'*Hathi*!'

Mahadur whistled softly. A tuskless female with a hide as

dark as polished ebony and small bright eyes fringed with long eyelashes, ambled slowly out of the shadows, her trunk extended in greeting.

'Isn't she lovely?' Mahadur said. 'Her name's Balmati. She's mine. She first carried me when I was only a baby. She's still young, but she's as gentle as a lamb.'

Violet gazed at her. 'She's the most beautiful creature I've ever seen. Can I stroke her?'

'Certainly. She loves having her chin rubbed. Here.'

Mahadur reached up and showed Violet how to stroke Balmati's soft leathery throat.

'Hello, Balmati,' Violet whispered.

Balmati put her trunk in the air and gave a little whistling cough. It reminded Violet of the old gentlemen she'd seen wheezing in her father's club in St James's Street when she was sent there once to meet him.

'She likes you, Vi. She's a bit of flirt. That's what she does when she's flattered.'

Violet's face glowed with pleasure.

All round her the other elephants restlessly circled the shadowy stable. Their huge feet, lifted and replaced as precisely as a ballet dancer's, rustled softly in the sweet-smelling straw. Slender trunks as delicate as fingertips brushed enquiringly across Violet's face, registering and examining the scent of an unfamiliar visitor.

'Balmati's part of my dowry. Like my husband, we'll never be parted. She'll carry my children.'

Mahadur tapped the elephant's left leg.

The magnificent animal went down on one knee, inclining her head for Mahadur to mount. The supple Indian girl took a firm grip on the ridge of the leathery ear and swung herself astride the broad shoulders. Balmati straightened her knee and suddenly Mahadur disappeared.

Violet looked up.

Mahadur's brown calves and bare feet dangled down on either side of Balmati's neck. She had pulled up her sari and knotted it round her waist to make a pair of billowing pantaloons.

Mahadur smiled down. 'This is where I used to sit when I

was little, like the mahouts. It's much more comfortable than riding in a howdah. My mother won't let me do it now I'm a woman. She says it's unladylike.'

Violet watched her with shining eyes. 'Oh, Mahadur, I wish I'd been born an Indian princess and had my own elephant!'

'Today you're going to be one. That's why I brought you here. This is the surprise I promised. We're going out into the jungle. You're going to ride Chandramala. He's safe as houses.'

Mahadur whistled softly again. A giant elephant with curving tusks standing in the shadows came forward and touched Mahadur's bare leg with his trunk.

'Good boy, Chandra,' Mahadur rubbed the chin he offered up to her.

She glanced down at Violet.

'Don't be scared, Vi. He's big, but he's very easy to ride. We always give him to visiting maharanees. He was my grandmother's dowry-elephant. The old warrior, we call him. Chandra, meet Violet.'

She reached over and tugged gently at the wrinkled ear. The huge elephant ambled towards Violet. He raised his trunk again as if to salute her. Then he turned his head to watch her, blinking one pink eye gravely.

'Hello, Chandra,' Violet greeted him apprehensively.

'Jemail, his mahout, says he's a hundred years old. Chandra knows he's an elephant Maharajah. I expect he thinks Balmati's just a servant girl. He's very conscious of his dignity – except when he's in *musth*.'

'What's that?' Violet asked.

'It's when elephants breed,' Mahadur replied. 'The males have a gland on their heads. When they come into *musth*, it runs with something oily and smelly. Sometimes they can become almost mad when it happens, but don't worry. Chandra should be much too old for that silly nonsense. Aren't you, old fellow?'

Mahadur stared at the elephant. She wrinkled her nose and sniffed. 'Well, I hope you are,' she finished uncertainly.

'Does Balamati come into *musth* too?'

Mahadur shook her head. 'The cow elephants don't. But if

there's a male in *musth* around, all the females get excited –
even you, my star, don't you?'

As if in answer, Balmati tramped over to one of the stone
water basins which stood at each corner of the stable. She
dipped her trunk into the clear pool. Then she raised it
gracefully in the air and blew a shower of droplets which
rained down over her rider.

'That's my girl!' A smile of pure delight ran over Mahadur's
face. 'She can tell we're off on an adventure. She hero
worships Chandra and she'll be as happy as anything as long
as he's in front. Tap his forehead so you can climb up.'

Violet did as she was told and the bull elephant dropped
obediently to one knee.

'Now, up, Violet, up!'

Her heart beating with excitement, Violet scrambled up on
to the elephant's neck.

29

'Settle down comfortably. It's a long ride,' Mahadur said as they moved quietly out of the darkened stables and made their way into the thicket of bushes which stretched beyond the palace grounds.

The jungle was warm and steamy after the monsoon rains.

Tangles of creeper veiled the dark pools where the forest animals came to drink. The moon was full. Pale silver light slanted through the high canopy on to the thick undergrowth beneath. They moved in a slow stately procession, the two elephants occasionally reaching out to snatch mouthfuls from a clump of young bamboo.

Chandra was in the lead with Balmati following. If she glanced back, Violet could see the scarlet slash of Mahadur's sari bright against the she-elephant's dark shoulders.

All Violet's senses were sharp and alert, heightened by the excitement and strangeness of the adventure, the stirrings of monkeys and the calls of night-hunting birds in the branches above. Her nostrils filled with the scent of wet foliage and warm heaving animal. If she closed her eyes, she was a child again in Africa – and then, not for the first time but never with such a poignant stab of loneliness, she wondered if she would ever see Billy again.

She had danced for him in the palace. He'd belonged in her arms then. Now he belonged with her in the jungle.

The elephants might be Mahadur's and Violet loved the Indian girl more than almost anyone she had ever known, but on Chandra's back she was in a world which only she and Billy truly shared.

Violet shook her head. She tried to dismiss Billy from her thoughts, and peered ahead.

Chandra swung his great haunches along the track, the tip of his trunk trawling the ground ahead, like a blind man tapping with a white stick. Three hours had passed and the moon was already on the wane when the path opened out into a clearing. The big grey beast came to a sudden halt, all his four feet planted firmly, and his trunk extended to sniff the night air.

Chandra blew through his nostrils in a sharp rush of air. Something was wrong.

Mahadur urged Balmati forward until the she-elephant was rubbing her flanks against the big bull.

Violet glanced down at her friend – Balmati's shoulders were at a least a foot lower than Chandra's.

'Mahadur, I think Chandra's worried.'

Mahadur frowned. 'Maybe he can smell tiger.'

She gestured towards a path which ran at right angles to the track they were following. The meeting point of the two jungle highways formed the clearing.

'That looks like a tiger track. They use the firebreaks to get from one side of the jungle to the other. If it's not a tiger . . .'

Mahadur broke off. Her expression changed. She flared her nostrils, her face at first puzzled and then alarmed.

Violet sniffed.

She noticed it now too – a strange musky scent, rank and powerful. Beneath her Chandra was restless, punching the ground irritably with his foreleg as his trunk swung backwards and forwards sifting through the night wind.

The scent in her nostrils, Violet guessed, could mean only one thing. She leaned forward. She could see it clearly, the dark oily discharge running down Chandra's wrinkled grey cheek. Mahadur had been wrong. The great bull elephant wasn't too old to breed.

Chandra was in *musth*.

An owl swooped low over the clearing, its pale wings a quick ghostly shimmer in the moonlight. Startled Chandra swerved, his four feet thumping sideways. He began to move, roughly shouldering aside the smaller bulk of Balmati.

Striding forward, Chandra raised his trunk in a curved arc and trumpeted once, and then again, and then once more. The screaming pealing burst of noise was so loud in the silent darkness it made Violet dizzy.

'*Makna hathi*! Hold him, Vi! Bring him round!' Mahadur shouted

Violet tugged frantically at the rope halter.

She knew even as she pulled on it it was utterly useless – she might as well have been an ant trying to halt a moving glacier. Beneath her she could feel Chandra's flanks quivering, a rippling contraction of muscle which threw her momentarily off balance. She pitched forward and almost fell. Somehow she hauled herself back.

The great bull heaved himself into a swaying canter. He was making a rumbling sound, a strange low-pitched murmur like the beginnings of an earthquake. Something inside him had snapped. He gathered speed and stormed down the pathway.

'Tiger! There's a tiger, Vi!'

Violet just heard Mahadur's warning scream over the thunder of Chandra's feet.

She gazed terrified ahead.

Dust was rising from the track. Through the spiralling choking clouds she caught a glimpse of the tiger – a flash of gold and black at the edge of her sight. At the same instant she was aware of Balmati beside her. The young she-elephant's ears were laid back against her shoulders as she raced neck and neck with the stampeding bull.

The tiger raced on towards them.

It was moving unbelievably fast – its legs bunching and stretching out in coils of muscle-driven power. It had almost reached them when it swerved. It seemed to squat for a fraction of a second, poised and balanced at the side of the path with its yellow eyes blazing. Then, snarling, it leapt upwards.

It wasn't interested in Chandra, Violet, or Balmati. Its target was Mahadur in her brilliant scarlet sari.

Violet opened her lungs and yelled.

The sound that came out was an animal sound, not of fear

or warning but of protection and defiance, a shout that seemed to rise from the depths of her being. She might have been a tigress herself protecting her cubs, and she was using her voice as a weapon.

Later neither she nor Mahadur could explain what happened next – how it was that the great striped cat jackknifed in midair and tumbled back with splayed claws to fasten on to Chandra's heaving rear.

Chandra himself was crazy now, crazy with *musth* and fear and aggression. The old bull, long past his prime but still the most powerful animal in the jungle, halted and turned. He stumbled and swung round. Regaining his balance he turned his head and tried to gouge the tiger with his yellowed tusks.

Clinging to his blood-stained rump, the tiger was out of his reach. Screaming, Chandra edged backwards towards a tree and started to swing his haunches against its trunk, trying to brush the tiger off.

On the elephant's back Violet felt no fear, only a frozen misty sense of confusion. The tiger was so close to her she could smell the rank stench of rotting prey on its breath. Blood spattered her as the talons raked down Chandra's haunches. He was trumpeting again, and she was being hurled backwards and forwards as the two animals battled.

'Jump!' Mahadur's voice rose in a frenzied cry above the clamour. 'For God's sake, Violet, jump!'

Violet heard her.

She let go of the rope and threw herself upwards, launching herself into space at the very moment when Chandra reared up and deliberately rolled on to his back, trying to crush the tiger beneath him.

Cold air rushed past her face and the lurching earth raced upwards to meet her. As she collided with the ground, all her breath was driven out of her lungs.

She lay still and unconscious.

'Violet! Violet – are you all right?'

Mahadur's voice seemed to come to her from a long way away. Violet struggled to open her eyes. Inexplicably the horizon was rocking. For a moment she couldn't remember where she was.

'Mahadur?'

She struggled to sit up through a haze of pain.

'Oh, Vi!' Mahadur threw her arms round her. 'For a moment I thought you were dead.'

Mahadur was sobbing. Violet tested her arms and legs. The pain was fading now, and as far as she could tell nothing was broken.

'I'm fine,' she said shakily. 'What about you?'

'Safe thanks to you.'

'Where's the tiger?'

'It's gone.'

The earth beneath her was damp. Violet felt Mahadur's warm hand in hers. She raised her head, searching for the elephants.

'Where are Balmati and Chandra?'

'They're here. Poor old Chandra's lost some blood, but the shock seems to have jolted him out of *musth*. I don't think Balmati and I would ever have caught him otherwise.'

The two chastened and shocked young women returned to the palace in the early light of dawn, both of them mounted on Balamati with Chandra tramping behind. The mahouts had long since realised the elephants were missing, and search parties had been out since midnight.

The girls, particularly Mahadur, were in disgrace, but it was her wedding day and, as the Maharanee said, there was nothing anyone could do about *that*. For Violet the experience had changed her life. The momentary terror of the tiger's attack had faded and vanished even before she and Mahadur got back to the palace.

Violet had rediscovered elephants.

For the first time since she left Africa she knew where she wanted to be and what she wanted to do. Chandra and Balmati were noble and graceful, but they had been tamed. No one had ever tamed Uhuru and the herd she led down to the river to drink.

With all the absolute certainty of her sixteen years Violet knew that nothing apart from the valley in Africa would ever matter – nothing *could* ever matter. All she had to do was convince her mother that she was serious, and from then on everything would fall into place.

Violet *did* have a dowry – a responsibility, just as the Maharanee had said. She had the valley. Where the Maharanee was wrong was that Violet didn't need a marriage to take possession of it.

It was already hers – hers and Billy's.

'Of course you can't, Violet. It's completely ridiculous! Who on earth put such a madcap idea in your head?'

Violet stared at her mother.

'No one,' she said furiously. 'I don't need ideas from anyone. I've got my own.'

She paused, controlled herself. She tried another approach. 'All right, I'll finish my exams. I'll do really well. How about then?'

'My dear Violet,' her mother's voice rose in exasperation, 'I've already decided not to send you back to school. I've discussed it with Miss Prescott. We both agree it frankly hasn't worked out. Instead, you're going to Paris, to the Convent of the Sacred Heart. You can work on your French and perhaps learn some reasonably civilised behaviour from the nuns. After that I'll find you a finishing school.'

'I don't want to go to Paris, Mummy, or to a convent or to finishing school. I've told you want I want to do.'

'For goodness' sake, be realistic, Violet! You'll do what all of your friends will be doing. A secretarial course after that and then the season. Don't you want to marry and be happy, child?'

'I've only got two friends,' She said bleakly. 'Nanny's always telling me I've got to forget the first of them. The other's just got married. Mahadur's husband may be a prince, but he's bald and he's got body odour and looks like a dummy.'

'Violet!' Margaret Somerset looked at her, shocked. 'You take the Maharanee's hospitality and say wicked things like that?'

'It's true,' Violet pressed on stubbornly. 'You don't know

him, you haven't smelled him. Well, I have. I don't want a husband like him, and I don't want to do the season.'

Mrs Somerset's mouth tightened. 'You'll do as you're told, young lady.'

'What if I don't?' Violet challenged her defiantly.

As soon as she'd spoken she regretted the question. She was sure it would provoke an explosion which, she knew, would get her nowhere. Violet was wrong.

Confronted with her daughter's obdurate stare, for once Mrs Somerset backed down. When she answered Violet her voice was cold but briefly conciliatory.

'We can't go on quarrelling, Vi,' she said. 'You're growing up. It's no secret to anyone that you're a fortunate young woman. One day you're going to be very handsomely provided for. Until then you depend on me. We should both of us work together to see you find a husband who'll make you happy, and look after your provision.'

Violet was silent for a moment.

So there it was. The Maharanee had been right. Her mother had indeed been making plans. The interesting piece of news was that it seemed she had her own money. Violet wanted to be sure.

'When you say "provision",' she asked carefully, 'does that mean money?'

'Of course. It's all rather complicated, but basically it's a matter of trust funds. Your grandparents were very generous. Then eventually my inheritance will come to you too. Honestly, darling, you're quite a catch.'

'I don't want to be a catch,' Violet retorted. 'It sounds like a fish.'

Once again Mrs Somerset stopped herself from bristling. She managed to laugh.

'You have a most odd way with words, dear,' she said. 'But you'll have to think about it. Money's a serious matter. Meanwhile, once you're back from Paris and through finishing school, we'll do the season together. It should be such fun.'

Fun, Violet knew, was her mother's highest accolade.

Violet hesitated again. Then she made a final attempt.

'I really want to go to Africa,' she said. 'I want to live in my valley and be with the elephants. Honestly, that's all I want to do.'

Even as she spoke Violet knew the plea was half-hearted. The conviction had gone out of her voice in the turmoil of what she was still trying to absorb from what her mother had told her.

Margaret Somerset smiled.

She knew she'd won. Now she could afford to make concessions. Whatever they were, they would be meaningless. By the time Violet was old enough even to remember them, her life would have changed direction entirely.

'One day, darling, of course you will,' she said. 'I bought you that land as an investment. Nice Uncle Finlay Hampton said it could be a very good one. In spite of all the problems out there, he was probably right. As my stockbroker wittily says: "You can't go wrong with land – they're not making it any more."'

She leant forward and kissed her daughter.

'But you and I, we're going to have a lot of fun before then.'

For much of the time Violet, with her strangeness, her oddity, her bloody-minded contrariness, drove her mother to the edge of distraction. She was also, Mrs Somerset knew and all her friends enviously or admiringly confirmed, the most beautiful young girl of her generation.

When she came to do the season, she would unquestionably be the debutante of the year.

Violet tensed as her mother's arms embraced her. She smelled her mother's expensive scent, and felt the coolness of her silk dress touch her neck. She opened her mouth to argue again about the valley, but she changed her mind.

'Yes, Mummy,' she said meekly.

There was no point in arguing. Mrs Somerset was no longer even listening.

For the moment it didn't matter. Violet had realised she would never break through to her mother. Africa, the valley, the elephants, none of them meant anything to her. If Violet was going to get what she wanted, she knew she would have to do it alone – alone, of course, apart from Billy Ramsden.

The valley was as much Billy's as hers. Billy would help her, Billy would know what to do.

All she had to do was find him.

30

'I'm looking for Billy Ramsden,' said Violet.

The little girl who'd opened the door wrinkled her face sullenly and squinted up at her.

'Ain't no Billy here, lady.'

The child was about five. She was wearing a torn and filthy dress, and her feet were bare.

Violet tried again. 'Is your mummy in?'

The child picked her nose. Without answering directly, she turned and screamed upstairs: 'Gran! Door!'

'What's he want?' a voice called down from above.

'It's a miss,' the child said, inspecting Violet again.

Then she screamed back up to the floor above: 'Dunno, Gran. She's not the 'ealth.'

'I'm putting on me gown. Tell her I'm coming down!' the voice bellowed.

'Gran's coming down,' the child said.

The little girl gave Violet a final blank and cross-eyed stare, then she vanished through a door at the end of the passage. As she pushed the door open an overpowering tangle of smells – stale stewed cabbage, coal fumes, carbolic soap, and urine – billowed down the hallway, and swept out into the street.

Violet recoiled.

She was already cold. In spite of the warm April day the little house looked dark and chill. Now, giddy from the stench and uncertain of her reception, all she wanted to do was turn and run away. Somehow she forced herself to wait.

'Yes?'

The voice, the same one she'd heard shouting down from above, came from the shadowy space inside the hall. It was truculent and wary.

Violet could barely see the woman. She realised she'd unconsciously retreated into the street as she'd waited for her to appear. Embarrassed she stepped forward on to the doorstep which gave into the dark and rank-smelling warren of the house.

Violet peered into the gloom.

'I'm looking for Billy Ramsden,' she said. 'I was told I might find him here.'

'Who might you be, then?'

'My name's Violet, Violet Somerset.'

The woman must have been studying her well before Violet knew she was there. In the silence that followed she continued her inspection.

Violet gazed back at her.

The woman was about sixty. Once, Violet thought, she must have been beautiful. Her body was full but still erect and graceful. Her hair was dyed a deep russet brown to conceal what was no doubt a fading grey-whiteness, but it still shone. Her face was proud and strong, with its fine-cut nose and dark level eyes that would have dominated any family, any street, maybe even any city.

Only one thing was wrong – her skin. The skin of the handsome old woman was dry and yellow. It had the colour and texture of death.

'You're after Billy Ramsden? What if I tell you there's no Billy here?'

Her voice was absolutely flat.

Violet stared into the old woman's eyes.

Forty years separated them in age. Much more, generations of wealth and class and history, stood between them as people. They came from worlds so different they might have been inhabitants of different galaxies.

'Billy is – was – my friend,' Violet answered. 'We knew each other a long time ago. In Africa. He may have spoken of me.'

The woman pursed her lips. Her face was implacable, giving nothing away.

'I 'eard little Steph tell you. There's no Billy here, miss.'

'Please call me Violet.' For some reason she felt impelled to plead.

'Why?' The old woman's voice was still suspicious.

Violet hesitated. 'I think I need your help if I'm to find him.'

'What would a fine young lady like you want with Billy?'

'Can I explain? Perhaps I could come in.'

The old woman glanced up and down the street. She stood aside.

'Nosy neighbours,' she snorted.

She led the way into the cramped kitchen. The smell was almost overwhelming now, and it was as much as Violet could do not to put her handkerchief to her nose.

Doris put the kettle on the hob and began to make tea.

It hadn't been easy to track Billy down.

Violet had started with the assumption his aunt had been called Ramsden too. There were dozens of Ramsdens with South London addresses listed in the telephone book, and she'd telephoned them all.

Her search yielded nothing. No one had ever heard of the orphaned son of a soldier who'd been killed in the Far East with Rattray's Sikhs. It was as if Billy Ramsden had vanished without trace, or never even existed. Then two thoughts came to Violet, and she cursed herself for her stupidity.

First, there were almost certainly Ramsdens in South London without telephones. Second and more important Billy's aunt was probably married and had changed her name long ago. The telephone book was useless. Finally as a last resort it occurred to her to try the regimental records department at the War Office.

She made an appointment and went along to Whitehall.

There she had a remarkable stroke of luck. Billy's return to Liverpool was logged under his father's name, and so was the colonel's request for a military policeman to escort him to London. There was no record of his aunt's name or where Billy had been taken, but the sergeant clerk she spoke to was also a South Londoner and like most South London men he went to the fights.

'I remember a Billy Ramsden on the club bills, miss,' he said. 'Fine young scrapper, he was. Strong, lovely footwork, and a good boxing brain. Last time I watched him he made it through to the London finals. That was, well, four or five years ago. Never turned up for the finals and haven't heard of him since. Of course, it may not be the same Billy Ramsden. Common enough name, after all. But it might be worth a try.'

Violet was absolutely certain it was the same Billy Ramsden, *her* Billy.

'How do I give it a try?' she asked eagerly.

'As far as I remember he fought out of the Crown and Garter.'

'What's that?' To Violet it sounded like a pub.

'Boys' club in the East End,' the sergeant answered. 'One of the best. They take promising lads from all over the smoke. Father Geoffrey was their most famous scout. He's gone now, the booze got him, but Len, the head trainer, he's still there. You could go and see him.'

'Thank you, Sergeant.' Violet smiled at him gratefully and stood up. 'I will.'

The sergeant looked at the beautiful and elegant young woman in her expensive clothes. She'd said she and this Billy Ramsden had been friends as children. He couldn't imagine how that had come about or why she wanted to find him again.

The sergeant frowned doubtfully.

'If I can give you a word of advice, miss,' he said. 'Lads like Ramsden, in the streets where they come from, they sometimes get into trouble.'

Violet wrinkled her face puzzled. 'What do you mean?'

'There'd have to be a very good reason for him to miss the finals. I don't want to say anything out of turn, mind you, but it might just be he was a guest of Her Majesty at the time. Could be he still is, miss.'

Violet stood there for a moment. She managed to work out what the sergeant meant.

'Billy Ramsden in prison?' She shook her head. 'Not if it's the Billy I know, Sergeant.'

She thanked him again and went out.

The address given for the Crown and Garter boys' club

was in the East End docks. Violet took a taxi there the next morning. She'd told Bobbity where she was going after making her swear not to tell Margaret. Bobbity had been appalled, but hadn't been able to dissuade her.

'Pickpockets, rapists, and murderers,' she had said miserably when she knew she couldn't change Violet's mind. 'That's all you'll find up there. I'm not having you going in your finery. You'll be an open invitation to Lord knows what. At least you can wear your oldest skirt and that darned coat we haven't had out for years.'

Dressed in the clothes Bobbity had insisted on, Violet sat back in the cab as it made its way through the city and into the docks.

They pulled up outside a grimy building off the Mile End Road. Over the entrance was a sign saying 'Crown and Garter Boys' Club 1924'. Violet paid off the driver and glanced round. She could see the morning sunlight shining off the river a hundred yards away. Tugs and barges hooted and gulls wheeled screaming overhead.

Most of the other buildings in the street were vast and barrack-like. They all seemed to carry signs carved in granite like the one above the boys' club door. She could see one which read Peabody Trust 1927, another for the Whitbread Trust 1931, and the biggest of all for the Bernard Baron Housing Settlement 1932.

She wondered briefly who they'd all been, the Whitbreads, Peabodys and Barons, who must have spent fortunes in endowing these charitable projects in what was the grimmest and most derelict area of London she'd ever seen.

Violet shivered and went inside.

She found Len without any difficulty. A boy in the entrance lobby led her through to the raftered gymnasium and took her up to him. The room smelt of rosin and sweat and cigarette smoke. Len was sitting on a bench against one of the walls.

He was a bald old man with a stubble of grey hair round his ears, heavy bowed shoulders, and a scarred and battered face. He was also the most laconic, unforthcoming person Violet had ever met. He listened without comment or question as she told her story.

Afterwards he sat for a long time in silence.

'The padre brought him in,' he said eventually. 'Could have gone the full distance, Billy could, right to the top. Might have been another Kid Hawkins, even another Mendoza. But he buggered us up, me and Father both. He let us down.'

The old man snorted. 'Know why? Father Geoffrey told me. I didn't believe it, I still don't believe it except the padre never lied. He said Billy was thieving for elephants. That's what they got him for, bleeding elephants!'

Len spat. 'He lived with his Aunt Doris. Ask at the desk. They'll give her address. But you won't find the little bastard. He's gone.'

Len stood up.

Boys were starting to drift back into the gym. Violet heard the clatter of skipping ropes whipping against the floor, and the thud of gloved hands on the swaying punch-bags. She must have caught Len in a break in the training. Now the break was over.

As he walked away, the old man looked back over his shoulder.

'Sorry for the language, miss,' he said. 'But Billy, he could have been the best. He never should have done it. It was right out of order. And for elephants, I ask you!'

Violet went to the desk.

She got the address of Billy's aunt. She took another taxi to Malplaquet Road in Brixton. Now she was sitting with Doris in the kitchen with cups of tea in front of them both.

'At least he hasn't knocked you up, Vi. Where he is, you don't get much chance of that!'

Doris gave a peal of laughter. Violet smiled back.

'How did you guess I'm called Vi?' she asked.

Doris chuckled again. 'It's not only gentry who call their daughters Violet, darling. You'll find lots of Violets round here in Brixton. And once they're Violet, of course they're Vi.'

Violet sat for a moment thinking.

She felt slightly abashed. Only a few people shortened her name – her mother, Nanny, Angie, Mahadur – and then only, she'd supposed, because they'd known her intimately for a long time.

She'd never thought of other people, people like Doris, assuming they could address her as Vi within ten minutes of meeting her. She looked at the older woman again and decided she didn't mind, she didn't mind at all.

In the short time they'd been together a curious intimacy had developed between them. Violet liked Doris, she trusted her. She sensed Doris trusted her too. Violet also sensed that in her own way, the way of South London's streets, Doris was wise.

'Listen, Vi.' Doris reached across the table and took her hand. 'You've told me about you and Billy as kids in Africa. I've told you about Billy. I've told you he's banged up – well, Len told you that. Those bloody elephants, they started it all, and look where they've got him. In the bloody nick. Len didn't tell you where, I'm not going to either.'

She paused. 'Billy's different now. I go and visit him. He's not what you remember. He's not a child, he's grown-up. He's a hard, strange, difficult man. You can't do anything for him, he can't do anything for you. Leave him alone, for your own sake.'

Doris dropped Violet's hand and drank from her cup of tea.

'Go back across the river, Vi. You've been looking for something that isn't here. It was just a dream, it's gone. Forget Billy, forget those fucking elephants – excuse my French. Get on with your own life.'

Tears blurred Violet's eyes. She wiped them away. She finished her tea and stood up.

She looked down at Aunt Doris. Aunt Doris! She smiled through her still watering eyes. Doris had no relationship with her, let alone as an aunt, but that was how in less than an hour Violet had come to view her. She knew Doris wouldn't mind.

'Thank you.' Violet leant forward and impulsively kissed her. She hesitated. 'If Billy comes back, tell him I was here. Tell him I was looking for him and the elephants.'

'If he comes back, I'll tell him what I think's best,' the old woman said grimly. She broke off. Slowly a smile spread over her face. 'And perhaps what I think's best for you too.'

She escorted Violet to the door. 'Come back again, darling, whenever you want. But leave the bloody elephants in Africa.'

Weeping uncontrollably, Violet stumbled away up the street.

31

Violet sat in her little bedroom under the eaves of her parents' house.

Through the wall she could hear the murmur of Bobbity's and Nanny's voices as they chatted together in the nursery. It was to be Violet's last night in the bedroom. In the morning she was leaving for Paris. When she returned her mother had promised to move her down to a much bigger room on the floor below.

'I'll have Sibyl Colefax do it up for you while you're away,' said Margaret. 'I know she'll make it enchanting. After all, you're almost grown-up now, darling, and you need a proper room of your own.'

Violet picked up teddy and stared at the raggedy little bear.

The tears she'd wept as she left Aunt Doris' house a week ago – Violet could still only think of her as Aunt Doris – had long since dried up. Now she simply felt numb and defeated.

She'd had a wild idea she could find Billy and he'd know how to help her escape from the misery that surrounded her. It was, of course, as Aunt Doris pointed out, only a dream. Billy had changed. He'd grown up, he'd become a man, he'd been sent to prison.

Once or twice over the week Violet had thought of going back to the Brixton house and pleading with Aunt Doris to be told where he was. That was a fantasy too. Doris wouldn't have told her. Even if she had and Violet had managed to visit him, it would have been a disaster. More vividly than anything else, she remembered Billy's pride.

It would have humiliated him for Violet to see him helpless

and caged in prison. The image of him she carried in her mind might only be a dream. It was better for both of them to keep it like that than have the dream shattered.

Violet hugged teddy to her.

Over the past week she'd learnt more about what her mother called her 'provision'. Her father was back on one of his increasingly rare visits from his postings abroad. He'd always been a remote and austere figure in Violet's life, and it had taken her several days before she plucked up enough courage to tackle him. Then one evening she forced herself to go to his study and confront him.

'What did your mother mean?'

He took off his glasses and repeated the question she'd just put to him.

'Well, Vi, your grandfather was a very rich man. He left most of his money to your mother, but he also left a considerable sum to you. It has of course grown very substantially since then. He was somewhat old-fashioned in his views – he believed young women would rush out and spend every penny they were given on clothes – and so he left the money in trust.'

'What does that mean?'

'In the case of your trust, that you don't get control of the money until you're thirty.' Her father smiled. 'By that age, he hoped, you'd be losing interest in dressing up.'

Violet's heart sank. Thirty was thirteen years away. It was an eternity. By the time she was thirty she'd be middle-aged and probably dead.

'I'm not interested in clothes, Daddy,' she said eagerly. 'Everyone knows that. Ask Nanny or Bobbity or even Mummy.'

'Unfortunately that makes no difference. Trusts are regulated by law. The law says your grandfather's wishes must be followed.'

Violet frowned and gnawed her lip. 'Does that mean until I'm thirty, I have to depend on you and Mummy?'

Her father nodded. 'In general terms, yes.' He paused. 'There's one exception. If you get married before then, you

– or in a more real sense, your husband – automatically obtain control over half the trust funds.'

Violet was silent for several moments. She tried to work it out. She shook her head.

'I don't understand,' she said. 'Who gets control, me or my husband?'

'Well, technically you, of course, it's your money,' her father replied. 'But for all practical purposes, it's always assumed the husband will manage it.'

'So I have to get married and then I get half the money and then my husband decides what to do with it – except it's still really mine?'

Her father laughed. 'Crudely but admirably put, Vi!'

'And if I don't,' she insisted. 'If I want to spend it myself, what then?'

Still laughing her father raised his hands. 'It would be most strange and unorthodox but frankly, I have to confess, no one could stop you.'

Violet came over to the desk. She bent down and for the first time since she was a child she kissed her father unprompted by either Nanny, Bobbity or her mother.

'Thank you.'

'Just don't tell your mother,' he replied.

As he put his spectacles back on and returned to his papers, Violet left the study. She climbed the stairs to her room. She knew exactly what she was going to do, and she felt a wonderful surge of energy and confidence.

She would go to Paris. She would attend the convent. She would come back, take a secretarial course, go through the season. She would do everything her mother wanted.

Furthermore – which was what her mother desired most of all – she would get married. Her mother wouldn't know or care why. Violet did.

She'd discovered it was the only way out.

Paris should have been lovely – beautiful, gay, and glamorous.

It wasn't. Paris was hell. Violet and the other *'jeunes demoiselles'*, mostly rich and silly girls from Venezuela, Switzerland, and Germany, tramped through the museums, visited the Comédie Française and the Opera, and sat every day through lectures of stultifying boredom on dead philosophers and even longer-dead writers.

Everywhere they went they were strictly chaperoned, and in the evening immediately after dinner they were locked in their rooms. Violet would gaze down from her window in the darkness and enviously watch the Parisian girls of her own age swing themselves on to their boy friends' Vespas, and roar away, eyes sparkling and hair streaming in the wind, to go to the latest Godard film and then sit up drinking coffee in a cafe on the Boul' Miche' until the early hours.

She lay in bed hating them, hating the convent, hating everything about her life.

Then she returned to Britain. The year at the Ascot finishing school which followed was if anything worse. At boarding school in the Malvern Hills she had always felt an outsider – but there had been Mahadur, and a few courses like biology and geography which she'd enjoyed.

At Ascot there was no Mahadur, no biology or geography.

Only the company of girls almost sillier than the ones she'd lived with in Paris, and tedious instruction in how to arrange flowers and organise a household. Violet had no interest in arranging flowers or running a house. All she wanted to do was to learn how to pitch a tent, like Ngoro, Billy, and the boys had done in the valley, how to bake bread in an oven in the ground, and how to make an open fire that would burn through the night.

Intensely lonely, Violet confided in an unguarded moment to one of the other girls what she yearned for. The girl didn't even answer. She simply looked wide-eyed at Violet as if she was mad – mad and possibly dangerous.

Violet never made the same mistake again. She gritted her teeth and silently survived the finishing school just as she'd survived the convent in Paris.

Her time at Ascot ended and she came back to London.

'Isn't it heaven, darling?' her mother said as she showed Violet her new bedroom. 'Sibyl's excelled herself. I'm really longing to move in here myself.'

Violet looked round.

The room was an elegant riot of richly swagged curtains, ruched bedspreads, plump low chairs upholstered in expensive copies of eighteenth-century chintz fabrics, and little low tables piled with magazines and silver-framed photographs.

'It's lovely,' Violet said uncertainly.

In her view it looked more like a tart's boudoir – one of the phrases she'd learnt from the now long-lost Angie – than a place where you shrugged off your clothes and threw yourself down to sleep.

Her mother beamed. 'I'm so glad you like it. I know it's going to be a haven for you. My goodness, we've got a busy year ahead of us. Come on downstairs, let's start planning and plotting.'

The year ahead was the year of the London season.

The season began in March with the announcement of the list of the models for the Berkeley Dress Show.

The list was a coded advance identification of the girls being launched on London society who were likely to emerge as the debutantes of the year. Violet wasn't just on the list, she was asked by the show's charity organisers to model the centre-piece of the collection, the wedding dress.

On the catwalk she was a sensation.

'Violet Somerset made an absolutely charming bride in Norman Hartnell's exquisite organza gown,' wrote Betty Kenward, doyenne of the society diarists, in the *Tatler*. 'It's hard to think of any girl in the post-war years who has made such an immediate and enchanting impression.'

The dress show was followed by a round of tea and cocktail parties given by the mothers of the year's debutantes. Next came the ritual of being presented to the Queen at court. Immediately afterwards the nightly balls began and the London season was in full swing.

Margaret Somerset had chosen to hold a dance for Violet at the end of September.

'It'll be the last of the season, darling,' she said as she arranged to hire the ballroom at Claridges. 'That always has a particular cachet. And who knows what may have happened by then?'

'You mean I may be doing what Lady Birmingham calls "delivering the goods"?'

Lady Birmingham was one of her mother's closest friends. Margaret Somerset studied her daughter for a moment.

'Sometimes, Vi, you're too sharp for your own good.'

Violet smiled innocently, but said nothing. She knew the remark had struck home.

It was in fact Lady Birmingham who was responsible for Violet's meeting James. There was a Saturday night ball in the country near Arundel in Sussex. Lady Birmingham's own daughter, Charlotte, had been invited to stay in the same house party as Violet, and Charlotte's brother was driving her down there. Lady Birmingham asked Violet to go with them.

To make up a four she suggested they take another guest, James Rippon, with them.

'He's Tommy Sedgehill's eldest boy,' she said to Mrs Somerset. 'He looks like a god and and he's quite delightful. I really think Violet might go for him.'

Lord Sedgehill was a handsome and wealthy Yorkshire landowner. He was master of the local hunt and widely known in the county by the nickname of 'Whipper' – partly for the aggressive way he rode to hounds, and partly because of his unusual but well-reported sexual habits.

His son, the Honourable James, had inherited his father's good looks – the aquiline features, reddish-blond hair and pale blue eyes of their Norse ancestors. He'd also acquired Lord Sedgehill's tastes and appetites on and off the hunting field. Both women and horses, James had learnt from his father, were all the better for a regular beating.

Violet knew nothing of that when the car drew up to collect her and James got out to open the door. All she saw was a tall, confident, and superbly good-looking young man who talked languidly and amiably to her as Charlotte's brother drove them down to Sussex.

In his turn what James registered was the most beautiful young woman he'd ever seen – golden-haired and full-breasted, with sleepy blue eyes and extraordinarily long and elegant legs – legs, he realised instantly, that would look even better against the flanks of a horse.

She'd already been declared the debutante of the year in the gossip columns. She had impeccable breeding – far better than his own even if the Rippon soap fortune had bought a title from Lloyd George – and she was, he'd been told, destined to become immensely rich.

Violet was everything his father had counselled him to look for in a wife. She would also be, he guessed from the sway of her hips as they danced and the rich musky scent that came off her, a rattling good goer in bed.

James proposed to her over salmon kedgeree in the gardens of Belvoir Castle as the orchestra in the marquee beyond was playing a final waltz at the end of one of the last of the summer balls.

'I fear I'm not very romantic, old girl,' he said. 'I suppose I should go down on one knee and all that sort of thing. But what I really want to say is – will you marry me?'

'Yes, James,' answered Violet without hesitation.

She smiled. She took a deep breath, sat back, and looked at him.

She hadn't the slightest idea whether she loved him or not – probably not, she thought on reflection. The only man she'd ever really loved was Billy and that she knew, as Aunt Doris had bleakly and firmly told her, was a dream, a fantasy. It had no place in the scheme of things. What James Rippon offered her was freedom.

That was enough.

'Wonderful!'

James put down his fork and wiped his mouth carefully.

He had a little blond moustache which gleamed in the moonlight. He leaned forward and kissed her. His chin felt pleasantly rough, his moustache tickled and his lips fitted nicely into hers. His arm circled her shoulders, holding her to him. It felt strong and safe.

Violet picked up his hand. She held it to her cheek, then she turned the palm over and kissed it. The palm tasted salty, a little damp. So he *had* been nervous after all. She felt protective. She laughed up at him, her eyes sparkling.

Teasingly she said, 'What shall we tell our parents?'

James pulled his hand back, almost as if the question irritated him.

'Well, of course, I've already consulted them.'

'You asked *them* before you asked me?' Violet stared at him in astonishment.

'Naturally. Had to ask permission first.'

'And what, if I may ask, did they say?'

Violet gaped at him. She was already beginning to feel herself go cold.

'On my side, total approval. Yours too, although your father and I have to iron out a few details. Men's talk. Nothing you need bother with, my dear little girl.'

'I'm not a dear little girl, James,' she snapped. 'And of course I'll concern myself. You seem to know more about my affairs than I do.'

'Well, obviously I do, darling – can I call you that now? I mean, it's natural, isn't it? You don't want to be bothered with things like money. Your father thinks so, so do I, so does everyone. You'll have much more fun doing what you really want to.'

'But—'

Violet's protests faded as he kissed her again.

This time she kissed him back. As she did she felt a tingle all down her body, in her nipples and the pit of her stomach and in all the places she knew she was supposed to tingle. James was warm and close. He was strong and male. She'd agreed to marry him. It felt natural to cling tightly to him.

Her doubts and uncertainties receded. Perhaps it would be all right after all.

Violet's father announced her engagement at the ball her mother gave for her in Claridges. The triumph in her father's voice gave her the second warning that marriage might not confer the hoped for freedom.

'Ladies and gentlemen, all of our friends gathered here, as any father knows the sad moment inevitably comes when a beloved daughter leaves one's care . . .'

The words washed over Violet like an icy wave of the sea

water Nanny had made her bathe in when they went on holiday to Frinton.

James was sitting beside her. He was grinning proudly and happily. She was the first of the season's debutantes to have her wedding announced. She was the first and richest and most beautiful, and he had won her. Violet glanced at him and gritted her teeth.

'Nonetheless, it's with great pleasure and confidence that I hand Violet over to James.'

Pleasure, Violet thought, what pleasure?

To transfer responsibility for a chattel from one man to another? Was that what it meant, this contract whose terms could be agreed without consulting the one person who was most affected?

The Maharanee's voice echoed in her head, and warning bells clamoured in Violet's brain. Her instinct told her that the position she found herself in was the same as Mahadur's. There was one vital difference. All of Mahadur's life had been a preparation for an arranged marriage. Violet's had not been.

She believed stupidly and naively in something called love, in the photo-romances that Bobbity bought. Violet wasn't getting love. She suddenly doubted whether she was even getting freedom.

'Say something, old girl.' Her father had finished speaking and James was prodding Violet to her feet. 'Doesn't matter what, just a courtesy to your parents and me.'

Violet stood up. Her gaze travelled slowly across the ranks of expectant faces she could see behind the wavering pools of candle-light. She was trembling, but she steadied herself and drew in her breath.

'I love elephants,' she said.

She stood there for a moment. Then she sat down. There was a short silence. Then a ripple of chuckles and clapping started at the tables closest to her. The ripple built up into a tide of laughter and applause. It spread out and filled the room, sweeping from table to table in a great joyous and unthinking wave of sound.

Her father came over and kissed her, James wiped his moustache and beamed, her mother was cheering.

Violet sat upright and very still.

There was a small bright smile on her face, a quiet and enigmatic smile, although no one noticed that. She was a Somerset, she was the beautiful and witty Margaret's daughter. She had said something deliciously audacious and funny, a wonderful nonsensical joke.

Violet had confirmed what everyone knew: she had inherited her mother's sense of style. She'd inherited it in trumps.

Violet looked at the candle flames and thought of Billy and the herd and the valley.

'Terrific stuff, old girl.' James pinched her thigh. 'You should be in the music halls!'

Violet married James Rippon at St Margaret's Westminster early in the new year.

'Lord Sedgehill's heir marries diplomatic heiress,' the *Evening Standard* reported on its front page on the morning of the wedding. The story was illustrated by a photograph of Violet holding a posy of her namesake flower.

She went through the ceremony in a trance.

Dimly she was aware of her white Hartnell gown swirling at her feet, the scent of the flowers that canopied the church, her father's melancholy but proud face as he passed her over to James, James' little yellow moustache quivering as he took her hand.

Then there was the reception, inevitably, like her coming out ball, at Claridges again. It too passed in a trance. Violet drank champagne, she heard the toasts to her and her new husband, she saw her mother's ecstatic laughing face.

Nothing had any meaning for her.

Violet went upstairs to change. Both Bobbity and Nanny were in the suite her mother had booked. They fussed around her, tears in their eyes, as they helped her into the clothes she would wear for her departure on her honeymoon. She thanked them, kissed them, and went down to the foyer.

She kissed her mother and father goodbye, waved at the crowd of eager sightseers gathered outside the hotel entrance in Bruton Street, and set off with her husband for the airport.

Four hours later a limousine delivered her and James to the Ritz Hotel in Paris, where they were due to spend their honeymoon night. James insisted on going straight upstairs to the suite. He waited until their luggage had been brought up and the bell boys had left. Then he started to wrench off his clothes.

'Fuck time,' he said coarsely. 'Let's buckle to it, Vi.'

A greedy slovenly grin slid across his face. He'd drunk a great deal of champagne at the reception and more on the flight between London and Paris. Now he stank of alcohol.

'Fuck time and spank time,' he added.

He grabbed her wrist with one hand and lashed out at her buttocks with the other. Violet gazed at him appalled.

The trance ended then and the nightmare began.

32

'Not tonight, James. I'm tired.'

James grunted. 'Fuck time,' he said.

It had become a ritual. His hand tugged up Violet's nightdress. He heaved himself across her, his hands cold and claw-like as he searched for her crotch. Now he was thrusting down between her legs.

Violet twisted away as one of his nails tore her skin.

'James, I mean it! I'm really tired,' she said sharply. 'Please don't.'

'Don't what?'

As usual he'd been drinking heavily at dinner, but the sudden note of anger in her voice momentarily sobered him. He took his hand away.

'Oh, come on, Vi,' he pleaded. 'It's only our fifth night. You've been such a wonderful little goer until now, everything everyone guessed about you. You've loved it, too, haven't you? Don't be a spoilsport.'

'How the hell do you know if I'm a goer? You pass out before either of us has a chance to find out.'

James raised himself on one elbow and tried to focus on Violet's face in the darkness.

She could see him clearly. His face, drunken and slack, was caught in the moonlight streaming in from the open window over the Rue Royale, but hers was lost in the shadows round her pillow.

'Pass out, do I? We'll see about that.'

He grabbed at her again. This time his hand didn't fumble for her legs. It plunged down swiftly and strongly through the neck of her nightdress between her breasts, ripping the silk. He began to fondle her nipples, his long powerful fingers switching from one to the other.

Violet tried to push him away.

'Please don't, James! Let's talk about it in the morning.'

'The hell with the morning! You're my wife, Vi.'

He was furious now. He pushed the bedclothes aside and stood up. His muscular body was bunched with rage and his features were taut and pale in the moonlight.

'"Fuck time's" all the conversation you'll get from me, young lady.'

He went over to the wardrobe and fumbled in the cupboard.

When he returned to the bed, she could see the whip in his hand.

'Naughty little filly needs a lesson, doesn't she?'

Violet caught the flash of white teeth as he grinned.

She felt her body grow cold. Then the whip descended – once, twice, and a third time across her breasts, and then a fourth across her arm as she threw it across her body to protect herself. Afterwards he was on top of her again, his hand clamped over her mouth to stifle her screams as he thrust down into her body.

She could feel there was excitement for him in the assault, a violence and brutality she hadn't imagined in her worst dreams. She struggled to fill her lungs, twisting her face until his hand broke free. She thrashed and heaved, trying to throw him off.

It was hopeless.

He was far too strong. It was like battling against a suffocating iron bar which had been placed across her chest. She forced herself to go limp. He came to a climax, his muscles relaxed, and the dizzying pressure eased.

Instantly she swivelled her head and bit savagely into his wrist.

James howled in pain. As he jerked away, she rolled out of bed and stood up. Blood, she knew, was trickling down her chin.

'For Christ's sake, Violet!'

'Bastard!'

Violet gazed down at him, her cheeks white with rage and humiliation. She glanced at the bruises and weals rising on her arm.

'You're drunk, James, blindly, crassly, idiotically drunk!' she stormed at him. 'If you ever do that again – *ever* – I'll leave you. Understand?'

John gazed back at her.

He was astounded.

He knew he was drunk. He was almost always drunk in the evening, so was his father, so was virtually every man he knew. As far as he knew every woman accepted that and they enjoyed being reminded who was master – and if that involved a little bit of horseplay and discipline, what on earth was there to make a fuss about?

'What the hell's the matter with you, Violet?' His voice was slurred but he looked genuinely shocked. 'You're married to me. I thought you were grown-up. I thought we understood each other.'

'I am grown-up, James, and I'm afraid I'm beginning to understand you.' Violet's voice was acid. 'All I can hope, for both our sakes, is that I'm wrong. Because what I'm starting to understand, I don't like one little bit.'

She snapped the words out savagely and icily.

'Go to sleep. Sober up. Tomorrow try to behave rather more like a gentleman and less like a squalid little thug.'

She went out and slammed the door.

She slept fitfully that night on the couch in the living-room of the suite. In the morning she did something she'd never done before. She went to the British Embassy and asked to see the Embassy's doctor. As the daughter of a senior diplomat – Violet's father had by then been posted to Bogota – she was given an immediate appointment.

She had just got married, Violet explained. It had been a highly charged and somewhat traumatic experience, and now on her honeymoon she was having difficulty in sleeping.

Could the doctor give her some pills to help her get some rest?

The doctor smiled with fatherly sympathy. He knew Violet's parents well from a previous posting they'd shared in Mexico City. He quite understood the stress she was under. He had no hesitation at all in prescribing her both tranquillisers and sleeping tablets. He was sure it was what Margaret Somerset would have wanted.

Violet didn't even have to go to the chemist to collect them, he said. They'd be picked up by an Embassy messenger. If the old hands at the Office couldn't look after their various dependants, he chuckled, then who on earth would?

He wrote out the prescription, and gave it to a uniformed messenger. That night Violet started taking the pills.

Three months after the honeymoon ended and when Violet was installed in the house James occupied on his father's estate, she discovered she was pregnant.

'In foal, are you, Vi?' James said when she told him.

He stared at her with an expression of mild dislike on his face which Violet had come to learn heralded one of his less attractive sallies.

'Lets you off the hook, old girl. Let's just hope for both our sakes it's a son.'

After the fifth night of the honeymoon James had been more careful about pressing his attentions on her, although he continued to drink as much as ever and she knew the violence was never far from the surface. When they did make love it was always, from Violet's point of view, an unqualified disaster.

She felt nothing except boredom and discomfort. Without any other information – sex was something her mother had never been able to talk about – Violet decided she must be frigid. She'd learnt enough from the other young Yorkshire wives to know it was quite a common condition, and nothing to be ashamed of.

It certainly didn't affect the man's pleasure, and that was all, she'd always been told, that mattered. Now for the moment, since she was pregnant, that wasn't an issue any longer.

Violet moved into a separate bedroom and settled down to prepare for motherhood.

By Christmas, when she was in the sixth month of her pregnancy, Violet was desperately lonely. She had nothing to do in the house – under the housekeeper, Mrs Boycott, there was a cook, a butler, and a parlour maid who took care of everything. She saw little of James who would drive himself to Leeds each weekday morning, where he occupied himself with the family business.

Weekends were spent overseeing the estate. The evenings brought a round of trivial social engagements which Violet sometimes joined, or more often avoided. The only breaks in the monotonous passage of the months were her mother's occasional visits – something which in the past Violet would have dreaded but now welcomed.

'You can't imagine how lucky you are, darling,' her mother said once as she glanced round the house. 'This lovely place, an adoring husband, as I'm sure James is, and a child on the way. You're the envy of everyone. I'm so glad it's all worked out.'

'Yes, Mummy,' Violet said, trying to keep the misery out of her voice.

Her mother departed to spend the winter in Capri, leaving Violet to cope with her swelling belly alone.

It was bitterly cold in the Dales.

The snow drifted in deep furrows which followed the lines of the long valleys, and even the dinner parties which sometimes enlived the weekends had to be cancelled, involving as they did long treks in four-wheel drive vehicles across the icy moors.

To James' irritation, Violet hadn't the slightest interest in the countryside field sports like hunting which were almost an obsession with him.

'I'm sorry,' she said. 'I just don't see the point in any of this hunting and shooting. I don't want to quarrel with you, but it simply isn't me. You can argue until you're blue in the face, I'm having no part of it.'

She thought of trying to explain to him about Africa and the valley and the elephants, but knew it would be useless. James would simply see it as another place to kill animals.

'And I thought you were a real goer in every way,' he said sourly. 'Just shows you how bloody stupid a man can be.'

He stormed from the room.

The one activity Violet did enjoy was exploring the Dales mounted on an elderly cob. She'd ramble across the moors and through the valleys, occasionally stopping off at the small Yorkshire inns and listening to the gossip of the sheep farmers as she drank half a pint of shandy.

Then the snows set in.

At the same time she became too cumbersome to ride and even that small pleasure was denied her. The cold grew sharper, Christmas came, and immediately afterwards, Boxing Day. The Boxing Day meet of the hunt was one of the most important social events of the year, the only day in the Dales apart from the summer agricultural show when everyone – landowners, farmers, and tenants – gathered together.

'We're breaking for lunch this year at the Bull and Crown,' said James. 'Everyone locally knows you're pregnant, but of course they'll still expect you to put in an appearance. For Christ's sake, you're only six months gone! Please be there by twelve o'clock sharp.'

'Yes, James,' Violet said wearily.

She had every intention of being there. Unfortunately on Boxing Day morning she had an attack of nausea. She swallowed a handful of pills – by now it was second nature to her – and fell asleep in front of the fire.

James found her there when he returned in the dusk at four. He was drunk – he must have emptied the huge silver flask he took out with him hunting – and enraged.

'I thought the least I could expect of a wife was that she didn't shame me in front of my friends.'

'I'm truly sorry, James.' Violet looked at him. Pangs of guilt were surging through her. 'I felt sick and tired, and I must have dozed off.'

'As far as I know it's been a long time since you felt anything at all, Vi.'

His eyes were glittering with rage as he advanced towards her. He was still in his muddy riding clothes with his whip clenched in his fist.

Violet tried to back away. 'James, please. It was a terrible mistake, but I really am sorry.'

He stopped in front of her, the whip tapping on his polished boot.

'Show me just how sorry you are.'

His voice was quiet but full of menace.

Violet hesitated. Her eyes were wide and frightened. 'What do you mean?'

'Show me how sorry!' he shouted. 'Get down on your knees and prove it. Here and now!'

He moved suddenly. He stretched out his arm, caught her wrist, and threw her to the floor. Dazed, Violet stared up at him.

'For God's sake, James, it's not safe. Not with the baby.'

'The hell it's not, Vi.' He lowered his face over hers, and she could smell the brandy on his breath. 'I'm bored of your excuses. Turn over!'

He wrenched at her again and fumbled at his fly.

'Please, James – what if the servants came in?'

'Fuck the servants!' He grinned. 'Door's locked. You're my wife. I want to bugger you. Now! Like this!'

He pulled up her skirt, and tugged down her underwear until she was naked from her waist to her knees. Then he thrust himself brutally between her buttocks.

Violet felt the bile rise in her throat, and choked. It was agonisingly painful. She opened her mouth to scream, but James was too fast for her. His hand clamped down over her mouth.

'Bitch!' he whispered. 'Foul, idle, careless little bitch!'

Violet felt the raging weight of him as he rode her, crushing her belly into the floor. Then she heard the swish of the riding crop. The pain seared through her as the thong cut into her skin. Again and again the crop lashed down – but after a while she no longer registered it.

She felt nothing except a fearsome anger of her own – anger and fear, not for herself but for her unborn child. Finally, in the darkness of the pain, she felt nothing at all.

Violet lost consciousness.

Violet knew she had lost the child as soon as she opened her eyes in the bedroom where James had carried her.

As she felt the life-waters trickling away between her bruised thighs, she knew she would never forget or forgive him. She refused to let James near her, in spite of the fact that he appeared stricken and contrite. He had called for the doctor, but it made no difference.

The child was dead.

All the doddery old man with the black bag could do was reassure her that the 'plumbing', as he called it, was still in working order, and that as soon as Violet had had a decent interval of rest, there was no reason why she and her husband shouldn't try again.

'In fact, my dear,' the doctor said as he left, 'there's no cause for panic at all.'

Violet hadn't the slightest intention of panicking. It was the very last thing in her mind.

What she did intend to do was leave James. She had tried to make the marriage work, partly out of a sense of obligation to her mother and partly out of her own pride. She had failed disastrously. Or perhaps James had failed. She didn't know. All she knew was that once again she wanted her freedom.

Half her fortune was now in her control. She didn't quite know what that meant, but there were solicitors who'd be able to advise her. She was free and independent – and not just independent, she sensed, but rich.

All she needed was a final trigger, a reason, to walk out of the Yorkshire Dales and the Honourable James Rippon's life forever.

Meanwhile, to insulate herself against the loneliness and monotony of her existence, Violet did what she was doing with increasing frequency.

She swallowed some more pills.

33

The miscarriage gave Violet a new source of tablets.

She'd repeated the prescriptions for tranquillisers and sleeping pills ever since she'd visited the Embassy doctor in Paris. Now, at the suggestion of the ancient little Yorkshire practitioner who looked after her in the months following the loss of her child, she began to use amphetamines.

'They're quite new, my dear,' he said as he wrote out the first scrip. 'To be truthful we in the medical profession don't really know a great deal about them. But my London colleagues tell me they can work wonders in perking people up after something like this. I certainly think they're worth trying.'

He peered through his glasses at Violet and beamed.

She started on the amphetamines. They seemed to act on her like champagne but without producing a hangover. She finished the bottle and asked for more.

She was young and exquisitely beautiful, she was the daughter-in-law of Lord Sedgehill, she'd been through a tragic experience. There was no question of the doctor's refusing. The old man smiled happily at being able to help her. The next prescription he wrote out was for multiple open-ended repeats.

Violet's days passed in a haze.

By day she buoyed herself up with the 'leapers', as she learnt they were called. By night she drugged herself with the 'sleepers'. At least between them the pills made her life tolerable, although she soon acquired a reputation for unreliability which meant that if she failed to arrive with James for a dinner party, no one was particularly surprised.

'Violet Rippon's thrown another wobbly,' the neighbours

would explain to each other, and prop up a teddy bear in the empty chair so they weren't left with thirteen at the table.

James didn't renew his demands for his 'marital rights', nor did he suggest a divorce. In her more coherent moments, Violet sometimes wondered why. She decided the reason was that if he had done and she'd chosen to contest it, the exposure in court of his private habits wouldn't have reflected at all well on him or his family.

Instead James acquired a succession of mistresses, chosen from the other young Yorkshire women who, unlike her, enjoyed the social merry-go-round and were happy to accept his tastes as part of the game. Violet was left in no doubt as to who was receiving his attentions. Almost everyone, it seemed, was delighted to tell her about his infidelities.

'I just don't know how you put up with it, Violet,' one of her neighbours remarked. 'You must be a complete saint. If Oliver did it to me, I'd reach for his cut-throat razor and re-model him for the next century when I'm told we won't have to breed any longer. It'll all be done by machines then.'

Violet worked out what she meant and smiled. She said nothing.

Later, in her room, she threw back her head and dropped some more pills down her throat. Oblivion from the whole ghastly charade – James, the loneliness, the bitter weather and mindless neighbours – came easier that way. All she had to do was bide her time and wait.

Sooner or later the answer and the release would come.

Both arrived soon after her twenty-first birthday.

They were called, or rather *he* was called because the two came together in the same person, Toby O'Brien. Toby was small, fair-haired, delightfully dishevelled, and had the bluest eyes Violet had ever seen – almost bluer than her own and certainly more sparkling and smiling.

He also had the warmest, softest voice Violet had ever heard – rich and low-pitched and beguiling with a cadence that ended every sentence as if he was about to burst into laughter.

'Toby,' he introduced himself at a party given by one of their neighbours. 'Fresh out of prison, sheltered for the moment under my beloved sister's roof, and looking for sex, drugs, and rock and roll. Or at least a rich woman who'll buy them all for me.'

He paused. His eyes shone mischievously. 'Are you by any chance rich?'

Violet felt helpless. She had no idea whatsoever how to reply. She laughed.

'Yes, I suppose I am.'

'Very rich?'

The blue eyes continued to dazzle her. She was choking with laughter now. 'Yes, I think so.'

'Wonderful! Let's make love immediately and then plan our future.'

'Toby, for God's sake, what fibs are you telling Violet?'

Their hostess, Toby O'Brien's sister, came across the room, smiling and scolding at the same time. She was a short dowdy woman who had married another of the local Yorkshire landowners. For some reason James had taken a fancy to her and made her, Violet guessed, his latest mistress.

Violet didn't mind at all, although she couldn't understand why he had picked someone so apparently plain and unappealing. Or she didn't until she met Toby. Then she saw in both of them, brother and sister, the same verve, the same energy, the same capacity to foster laughter and gaiety.

Perhaps, Violet thought long afterwards, James wasn't quite as insensitive as she'd believed.

'No fibs at all,' Toby protested indignantly. 'I said I've just come out of the slammer. I've discovered she's rich. I've asked her to marry me. What could be more truthful and honorable than that?'

His sister slapped his face. The slap was at once playful, affectionate, and yet hard enough to be a warning.

'Violet's married,' she said firmly. 'Stay away from her.

'And you—'

She turned to Violet. 'Don't you have anything to do with my wretched little brother.'

She smiled at both of them and went back to look after her other guests.

'Yes, madam,' Toby said behind her back as she left.

'Of course, madam,' Violet echoed.

They gazed at each other. Violet began to laugh again. As the laughter spilled out she did something, said something, she would never have believed possible for her.

'Do you really want to make love to me?'

Toby lifted his head and stared thoughtfully at the ceiling. 'At this moment,' he said, 'and probably forever, yes, more than anything in the world.'

'I'm frigid, you know.'

'No, I don't know.' His gaze returned to her face. 'And I very much doubt it. I'll take the gamble. I have a feeling I'm on the seven-to-four favourite at Cheltenham when the favourite comes in.'

Violet had no idea what he meant, but she reached out and took his hand.

'Why don't we go outside?'

He kissed her. Each time he touched her it was like an electric shock, almost knocking the breath out her body.

'How often have you done this?' Violet asked.

They were both lying naked on a mattress in the summer house at the end of his sister's huge rambling garden. It was a warm May night and over his shoulder Violet could see stars through the little gothic window. The sounds of the party drifted faintly across the long expanse of lawn that separated them from the house.

'With other men's wives? Hundreds and hundreds of times,' he answered. 'And, the Good Lord and the Mother of God permitting, I'll do it hundreds more – particularly with you.'

He nibbled her ear.

'You're mad, Toby!'

'All the best asylums are run by lunatics and this is a glorious asylum – it's got you in it.'

Violet laughed. There was a lovely Irish lilt in his voice. It was almost certainly faked, she knew that. She'd heard him speak at his sister's party and he'd talked with the clear precise accent of a native-born Englishman.

Violet didn't mind. She didn't mind anything about him. Not even that he was a rogue and that he had indeed just come out of prison after serving six months for fraud.

He had made love to her and she'd discovered she wasn't frigid and it had been the most wonderful experience of her life. Half an hour later she was still tingling lazily with warmth. When she came to a climax she thought she was literally going to melt. She felt her whole body turn to a joyous softness which started in the pit of her stomach and spread upwards, and downwards from the tips of her fingers to the ends of her toes.

He looked at her now and his teeth flashed white as he smiled in the darkness – and to Violet it seemed as if the smile promised everything in the world she wanted. An understanding of her needs, an acceptance of her uncertainties, a confirmation of her womanhood.

'We'd better go back before the chief warder, my darling sister, sends out armed search parties.'

He pulled Violet to her feet. They dressed quickly and headed back towards the house. Just before they went in he stopped.

'Are you going to live with me forever?'

'I think so,' Violet replied.

'I should warn you: I'm an incorrigible liar, a spendthrift, a hopeless driver, and congenitally unfaithful.' He paused and asked earnestly, 'Does that matter at all?'

'Not a bit!' Violet burst into laughter again. 'Stop teasing me, Toby! Your sister's right. You're utterly impossible. The trouble is, I probably love you.'

He didn't answer.

He simply drew her into his arms and kissed her – a long slow kiss that turned all the other kisses she'd ever had into nothingness. It was as if he was tasting and savouring her like a fruit, like some ripe and exotic peach he'd plucked from the sun-warmed corner of a garden wall.

Violet knew she was already lost. If she hadn't been, she would have been lost then.

* * *

She ran away with Toby on Derby Day.

The servants had the day off – all except one young house-maid whose duties were to lay the fires in the drawing-room and fold the covers down in the bedrooms.

Violet left a note for James on the hall table. 'Dear James,' it said, 'I'm leaving. Your dinner is in the oven. Ask the housemaid where the oven is.' As an afterthought she added: 'PS. I shall be happy to provide evidence for divorce. Naturally, I shall make no claim on you.'

James obliged swiftly, filing for divorce on the grounds of her adultery. He had had enough of Violet to last him a lifetime.

Her happiness lasted for four whole years.

She was, as she'd suspected and her lawyers had confirmed, a very rich woman. She yearned for the sun and there was nothing to keep her in Britain. She moved to southern France and bought a pretty *mas*, a rambling white-washed farmhouse, on the edge of the Camargue in Provence. One of Toby's passions was horses. Violet gave him the money to buy a breeding stock of the beautiful white Camarguais animals, and settled down to decorate the house while he ran the stud farm.

It didn't matter at all that each time one of the mares produced an outstanding foal, it would mysteriously be sold and the proceeds would apparently slip through a hole in Toby's pocket – requiring him to ask her to top up the bank balance once again.

The sun was warm on her face. She was alive and in love. For a time she even gave up her pills.

For three of the four years Toby was a delightful and attentive companion, both in bed and out of it. By the fourth year he was spending more and more time in bed. The trouble was it wasn't Violet's bed. When she first discovered he was being unfaithful, she impulsively insisted on marrying him – something that hadn't seemed important until then.

It made no difference.

Toby started disappearing not just for a night but for days and then weeks at a time. He always came back with his enchanting smile, a plausible story, and his feckless charm, but somehow none of it worked on Violet any longer. She returned to the pills. Then as his absences grew longer, she began to look for companionship elsewhere.

By now Violet had discovered a taste for champagne. Combined with the pills, the bubbling straw-coloured wine made a wonderfully potent and heady cocktail – one that obliterated everything awkward and unpleasant in life, like Toby's infidelities, and instead gave her a surge of confidence and optimism.

If there was any one thing above all else Toby had taught her, it was that she enjoyed making love. She wasn't frigid. She was a passionate sensual young woman – and the bars of Arles, Aix, and Les Saintes Maries de la Mer were filled with young Camarguais cowboys who could make love three times a night.

Violet made them hang up their leather riding chaps behind the door, and turned a blind eye to their petty pilfering of her possessions. Toby was often away on 'horse business'. There was no reason for her to sleep alone, not when she could have the choice of a dozen whipcord-hard bodies lying against her.

And still she refused to give Toby up.

He had given her so much that she continued to tolerate him. He was after all her husband. Violet went on buying him Cartier watches, van Cleef & Arpels cufflinks, shirts from Charvet, and even a Porsche. The jewellery had to be reclaimed at intervals from the London or Marseille pawnbrokers, but at least her fortune was big enough to absorb the ruinous interest rates.

And, of course, whenever she despaired, whenever the whole circus of Toby's profligacy and philandering and her own madcap adventures threatened to overwhelm her, there was the shining champagne and the even more shining pills to shore her up.

Seven years after she fled from Yorkshire, Violet met Curro Lopez. This time she didn't hesitate. She made a handsome settlement on Toby, divorced him, and married Curro.

Curro Lopez was a bullfighter.

34

Eight years earlier the violence and savagery of the bullfight would have horrified Violet. She loved animals and the thought of watching them wounded and killed before crowds of applauding spectators would have repelled her.

Like so much else in her life, that had blurred and changed.

Violet didn't see the cruelty. Instead she responded hungrily to the drama, the ritual and pageantry, the exhilarating art of the sculpted passes with the cape and *muleta*, the stomach-churning excitement of the moment of truth when the matador profiled with his sword and went in over the horns to kill.

To Violet, Toby had always been irresistibly appealing with his wayward boyish charm. She had loved him but it was, she realised, in a way the love of a mother for a mischievous child. Curro Lopez was utterly different. He was remote, strange, and majestic – a haunted, almost tragic figure in his glittering suit of lights.

Toby was a boy. Curro was a man. Curro was a hero.

Born in Triana, the gypsy quarter of Seville, he had almost all the classic attributes of a Spanish *matador de toros* – a killer of bulls. He was immensely brave. He had curling black hair, dark lustrous eyes, and a slim athletic body with the balance and reflexes of a hunting cat. Unusually for a bullfighter, he was also educated.

What Curro lacked, what held him back from being another Belmonte, Manolete or Ordonez, was a love of the bulls. In spite of all of his courage, all his vast natural gifts, he neither knew nor understood the great raging animals. It meant he neither understood nor loved people too.

Violet only discovered that much later.

She saw him first by chance at one of the spring bullfights in Arles – ironically she'd been taken there by her latest cowboy lover from the Carmargue. Lopez had spotted the vibrant blonde-haired young woman in her *barrera* seat. On impulse he dedicated his second bull to her, throwing her his tricorn hat as he went out to face the animal.

That afternoon Curro Lopez gave the finest performance of his entire career. Afterwards, as he was carried round the ring on the shoulders of the members of his supporters' club, his *pena*, he stopped in front of Violet.

'*Como te llamas?*' he called out. 'What are you called?'

'Violetta,' she shouted in Spanish, tossing back his hat.

'I have a lovely garden on my *finca* in Sevilla. Come and grow in it, Violetta!'

Intoxicated by his triumph, he laughed and waved.

Three months later Curro was badly gored in the Las Ventas bull-ring in Madrid. Violet read of the accident in *Arles Matin*. She flew to Madrid, argued her way into the hospital, hired a private ambulance, and escorted Curro back to Seville to recuperate.

The following year she married him.

Curro's wounds were so bad, he was forced to retire from the ring. That suited Violet admirably. In the months since she'd first watched him, she had followed him across France and Spain and briefly to Mexico. She adored his grace in the ring, the splendour of his physical presence, the delicacy with which he fought, but each time he walked out to confront a new bull her throat dried and she almost vomited with fright.

Now that was over. Now Curro belonged to her. Just as good in a way was her discovery that the finca, the ranch, where he'd invited her to 'grow', was a barren wasteland in the Andalusian sierras. Whatever money he'd made had long since been wasted or gambled away.

Financially Curro Lopez was entirely dependent on her. Violet didn't mind at all. She loved looking after him, she loved giving him things just as she'd loved giving them to Toby. And it gave her a measure of control – almost of power.

It took five years for Curro to begin to stray.

Violet wasn't aware of it at first any more than she had been with Toby, but she did vaguely notice – she remembered afterwards – a particularly beautiful young gypsy girl who always seemed to be hanging round their hotel when she and Curro went back to the Camargue for the May pilgrimage to the sea.

A year later the girl arrived on their doorstep on the new ranch Violet had bought close to Granada.

Toby's hobby had been breeding horses. Curro's was breeding bulls. Violet was rich enough to indulge them both. She was called down to the door that day by one of the maids. She frowned, then she recognised the girl. Squawling in her arms was a tiny child.

'Take the senorita to the kitchen,' Violet said crisply. 'Give her a coffee, and the baby whatever it wants.'

'How would you have me, Violetta?' Curro shrugged when he came back from riding round the ranch. 'You want me to be a *maricon?*'

In Spain to be called a *maricon*, a male homosexual, was a disgusting insult. Curro had used the word deliberately to provoke her. It succeeded.

Violet flared. 'I didn't marry a *maricon*, Curro. I did marry someone I trusted not to litter the countryside with his bastards.'

Curro shrugged his shoulders again. 'Sometimes by accident it happens. Now maybe I have to pay her.'

'You mean *I'll* have to pay her?' Violet snapped.

Curro said nothing.

When he'd left the room, Violet called the girl in from the kitchen. Briefly Violet discussed the matter with her. Then she wrote out a dozen cheques, post-dated at six-monthly intervals over the six years ahead. Long before they were up, Violet guessed, she'd have found a husband to support her.

She embraced the young woman, kissed the baby, and sent them on their way.

That night in bed she looked at Curro.

'Perhaps we should have a child?' she said.

'At your age I'm told it can be difficult,' he answered.

'What on earth do you mean?' She propped herself on one elbow and stared at him. 'I'm only in my early-thirties.'

'I looked at your passport, *cara*,' Curro grinned. 'It says next birthday you will be thirty-seven.'

Violet swore.

She raged at him, she beat him with her fists, she kicked out at him with her feet. Then, when she was exhausted, she folded her arms round him and pressed him to her.

He was a swine but she remembered him standing in a shaft of sunlight in the Maestranza ring as death, violent murderous death in the shape of a vast Mirua bull, swept towards him, and Curro in his glittering suit of lights never flinching – only brushing death away in a series of gay and elegant passes with a cape that billowed out like a joyously tossing bell.

She felt him harden. She felt his seed pour into her. Afterwards she slept.

Nine months later Rose was born.

If the child had been a son, Violet thought, her marriage might just have worked. As it was, Curro Lopez already had a son by the gypsy girl. Sons were all that mattered. Violet had undertaken to pay for the boy. There was really nothing left to keep her and Curro together.

He drifted away and Violet found herself alone again.

Well, this time not quite alone. On her hands was a troublesome girl-child whose birth had solved nothing. Violet engaged a nursemaid and returned to her cocktail of pills – washed down now with the best champagne the Madrid wine-merchants could send her.

She was never quite sure what happened in the years that followed.

The Camarguais cowboys in her bed were replaced – and she cringed much later as images of this time floated back to her – by a succession of waiters and farmhands. She fuelled herself on brandy and anis, the fiery liquorice-based drink of the southern Spanish hills.

She parted her legs and heaved rhythmically in bed, frantically clasping to her whatever body she'd picked up late at night in the Seville or Granada cafes and alleys. In the morning she hurled the man away in disgust. She rose, she rubbed her sunken cheeks and shadowed eyes, she reached for another bottle of brandy. Then, as the liquor warmed her, the cycle started again.

What saved her – saved her possibly from suicide and certainly from an irreversible physical collapse that would have amounted to the same thing – was Rose.

Rose was both her salvation and then increasingly her burden.

Although Violet organised her life so that her servants took physical care of the child, she could not avoid the little girl. Rose was always *there*. She was there when Violet came back from an evening out, she was there when she returned from a month away.

Strangely Rose seemed to have inherited nothing at all from her father. She was exactly like her mother. She had the same sleepy blue eyes, the same cascading yellow hair, the same sensuous willowy body although in a child's frame. Every time Violet looked at her she saw herself and her past.

At the age of forty it wasn't what she wanted to be reminded of.

As soon as the child was of school age Violet sent her back to a boarding school in England. Violet's mother had died the year before but her father, recently knighted and retired from the diplomatic service, was still healthy and vigorous. He was delighted to look after his only grandchild while Violet was abroad.

Rose's departure brought Violet both relief and, for the first time since her incarceration in Yorkshire, loneliness. A change of location was the obvious answer. She sold the ranch in Andalusia, and bought an apartment in SoHo in New York.

She had tried almost everywhere else. Manhattan, it seemed, was where everyone was heading for, just as in the thirties they'd gravitated towards Paris.

New York was full of new drugs and old drink. Bourbon replaced champagne. The drugs were harder to distinguish one from the other – there seemed to be such an immense range of them. Violet took everything her money could buy

– and what her money could buy by way of narcotics in New York was limitless.

It could buy buy oblivion. Oblivion and young men from Harlem – gorgeous and black and happy to supply her with everything she wanted in one glorious technicolour cocktail.

Cocaine and the black boys pushed her to the edge of the precipice.

'No, man, don't give her any more of that shit!'

Violet heard the voice through a dull aching haze.

She had taken to zig-zagging crazily between smart dinner parties in mid-town Manhattan and the dives and bars of the upper east side where, after the dinners ended, she finished up in the early hours of the morning.

She hadn't the slightest idea what she was doing, only that she was appallingly lonely, lost, and isolated, and the sleek plump bankers she sat between at the candlelit tables offered her nothing. At least the young Harlem studs were bold and dangerous and vigorous. They reminded her of Toby entering her under the stars, and Curro whirling on his feet as one of the great bulls reared and lashed at him with its scything horns.

Violet coughed.

She didn't know where she was, except she was lying in a bed. Beds had bedside lights beside them. She reached out. In a mist of nausea and pain she fumbled for the switch.

'Where the hell am I?' she demanded as the light came on.

'Just resting, resting easy,' a voice replied.

'Shit!' She managed to prop herself up on her elbow. 'I feel terrible. For Christ's sake, give me something!'

'No more, lady. You got it bad.'

'The hell I have. Who the fuck are you?'

There was a shadow by the window. She peered dizzily at it. The shadow came into focus. It was a young black man and he was grinning.

'Call me darlin', darlin'.'

'Bastard!' she shouted. 'Where's the stuff?'

She registered another shadow then. There were two men looking down at her.

'No way,' the second man said. 'You done enough, lady.'

'I paid you.' Violet was almost screaming as the tremors racked her body. 'Just give me something to stop it!'

The white teeth flashed again, nervously this time.

'You got what you paid for, lady,' the first man said. 'Both of us inside, front and back of you. But you ain't getting no more of the shit. You'll just burn. That we don't need, nor you nor us.'

Violet slumped back on the pillow. Her head felt terrible. She had to think clearly. She knew she was cunning, she knew how to get what she wanted. She forced herself to sit up again.

'How much?' she demanded.

There was only one man beside her now. The other was somewhere over in the shadows, watching her. Bastard, she thought. Black bastard.

'Come on,' her voice was wheedling. 'Just a little one. For mommy?'

'Lady, you ain't getting nothin'. You just going to lie there like a good girl until the stuff you took last night works its way right out of your system. Otherwise,' the face came close to hers, 'you are going to *die*. And that, momma, is bad for business.'

Violet began to scream. The last thing she knew was that the two men in her room were holding her down. Then blackness overwhelmed her.

Her screams were still ringing in her ears when she opened her eyes again. This time she wasn't in her own apartment but in a hospital bed, and there was a stranger – a tall and elderly white man – sitting upright on a chair beside her.

'Hullo, Violet,' he said.

She peered at him. She felt worse than she had ever done in her life. Her whole body ached, her head was throbbing, and she felt sick and giddy.

'Where am I?' she asked huskily.

'In the Good Samaritan Hospital for the Victims of Addiction,' he answered. 'You're safe now.'

'Am I going to die? I certainly feel like it.'

He smiled. 'No. With any luck you're going to live for years and years yet.'

Violet tried to haul herself upright. She was too weak. She fell back on the pillow but managed one last question.

'Who the hell are you?'

'My name's Cameron,' he said. 'Boy Cameron.'

She tried to focus on his face, but the darkness invaded her again and she lost consciousness.

The Garden of Eden

The Forbidden Fruit

'Close your eyes!'

The woman's voice was teasing and full of laughter.

'Why?' the man asked.

'Because I say so.'

He hesitated.

The man never closed his eyes except when he slept and then only when he was safe. It was instinctive. He was both hunter and prey for the other larger and swifter predators of the savannahs – the black-maned lions and the giant sabre-fanged tree leopards which ranged between the forest and the plains.

The woman closed her eyes to heighten her senses. She did so when she scented the breeze, when she felt in the ground for the hidden tubers, when she listened for the noise of the bees and insects which would lead her to their nests.

The man's eyes were always open and alert. His life – and hers too – depended on his sight.

She was telling him to suspend it.

'Why?' he said again, bewildered.

She had never asked anything like this of him before.

She was standing in front of him with her hands behind her back, hiding something.

'Trust me,' she replied.

Still perplexed, he studied her for a moment.

'Are you sure?'

She nodded.

The man bowed his head and closed his eyes. He waited.

'Don't move!'

The man tensed. However odd the instruction, he knew he had to obey it. She might be his companion but she had power over him. She had done from the start.

'Now!'

He started involuntarily then.

Something was cascading down over him. It was liquid and it had the sweet fragrant scent of juice from one of the valley's fruits. Some of the juice trickled over his lips and he licked the drops into his mouth with his tongue. He recognised the taste. The juice came from a plump yellow tsama melon.

At the same moment he felt the woman wind herself round him. She had other melons in both hands and as she pressed herself against him, she was rubbing them over his back, his chest, his stomach, and down between his legs.

He half-broke away from her. He shook his head, shaking off the liquid in sprays that shone in the sunlight and blinking his eyes until he could see again. He gazed at her. The woman was laughing.

'Taste!' she said.

She reached down and picked up another melon. His eyes followed her hand as she bent down. There was a whole pile of fruit on the earth at her feet. She stood up again. He took the melon from her and bit into it.

The fruit was milky yellow-green, fragrant, and the size of an apple. Bemused, the man broke its skin with his teeth. His tongue curled round the sweet juices of the flesh. In the humid heat of the African late-afternoon it tasted wonderfully invigorating and refreshing, but it was no different from any other ripe tsama she'd gathered when the season came round.

Puzzled he took another bite.

Then the man stiffened.

The season. The tsamas fruited in the two moons after the rains. The rains had finished more than six moons ago. There should be no more melons until the rains came again.

He looked at the woman, bewildered.

'Come with me,' she said, her face losing its laughter, now serious.

She led him down to the river.

There on the bank she showed him a small oval plot of red-brown earth, cleared of the river grasses and reeds and planted with clumps of fruit-bearing tsamas. The plot was irrigated by little ditches bringing in water from the river. There were more melons lying on the ground below the tsama plants.

Together with everything else they could hunt or gather there was enough fruit, the man realised, to support them until the rains came round again. Not merely enough for survival, it dawned on him, but enough to provide a surplus.

He turned to the woman. 'How did you learn this?' he asked.

'I watched the elephants,' she said simply. 'I saw where they went, how they broke down the trees, how the land flowered when they had gone and light came in. I gathered some melons and buried them in the earth where the elephants had opened it. When the rains came, they grew. I knew then they needed not only light, but water.'

She lifted her shoulders in a small uncertain shrug.

'Afterwards I buried some more melons here. I gave them water. I waited and they grew. These are the first. I think now melons will grow with light and water even in the hardest of the dry months.'

The woman swung round to him and laughed again. 'I wanted to bathe you in their juice to show you!'

Now the man laughed too, the taste of the juice sweet as honey on his lips.

'I too have something to share. Come.'

Eagerly he tugged her behind him as he hurried up the river bank. It had been a secret, a surprise for the woman. This was the moment to share it.

The man had made a small enclosure in the roots of an overturned tree. Here, protected by a thick hedge of woven thorn branches, he had coralled a young female duiker, a little antelope. He had found her in one of the pit-traps he set in the forest, and was about to dispatch her when he noticed that the creature's belly was swollen with young.

He thought of the woman, and the thought had stayed his hand, not so much for pity, but for the practical reason that it made no sense to kill one prey animal when with a little patience he might have two. Here, in the enclosure which not only imprisoned the little antelope but kept her safe from other predators, he had fed the creature daily, waiting for the moment when she would give birth.

That morning the moment had come.

'Open your eyes,' he said. 'And see what I have done.'

The woman looked, and laughed, and loved him for what he had done.

That night, joyful in the knowledge of what they had made, the man and the woman lay down together as always.

As dawn approached they woke together in the reed nest. Both had been dreaming, dreaming of the moment when they would no longer have to hunt and gather, but could stay in the valley and live off the tending of the land.

Now, for the first time since he'd slept with her, the man's penis was swollen and erect. He rolled urgently on top of the woman and started to part her legs with his hand.

There was no need for further persuasion. Her thighs opened before him and the fluids were flowing down from her, eagerly, hungrily, even before he entered her.

They clung together, rhythmically heaving and swaying until at the same instant they both came to a climax that blotted out the incandescence of the stars and the roaring surge of the river. The man shuddered as the woman screamed. Then, moaning and whimpering the man toppled over on to his side.

The woman lay back too. She reached down between her legs, scooped up some drops of the semen that had been spent outside her body, and licked it from her finger. It was strong, sweet-scented, salty.

She laughed and licked again, tasting once more the flesh, her mother's heart's blood, which had sustained her on the long journey to the valley.

As the sun rose over the valley, the elephant herd began its morning passage down to the river to drink. She listened to the delicate placing of the great grey feet on the earth and the rustle of the thorn bushes as the columns passed by.

Leading them, she knew, would be the herd's matriarch.

As she listened, she smiled. She too was a matriarch. She too was the guardian of the knowledge of all her tribe. But unlike the elephant mother, unlike any other living creature on the planet, she understood the power of that knowledge.

She possessed the secret of life itself.

In her belly was the seed of all humanity. For a moment she wondered whether, when it grew and struggled scarlet-faced and gasping out between her legs, the child would be male or female. It didn't matter. There would be more. Her seed would form new seed, just as the tsama melons the woman had learned to tend, just as the little antelopes the man had learned to husband. As the millennia passed, there would be a thousand thousand two-legged creatures in the valley.

Gently she touched the cheek of the spent and sleeping figure beside her, her fingers soft as the wings of a moth so she didn't wake him.

In the slumbering heat of the garden the woman kept watch over the man, not only knowing but understanding.

The seed within her began to grow.

PART FOUR

Cameron's Story

36

'Who are you?'

Violet's question in the New York hospital echoed through Cameron's head. He had answered it simply and straightforwardly by telling her his name. It was the obvious answer – but it wasn't the whole answer.

To provide that he would have to go back a very long way. Cameron, after all, wasn't his own name.

In his seventy-four years the question of who he really was, and the many other questions that followed from it, had been put to him often. Where do you come from? Where were you born? What was your real name? What language do you like speaking best? How did you start in Africa? What still drives you on? Who do you support? What do you believe in? And is it true that—?'

The last had endless variations.

Like all the other questions it was asked by presidents and prime ministers, journalists, television interviewers, businessmen, the many women who'd been his companion over the years, even by the workers on his estates.

Cameron gave the answers that suited him and his interests at the time.

Frequently they didn't square with other replies he'd given at other periods of his life. It didn't seem to matter. No one was able to pin down the contradictions, and Cameron often wasn't sure of the truth himself. There was only one point on which he consistently and knowingly lied.

He claimed he preferred speaking English, which he did faultlessly in his deep patrician voice without a trace of any accent. It wasn't so. Everyone, someone had told him once, counted, swore, prayed, and made love in their first language.

Silently and privately Cameron calculated, cursed, petitioned Jahveh, and embraced his women in German. In his mind he did it not in the name of Cameron – that was simply a flag of convenience he'd flown over his life – but in his own name.

He was Karl Mayersdorf. He was Jewish. He came from Berlin.

'Look at the lad.' Proud but puzzled, Frau Meyersdorf shook her head. 'Where did he get it from?'

She was standing with her friend, Else, looking out over the municipal garden that ran back from her house in Berlin towards the great thoroughfare of the Kurfurstendam.

The Berlin Olympics had finished a month earlier and her sixteen-year-old son, Karl, was practising sprint starts with a group of his friends in the open space below. All the boys had become obsessed by the games, and the current teenage obsession was to become a member of the team that would go in four years' time to Los Angeles.

Else glanced at her neighbour.

It was strange, certainly, very strange. Frau Meyersdorf and her husband, an accountant, were both small and sallow with dark eyes and tightly curled hair. In total contrast Karl, their only child, was tall and fair-haired with vivid blue eyes. He could almost have been a model for what the Chancellor, Herr Hitler, was demanding as the racial stock of the country's future.

Else wondered briefly about the janitor at apartment block six, just up the street. He was also tall and blond. She dismissed the idea almost as soon as it crossed her mind. Middle-aged, plump and dowdy, Berthe Meyersdorf was hardly likely to have had a fling with someone who'd then been barely an adolescent.

'Just be happy, Berthe,' Else said. 'He's a lovely boy.'

Herr Mayersdorf, Karl's father, thought so too.

Karl wasn't just the centre of the little accountant's life – he virtually *was* Mayersdorf's life. Without his son, existence would have had little meaning or purpose. Until the early-1930s there didn't seem to be any threat to the boy apart from the usual hazards every child faced in simply being born.

With the rise of the Nazi Party and Herr Hitler's accession to the Chancellorship, everything changed.

Jews, at first by innuendo and then openly, became targets for the anger and frustration of Hitler's power-base, Germany's labouring and middle classes. Germany had failed them. Their old proud society was in economic and political chaos. There had to be a reason. It wasn't hard to find. The Jews – the greasy alien usurers and merchants who'd infiltrated themselves into the ancient Aryan land – were bleeding the country to death.

By 1936 vigilante groups of 'heritage' Germans were attacking, wrecking, and burning local Jewish-owned businesses. For a while Mayersdorf felt safe. He had no office. As an accountant he carried his skills round with him in his head as he visited the various companies and families whose affairs he looked after. The few files he needed, he kept in the front room of the little family house.

Then as the tide of anti-Semitic propaganda rose, Mayersdorf realised it made no difference. Soon the black-shirted party thugs would turn their attention to the Jews' homes. He wasn't afraid for himself, nor even for his wife.

He was terrified for Klaus.

One of the families Mayersdorf advised was called Heiligenkreuz. They came from old Prussian stock and lived on a small estate to the north of Berlin. Once they had been rich landowners. Most of their fortune had been squandered over the centuries, but they were still comfortably off – not least, Mayersdorf prided himself, because of his prudent management of their remaining investments.

The von Heiligenkreuzs had been among his first clients. Over the years the elderly husband and wife and their middle-aged widowed daughter had become more than clients – they had become his friends. Early in 1937 Mayersdorf went to see them.

'Graf and Grafin Heiligenkreuz,' he began.

In spite of their long association, the relationship between them remained formal, and he used the old princely titles which they'd inherited from their past.

'This will perhaps sound a strange request. However, we live in strange times. I wish to speak about my son Karl.'

He paused for a moment then went on.

That spring the Heiligenkreuzs' only grandchild, the son of their widowed daughter, had been killed in Berlin when a car driven by three drunken Nazi youths returning from a rally at the Hindenberg stadium had careered off the road and crushed the young man against the street railings. In the wake of the tragedy Mayersdorf had made changes to the grandparents' will. He'd also seen with anguish the grief in the faces of the old couple and the boy's mother.

The boy was the same age as Karl and had looked astonishingly like him – tall, fair-haired, blue-eyed, and athletic. The two boys had come to know each other well. They were members of the same youth adventure club and for the past few summers they'd shared a tent on camping trips in the Black Forest.

'I ask if you will take Karl into your house and allow him to live with you?' Mayersdorf said. 'Naturally I will provide money for his support. To me that is the least of the matter. All I care about is his safety. I fear he is not safe with my wife and me in the times we live in. With you it would be different.'

There was no need to say why it would be different, that the von Heiligenkreuzs were of pure ancient German blood while he and his son came from wandering Jewish stock, the disgraced scapegoat tribe in Hitler's new Germany. They knew that as well as he did. All Mayersdorf could do was to trust to the bond he'd forged with them over the years.

'I have thought deeply about this,' he finished. 'Karl can never replace your grandson, but he is a bold and intelligent boy. It may be that in some way he can fill a small part of the great emptiness left by your grandson's death.'

Graf Heiligenkreuz was silent. He had flowing white hair and a trim Prussian beard. He glanced at his wife. She wrinkled her face in thought. Then she gave a swift emphatic nod.

Heiligenkreuz looked back at Mayersdorf. 'Send Karl to us,' he said.

He went to live with the von Heiligenkreuzs the following day. It was 30 June 1937.

Exactly one week later Hitler's supporters stormed through Berlin burning and looting every Jewish house they could find. The home of the Mayersdorfs had long since been identified by a neighbourhood Nazi activist group as belonging to 'degenerate foreign scum'. It was one of the first to be put to the torch that night. Both the Mayersdorfs died in the blaze that engulfed their house before they could even leave their bedroom.

Many others died in the maddened violence, in the frenzy and blood-lust of the infamous *Krystallnacht*.

Klaus Mayersdorf – Boy Cameron – survived.

37

'Okay, men, what's it going to be?'

The young clerk in the South African passport office in Johannesburg looked up from the form he was completing.

'Doesn't matter a bugger to me, mate,' he grinned. 'You got credentials and clearance, that's all that counts. Napoleon, Frankenstein, Caligula. Just give me a name.'

Klaus thought. 'Cameron,' he said.

'Cameron it is,' the clerk wrote. 'We need a first name too. Any offers?'

Klaus thought again. 'How about "Boy", or has it got to be Christian?'

'Christian, for Christ's sake!' The clerk shook with laughter. 'This is kaffir country, man. Anything goes, or it will be when the monkeys take over. Mr Boy Cameron, that's what I'm writing down. Here.'

He completed the form and tossed it across to Klaus. He signed it and handed it back. Twenty minutes later he walked out on to the streets of Johannesburg with his new passport in his pocket.

He was no longer Klaus Mayersdorf. From now on he was Boy Cameron.

Before their fortune dwindled, one of the benefits the von Heiligenkreuzs had been able to give their daughter was to pay for a nanny for their grandson.

Like many other wealthy European families, they'd employed a Scotswoman. English was an essential social requirement and no one, they knew, spoke better English than the Scots. The woman they hired was called Miss Cameron. She had stayed on in the household after their grandson grew up.

She was still there when Klaus went to live with the von Heiligenkreuzs after their grandson's death.

By then Miss Cameron was old and irritable. She could speak kitchen German, but much preferred to talk in her own language. Whether she was angry or affectionate, she always adressed Klaus as 'Boy'.

'Wipe your boots, boy, for the good Lord's sake,' she would say. Or, 'Eat your dinner, boy, ye wee hen, there's no knowing where the next will come fra'.'

Klaus lived with the von Heiligenkreuzs for four years. Much of his time there was spent in the kitchen with Miss Cameron. In his mind 'boy' became his first name. When asked to give a name for his new passport, Cameron was the obvious choice, with Boy coming before it.

It was now 1945.

Six years earlier, at the start of the Second World War, he had enlisted in the Luftwaffe, the German Air Force. By then he was no longer Klaus Mayersdorf – that was another of the identities he'd been forced to shed. Instead he was Gunther von Heiligenkreuz, the 'nephew' and adopted son of the Prussian family with whom he lived.

He proved to have an exceptional talent for flying. He graduated top of his class of trainee pilots, and was sent out to North Africa with a fighter-bomber squadron providing air support for Rommel's army. For three years he fought with distinction in the desert campaigns, and rose to become one of the Luftwaffe's youngest wing commanders.

Then after the battle of Alamein was lost and the Germans began to retreat before the Allies, he was given a new task. This time it wasn't a combat role, it was in special intelligence.

At the other end of the African continent Germany still had its colony, Namibia. It also had many links with disaffected Boers of German descent in neighbouring South Africa, who'd always opposed their country's support of Britain and cursed the British as devils incarnate.

North Africa might have been lost, but Hitler still clung to the belief that Germany would win the only victory that really mattered – the Battle for Europe. If it did, the post-war years would see a period of unparalleled industrial expansion. For that Germany would need minerals – and the greatest concentration of mineral wealth in the world was in Africa.

Hitler despatched one of his most trusted aides, Wilhelm Meister, a geologist, fanatical Nazi, and brother-in-law of von Ribbentrop, to southern Africa to analyse and report back on its mineral resources. Meister travelled under a Swiss passport. So did the pilot who flew him on his mission.

For the third time in his life he had a new identity.

They started in Namibia. From there they flew to Capetown, and then north to Johannesburg. After Johannesburg they headed north again for Bechuanaland, then east to Rhodesia, north once more to Kenya, and back south-west to Uganda. At every stop they had clandestine meetings with groups of Germany's supporters. In Nairobi they stayed at the famous bastion of Britain's African empire, the Muthaiga Club.

Every white settler who dined with them there swore undying hatred of Churchill and drank to the health of Herr Hitler. The German Chancellor knew what to do with the blacks, and Rommel was a gentleman. Churchill was at best mad and at worst a communist.

'I believe we have covered it all,' Meister said to Klaus as the plane taxied to a halt at Johannesburg again, and they waited to be called to the marshalling area for disembarcation. 'With this the Führer knows everything.'

He tapped the bulging leather briefcase on his knees.

Meister was an obsessive note-taker. The dossier he'd assembled, together with its maps and secret data, contained the most detailed and comprehensive package of information about southern Africa's minerals that had probably ever been compiled. As a weapon in the economic war that would surely follow the combat on land it would literally be priceless – whoever won the military battles.

Through his earphones Klaus received instructions to enter an unloading bay.

He taxied forward again and stopped. He and Meister climbed down the steps on to the tarmac. They cleared customs, took a taxi into the centre of Johannesburg, and checked into separate rooms in a hotel near the Swiss embassy – the Swiss were acting for Germany as what the diplomatic world called a 'post-box' until the war ended.

Klaus was just emerging from a shower when he heard a knock on his door. He knotted a towel round his waist and answered it. Meister was standing outside.

'I have arranged a meeting with our chargé d'affaires for nine tomorrow morning,' Meister said. 'The Swiss accommodate him in the Embassy. He will arrange secure transport of my report to Berlin. For tonight I will leave it with you. You will remain here and keep it safely.'

Meister handed him the briefcase. 'You have done well, Gunther. I will personally make sure the Führer knows. We are both due some relaxation, but I think my white hairs give me priority.'

He smiled.

Klaus gazed at him in astonishment. Meister was wearing eye-shadow, his cheeks were rouged, and there was a light patina of coral-coloured lipstick over his mouth. Klaus had travelled and lived with the man for five months, and had never had the slightest suspicion. Now he knew. Meister was a homosexual.

He was going out into the Johannesburg night to celebrate the end of their mission by picking up a homosexual partner.

Klaus took the briefcase. He was about to say: 'Please be careful, Herr Meister, Johannesburg is a dangerous city.' He never had the chance. Meister closed the door and was gone.

Klaus stowed the briefcase under his bed. Then with the towel still knotted round his waist, he gazed bewildered out of the window.

The police called him at four in the morning.

A white man had been found stabbed to death in a Johannesburg suburb, notorious as a place where the city's male prostitutes serviced their clients. Most of the man's possessions had been stolen, but the police had found a hotel registration slip which gave the name of his companion.

Klaus dressed and went down to the police station. He identified Meister in the police morgue and gave a brief statement about how they came to be together. Then he was allowed to leave. Back in his hotel bedroom he pulled out the briefcase and began to study its contents.

He was still working through the papers when the telephone rang. It was the German chargé d'affaires calling from the Swiss embassy.

'I am looking for Herr Meister,' the voice said. 'He was due here almost an hour ago. The switchboard referred me to you. Can you tell me if there is a problem?'

Klaus glanced at his watch. It was nearly ten am. He had been up all night and he had entirely forgotten about the appointment.

'Yes, I'm afraid there is,' he replied. 'There has been a tragedy. Herr Meister died last night in what appears to have been a savage and senseless murder.'

Klaus glanced at the papers from the briefcase strewn round him on the bed.

'Everything with him was stolen. Perhaps I can come down and tell you what little I know.'

Klaus walked the three blocks to the Swiss Embassy.

The German chargé d'affaires, an alert balding young man with a crisp manner and cold questioning eyes, had already spoken to the Johannesburg police department. They confirmed what Klaus had said. The young man still wasn't satisfied.

'Herr Meister was bringing us certain papers, important papers,' he said. 'Where are they?'

'I was only his pilot.' Klaus shrugged. 'Maybe he left them in his room? I would not know.'

'The police have searched his room. They are not there.'

'Then he must have had them with him when he was killed. No doubt his murderers disposed of them along with everything else.'

'Yes.'

The bald young man rubbed his chin. He still wasn't happy, Klaus knew that. He also knew there was nothing else the diplomat could do.

'Thank you. I will contact you if anything else emerges.'

He stood up and held out his hand.

Klaus knew he'd been dismissed from the German's own

line of inquiry into the disappearance of Meister's dossier. The young diplomat might have finished with him. Klaus hadn't finished with the young diplomat.

'I travelled with Herr Meister under a temporary Swiss passport,' he said.

'Yes?'

'It expires next week. I will have to stay here for at least ten days until the police complete their inquiries. By then I will need other documents to travel on. I serve the Reich. I am entitled to ask for them.'

'Ah.' The young man rubbed his face again. 'Of course. Here.'

He pulled out a piece of headed paper, wrote a few lines, and signed the page with a flourish. He put the letter in an envelope and gave it to Klaus.

'The head of the passport section in the Foreign Affairs ministry is a Menheer Blaukampf. He is a good friend of ours. Take this to him. He has the authority to issue passports at his discretion, British passports of course. I have no doubt he will give you one.'

'Thank you, mein Herr.'

Klaus clicked his heels in the gesture of respect he'd been taught in the pilot training school.

Three days later he walked out of the Foreign Affairs ministry with his new passport in his pocket.

He was no longer Klaus Mayersdorf. He wasn't Gunther von Heiligenkreuz. He wasn't Otto Schwarz, the Swiss-German pilot who'd flown Herr Meister. He was Boy Cameron, a British-South African squadron leader who'd been flying missions against von Ludendorf's troops on their retreat through Tanzania.

He went back to his hotel.

He sat down at the dressing-table in his room and wrote his new name over and over again on the notepaper the hotel provided for its guests. At the end of an hour his wrist was shaking with tiredness and he'd used up every scrap of the paper. In his mind he'd also obliterated every trace of his former identities.

He stood up wearily and walked downstairs to eat. In the

restaurant the waiter took his order and asked him what room the bill should be booked to.

'Number 429,' he said.

The waiter tore off the small white docket and placed it on the table for him to sign.

Unhesitatingly he signed it 'Boy Cameron'.

Two weeks later Cameron flew north.

The police investigation into Meister's death had got nowhere. It was obvious Cameron had nothing to do with the murder, and equally obvious that the German had been killed for his money by one of the gangs that roamed the quarter and preyed on the rich homosexuals who went there to pick up young black boys.

'You want to bugger, man,' the Afrikaans airport police sergeant said laconically as he prepared Cameron's clearance-to-leave paper, 'you liable to get buggered. I got five sons, man. Know what I tell them? Stay away from bum-boys. You can bugger them, but they bugger you worse. Understand me, man?'

Cameron didn't answer. He watched the sergeant complete the form and stamp it.

'Bum-boys!' the sergeant spat. 'Fucking perverts!'

He handed over a copy of the clearance document. Cameron stuffed the paper into a pocket and walked out. He climbed into the plane and took off.

The plane, a twin-engined Messerschmitt 224, was on charter from Namib-Luft. The monthly charter and fuel bills were being sent to the German High Commission in Windhoek. As far as Cameron knew they would continue to be paid indefinitely, or at least until Berlin, which had authorised the charter, countermanded its instructions.

Cameron wasn't concerned about the long-term, the medium-term, or even the short-term. He was only concerned about the next twenty-four hours. At the end of that, he'd have no need of the plane again.

He set his compass and headed north.

On the passenger seat beside was the leather briefcase containing Meister's dossier.

38

From his travels with Meister, Cameron knew that dotted across southern and eastern Africa, often far out in the wilds, there were a number of makeshift runways.

They had been built by companies prospecting for minerals, and he and Meister had used several of them on their criss-crossing of the continent. Many, although abandoned and far from any human settlement, were still serviceable, and Meister had recorded them all on his maps.

Cameron's plan was to land on one of them within reasonable distance of the Kenyan capital of Nairobi, set fire to the plane, and make his way on foot into the city.

The young diplomat in Johannesburg might still blindly believe in victory for Germany. To Cameron it was a fantasy. That had become clearer and clearer with every report of the Axis defeats that reached him and Meister along their way. The invasion of Normandy was the last nail in the coffin the Allies had built to bury the Reich.

The formal end might not come for months or even a year yet, but the war was already effectively over and Germany had lost.

The impending collapse of the Reich barely touched Cameron. When he thought about it at all, he knew Hitler's Reich was just another 'system' and that he, socially, politically, and racially, was an outsider from all systems. Hitler had murdered his mother and father, but the Nazis had advanced his own career to a degree that would never have been possible if he'd simply grown up as the son of the little accountant.

Cameron was a Jew, and by instinct and upbringing a trader.

His father had supplemented the family's income from his accountancy by dealing in bonds and notes of hand. Cameron had learnt from him. He was determined, ruthlessly determined, to become rich. Even more than that, he was a survivor. The Jews had always had to be that.

Cameron was going to survive.

In everything else, his country, his family, his background, the war, he had little interest. He wasn't even moved by the emerging story of the holocaust. Coldly and dispassionately he was determined to rise from the ruins of the Reich and make his fortune. He was going to deal and manipulate, cajole and coerce, plot and bribe, lie, bully and deceive in a world that had been changing since his childhood and now, as the war approached its end, was changing again almost daily.

His father had been a loser, so had his entire race. Cameron was going to win. And he knew how.

What hadn't changed as peace came closer was the massive economic reconstruction which would follow the war's end. Germany wouldn't be directing it now, that would fall to the victorious Allies, to the United States, Britain, and France. They would still need what Hitler had sent Meister out to reconnoitre – Africa's minerals.

The secrets of those were with him as he flew north.

He intended to present himself in Nairobi as a pilot of the South African Air Force whose plane had crash-landed in the wilderness on an intelligence mission. He had all the supporting documents and spoke English with the light Scottish accent his name suggested. If anyone checked on his story – in the turmoil of the war's imminent finish it was unlikely they would – the records in Johannesburg would bear him out.

Cameron would stay in Nairobi until peace was declared. Then armed with Meister's research he would set to work. It might take him ten, twenty, or even thirty years but at the end, he was sure, he'd have made himself one of the richest men in Africa.

Cameron was right, although it didn't happen exactly according to his plan.

*   *   *

He saw the first sign of the storm as he flew across the border between the old British colonies of Bechuanaland and Nyasaland.

The clouds rose in front of him in great cones of rolling blackness with spears of forked lightning flickering between them. Within minutes the Messerschmitt's cockpit canopy was sheeted with driving rain. Cameron pulled the joystick back. Although he'd never experienced one before, he'd heard about the violence of southern Africa's sudden devastating storms.

The conventional wisdom of veteran African pilots was to gain altitude and fly over the storm's centre. The plane should have slanted upwards as he moved the controls. It didn't. Instead the nose cone dipped. Cameron glanced to left and right. The starboard engine seemed to be functioning normally, but a stream of scarlet sparks was spiralling away on the port side.

As Cameron watched, the port propeller shuddered to a stop and sheared off.

His eyes flashed to the instrument panel. It told him something he already knew – the port engine had gone – and something he didn't. The starboard engine was also faltering.

He fought to regain control of the plane. It was still plunging down, but by forcing the joystick back against his ribs he managed to slow the angle of its descent until the flight path was almost level.

The next two hours were the worst of his life.

The canopy was blind.

The storm lashed and savaged the plane like some frenzied wild animal. The one remaining engine stuttered, choked, and fell silent, and then each time Cameron thought it had failed completely, it suddenly coughed back into life again. All the time they were losing height. In the few moments when he could think about it, he guessed the cause.

At his last refuelling point, the tanks had been filled with a rogue consignment of aero-fuel. He knew it could happen in Africa's remote airfields, and had been warned against it.

In his urgency to get to Nairobi with Meister's briefcase, he hadn't made his usual careful checks.

Now he was paying the price.

Somehow the plane kept airborne and he flew on. Suddenly, as quickly as the storm had enfolded him, he burst out of it into the clear golden light of an African late-afternoon. Cameron had no idea where he was, although from the position of the setting sun the storm had hurled him far to the west of the strip that had been his intended destination.

All he knew was that he was barely skimming the tree tops. He fought for the last time to hold up the flaps, and searched for a place where he could try to put down. He saw a winding river bed below with a cluster of mountains beyond. Beside the river were banks of earth trampled flat by great rounded footprints.

Cameron aimed for one of the banks.

As it turned out he had no choice. The engine spluttered and fell silent for what he knew was the last time. He released the wheels and dipped down. It was the last response he got from the controls. The power-generating alternator had failed and the electrical supply had been drained dry. The wheels touched the ground, and bit into the crusted surface of sand.

Cameron pumped helplessly at the brakes.

Nothing happened. The plane skidded forward. Its port wing slashed against a tall acacia tree, and the plane was thrown on to its back. A moment later its tanks, still half-full of the contaminated aero-fuel, exploded.

Just before they did, Cameron managed to unbuckle his harness and leap clear.

As he jumped he grabbed Meister's briefcase.

The explosion blew him into the river. He surfaced with his lungs heaving and water spraying from his mouth. The heat from the wreckage of the blazing plane scorched his face. He stumbled away and waded out. He was stunned and dizzy, blood was pouring down his face, and he sensed one of his legs was broken. The briefcase was still in his hand.

He collapsed on the bank.

It was dark before he'd recovered enough to climb to his

feet. He stumbled and lurched. His leg throbbed painfully and he clung to a tree for support. Cameron peered into the night. In the far distance, in the direction where he remembered noticing the mountains just before he crashed, he could make out what he thought was a light.

He picked up a couple of dry branches from the shore. Using them as crutches to support him, he set off towards the light.

'If it's any comfort,' Finlay Hampton said, 'Dr Robbins reckons you'll live. Some might say that's no consolation at all. You may be one of those sods who disagree.'

He chuckled.

Cameron peered round.

He was lying on a wicker bed in a white-walled rondavel, the elegant European version of an African hut, with his leg encased in plaster propped out in front of him. A tall and burly grey-haired European, the man who'd spoken to him, was standing at the bed's foot and an African servant in a white robe was waiting by the door.

'Where am I?' he asked, confused.

Hampton laughed.

'The Laager game lodge,' he said. 'North of Nyeri in the Aberdare Mountains. You hobbled up here with your broken leg a couple of days ago, remember? A nasty double fracture, Dr Robbins said. Anyway, he did his bone-setting tricks and knocked you out with some of his magic pills to see you got some rest.'

It started to come back to Cameron now.

The flight from Johannesburg, the storm and the crash, the four days and nights he'd spent swinging himself on his crutches towards the cluster of lights in the mountains. The journey had been painful and agonisingly slow. Heat and flies had tormented him by day, at night the cold had been icy, and several times he'd lapsed into unconsciousness.

He couldn't remember his arrival but suddenly felt ravenously hungry. He said so and Hampton spoke to the Kikuyu servant.

'Joshua will bring you up a tray. Two days more and you should be well enough to eat downstairs with me.'

He went out.

The servant came back with a tray of food. Cameron ate and slumped back on his pillow. Just before he slept again he managed to heave himself upright and search the room with his eyes. The briefcase was on the chair beside his bed.

He closed his eyes in relief.

'I can have you run down into Nairobi,' Hampton said, 'or you can stay up here until Dr Robbins is ready to take the plaster off. Take your pick. If you want my advice, stay here. Nairobi's a hell-hole at this time of year and the Doc's the best in Kenya – Nairobi's got no one to touch him.'

It was five nights later.

Cameron was sitting with Hampton on the verandah overlooking the forest. They'd finished dinner and the barefoot Joshua was padding round the table removing the dishes. Hampton was leaning back in his chair with a cigar in his mouth and a glass of whisky at his elbow.

Cameron glanced up at the stars shining between the slats of the verandah roof.

The night was cool and quiet and sweet-smelling. His leg was healing but he still felt sharp twinges when he moved. Nairobi, he knew, could be a noisy furnace in the heat of the African summer. He had no reason to go down to the plains until the war was finally over. From the last reports he'd listened to on Hampton's wireless, that was still several months away. Until then he was better off where he was.

'If it's no inconvenience,' Cameron said hesitantly, he'd learnt the hotel was officially closed for the war, 'I'd very much like to stay on.'

'Bugger inconvenience! Look at all these idle sods like Joshua. Not enough to do. What the hell's going to happen when the visitors come back? Getting out of practice, all of you lazy swine, aren't you?'

He waved his cigar benevolently at the Kikuyu. Joshua grinned.

'Yes, bwana.'

'Of course you are.' Hampton turned back to Cameron. 'I'd be glad of the company. In fact, after four years' closure I got rather a taste for it again just before you pitched up. I had a wartime refugee party landed on me. A delightful young woman with her servants and a couple of children. Regular little monkeys, they were, but she was a real handicap chaser. When the stallion's away, the fillies will play.'

He winked.

'At least that's what randy old men like me like to believe. It never works out of course but at least we can dream. And when we're not dreaming it stimulates us to get on with our own pet projects.'

Hampton paused. Then he asked abruptly, 'Ever thought where man comes from, Cameron?'

Startled, he shook his head.

If the question had ever entered his mind, it had only been through his childhood reading of the Jewish scriptures and then through Hitler's pronouncements about the origins of the Aryan people. Strangely, both in their different ways fitted together. People were naturally white, or at least olive-skinned. They'd been so from the beginning of time.

The Jews might be degenerate, corrupt, hateful, the Germans might be the noble breed nature had designed to dominate and replace them, but both came from the same root-stock – and that stock was white.

'Come with me.'

Hampton led Cameron, swinging on a pair of proper crutches now, through to his office at the front of the hotel. Running along one wall was a large glass-fronted display cabinet. Hampton opened its door. He took something out and handed it to Cameron.

'I'll wager you don't know what that is.'

Cameron studied the object. It was obviously bone and there were worn empty sockets which might once have held teeth.

'An animal's jaw?' he suggested.

'Not bad. Except it's not an animal's, it belonged to a man,' Hampton answered. 'Old Ngoro, my tracker, found it out in the back country beyond the mountains. I sent it down to

Professor Dart in Jo'burg. He came up here once years ago and got me interested in the whole business of where the human race began. Dart says that's one of the most interesting finds to come his way. He reckons it could be a million years old.'

Cameron looked at it again in astonishment. It had never occurred to him man could be a million years old.

'But how's it survived that long?' he asked.

'It belonged to a hunter, that's Dart's theory. He may have been killed by an animal. Before other animals broke up his body, there was probably a flash flood and he got buried in silt. The silt built up over hundreds of thousands of years, then it began to wash away again until he came back to the surface and Ngoro found his jaw.'

Cameron placed the bone back in the cabinet as carefully as if it had been porcelain. The shelves were full of other fragments of bone together with stone blades and axe-heads.

Cameron glanced round the room. A table by Hampton's desk was piled with books and journals. The author's name on the topmost book was Professor Raymond Dart.

He heaved himself over and picked it up.

'Could I borrow this?' he asked after flicking through the pages for a moment.

'Stirred your interest, have I?' Hampton chuckled. 'By all means, and anything else, too. Up here there's not much to do but read. Just be warned. You get involved in bones and stones, as Dart calls them, and they'll never let you go.'

Cameron went back to his rondavel with the book under his arm.

At three the following morning he was still reading by the light of his paraffin lamp.

39

Cameron knew that Meister's dossier would change his life.

It came about because of a calculated decision on his own part once he knew Meister was dead, and because only he, Cameron, knew what the dossier contained. There was nothing careful or calculated about his reaction to something else that happened in the very same week, something which was to affect his life just as deeply.

Cameron didn't even make a decision about it.

It crept up on him, it insinuated itself into his mind, almost without his knowing. Years afterwards he still wasn't sure how it happened. All he knew was that just as Hampton had laughingly warned him, it swiftly turned into an obsession.

Cameron became fascinated by the question of man's origins.

Possibly, he sometimes thought, it had its roots in his own exposure from childhood on to Herr Hitler's maddened paranoia about the issue of race. By Hitler's criteria Cameron had done something extraordinary, even unique. He had crossed between not just two worlds but four.

His physique, tall and powerful, fair-haired and blue-eyed, had allowed him to change from a Jew into an Aryan. And then language and an accident of fate had allowed him to change once more from a Swiss into a Briton.

Sometimes Cameron would speculate again that it was due to the isolation of the months he spent at the Laager. Hampton was right. There was little to do there except read, particularly for someone virtually immobilised by a broken leg. Cameron read everything in Hampton's library from Professor Dart to the scholarly journals Walker had sent up from the Cape.

Or perhaps it was due to Hampton himself. They met every night for dinner. Almost always the talk turned to the subject Hampton had introduced the first evening they sat down together.

'So, Cameron,' he would say, 'what have those irritating buggers, the bones and stones, come up with today?'

Cameron would tell him what he'd been reading. They would discuss it, argue, sometimes quarrel – Hampton was naturally quick-tempered and after a few whiskies was liable to start shouting.

Always by the next night they'd have made peace again. There was a curious innocence, Cameron discovered, in the old hunter. He venerated scholarship and Professor Dart was his idol, but he believed himself totally uneducated. Even as he was about to launch into a tirade about some particularly obscure branch of palaeontology, he'd protest he knew nothing about it.

'I can't even pronounce the bloody words, young man, let alone spell them,' he'd say. 'But let me tell you this . . .'

He'd start to talk.

In fact Hampton had one of the shrewdest minds and certainly the sharpest eyes Cameron had ever encountered. When Dr Robbins took the plaster off Cameron's leg, Hampton began to take him out for short walks in the surrounding forest.

He saw things in the landscape that Cameron knew he'd never have noticed if he'd spent his entire life there. The old hunter would spot what to Cameron, even if he'd seen it, was an apparently random scratch in the earth. Hampton would squat on his haunches for a moment to examine it. Then he'd stand and explain.

'The pug-mark of a female leopard. The dew and the breeze have broken the print down, but she came by here at dawn seventy-two hours ago. She'd been hunting but without any luck. She was hungry and restless. Take a look round and you'll find she'll have claw-marked some of the trees.'

Hampton moved on down the path peering from side to side.

'There.'

Pointing, he guided Cameron's gaze to an acacia trunk. Cameron could just make out some faint incisions where the bark had been raked at shoulder height.

'That's a warning for other leopards to stay out of her territory. And because she's a female, I'd guess she's coming into oestrus. They're always most aggressive then. Look!'

He stooped and picked up a dead leaf.

Cameron gazed at it. It meant nothing to him at all. It was just a leaf, brown and veined and curling from where the sun had caught it as the light slanted down through the branches.

'Here, right by the stem.' Hampton pressed it into Cameron's hand. 'That little brown spot. It may look like leaf-rust to you, but it's not. It's dried blood from uterine discharge.'

Even with the leaf in his hand Cameron could barely make out the speck. The old hunter had spotted it from eight feet away.

Cameron stared at him. 'How do you know?'

Hampton laughed. 'I was a hunter. Good hunters learn, bad ones don't. That's why I sleep at the Laager, and the others have beds three feet under in Nanyuki churchyard. You haven't met Ngoro yet, have you?'

Cameron shook his head.

'I'll see you meet the old rascal. Compared to him, I'm a novice. He'd be able to tell you that damn' leopard's birthday, the size of her headache, the names she gave her cubs, and what she feels about tribal land rights. But compared to early man all of us are children, even Ngoro.'

He paused. His craggy square-jawed face was wrinkled in thought and his eyes were narrowed.

'Perhaps that's why I became interested. That first man, he knew so damn *much*. He had to to survive. He must have had secrets he kept to himself. If we knew who he was, maybe bit by bit we could learn his secrets. It might even lead us to the secret of life itself.'

Hampton stopped again. He lifted his head and laughed.

It was a great jovial sound that rang round the trees. Cameron sensed it was produced to cover his embarrassment at what he'd just said. Hampton was not only more intelligent than he portrayed himself. He was also, Cameron realised, much more sensitive.

'I'm just a sentimental old buffoon who thinks he might have killed more animals if his field-craft had been better,' he continued to chuckle. 'Ask Ngoro. He'll tell you the truth. He thinks I'm an idiot. Christ, after more than forty years with me, he should know!'

Cameron met Ngoro the following day.

Hampton led Cameron out of the hotel and on to the wooden porch. Ngoro was squatting on the beaten earth below with his spear upright in the ground beside him. As the two men appeared the old Masai rose to his feet.

'I salute you, Ngoro,' Hampton said.

'I salute you too, bwana,' he replied.

'Ngoro, this is bwana Cameron,' the hunter went on. 'I've woven the old spell and got him interested in our bones and stones. I want you to tell him what the Masai think.'

Ngoro nodded. 'Very good, bwana.'

'Then I'll leave the two of you to it.'

Hampton went back inside and Cameron sat down in the shade of the porch. Ngoro pulled his spear from the ground and hammered it fiercely back into the earth.

'I am Ngoro. I am Masai, so listen well,' he said.

The old man squatted down in the sunlight outside the rim of the shadow and began to speak.

Ngoro talked for two hours. He told Cameron the same legends he'd told Violet and Billy only a few weeks before about the beginning of the world, about the lion and the clay he had baked and the elephant he had made. He spoke in the same chanting voice and used exactly the same words and images that had been passed down through generation after generation of his tribe.

Cameron listened as mesmerised as the children had been.

When Ngoro finished Cameron thanked him. He went back to his rondavel and lay down on his bed. His mind was spinning.

Ngoro's stories were so vivid and detailed they had to come from somewhere. They might have been changed and elaborated over the millennia until now they were told in symbols like the lion and the clay oven. But was it just possible that somewhere in the remote past, in the pre-history of man's beginnings, they were rooted in fact.

Was it even possible, it suddenly occurred to him, that all the world's creation myths had a common source – even the greatest of them all, the one he'd been taught as a child, the legend of Adam and Eve, of the serpent and the apple?

Could the Garden of Eden once have been historical reality?

It was an extraordinary, dizzying thought. Cameron raised it that night at dinner on the verandah.

'I knew old Ngoro would tickle your fancy,' Hampton laughed. 'Yes, I think it's possible but then, as I told you, I'm just an ignorant old buffoon with an old man's hobby. You should be asking Dart and the other younger pundits.'

He paused. 'You could do better than that. You could make yourself rich and try to find it. You'll need to be rich. Over the next fifty years, I'd guess, we'll learn more about the past than we have in all of recorded time. That's what Dart says. It's going to mean digging and expeditions and collecting, and then hiring bright sparks in universities to sort it all out and stitch the stuff together. In a word it's going to mean money.'

Hampton chuckled. 'Have you got a secret path to a fortune, Cameron? You'll need one, man.'

He thought of Meister's dossier tucked safely away under his bed in the rondavel.

He smiled but didn't answer. Instead he said, 'Ngoro says the Masai believe it all began in the back country out beyond here, where he found that jaw-bone.'

'The valley of the elephants?' Hampton nodded. 'It's one of the oldest legends in Kenya. I used to run safaris there.'

'Ngoro said a white woman had bought the land?'

The old hunter nodded again.

'Remember that delightful lady I told you about, the one who was here a few months ago? Ngoro took her daughter and another young scamp out to the valley. Little Violet fell in love with the elephants. Mrs Somerset, her mother, is a very rich woman. She wanted to do something to mark their visit here. I suggested she bought the land for her daughter.'

Hampton drank from his glass of whisky.

'I said it was a good investment. I believe it is. There was something else.' He grinned, slightly shame-faced. 'None of us knows what's going to happen when the war's over. Christ, if you believe everything you hear, one day we could even end up with the blacks running this country. They might try to expropriate land. The Somersets are an influential bunch. If anyone's going to protect the valley, it'll be a member of a family like theirs.'

He spread out his legs and sat back defiantly.

Cameron didn't notice. He was writing the name Somerset down in his notebook. He looked up.

'I'd really like to see the valley.'

'Old Ngoro can take you out there, but it's one hell of a trek.' Hampton glanced at his leg. 'Wait until you've had a few weeks to build up the muscles again.'

Joshua padded in with the silver coffee tray, and they returned to discussing the legends of the Masai.

Cameron never went to the valley.

He spent three weeks more walking and exercising in the forest round the Laager. On the very evening he was about to suggest to Hampton he was ready to make the journey with Ngoro, the news came through on the BBC's World Service – Hampton tuned into it every night – that the war was over.

Hitler, it seemed, had committed suicide in a bunker in Berlin.

The last of the German resistance had crumbled and the Allies had won. In a short report after the news, the BBC commentator said the Allies' immediate priority would be the reconstruction of the ruined western European economies. Cameron knew as he listened what that would mean for Africa's mineral resources.

Next morning Cameron headed down towards Nairobi in one of the Laager's four-wheel trucks with Meister's briefcase once again on the seat beside him.

He left the old hunter and the lodge in the mountains with

a driving determination – to make his fortune – and also with an obsession that had been born in the Aberdares. Cameron wanted to solve the riddles of the bones and stones. He wanted to know where man had been born. He wanted to find the Garden of Eden.

The fortune he desired was part and parcel of the quest.

40

The man was still there when Violet woke again.

She opened her eyes and blinked as she scanned the room, her head turning drowsily on the pillow. He'd been sitting when she saw him first. This time he was standing by the window. Above him on the wall was a clock. Violet frowned. Dimly she remembered it had been midday when she saw the clock's hands last. Now they showed it was almost six.

If he hadn't left the room, he must have been there for six hours. She stared at him.

He was a tall heavily-built man wearing a white silk shirt, a silk tie, and an expensive dark suit with a flamboyant gold and scarlet handkerchief tucked into the breast pocket. Violet knew about men's suits, she'd paid for enough of them in her time. This one had originated in Burlington Street or Savile Row, the home of the best men's tailors in the world. The handkerchief and tie could only come from Hermes or Charvet.

He was in his late-sixties, she guessed. He had grey-white hair, a strong deeply lined face, and his hands were mottled with age spots, but there was an extraordinary vigour and alertness in the way he held himself. Most striking of all were his eyes.

They were pale blue and fringed with long grey lashes, and more penetrating than any eyes Violet had ever seen. He had seen her wake and the intensity with which he was gazing at her was almost frightening.

'Who are you?' she asked.

He stood up and came over to the bed. Even before he answered, Violet remembered. He was called Cameron, Boy

288

Cameron. He'd told her so when she saw him first before she drifted back into sleep.

He repeated his name and smiled. 'How are you feeling, Violet, if I may call you that?'

The effect of the smile – warm and magnetic and direct – combined with the almost-tangible strength of his physical presence was somehow immensely reassuring.

She knew she had lived and dreamed nightmares, like the raw needle punctures on her arms, that were too close for her to look at. This man, this stranger, didn't belong to them. He belonged to another safer world.

'Of course,' she said. 'Do I know you?'

She stopped.

The scent of flowers was billowing towards her. Startled she managed to prop herself up. She gazed round. The room was heaped with blossoms: roses, lilies, lavender, phlox, They were everywhere – on the tables, on the shelves, even the floor.

Her glance swept across them. She sank back on the pillow. Wide-eyed her gaze returned to Cameron's face.

'Are they from you?'

He didn't answer directly, simply said, 'I've always believed flowers help heal people.' Cameron smiled again. 'And in answer to your other question, yes, in a way we do know each other. At least we've met. We had dinner together some months ago in the house of your friend, Naomi Rothschild.'

Violet struggled to remember.

Naomi Rothschild had been a friend of hers for years. She must have dined at Naomi's elegant brownstone house on the upper east side on countless occasions. She tried to recollect meeting Cameron there. She couldn't. Like so much else it had been plucked down into oblivion in the dark whirlpool of the past.

'I don't understand,' Violet said. 'Why are you here?'

Cameron was silent for several moments. 'Maybe because I like floating life-rafts to people,' he said. 'Bold and strange and interesting and beautiful people who wade out of their depth into rivers where they can't swim. I think you're one of them.'

He walked away from the bed.

At the door he turned. 'I'll be back tomorrow with a life-raft in my pocket. I'm going to toss it on to a river we both know. If you don't grasp it,' Cameron looked steadily at her, 'at least there'll be some more flowers.'

The door closed.

Violet lay back on the bed. A great surging wind seemed to have swept through the room, cleansing, exhilarating, and terrifying. She felt numb and bewildered.

The night nurse came in with pills to make her sleep. Violet swallowed them but it was hours before she slept. She lay awake trying to work out what river she and Cameron might conceivably both know. There was none she could think of.

When she did finally sleep she dreamt. For the first time in years she dreamt of Billy and the elephants coming down to drink in the valley.

Next morning Violet felt better. As soon as she woke she telephoned her friend Naomi.

'Violet, for God's sake, where are you?'

There was alarm in Naomi's voice. 'Everyone's been looking for you. There's been no reply from your apartment for weeks. Someone, I think it was Morton, went round and the doorman said you never came back after Peggy Krantz's party. Are you all right?'

Violet tried to remember Peggy Krantz and her party. Like so much else over the past months it had vanished.

'I'm fine, Naomi,' she answered. 'Or at least I will be soon. Right now I'm in hospital. I'm afraid I dropped off the edge again. It's going to be the last time, I promise you.'

Violet knew she didn't have to explain what she meant by 'dropping off the edge'. It was a phrase she used to her friends to describe what happened to her when the darkness seemed to invade her life as it had done more and more often lately. Naomi was one of her oldest friends. She'd know exactly what had happened.

'But, darling,' her alarm increased, 'I must come and see you immediately.'

'No, Naomi,' Violet interrupted her. 'Not just for a while.

It's sweet of you, but please give me a little time to get well first.'

'There must be something I can do.' Naomi insisted. 'Is there anything I can send you?'

'Darling, there's something you can *tell* me,' Violet said. 'I've had a visitor, a man called Boy Cameron. He's been very kind. He says he met me with you. I vaguely know his name, but I can't remember anything about him. Who is he?'

'Boy Cameron? Darling, of course you know who he is! I put you next to him at dinner, I knew you'd like each other. Oh, Violet, don't you remember? He's the tycoon from Africa.'

Violet lay back and listened as Naomi explained. She was a gossip, but a wonderfully well-informed one.

Violet had been almost right about Cameron's age. He was apparently a little older than she'd thought, in his early seventies perhaps, although like so much else his age was something of a mystery. He hadn't been born with the name Cameron, he'd acknowledged that often in interviews. His original nationality was German.

According to his own account – and no one had found anything to contradict it – he'd been a pilot with the Luftwaffe in the North African desert. Disgusted by the wartime reports that began to filter out from Germany about Hitler's genocidal pogroms against the Jews and gypsies, he'd defected to the Allied side well before the war's end and had been granted British nationality in South Africa.

After the war the path of his career was clearer. In the past forty years he'd made himself one of the richest men on the African continent.

His fortune was built on minerals. No one knew how he did it but Cameron seemed to have some instinct, some magic touch, about where Africa's wealth was hidden. Almost every time one of the west's great mining companies discovered a new mineral vein, it would turn out that Cameron had a concession over the area. He would sell out his rights – he was a ruthless bargainer – and move on.

Minerals still remained the main source of his wealth, but his business empire had expanded far beyond them. He had holdings in ranches, timber, shipping, newspapers, property, and a dozen other activities. Rumours about the way he worked abounded. He was known to be a close friend of several African presidents, and, it was whispered, paid them huge bribes to advance the interests of what had once been a tiny private company, and now was a giant international conglomerate.

'What else can I tell you?' Naomi said.

She loved talking and prided herself on knowing everything concerning the person she was talking about.

'His private life's a mystery, too. He's tall, handsome, charming – charismatic is the word, but you'd know that, darling, wouldn't you? He's never married and I don't *think* he likes boys, although one can never be sure. He's just a delightful and intriguing enigma.'

Naomi paused. Violet knew she was searching for something else to say. Naomi was always reluctant to bring her stories to an end.

'Yes, of course,' she added eagerly. 'How could I have forgotten? He has a hobby, or rather a passion, so people say. He collects things from the past, old bones and flints and spears and so on. I can't think why. He'd be much better off with paintings. Now, there I could help him . . .'

She finally stopped.

'Thank you, darling,' Violet said. 'As always you've been wonderful. Everything I wanted to know and almost more. I'll call you just as soon as I'm up to a visit.'

She put the telephone down without giving Naomi a chance to add anything else.

As she lay back Violet smiled. She'd even managed to avoid telling Naomi where she was. There was only one person she wanted to know that, and he already did.

Cameron came back at midday. He glanced round the room and frowned.

Without even saying hullo he asked, 'Where's your telephone?'

It wasn't so much a question as a demand. Surprised, Violet pointed to the telephone by her bed. He strode across, picked it up, and dialled.

'Morgan?'

When he'd spoken to her the day before Cameron's voice had been warm and gentle. Now, although still deep and resonant, it was angry.

'It's me,' he went on. 'I'm at the hospital with Mrs Somerset. I said I wanted her flowers changed every day. They haven't been. What the hell's happened?'

He listened for a moment. 'Then make damn sure they're here within the hour. And if they're not, find another florist or another job.'

Cameron slammed the receiver down in its cradle. As he glanced at Violet the flush of anger faded from his face.

'I'm sorry, my dear. Morgan's my personal assistant. I told him to see you had fresh flowers each morning. He let me down. He won't do it again.'

Violet looked up at him.

'Thank you. I've discovered who you are, Mr Cameron.'

He shook his head. 'I doubt it. I guess you've probably telephoned around and been told a few things people think they know about me. And it's not "Mr Cameron", it's Boy – even my enemies call me that.'

Violet smiled. 'But I still don't know why you're here.'

Cameron thrust his hands into his pockets and walked away.

He stood gazing out through the window on to the Hudson River. He didn't reply. Even silent and still there was a powerful charge of energy in the set of his shoulders as he tilted his head to look down on the ice-floes below.

'Is it because of me or something else?' Violet said. She hesitated. Then she added quietly and tentatively, 'Boy?'

She knew men. She knew their vulnerabilities. One of them was over what they were called. She was using his name to provoke him into an answer. Cameron still didn't reply.

The silence went on. Violet let it continue for several minutes. Then, weak as she was, she tried again.

'My mind still doesn't work too well, but yesterday you mentioned a river and a life-raft. You said we both knew the first, and you'd got the second in your pocket.'

She glanced away from him.

'Won't you give me one of them?'

Cameron stiffened. He swung round from the window and came back to her bed. He took her hand, holding it between the mottled and splayed fingers of his own.

'I'm keeping the life-raft in my pocket until you're well again,' he said. 'Our river can wait. As for the rest, I've decided to marry you. At least, if you will agree?'

41

'It's a skull,' Violet said.

She felt foolish as soon as the words were out of her mouth. Of course it was a skull. There was nothing else it could have been. The empty eye sockets, the upper jaw with its teeth, the dome of the cranium that had once shielded the brain.

She glanced up at Cameron. 'I mean, it's a human skull,' she added.

He said nothing. His face was expressionless. He hadn't said anything since he came into the room, handed it to her, and asked her what it was.

Violet felt even more embarrassed. Obviously it was a human skull. A child would have known that. Trying to cover her confusion, she studied it again.

She hadn't seen many human skulls before, probably less than half a dozen in her entire life. They had been mainly in displays in almost-forgotten museums. She tried to bring them back to mind. As far as she remembered they'd been whiter and more sharply defined than the cage of bone-matter she was holding in her hand now.

'Oh, for heaven's sakes, Boy, I don't know,' she said defensively. 'It's a funny thing to bring someone in hospital. People must be dying all round, and you bring me a skull. Most people would bring flowers.'

The words were barely out of her mouth before she flushed at the idiocy of what she'd said.

The room was packed wall to wall with flowers, the freshest, the loveliest she'd ever been given. It looked much more like a wonderful scented conservatory than an invalid's bedroom in an expensive New York hospital. It had done so ever since Boy Cameron had started to visit her. The flowers were changed every day when the daily deliveries of champagne, fruit, magazines and books arrived.

She'd never been so well and carefully looked after in her life.

Violet laughed awkwardly and apologised. 'I'm sorry, Boy. I must be going mad. But I truly can't think of anything else.'

Cameron smiled back at her. 'You're not going mad. You're getting better all the time. But try again.'

Violet frowned. She studied the skull once more.

'It's old,' she said suddenly. 'Very old.'

'How did you guess?'

'Because it's yellow,' Violet answered. 'And everything's been worn down all round it. Perhaps it's been buried in sand. Could that have made it yellow?'

Camereron nodded.

'Very good,' he said. 'Anything else?'

'This is a real guess,' she replied. 'Somehow it looks small to me. I mean, smaller than I think of a man's skull being. Is it a woman's?'

He smiled approvingly. 'Excellent. You've done so well I'm almost tempted to ask you the woman's name. As she died about two million years ago, that wouldn't really be fair, would it?'

'Two million years?' Violet frowned. 'That's long before history began. Surely people didn't even have names then?'

'Two of them did.'

The smile was back on Cameron's face, the teasing enigmatic smile Violet had come to know so well. This time it contained a charge of excitement, even of triumph.

She shook her head. 'I don't understand.'

He took the skull back from her.

For several moments he held it silently in his hands, cupping it as gently as if it had been some priceless chalice. Then he raised it towards the window. The chill clear light of the setting February sun filled it with an extraordinary radiance, turning the ancient and worn cranium into a beacon lantern.

'The two who had names were of course Adam and Eve,' Cameron paused. 'This was Eve's skull. Here, hold it again.'

Violet had barely taken in what he'd said. She'd heard the name Eve and could see the light shining through the pale bone. For some reason she recoiled, pushing herself back against the pillows.

Cameron gave another smile. Beneath his mane of grey-white hair his powerful craggy face was more animated than she'd ever seen it.

'There's nothing to be frightened of. Most of the world would give almost anything just to see this, let alone hold it. It's almost certainly Eve's skull, but it's possibly more than that. If the original creator, the fountain of life, was a woman as the genetic readings increasingly suggest, then this may be God's skull too.'

He placed it in her hands.

For an instant Violet lay very still. The skull seemed lighter than before. It looked and felt more like some strange shell from the depths of the sea. An image of Botticelli's Venus flashed through Violet's mind.

Venus had come from the sea and she had been borne up through the waves on a shell.

'Yes, God probably was a woman,' Cameron said. 'You could have all that's left of Her right there in your hands.'

As he started to speak, Violet began to shiver uncontrollably.

'Of course, we can't be sure in a specific sense,' Cameron said. 'Not that this single woman's skull was actually God's skull. But in a wider, more symbolic framework, it seems very likely.'

Cameron opened a bottle of the champagne he'd had delivered. He filled two glasses. Then he pulled up a chair beside her bed, sat down, and explained.

Violet knew from her friend Naomi about Cameron's lifelong obsession with what she discovered was called palaeontology, or 'bones and stones' as he usually referred to it. She was astonished to learn it had started with Finlay Hampton at the Laager lodge in the Aberdare Mountains, and that Cameron had arrived there within days of Mrs Somerset, Violet, and Billy leaving to return to Britain.

'Hampton introduced me to his old Masai tracker,' Cameron

said. 'He told me he'd taken you out into the bush to show you the elephants. His name was Ngoro, but you've probably forgotten that.'

Violet shook her head. 'No, of course I remember.'

She would never forget Ngoro's name or what he looked like, the tall ebony-skinned stork-like figure, or the stories he'd told her and Billy. Unlike so much else in her life, they were held indelibly in her memory.

'Ngoro told me the Masai creation stories. I found them fascinating. Those and the books I read at the lodge started me on something I've pursued ever since. It's a theory that's known as the African genesis.'

Cameron paused and looked at her to see if it meant anything to Violet. She looked back at him blankly.

'It sets out to explain where we all came from,' he went on. 'Scientists know from the fossils which occasionally turn up that very early man lived in a number of places as far apart as Java, Peking, Mongolia, and above all Africa. The crucial question is: did we evolve in all of those places at about the same time, or were we born in just one place and spread out from there to colonise the rest of the world? The African genesis theory says it was one place, and the place was in Africa.'

Violet frowned.

It was a subject she knew nothing about, but so far she'd followed Cameron although she couldn't see where he was leading. Africa was vast. It wasn't a country, it was a continent, almost a world in itself. It didn't seem to get the theory much further forward.

She said so and Cameron nodded.

'Exactly, my dear,' he said. 'You're very perceptive. If we were born in Africa, where in that huge continent was it? It's safe enough to guess it must have been somewhere where two million years ago there was grass and trees, fruiting plants, animals, and of course water. Without dependable supplies of water nothing can survive.'

Violet thought for a moment.

Then she said, 'I was hopeless at school but I did geography and I do remember a few things. Where there's water and trees today, it doesn't necessarily mean it was the same two million years ago. Everything's changed. Surely,' she objected, 'no one's ever going to be able to find that sort of place now? There's no way you can go back two million years.'

She stopped.

She felt naive and uneducated. She often did in the presence of someone obviously much better informed and more intelligent than herself.

The someone, like Cameron, was always a man.

Violet remembered her mother's pronouncement long ago when Violet was quarrelling with her about school. 'Men don't like intelligent women, darling, it frightens them. Whatever you may think, it's much better just to agree with them.' Over the years Violet had discovered Mrs Somerset was right. She had tried to follow her advice. In spite of her best attempts she had almost always failed.

There was something inside her, Violet reluctantly came to acknowledge, too stubborn, too combative, too contrary to accept as truth what she knew was false. She was meant to listen to men wide-eyed and admiring; she was meant to agree to whatever men told her. She didn't. She never had done. She wasn't doing so now.

As Boy Cameron continued she discovered she was wrong. Not wrong in making her point, but wrong in thinking he'd laugh at and dismiss it. Cameron was different. He took her objection not as stupidity or ignorance, but as thoughtful and well-founded.

'Of course,' he said, 'once again you're right – or you would have been until very recently. Over the past twenty years there've been two technological developments that have revolutionised our ability to reach back into the past, even the infinitely remote past. One, to use appropriately the language of the camera, is in long-shot. The other in close-up.'

Violet relaxed.

A wonderful sense of relief and well-being flooded over her. For once someone, a man, and a powerful influential man at that, hadn't contemptuously dismissed her. She was being taken seriously.

She smiled. 'Tell me.'

Cameron told her.

He explained about satellite photography.

He described how for years he'd been acquiring images from the ever-increasing number of manned and unmanned capsules orbiting and photographing the earth from space. From the Americans out of Cape Kennedy, from the rockets fired by the French-led European consortium from Guyana, even from the Russian space craft thrust up from the launching-pads near Tbilisi.

With a few exceptions – the so-called sensitive national security data the cameras sometimes obtained – everything the orbiting satellites sent back was available to anyone able to pay for it. With Cameron's immense resources, he'd built up, he told Violet, the most detailed profile of Africa seen from the sky that existed anywhere.

Computer-enhanced and translated into three-dimensional models, the photographs didn't just show the continent as it was towards the end of the twentieth century. Analysed and interpreted – and his private foundation employed the best satellite photography interpreters in the world – the penetrating infra-red pictures revealed Africa as it might have been two million years earlier.

'We came up with three sites,' he said. 'They were obviously conjectural but they were the only ones that met all the criteria. And that was as far as the satellite cameras could take us, the long-shot. We needed a close-up, a tight focus to show us which – if any of them – might be the place we were after. Otherwise we'd be faced with excavating hundreds of thousands of square miles of remote bush.'

Cameron laughed. 'Compared to that, finding the proverbial needle in a haystack would have been the easiest task ever assigned to a man.'

'But didn't you say there was something else?' Violet asked.

'There is. It's called a geomagnetic survey. It came from Troy.'

'Troy?' She blinked in bewilderment. 'I thought Troy was

that lost Greek town with Homer and Helen and the wooden horse and all those gods fighting each other?'

Cameron chuckled.

'I always say it came from Troy because that's where the technique was first used in archaeology. It's very new. Basically it involves machines called magnetometers. They can probe and map the earth twenty feet down and increasingly much deeper. If something "unnatural's" happened there, if the landscape's been interfered with, if man once made a hunting cache or built a shelter or cultivated a field, they reveal it.

'It doesn't matter how long ago. Magnetometers know, as the politicians say, where the bodies are buried. At Troy they showed Schliemann's famous find wasn't the city itself, just a palace and fort on a hill to the west. The real Troy is much bigger and older and deeper. Under it one day someone's going to find Helen, Paris, Agamemnon and Achilles – maybe even the wooden horse.'

'But what's that got to do with you and Africa?' Violet asked.

'I took the technology to the three sites we'd identified as possibilities,' he replied. 'The first two proved blank. There was nothing under the surface except the natural undisturbed build-up of the millennia. The third was different. It was so different that the patterns of the magnetometers' waves, the electronic pictures the machines sent back to us, amazed even the most hardened sceptics who work for the foundation.'

Violet tried to absorb it all. It was immensely difficult and she frowned.

'What is this place, Boy, and where is it?'

'We won't know what it is until we excavate it, but there's already enough evidence – geological, core-drilled samples of ancient plant spores, human and animal remains – to indicate it's what we've been searching for.'

Uncharacteristically he hesitated.

'Schliemann had a dream of finding Troy. Lord Carnarvon had a dream of finding the Valley of the Kings and Tutankhamun's tomb. I had a dream of finding the oldest, most important place of all. Our birthplace, our cradle, our nursery. I think I've found it.'

His words were coming slowly now. Again Violet was aware that his voice had lost its confidence and authority. For once it was quiet and wondering, not as if he doubted what he was about say but as if the sheer magnitude of its significance overwhelmed even him.

'It's the Garden of Eden,' he finished. 'I believe it's buried below the valley and the river your mother gave to you as a child all those years ago.'

Violet said nothing. She stared at him. After a while her gaze moved to the skull which he'd carefully placed on the table by her bed.

Eve's skull. The first skull of creation. The ancestral skull of all humanity.

The skull which had encompassed and shielded in its helmet of bone the mind of God.

Violet closed her eyes and lay back on her pillow. She felt numb.

It was several minutes before Violet could organise her thoughts so she was able to say anything.

She'd never forgotten her mother's announcement that she was buying Violet the valley where Ngoro had taken her and Billy. Equally vividly she remembered tearing in two the paper her mother had given her, and giving one half to Billy.

It was an absurd gesture, of course. The paper meant nothing. Only the title deeds mattered. When they eventually arrived in Britain, they were in her name alone, although she didn't discover that until she was thirty and her solicitor carefully took her through all the holdings being passed on to her now that her trust had matured.

At the time, as a child on the ship, it had seemed vitally, passionately important. More than once, long afterwards, Violet ruefully wondered if it hadn't set a pattern for her life – giving a man something to keep him, giving him something else to get rid of him.

No, she'd decided. Billy was different. He could never have been bought or sold like her husbands and boy friends. Violet and Billy were equal and that one gift, so fiercely pressed on him, so different from all the others which followed, was true and honourable – the valley *did* belong to them both.

Sentimentally she had always kept her half of the paper with her wherever she went.

It was with her now, neatly folded in a transparent envelope in the Gucci bag by her bedside. Apart from that she had long since almost forgotten she owned the valley. From time to time, when she met her lawyer, it cropped up as a footnote to her investments.

'To be frank,' he'd said the last time they met, 'while it's a very large area of land, it's entirely worthless. Africa has changed in ways no one could have foreseen when your mother made the investment – although happily even then it involved a very small sum of money. I could instruct an agent in Nairobi to try to sell it but even if he succeeded, we'd virtually be talking pennies.'

'I don't want to sell it,' Violet said abruptly. 'I want to keep it.'

'Very well,' the lawyer went on smoothly. 'It won't affect the accounts. We wrote its value down to nil years ago. There are no contingent liabilities. We'll simply let it lie in the portfolio.'

He smiled. He made a note and went on to more important matters.

And now suddenly, according to Boy Cameron, buried below her worthless valley might lie the Garden of Eden. So many thoughts were jostling in confusion through Violet's mind, so many calls from the past, so many echoes of her mother and Finlay Hampton, of Billy, Ngoro, and the elephants, they dizzied her. She couldn't make sense of any of them.

There was one, though, that dominated all the rest. The possibility of its being true chilled her. Cameron knew what it was. He saw her shiver and he pulled his chair even closer to her bed and took her hand.

'No, Violet,' he said. 'I know what you're thinking. It isn't so.'

'But I own the valley.' Her voice was quiet and puzzled. 'No one else does. Isn't that the reason?'

He shook his head.

'I've known you owned the valley ever since I first went to the Laager. It's always been in my files and somewhere at the back of my mind. When the geomagnetic survey told us what was there, it came straight to the front. Of course, I was intrigued. My people searched and found you were a friend of Naomi Rothschild. I asked Naomi to bring us together.'

Cameron stood up.

He plunged his hands into the pockets of his trousers and walked to the window.

He stood there with his back to her, looking down over the grey-brown ice-floes in the Hudson River. Violet watched him. She could see the knuckles on his heavy fists pressing against the cloth. Even his back, silhouetted against the grey sky beyond the glass, conveyed strength, energy, and authority.

'I had various ideas,' he went on. 'To buy the land from you. I knew it was worth nothing and you'd probably jump at the chance to get rid of it. Or to tell you what I thought was underneath the river, and ask you to let the foundation excavate the gorge.'

He pulled out one hand and snapped his fingers.

'Oh, there were many options. Then I sat next to you and I discovered three things. One, you were far more intelligent and beautiful than even Naomi had told me. Two, you were ill. Three, you needed looking after.'

He swung round to look at Violet again.

'I had you watched and followed, I had you picked up when you collapsed, I had you brought here. I came to see you the night you arrived. You were unconscious. I looked down at you. You were pale and shuddering with a drip in your arm. You were still the loveliest woman I had ever seen. I've never been married. I decided to marry you. Not for the valley, I could get that any number of other ways. I wanted you for yourself.'

He came back to the bed. 'Will you marry me, Violet?'

She closed her eyes.

She had been terrified. She wanted him desperately. Not for his money. Although her fortune was dwindling – for most of her adult lifetime she had, she knew, been throwing it wildly and recklessly to the winds – there was still enough left, she was still a rich woman. No, not for his wealth or his vigour and power. Not even for himself. Perhaps in time she could learn affection for him, although she doubted she'd ever feel love, let alone passion.

Violet wanted him for safety.

She could have accepted him for that on any terms except one – that he wanted to marry her for the valley. She had bought people, no one had ever bought her, least of all for the most precious possession she'd ever had. That could only be given as a gift.

She believed Cameron. He might want to marry her for all sorts of complicated reasons, many of which she might never know, but it wasn't to buy her, it wasn't for the valley.

She let out her breath and opened her eyes.

'Thank you, Boy. I'm grateful. I can't think for the life of me why you want me, but, yes, if you're really sure, nothing would make me happier.' She paused and gave him a quizzical, self-deprecating smile. 'Maybe your wonderful champagne's got to you. Wouldn't you like to think about it again tomorrow when it's worn off?'

Cameron laughed. 'I've a head like an ox. Nothing wears off me, nothing ever needs to. I just want you.'

He leant forward and kissed her on the forehead. Then he stood up. As he got to the door, Violet called out: 'Boy, you've given me so much already, I'd like to give you something. I should really save it for a wedding present, but I'm not going to. I want to give it you now to celebrate.'

Her eyes shone. She felt immensely, impossibly happy.

'It should come tied up in scarlet ribbon with a bunch of forget-me-nots pinned to it,' she said. 'You'll have to imagine the ribbon and the flowers, but from now on the river and the valley belong to your foundation. They're yours.'

Cameron came back. He picked her up and held her to him. His arms were the strongest and most comforting that had ever embraced her.

That night for the second time Violet dreamt of Billy.

The dream was very simple and very vivid. In fact it

was barely a dream at all, more a piercing memory of the past. They were on the final stage of their journey back to Britain. Violet was standing by the lifeboat muster station on the ship with her mother, Nanny, and Bobbity, after the U-boat's attack.

Billy came up to her through the mist and smoke with the brass shell-case in his hands. As he put the shell-case down on the deck at her feet, she saw – as she'd seen then – that his hands were blistered and bleeding from the heat of the brass. He looked at her through his impenetrable stony eyes. Then he walked away with the ragged and scuffed ends of his man-sized army trousers trailing round his ankles.

As he disappeared Violet saw in her dream not the smoke and cloud enveloping him, but the towering grey silhouettes of elephants.

She woke in the morning to the early duty nurse clucking her teeth and scratching her head in bewilderment.

'They're not just in here,' she complained. 'They've filled up half the passage. I don't know what your Mr Cameron's up to, Miss Somerset. I think he wants to drown us.'

Violet sat up. She had long ago reverted to using her maiden name. Sometimes people addressed her as Miss and sometimes as Mrs. She didn't mind which. That day she was so happy they could have called her anything in the world for all she cared.

She glanced round. The room was filled from the floor almost to the ceiling with red roses. Through the little round window in the door, Violet could see there were hundreds more bunches stacked outside. The scent was so rich it was almost overwhelming.

Violet smiled and dropped back. She'd forgotten about her dream. She lay with her head on the pillow letting the fragrance drift across her face.

Four weeks later Violet and Cameron were married by the registrar at the fourteenth district Office of Weddings in central Manhattan.

Afterwards, at Violet's request, they walked together down to the nearby Episcopalian church where the priest pronounced a short blessing. Then a limousine took them to the Carlisle Hotel where Cameron had organised a small party to celebrate the wedding.

Violet was still recovering from her collapse and wanted to keep the party small anyway. With three failed marriages behind her, it seemed like tempting fate to trumpet a fourth. Besides, if this was going to be the final one, the one that lasted, it didn't need flaunting. Cameron was content with whatever she decided. He didn't really appear to have any friends, only a handful of business associates Violet was delighted to have there.

Naomi, her only close friend in New York, was there. Midway through the party, leaving the guests talking and drinking champagne, Violet and Naomi walked out onto the balcony. They stood together with ripples of laughter and conversation drifting out through the open doors behind them.

'You look wonderful, darling,' Naomi said.

Violet gave a graceful little curtsey in acknowledgement.

She was wearing a simple and elegant tailored suit in grey shantung silk with a plain deeper grey cashmere shawl thrown casually over her shoulders – in spite of the warmth she still shivered at every gust of breeze. Round her neck was the choker of huge turquoises she'd inherited long ago from her mother. The blue fire buried in the pagan stones flared in the spring sunlight and echoed her eyes.

Her face was pale but she felt radiant. She knew she looked radiant too.

'When I said you and Boy would get on together, I didn't quite mean this,' Naomi laughed. Then she went on, 'It really is what you want, isn't it? Just reassure me for the last time, darling.'

Violet thought for a moment. She smiled and nodded.

'Too many years, too many mistakes, too much mess, too much damage,' she said. 'Sometimes it was fun, but the fun's gone. It's all over, Naomi, it's behind me. I woke up. I'm a grown-up now and I'm starting again. It's as if nothing in the past ever happened. It may sound trite but with Boy I feel I've come into harbour. I feel safe.'

She paused. 'Yes, it's what I want.'

Naomi looked at her. 'Can any of us really throw away the past?'

'I can. I can bob up like Venus from the waves. A virgin every time.'

'And you're not going to regret anything, miss anything?'

Violet laughed. 'Naomi darling, I can't *remember* anything.'

'Nothing?' Naomi insisted.

Violet stared back at her. Naomi was shrewd and tough and loyal. She was also uncomfortably, sometimes frighteningly, perceptive. Violet hesitated uncertainly. Then she shook her head.

This was her day, not Naomi's. She wasn't going to let her friend spoil it.

'Nothing!' she said defiantly.

Cameron's voice called from inside, asking for Violet to come and say goodbye to their departing guests. The two women went back in.

Violet and Cameron had a quiet dinner that evening in the hotel restaurant. He had booked separate suites for each of them. He escorted Violet to hers soon after they finished eating. She was tired and needed to sleep early as she would for weeks to come while her strength slowly came back. He, on the other hand, would be up until the early hours making business calls around the world.

At the door to her suite, Cameron paused and smiled quizzically.

'Was it the excitement or did you just forget?'

Violet frowned. 'Forget what?'

'To ask where we're going on our honeymoon.'

Violet closed her eyes in anguish.

A week after she'd agreed to marry him and the date had been fixed, Cameron said he'd chosen where they'd spend their honeymoon but it would be a secret until the day of the wedding. Several times she'd laughingly tried to tease the secret out of him. Always Cameron had refused to tell her.

Today, of all days, it had simply gone out of her mind.

'Oh, Boy, I *am* sorry. Excitement, yes, tiredness too, if I can make an excuse. But most of all because I don't mind where it is as long as it's with you. Forgive me, tell me now.'

Cameron smiled indulgently. Then his expression changed. His face was still tender and thoughtful, but his eyes were penetrating.

'Because of you, to be with you, I've stayed in New York for six weeks. Every second of them was the most precious I've ever spent. Now I've got to catch up on what's been happening everywhere else. We're going to spend a month going round the world. We'll take it slowly. I'll have my meetings. You'll be with me. But while I'm busy, you'll be resting, swimming, eating, doing whatever you want, at the best hotels in some of the most beautiful places on earth. Except . . .'

He raised his hand.

'All of that comes afterwards. First, and this was the secret, we're going to Africa. I'm going to take you back to the present you were given and the gift you gave me. We're going to visit your valley.'

He leant forward and kissed her on the cheek. Violet felt his mane of grey-white hair brush across her forehead.

'Sleep well, my dear.'

He turned and strode away down the thickly carpeted corridor. Even when he'd disapeared into the elevator, the aura of power and confidence seemed to hang in the air.

Violet stood at the open door to her suite.

For some inexplicable reason she was unsettled and suddenly felt apprehensive. Had Boy invaded her privacy and plundered something from her? She shook her head. He couldn't have done. She'd given him that remote lost wilderness, that worthless wilderness, lovingly and freely, in partial return for what he was giving her.

Then she remembered Naomi with her acute watchful eyes. She'd told Naomi the past was gone, and she couldn't even remember it. It was true. She tried to recall James Rippon and Toby and Curro Lopez and so many others. All of them stubbornly refused to come back to her. They might almost never have existed except as irrelevant and evermore blurred intrusions in a life Violet disowned, a life she'd bundled up and tossed away.

For once Naomi was wrong. Violet was Venus rising from

the waves. The world had started today with Cameron. There was nothing before.

Violet closed her door. For some reason – just to be completely safe, just to make absolutely sure she slept on her wedding night – she took a triple dose of sleeping tablets before she climbed into bed.

She fell asleep almost immediately. She didn't dream and in the morning she woke refreshed.

At midday she left with Cameron for Africa.

The Garden of Eden

The Expulsion from the Garden

The woman's time was nearly upon her.

The man knew it too. Anxiously he watched and waited, knowing it could not be long.

In the nine months it had taken the child to grow in the woman's belly, the man had husbanded all the small antelope he had trapped which were in fawn. A dozen of them were coralled within easy access of the nest, no longer just a heaped circle of reeds but shadowed by a roof of branches woven together and laid over hoops of saplings fixed in the earth.

The woman tended the crop of tsama melons which provided food for the penned creatures, just as they provided food for the woman, the man, and soon for the child the woman now carried in her womb. Soon they would no longer need to scavenge and gather, but could live off what they grew and tended. Soon they would no longer need to share the bounty of the valley with the creatures who had made it their home.

They would claim it for their own, for their children and their children's children.

That night, for the third time in four million years, the weight of the heavens bore down on the valley. This time the very bedrock of the earth heaved and shook under the thundering sky. A great anger rolled out of the west. Then fear came on the man and the woman, fear for the fruit they had grown, fear for the flesh of creatures they had husbanded. They feared for their child as yet unborn.

Terrified, the man and the woman fled.

In the morning, when the sky at last lifted its weight from

the earth, their home place, green as a garden, was left behind.

On that morning, the first morning of their endless wanderings, the woman and the man together gazed in wonder on their newborn child. Conceived in joy, born in sorrow, the firstborn of all mankind.

In the nameless place which was now at last a valley the great grey creatures moved slowly through the dappled shade at the river's edge as they had done since the beginning. There were other creatures in the valley, but the elephants were the most ancient of all.

Green as a garden, the valley drowsed in the midday heat.

PART FIVE

The Valley

44

Billy walked into Le P'tit Canard and threaded his way between the chairs to the zinc-covered bar.

It wasn't yet ten in the morning and the cafe in a side-street off the Canabière, Marseille's main thoroughfare, was almost empty. The barman was rinsing some glasses in the old porcelain sink by the entrance to the kitchen. Billy swung himself up on to a stool.

As he waited he glanced round.

He hadn't been there for what? Four, even five years. Nothing had changed. There were still the same yellowing photographs of Marcel Cerdan and Edith Piaf on the walls, the same cheap newspaper print of the great Louison Bobet climbing the Alps in the 1954 Tour de France, the same scornfully framed wartime Nazi poster offering a 'magnificent reward' for information leading to the capture of the 'criminal known as Vercors', one of the many heroes of the French resistance.

The *képi blanc* of the Legion – not the smart new cap, but one of the old cotton neck coverings of the North African desert – was still hanging there too above the rows of bottles of pastis. Billy smiled. He was glad of that. To him, as to every generation of post-war legionnaires, Le P'tit Canard was an unofficial headquarters, a post box, meeting place, and private club.

It was good to see it still flew the Legion's emblem.

'M'sieu'?'

The barman came over. Billy ordered a 51 with ice. As the barman poured it out Billy asked, 'Where's Thierry?'

The barman glanced up and frowned. 'Monsieur Thierry died three years ago, m'sieu'.'

'I'm sorry, I didn't know that. It's some time since I was here.' Billy paused awkwardly. 'What about Madame Delphine?'

Old Thierry had owned the bar for as long as Billy had known it. Delphine was his wife.

'She's in the kitchen.'

'Could you tell her I'm here? My name's Roget, Bernard Roget.'

The barman went away. A moment later Delphine appeared.

'Bernard! My favourite *rosbif*! You deserted me, but wherever you've been, welcome home!'

She came round the bar and embraced him, her bare arms dusty with flour and her face shining with pleasure.

'Delphine!'

Billy hugged her. She was older and plumper than he remembered. Her hair was white and her body bulged against the widow's black she would wear until she died, but her eyes were still bright and her smile as welcoming as ever.

'Come into the kitchen,' she went on. 'Thierry has gone, but the work goes on.'

'I just heard about Thierry. I'm so sorry, Delphine.'

She shrugged. 'He was a good husband. We had many good years together. He died happily drunk in his sleep in his own bed. What woman can ask more for her man than that? Now I run the bar alone. I survive.'

Billy sat down at the kitchen table as Delphine busied herself by the stove.

'How long is it, Bernard? Six years, no? What have you been doing, and what brings you back to Marseille?'

He told her.

Delphine's memory was better than his. Now he thought about it, his last visit to the bar had indeed been six years ago. It was the year he left the Legion after twenty-eight years' service. He was a sergeant-major by then, the highest rank he could reach. A year later the system changed. Had Billy still been serving he could have applied for a course at the French staff academy, and acquired a full commission as an officer.

In retrospect he doubted he'd have taken the opportunity

at the time even if it had been available. He'd thought he'd had enough of the Legion, of sudden missions to brush-fire wars, of discomfort, mosquitoes, and charred food cooked over a heap of smouldering branches in the jungle or desert, of the lonely hierarchical life of the barrack block in the long periods between.

He'd saved a considerable amount of money, he had his French passport, and he spoke the language fluently. When his fourth term came to an end, he decided to try something else. He spent six months looking round before he bought an olive farm in Provence.

Barely a year later Billy knew he'd made a terrible mistake.

There was nothing wrong with the farm or the olive harvest, the oil earned him a good income. What was wrong was the sheer grinding boredom and loneliness of the life. It had never occurred to him how much he'd come to depend on the Legion as a substitute for the family he'd never had in childhood. At its best the Mally house had been a poor and late second best.

Like any family the Legion had its tensions, quarrels, and monotonies, but far more important it had given Billy companionship, support, songs and laughter, the rituals of feast days and fasting, the moments of exhilaration and excitement. All of that had now been swept away.

A prisoner of his land, Billy forced himself to continue with the farm for another four years. Then came a winter so bitter it rivalled the winter of 1954, which had virtually ruined the Provençal olive oil industry. Most of Billy's trees were killed by the frost.

By the spring the French government was offering large grants for replanting to farmers who'd been stricken as he was. Billy declined. To him the winter had been far more of a release than a disaster. He sold the land to a neighbouring farmer who planned to use the subsidies to turn the devastated groves over to asparagus cultivation.

'So that's what happened, Delphine,' he finished. 'We tied it up last week.'

She turned from the stove.

317

'Tourists and *les gens de Paris*, they come here. They think Provence is warm and easy. They don't know about the mistral and the ice, they don't know the land is hard. You learned.' She gazed at him shrewdly. 'But that's not why you came here. Your farm's history, Bernard, like Thierry dying. What now?'

Billy had finished his pastis. Delphine bellowed for the barman and his glass was refilled. Billy sat for a moment thinking.

'I have some money, Delphine, not as much as before but enough,' he said. 'I can't go back to the Legion. I'm too old, but I'm still a soldier. It's what I know best. I want something to do.'

'Men!' Delphine heaved her shoulders and returned to the stove. 'You bugger up your lives, then you come to us and ask us to give you a fresh start. Isn't that so?'

Billy laughed. 'Maybe.'

She shook her head, her back to him. 'Not maybe, the truth. Thierry was just the same. He came out of the legion and he was lost. I found this place, I made it work, I gave him a life. And now you . . .'

Delphine stood with the ladle in her hand.

'There's a man called Fernando Guitarrez. He's a Portuguese from Mozambique. He served with the Legion, but he was thrown out. He tells good jokes and Thierry liked him. I think he's *merde*, but I put up with him for Thierry's sake. He's made money and he's started coming back here again. He'll be in tonight. He calls himself a business consultant. He says he's recruiting what he calls "experienced security officers" for East Africa.'

She swung round from the stove again. The ladle sprayed drops of the *soupe du jour* on the floor. She gazed at Billy in exasperation.

'Oh, Bernard, why don't you go home? Why don't you find a nice girl to marry? What is this silly nonsense of becoming a soldier again?'

He turned away from her accusing stare.

'I can't go home,' he said. 'That's why I'm a legionnaire. You know that, Delphine.'

'Then meet this shit Guitarrez in here tonight!'

She plunged the ladle angrily back into the cauldron simmering on the stove.

Billy stood up to leave. Delphine heard the scrape of his chair on the floor. She wiped her hands on her apron and confronted him as he headed for the door.

'Were you ever in love, Bernard?'

Startled, Billy checked. No one had ever asked him that before. He stood in front of her, wondering.

'Maybe once,' he said doubtfully. 'It was a long long time ago. I was only a child. I'm not sure that counts.'

'It always counts,' Delphine said. 'Any little blonde who flashed her tits at Thierry, he tried to get between her legs. Mostly he did. I thought I minded at the time. I shouldn't have. It's better than guns, much better.'

She stabbed the ladle towards him. 'Try to find it again.'

Billy laughed uncertainly. He embraced her once more and went out.

Billy met Fernando Guitarrez that night.

The bar was crowded when he returned, but Delphine had obviously told the Portuguese about him. As Billy stepped inside the door and scanned the throng, a man pushed his way forward and stopped in front of him.

'Bernard?'

Billy nodded.

'Let's have a drink.'

There was a table in the corner at the back of the room which Delphine reserved for her special friends. She must have kept it that night for Billy and Guitarrez. Two chairs were tilted up against it to show it was taken, and a bottle of Pernod and a couple of glasses were standing on top.

'*Salud, pesetas, y amor*!' Guitarrez filled the glasses and gave the Spanish toast.

Health, money, and love. Billy nodded. As he drank he looked at the Portuguese.

Guitarrez was small and sinewy with dark oval eyes and wavy silver hair. He was wearing tasselled shoes, cotton chinos, and an open-necked shirt of heavy blue silk, unbuttoned halfway down his chest. Hanging from his neck was a gold cross on a gold chain.

Billy understood why Delphine didn't like him.

Guitarrez looked confident, plausible, and shifty. He also looked dangerous. Few people wore gold in the side streets off the Canabière. Billy wouldn't have liked to have tried to take the cross and chain from Guitarrez. He would have ended up, he guessed, with a slashed face and a knife in his groin.

'I'm happy to meet you, Bernard, very happy,' Guitarrez said in French, flashing him a warm smile. 'Often I have to make inquiries. With you there is no need. You are so well spoken of everywhere there is hardly a reason for us to meet except for pleasure. But you are here, so am I, let us see if we can do business.'

Guitarrez leant forward and explained.

45

Billy raised his hand.

Behind him the other members of the patrol froze. Billy glanced left and then right. There was nothing except the endless grey-green waves of the mopane bush, and the occasional pool of shadow under a camel-thorn acacia. He flared his nostrils and sniffed the air. Still nothing. He looked up. A pair of batteleur eagles were lazily patrolling the pale African sky.

He waited.

Behind him the patrol shifted impatiently from foot to foot. There was no reason not to go on – except that there was. Something was wrong. Billy didn't know what it was, he simply sensed it. Then it came to him.

The birds had stopped singing.

The Kalahari robins, the shrikes, starlings and larks were flying silently back over his head. They were being pushed forward by a presence somewhere close ahead.

Billy swung round.

He gestured urgently for everyone to scatter and get down. Billy himself stepped off the winding antelope path and crouched with his Kalashnikov across his knees. With his head cocked to one side to pick up the slightest sound, he waited.

It was almost a year since he'd met Guitarrez in the Marseille bar.

Guitarrez' offer had been straightforward. Years after independence in southern Rhodesia, Zimbabwe as it had been renamed, the white ranchers in the south of the country were still being plagued by black bandit gangs who'd never handed in their weapons. Their stock was being rustled, their farm-hands blackmailed and terrorised, occasionally they and their families were attacked and murdered.

To combat the lawlessness, the ranchers, with the government's approval, had formed their own security force. Guitarrez was hired to recruit men to staff it. Most were young whites from South Africa or Zimbabwe itself, but he needed experienced English-speaking former soldiers as patrol leaders. He offered Billy a round-trip ticket and a year's contract.

He accepted.

Billy operated out of the little town of Beit Bridge in the extreme south of the country on the South African border. The assignment was difficult and dangerous. The black gangs were greedy and ruthless. They were well-armed, they had years of experience of guerrilla warfare against the whites, and they knew every inch of the countryside. They also terrorised the native villages, making intelligence about their movements almost impossible to obtain.

Whenever the gangs and the patrols met – Billy's patrol had seen action half a dozen times – the engagements were short and savage. There was no question of taking prisoners. Any bandit who survived the firefight and was captured was executed with a bullet in the back of his head.

Billy was used to it all, the danger, the discomfort, the savagery. It had been part of the fabric of his life for almost as long as he remembered. Zimbabwe was little different from Chad or Guyana. But he'd already decided not to extend his contract. The reason was simple: he despised the men he led.

They were scum.

Many of the legionnaires he'd served with were coarse and brutal, but they had also been disciplined. They held fast to the white *képi*, they supported each other with laughter, song and freely shared wine, they risked their lives for each other. They belonged to the same family. The young whites he commanded now were different. They were a rabble of trigger-happy murderers and braggarts.

All Billy could say for them was that they shot straight – they'd been used to guns all their lives. It was their only virtue. Apart from that they were vain, insolent, and in some cases downright cowardly. Once or twice, Billy knew, if he hadn't been there when they'd encountered a bandit gang, at least half of them would have broken and run. His leadership and his lacerating tongue had held them together.

He wasn't prepared to do it any longer. He'd had enough. There might be one or two patrols left for him to lead, but that would be the end. Meanwhile there was this mission to complete, and this was poised at a moment of the most extreme danger – the approach of what could only be a bandit group.

The sun was slanting down.

Billy narrowed his eyes against the light and gazed up the path. He felt cold and still and intensely alert. He'd always felt like that in an ambush. This time, even as the hairs were prickling on the back of his neck, he knew there was something wrong, something odd.

The birds were still being pushed back over his head. If a human presence was moving them on, they should have remained silent. They weren't. They were starting to sing again.

An instant later Billy realised why.

Through the bush emerged the huge grey shape of an elephant. It stopped. It raised its trunk, and flared out its nostrils in a dark tulip, testing the air. The light afternoon breeze was blowing from behind the elephant and it didn't register the patrol. Slowly the great animal came on.

Billy gazed at it astounded as it ambled forward.

There weren't supposed to be any elephants left in that part of the country. The herds had either been wiped out in the civil war, or driven far to the north. This one, Billy could only guess, was a freak survivor of the man-made carnage returning by some navigational instinct to its ancestral homeland.

It came on, slow and majestic, haloed against the fading light behind. Its ears flapped rhythmically, its trunk swung gracefully from side to side, its massive feet parted the branches of the thorn bushes as delicately as a dancer stepping through the artificial roses of a ballet set. The sun gleamed off its tusks and every inch of its smoke grey hide pulsed with veins of life.

It was the most beautiful creature Billy had ever seen.

The elephant was only yards from him when it turned aside and swayed unhurriedly away towards the east. It still had no idea, Billy knew, that he and the patrol were there. It had covered about twenty yards when Billy suddenly heard the crackle of breaking twigs behind him followed by a jeering shout.

'Hey, Jumbo! Look at me, you ugly old bastard!'

Billy's head jerked round.

One of the patrol was on his feet with his Kalashnikov in his hand. He was a young South African called Heini. All Billy knew of him was that he'd worked in a slaughter-house in the Transvaal, and he was a sullen foul-mouthed trouble-maker. Heini was waving to attract the elephant's attention.

The elephant hesitated and began to turn towards the shouting, gesticulating figure.

'For Christ's sake!' Billy shouted.

He leapt up and ran towards the man. For the first time Billy had ever seen, Heini was laughing. With a sickening sense of certainty, Billy knew what he was going to do.

Billy was too late.

Confused and alarmed, the elephant had stopped broadside on to the South African. Heini raised his gun. Billy heard the regulator catch being snapped on to automatic. Heini started to fire. The high velocity bullets tore into the animal and raked through its heart and lungs.

The elephant screamed and staggered. Sprays of blood rose into the air from the severed arteries. It pitched forward on to its knees, shuddering and fighting for breath. Then it crashed on to its side.

Heini looked at Billy. 'What's the worry, man?' He was still laughing. 'Better sport than bloody ters!'

Billy came to a halt. He gazed back at the South African. He could see the smoke still rising from the Kalashnikov's muzzle and the mindless gloating sadism in the man's face. Something in Billy snapped and a tide of uncontrollable anger flooded over him.

He swung up his own gun and fired a short burst into Heini's chest. The South African was hurled back as if he'd been kicked. He spun round, dropped on his front, and lay still.

Billy looked down at him for a moment. Then he rounded on the other members of the patrol. They had witnessed everything, and were standing staring at him with their eyes glazed and expressions of shock on their faces.

'Heini's had an accident.' Billy spat the words out, his voice low and menacing. 'So will anyone else who breaks security, and puts the whole fucking lot of us at risk from the ters. I want him buried. Then we're heading back to Beit.'

He paused. The men were still standing frozen. 'Move!' Billy shouted.

They ran forward, unslung their folding spades, and started digging.

46

It was well after dark when they reached the dropping-off point where they'd left the three Kudus, the armoured vehicles that took them out into the bush, and two hours later before they returned to Beit Bridge.

Billy sat in the front of the lead vehicle beside the driver.

Normally on their way back after a bush patrol, the men talked and laughed behind him. That night they squatted in silence, shaken and confused. Nothing like Heini's death had ever happened before. Billy knew that for the moment they'd accept his explanation. They were too numbed to challenge it. It wouldn't last. They'd start to question it, they'd talk among themselves, rumours would begin to filter out.

Heini hadn't died in an accident. He'd been killed by their patrol commander because he'd shot an elephant.

Billy knew he had a reasonable chance of justifying it. In a brutal bush campaign against terrorists, none of the rules of war had any meaning. Except it didn't matter whether he was believed or not.

Billy wouldn't be there.

They reached Beit Bridge. The men, still silent, trudged away in the darkness to their quarters. Billy went into the command post and wrote out a short report of the patrol and the accident. He handed it to the duty clerk, went back to his room, and packed his few belongings. Then he walked out onto the main road that headed north through the little town.

'Where are you heading, man?'

The driver of the third truck Billy had flagged down – the first two were returning to nearby ranches – was leaning out of the cab window.

'All the way to Harare,' he called up. 'Any good?'

'Sure, man. Hop in. Glad of the company.'

Billy clambered aboard and the truck ground away. For a while he and the driver talked. Then Billy slumped back in his seat. The headlamp beams jolted and wavered through the African night.

Billy thought.

The terrible anger had passed. Instead, in an utterly different way, Billy felt as bewildered as the patrol had done as the echoes of his gunfire were lost in the thorn bush.

Not because of killing the man. Billy had no regrets about that. He had been shooting people at intervals all his adult life. Like any soldier, and a legionnaire above all, it was a central part of the trade he'd been taught, the only trade he knew. Over the years since Chad he must have killed many men much less deserving to die than a murderous psychotic bully like Heini.

No, it wasn't that.

It was the elephant.

More than fifty years. Was it really that long? Was it really half a century since he'd stood with Violet and Ngoro on the cliff above the valley, and watched the great matriarch Uhuru lead the herds down to drink? He'd been a child then. Now his hair was sprinkled with grey, his face was scarred and lined, and strong as he still was, he knew his muscles were stiffening. In between he had lived through what to most of humanity would have been an entire lifetime.

It seemed almost unbelievable, but it was true.

He'd grown up in Brixton. He'd boxed and thieved and been sent to prison. He'd enlisted in the army and been sent to prison again. He'd worked for the Clarks, driven on the wages raid, been arrested, and sentenced for a third time. After his escape there'd been the endless years with the Legion, the unhappy interlude with the olive farm, and finally this abruptly ended episode – leading young thugs through the Zimbabwe bush in guerrilla operations on behalf of rich white ranchers he'd never met.

And now this.

'Coffee and a hamburger, man,' the truck driver said.

He pulled into an all-night motel. They were still in bandit country and the motel compound was ringed with arc lights and a high barbed-wire fence.

Billy and the driver stood outside eating and drinking in the warm African darkness as dust from passing trucks billowed over them. Then they pressed on.

Billy's thoughts ran on.

In the early years Violet, the elephants, and the old Masai, the three twined together in his mind, had been so vivid they were almost more real than his surroundings in the Mally house. In the misery of that first icy winter in Britain he'd lain awake at night wondering how he could escape, find Violet, and make his way back with her to the valley.

Later, at some of the worst and loneliest moments of his life, during his prison sentences or cooped up for months on end in one of the Legion's remote outposts, he remembered thinking the same as an adult. It had always been a fantasy, of course, but he'd clung to the memory like a talisman across the years. Then, as Billy knew it would, in the nature of the passage of time the memory began to fade.

Ngoro went first.

The Masai had been very old when the children met him. Lying on his bunk in prison at the age of twenty and thinking of Ngoro's stories of the valley, Billy realised the old man would be long since dead by then. Ngoro gone, the elephants faded next. Once or twice Billy had chuckled to himself, thinking of Father Geoffrey, the tipsy black preacher, and the money he himself had stolen to save the elephants.

Even twenty years after his visit to the valley, Billy remembered his excitement at hearing as a young legionnaire that he was going into combat in Chad. It wasn't just the fear and anticipation of battle for the first time. Chad was in Africa. Africa meant elephants. Surely there would be elephants in Chad?

There weren't, of course.

There had been once, but Chad's elephants had disappeared in Roman times. Instead there was stunted thorn, baking grey-white sand dunes, dust, flies, the stench of cattle dung and human excrement, and the look of stricken terror on the face of the first man he had killed. After that Billy was posted to Guyana. In Africa he left behind both the dream of elephants and the part of his mind which had obsessively harboured them.

Lastly there was Violet.

In a way she had never really gone. Even now Billy would wake after some troubled dream to find images of the child with her tousled yellow hair and her bold blue eyes, printed on the darkness inside his mosquito net or on the shadowy plaster wall of some cheap rooming house. Like every image from a dream they hovered tantalisingly for an instant, and then vanished before he could store them in his conscious mind.

In every other way Violet was lost to him too. She came from a different world. Billy had sensed it at the time. As he grew up in Mally and occasionally glanced at Aunt Doris' magazines with their photographs and stories of London society, it dawned on him quite how different it was.

Violet was rich and high-born.

She was like the daughters of the colonel's lady at Lucknow, except Violet was richer and grander still. In the barracks the colonel's daughters were treated like princesses, but unlike Mrs Somerset his wife didn't have British maids and nannies, only native ayahs.

Long ago Violet would have married a young man of her own background and breeding. She'd have settled into some stately home – Billy had learnt all the phrases from the photograph captions – and raised a family. Her children would have grown up like her. By now they'd have married too, and Violet would be adopting a third life as a stately and smiling matron wearing long elegant gowns and her mother's jewels.

Billy frowned.

Everything fitted except his last picture of Violet. Even with all he knew from the magazines, he couldn't see the turbulent anarchic child he remembered as a decorous matron. Billy chuckled. Then his face became sombre again.

It didn't matter what had happened to Violet. She and Ngoro were the past. They were both irrecoverable. Until that afternoon – in fact, it was yesterday because it was now long after midnight – he had thought it was the same for Uhuru and the valley.

Then for the first time in over fifty years Billy had seen an elephant.

The vast creature, so powerful and yet so fragile and vulnerable, had strolled out of nowhere across Billy's path, out of a landscape where it should not have been. It might have come out of his dreams like the fugitive images of Violet, but it hadn't. The animal was real and pulsing with life. It was alone, it had withstood all the devastation the ranchers and the ters had wrought on the bush, it had survived.

It was the creature Ngoro had taught Violet and Billy about. An engine of destruction and regeneration, baked of clay in the primal oven by the lion of the spirits in his wisdom, which had opened the valley to man. Heini had slaughtered this one, and the South African had paid the price for what he'd done, but there were other elephants.

Everywhere their numbers were dwindling. They were being massacred for their ivory and systematically driven from their ancient pastures so the land could be seized and cleared for farming.

Suddenly, it came to Billy. He had to go back to the valley.

He had no idea whether the place was as he remembered it, the magical gorge lit by glittering rainbows as the rising sun played through the spray of the plunging river over the quartz-embedded layers of sand. He had no idea if Uhuru's herds still came down to drink. He knew nothing for certain any longer, he thought bitterly.

Ngoro and his legends had gone. Violet had gone. Lucknow and Mally Road had gone. So had Father Geoffrey and the boxing, the Coldstream Guards and the Clarks, the Legion and Zimbabwe, everything had gone. All he was left with was the elephants and a memory of the gorge.

'Here we are, sport.' The driver pulled into a truck parking lot on the outskirts of Harare. 'Where are you headed next?'

Billy blinked and glanced up.

For the past few hours he must have been dozing. The sky was lightening with the approach of dawn. He saw the violet flash on the wing of an early-hunting roller as it dived to pluck an insect from the truck's hood.

'Nairobi,' he yawned. 'What's my best way to the airport?'

'Take a cab, man. But watch it when you get to Nairobi. They got real bandits up there.'

Billy smiled. 'I came across a few in Zimbabwe, but thanks for the warning.'

He swung himself down on to the ground. He waved and set off for the nearest cab-rank.

Six hours later Billy landed in Nairobi. He spent a couple of days in the Kenyan capital, buying equipment and familiarising himself with maps of the Aberdare Mountains and the back country beyond. Then he rented a Landrover and set off north-west.

47

Billy knew he must have travelled the road on the way from Mombasa to the Laager fifty years before, but he remembered nothing of it.

He reached the gates of the lodge and drew up outside. He'd been told in Nairobi that the place had been entirely rebuilt twice since the war, once after Finlay Hampton's death in the sixties and then when it changed hands again ten years after independence.

He might have been arriving here for the first time.

Everything was strange and unfamiliar – not even the old ironwood trees, which must have been there for two hundred years, evoked the smallest echo in his memory. Billy wasn't surprised, but he felt a quick stab of disappointment as he started the engine again and drove into the courtyard.

The rains had just ended, the tourist season had barely begun, and the lodge was almost empty. Billy booked a rondavel. Even these had changed. They were much smaller than he remembered, and they had hot and cold running water and generator-powered electric light. A Kikuyu servant carried in his baggage and Billy went outside.

He walked slowly towards the edge of the forest. And then at last something did slowly start to come back.

The grounds and the paths that threaded through them hadn't been altered. He recognised a long flat stretch of gravel where Finlay Hampton had taught him and Violet to play bowls with metal balls so heavy they had to use both hands to throw them. He saw a group of flame trees. They weren't in flower now, but Billy remembered the scarlet blossoms that hung from them and the scent that swirled across the carefully watered lawn.

He found the wooden trough which he and Violet had filled every morning with maize for the tame and stately Kavarondo cranes, taller with their crowned plumes than the two children. The trough was planted with flowers now, but it was the same one. Then just before he reached the forest, Billy checked. In front of him was a towering acacia tree.

He hadn't remembered the ironwoods at the front. He would never ever forget this tree.

Finlay Hampton had hung a wooden-seated swing on two ropes from one of its highest branches. Pushed by one of the native servants, he and Violet had played there for hours. The swing traced huge arcs from the shadowy tree canopy at the top, down in a racing stomach-churning curve to skim the sunlight-dappled earth below, and then up into the rustling darkness of the leaves again.

It had enthralled both of them. It was like flying. It was to break from the earth and soar towards the clouds, to know for a few terrifying and exhilarating instants what it was to be a bird.

Tentatively, almost disbelieving the tree was still there, Billy walked forward and gazed up.

The ropes had long since rotted away, but high above his head he could just make out the rusting iron pulleys on which they had swung.

'No, Billy, my turn, my turn! You've had enough!'

He could see Violet turning in a frenzy of impatience to the servant and stamping her foot.

'It's not fair! Stop him, Nkane, stop him!'

'Yes, missee.'

The servant grinned uncomprehendingly. He pushed Billy higher. At the top of the arc the branches whipped across Billy's face. He didn't care. He just wanted to fly, he wanted to fly for ever.

'Get off!'

Violet had resorted to her usual trick. She used her little steel-capped bush boots to kick the Kikuyu away. The swing slowed to a halt and she pushed Billy off the seat.

'You're a bastard, Billy!' she shouted angrily. 'Now I get a double-turn. Push, Nkane, push!'

Now, fifty years later, Billy saw in his mind's eye the swing gathering momentum again and Violet, her dress blowing up round her waist and her eyes narrowed against the wind, soaring up to fly where he'd just flown. Often he'd wished the seat had been big enough to take the two of them, so that they'd both been able to hurtle together into the sky.

It wasn't. The swing could only hold one.

As Nanny had said crossly and fearfully when she'd found them playing on it after the servant had gone and they'd pleaded with her to push them both, 'Of course I won't. You can't sit there together. It's much too dangerous.'

Billy reached out and touched the trunk, closing his eyes and exploring the bark with his fingers.

Violet and him together – of course it had been much too dangerous.

For a moment Billy felt the utterly unaccustomed prick of tears in his eyes. He shook his head. Then he turned and walked back towards the lodge.

That evening one of the few people in the Laager bar was a stocky young man sitting alone on one of the stools by the window.

He was wearing a bush shirt and shorts, knee-length stockings, and well-used safari boots. It was, Billy knew, the uniform of a professional African guide. Billy went up to him. He bought the man a beer and sat down to talk.

Years ago, Billy said, he'd visited the Laager. It had been in the last days of Finlay Hampton's ownership of the lodge. Hampton had taken him out to look at elephants in a valley somewhere to the north-west of the lodge. As far as Billy remembered there'd been a primitive campsite near a cliff above the valley.

Did the young man know anything about it? Was the campsite still there? Was the rough track to it still in use?

'Bloody Finlay Hampton!' The young man laughed. 'I never met him but, Christ, man, I heard enough about him. If it had horns, shoot it, if it had a skirt, screw it. They say he tumbled every wife in Happy Valley. When the husbands chased him out, he came up here.'

He went on chuckling.

'Sure, I know where you mean. After the old bastard died they went on running what they called rough safaris out there for a while. Then, way back before my time, they stopped. I mean, take a look.'

He gestured across the room.

An early-season group of tourists was sitting at one of the tables. There were eight of them and they were German. They were all in their mid- or late-sixties, white-haired, short-winded, overweight, and sweating in spite of the coolness of the evening.

'That's what we get up here now. No way are those guys going to go bush-whacking. They want a salt-lick slap up against the lodge, bait to bring a leopard in, and a glass of booze on the table while they zoom-shoot it in flash.'

The young man paused.

'I don't know about the track or the campsite, I guess the bush will have buried them, but the elephants should still be there if the fucking Somali poachers haven't gunned them out. They should be. It's wild country even for Somalis. Give me a shout and tell me when you get back. You'll be the first person out that way in years.'

Billy bought him another beer.

Early next morning he set off. The journey took him two days. The track, as the young man said, had long since been lost in the bush. Often even the Landrover couldn't force its way through, and Billy had to clear a path with his machete.

Finally, late on the second day, he came to a halt.

From his maps and the contours of the land Billy knew the gorge was close ahead. He climbed stiffly down from the vehicle and walked forward. Half a mile on he pushed through a thorn copse and stopped on a sandy ledge.

Billy gazed down.

Below him a river wound between almost vertical cliffs before spreading out in a series of oxbow bends towards a distant plain. The last of the light was fading from the sky and reflections of the first stars shone in the water. It was utterly silent. Not even an owl or a jackal was calling. As he watched something splashed to his right.

Billy's head jerked towards the noise. He saw silvery ripples. Then a huge shape, its hide dark and glistening, clambered out of the water and seemed to float soundlessly away until it vanished in the trees beyond. It was an elephant.

Billy stiffened and inhaled the night air.

Once long ago after he'd taken Father Geoffrey the weekly sixpences for the elephant fund and they'd talked for a while, the priest had glanced at his watch and told Billy it was time he went home for his tea. Billy had quarrelled with Aunt Doris that morning before school over what he thought was an unjust accusation about some mischief she claimed he'd led the other children into. The unfairness of it was still rankling. Sullenly, repudiating Aunt Doris and the Mally house, he told Father Geoffrey he hadn't got a home.

Father Geoffrey looked at him.

'Breadcrumbs and bream-bait!' the priest said crisply, using his favourite phrase for what he regarded as nonsense. 'Everyone's got a home. The trouble is some people never realise it. It doesn't have to be where you were born, or where your family live if you've got one. It's where you choose, it's where your heart and instincts tell you it is. I chose Brixton.'

Father Geoffrey paused. 'You've got a home like everyone else, young man. One of these days you'll recognise it.'

Standing very still above the valley, Billy knew he had come home.

He camped that night where he and Violet had slept on top of the gorge. The following morning he carried his supplies and equipment down to the river and ferried them on an improvised raft across the water. Billy set up a new camp on the bank on the far side.

Three days later he heard the sound of the helicopter.

48

Billy sat very still on a boulder opposite Violet.

When he'd led her there out of sight of the others, he'd thought he wanted to talk. He didn't. For the moment words meant nothing to him.

Alone with Violet all he wanted to do was to look at her.

She was wearing a crisp safari blouse and a calf-length divided skirt, both of them in expensive olive-coloured cotton. In spite of the heat they were almost uncrumpled. Round her neck was a heavy but simple gold chain, and a diamond brooch in the shape of a spray of the Prince of Wales' feathers was pinned to her breast. On her feet were a pair of lightweight leather bush boots, polished to a mahogany shine and almost unscuffed.

Even as a child she had been extraordinarily elegant. It was one of Billy's abiding memories of her. She was wild, she raced and fought and swore like a street urchin, she would tumble through the scrub or soar on the swing with her dress around her neck. But in seconds, without apparently doing anything, she could transform herself into the poised and graceful little girl Nanny had sent out to play.

The grace had bewitched Billy then. None of it had been lost with the years – if anything its presence was even more vivid now – and it held him spellbound again.

It was her face that fascinated him most.

He tried to match it with the print his mind had held across the half-century since he'd seen it last. Then it belonged to a child. Now it was the face of a mature woman. To Billy's astonishment the two fused effortlessly into one.

The fifty years had left their mark of course. The golden mass of hair was still tousled and shining, but it was thinner and touched at the roots with grey. Her cheeks were slightly hollowed, and her nose and jaw were etched more finely. There were lines down her neck, the veins stood out on the backs of her hands, and a few crowsfeet wrinkles were beginning to web her eyes.

The eyes themselves – and that was the most astonishing realisation of all – were unchanged. Sleepily downturned at the corners, dreaming but determined, and still somehow mischievous, they had kept all the deep lustrous colour of her name. Billy looked at them and knew he didn't have to search or puzzle or wonder.

She was Violet. *His* Violet.

'Do you speak first? Or do I? Or do we just sit here until we're both covered in moss? I'd be quite happy if we did, but I'm not so sure about the others.'

It was Violet who broke the silence. She pointed in the direction of the helicopter and smiled at him teasingly.

Billy shook his head, bemused.

'You've got friends,' he said. 'I'm here on my own. You'd better tell me.'

'My friends, as you call them, are the pilot, our guide, the scientist, the native boys, and of course my husband.'

She paused fractionally over the word 'husband' as if she was both drawing it round her like a protective cloak, and also in a way as if she was wary of it.

Billy sensed the ambiguity, but had no idea what it meant.

'My husband's called Cameron, Boy Cameron,' Violet said. 'I don't know how well you know Africa, but perhaps you've heard of him?'

Billy thought for a moment. 'He's the big industrialist, isn't he, mines and newsapers and so on? I read about him in Zimbabwe.'

Violet nodded.

'We got married in New York a few months ago. Boy's hobby is palaeontology, the search for man's beginnings. When he hasn't been working, he's devoted most of his life to it. He discovered this valley could be a very important site. We flew out here on the first stage of our honeymoon so Boy could take a look at it. We're just going to be here for a couple of nights. Then we're heading back to Nairobi and on to Bombay on business. Unless—'

She broke off abruptly.

Billy was aware of her eyes gazing steadily into his. The dreaming beguiling cast to them had gone. They were both haunted – which was something he'd never seen – and also implacable. That Billy had seen. He knew it meant trouble, it had always meant trouble on all of their escapades, and he'd never been able to deter her, any more than had Mrs Somerset or Nanny.

Violet had made her mind up. It would take portents and movements of the stars to change whatever decision she'd taken.

'Come on, Billy, we're going back to join them.' She stood up and took his hand. 'Boy will be wondering what the hell his wife's doing out of his sight with some man she's just met in a remote Kenyan valley. He won't even have to ask. I'll tell him the truth.'

She glanced at Billy and smiled. 'We knew each other as children. We were catching up on our childhood. For the rest, well, you can leave it to me.'

Billy didn't answer.

Nothing had changed. Violet had always been the leader when they were together, and he'd always left it up to her to decide what they should do. He didn't know what she had in mind now, but he knew he'd be helpless to challenge it.

They rounded the bend in the river which had hidden them from the helicopter's landing site. The native boys under the direction of the guide were already setting up camp. The tall white-haired man was talking to the pilot. As Violet appeared she let go of Billy's hand.

She ran forward and embraced her husband. Then she beckoned to Billy and introduced him to Cameron.

'So you're a soldier, are you, a legionnaire?' Cameron asked.

Darkness had fallen an hour and a half ago, and they were sitting round a fire in the middle of the camp the boys had set up. The helicopter pilot, the guide, and the palaeontologist had joined them for supper, but they'd retired to their tent as soon as they'd eaten. Now the three of them – Violet, Cameron, and Billy – were alone.

'I was,' Billy replied. 'Not any longer.'

'They produce some good men, the Legion,' Cameron said. 'I used to employ quite a number in West Africa in the old French colonies. They spoke French, of course, and they took no rubbish from the natives. God, did they take no rubbish!'

He chuckled at some memory. Then he added, 'And what now?'

Billy shrugged. 'I had an olive farm in France for a while. I got tired of it. I decided to travel for a while.'

Deliberately he didn't mention his year in Zimbabwe.

'My wife tells me you both came here as refugee children at the end of the war? A sort of sentimental pilgrimage back, is it?'

Billy glanced at Violet.

Her eyes had seldom left him since the three of them had pulled their chairs closer to the fire and started to talk. They'd had no further chance to speak alone together. She was learning about his past not directly from him – she had no knowledge of his years in the Legion – but in the elliptical answers he was giving her husband.

She seemed fascinated by them, absorbing hungrily the smallest fragment of information he parted with.

Billy looked back at Cameron.

'I suppose so,' he said. 'As a kid the valley made a strong impression on me. I wanted to see it again.'

'Yes. It's a most interesting place.'

Cameron studied Billy. Then he drew on his cigar and leant back, staring up at the stars. There was a moment's silence.

Billy's gaze remained fixed on Cameron's face. The man had an extraordinarily powerful and commanding, almost overwhelming, physical presence, and immense charm, too. Billy had seen it in Cameron's easy banter with the pilot and the guide, in the solicitous way he'd made sure Violet was warm and comfortable – he'd spotted her shiver once and demanded a blanket for her shoulders – in the casual friendly manner he'd questioned Billy.

340

He was also shrewd and ruthless.

Under his mane of white hair, Cameron's stone grey eyes were cold and pitiless. Billy knew he'd been interrogated, examined, and summed up. It was what Cameron always did, he guessed. Billy had been dismissed as being of no account, a veteran legionnaire on a tiny pension, a piece of flotsam from his wife's childhood who happened by chance to be in the valley where his helicopter had landed.

Billy looked at Violet again. Her eyes were still locked on to his, but her face was expressionless. The hairs on Billy's neck bristled. Cameron began to speak again and Billy turned back towards him.

'Have you ever considered where we came from, Mr Ramsden?' Cameron asked.

Billy shook his head.

'It's a fascinating study. I've been working on it for years. That's why we're here.'

'Violet told me that,' Billy said. 'I'm afraid I don't know much about it.'

'It's like an enormous jigsaw puzzle. Those of us trying to put it together call the pieces "bones and stones". They've been scattered and buried all over the world, but most of them seem to turn up here in Africa.'

He continued to talk.

He spoke of a man called Professor Dart and the fossil finds he'd made in the Transvaal years earlier. He described the excavations of the Leakeys in the Olduvai gorge – Billy had vaguely heard of the Leakeys – and the discovery of a two-million-year-old skull belonging to a girl christened Lucy by its young American finder, Don Johannson, in Ethiopia.

He outlined the various fiercely contested theories about human evolution. About whether the great apes, the primates Cameron called them, had swung down from the trees as the forest dwindled and learnt to stand upright, to hunt and gather in social packs. About which branches of the tree of man's descent might have withered and died, and which might have survived.

He used terms like *Australopithecus* which, he explained, meant 'southern man'. He described how analyisis of the calcium structure in fossil teeth indicated what the first humans must have eaten, and where, from the layered evidence of the earth, the seeds and tree spores, the animal debris sunk in the ancient silt and preserved across the millennia, they must have lived to have survived.

Billy listened fascinated.

Part of the fascination came from the knowledge he was listening to Violet's husband. She had married him. She'd chosen to share his life. In hearing Cameron speak, Billy was learning about her, was hearing the answers to questions he'd never have thought of asking.

But there was more to it than that. Cameron was a magnetic talker.

The white-haired tycoon with his craggy face and chilling eyes was a man in the grip of a passion, almost an obsession. It was as if he didn't just want to know where man came from. Under everything, Billy sensed, under the mantle of power and achievement, under the wealth and success, Cameron wanted to know where *he* came from.

It made him, Billy thought, at once vulnerable and infinitely more dangerous than he'd realised.

'My goodness, it's almost ten!' Cameron glanced at his watch and stood up. He spoke English fluently and idiomatically, but Billy knew it wasn't his first language.

'I do hope I haven't wearied you with my hobby, Mr Ramsden. If I have, forgive me. While it's one of those subjects that can consume one, it can also leave the rest of the world shedding tears of boredom.'

He smiled. Billy smiled back and shook his head. 'It was interesting. I was just wondering how the valley here fitted in?'

Cameron frowned. 'A good question. I'm honestly not sure. There've been one or two fossils dug up here. I wanted to take a look at the place, but I doubt it's going to be a piece in my jigsaw.'

He took Violet's arm and smiled again. 'I hope you'll dine with us again tomorrow. Goodnight, Mr Ramsden.'

As they walked away towards their tent, Violet glanced back at him. The moonlight caught her face. Her features were set in a curious expression, apprehensive and somehow signalling a warning. Then they both disappeared under the tent's flap.

Billy walked down to the river. He stood for a long time gazing at the water as the moon rose over the cliffs of the gorge, and spears of silver light clashed silently across the ripples. Then he returned to his own little camp-site a hundred yards upstream.

He slid into his sleeping-bag and slept under the stars.

49

Next day Billy deliberately stayed away from the helicopter camp until the sun was high.

When he paid a courtesy visit at ten am, Cameron and Violet had been gone for an hour. According to the head boy, they and the other Europeans had set off to explore the gorge. They were due back for supper in the evening.

Billy returned to his own small tent.

The day that followed was one of the strangest he'd ever spent. He carried out the usual camp chores. He raked out the fire, he collected water from the river, he gathered wood to burn that night. He checked his provisions – he had more than enough to last him for a week. He oiled the hunting Mauser he'd bought in Nairobi, he waxed his boots, he honed his set of knives, grinding them all to a razor edge.

For thirty years they were tasks he'd done every day in the bush. Normally they took him an hour at most. That morning he managed to spin them out until midday. Finally, with nothing left to occupy him, he walked down to the river again.

The sun was high.

Bearing suffocatingly down on the river's surface like the clamp of a steel vice, it had squeezed and drained the colours from the water. The few eddies coiled in slow grey tinges like oil. The sky was white and the air parched and still. An occasional jacana, an African lily-trotter, skittered delicately across the surface close to the bank. Even the bird's chestnut and ivory plumage looked drab and worn.

Otherwise there was nothing. No sound, no movement, not even the call of a fish eagle. Billy wouldn't have heard it if there had been. Everything in him was concentrated on Violet.

He couldn't rid himself of the certainty that she belonged to him.

One half of his mind, the sane realistic half, told him it was madness. He'd been her companion for a few short months when they were children. They'd separated, their lives had passed, by some extraordinary chance they'd met again – for forty-eight hours according to what Violet had told him of her plans.

He knew nothing about the past fifty years of her life. Her childhood, her growing up, her friends, her interests and beliefs, her former husbands and perhaps her children – something told Billy there were both in her past – all were part of an unknown and unmapped country.

He couldn't set foot in that country. It belonged to her and he was a stranger; entrance to it was barred to him. She had a husband, too, a rich and powerful husband. Cameron was another barrier but only one more among many.

Time and the habit-forming barnacle-like accumulation of experience divided them. So did society. It always had done, it always would. To think the different worlds could be bridged now was a fantasy.

A pied kingfisher rose from the reeds.

It hovered above the water, and plunged in a darting flash of black and white. At the sound of the splash Billy's head came up. He gazed at the ochre-coloured cliffs on the far side of the river. When he'd seen them first they'd been wrapped in rainbows of light in the damp morning mist, and they'd dazzled with flecks of quartz.

'This is fairy land,' Violet had whispered at his side.

Another fantasy. It wasn't fairy land. It was a three-dimensional sandstone valley, an ancient deep-cut fissure in the mantle of Africa's landscape.

Yet somehow the memory of it, the memory of that first shining sight of the gorge and cliffs, the cascading water and the winding columns of elephants, had sustained and nourished him through the years that followed. Violet stood at its centre, and she'd travelled with him across the years too. Now the two had come together. The memory had returned to him as a reality and so had she.

With a blind obdurate determination, Billy knew he wasn't going to let either of them go.

Cameron and the others got back just before dusk.

Billy was back in his camp. He lifted his head and heard the sounds of their return echo down the river in the stillness of the evening. He thought he heard Violet's voice and his stomach contracted. Then there was only a distant clamour and the shouts of the boys.

Billy remained where he was. An hour later he heard the approaching pad of bare feet on the sand.

'Bwana?'

He looked round. It was Cameron's head boy.

'The bwana says would you eat at his fire?'

Billy followed him back along the bank.

In a different way the evening was almost as strange and dislocated as the day. All the party were happy, tired, and relaxed. The pilot and the guide were glad to have been able to stretch their legs in the bush. Cameron's palaeontologist was delighted with the sandstone cliff sections he'd found – they held, he said, remarkable possibilities for excavation.

Cameron himself sat at the head of the table smiling and talking easily as the staff served dinner under the stars. The evening before Billy had been aware of the acuteness of his gaze and the sharpness of his questions. Tonight he was benign and affable.

Violet sat at his side.

During the day, as Billy's thoughts had endlessly dwelt upon her, he remembered something he'd overlooked when he first saw her – her skin was pallid, almost grey, and her cheeks were sunken. He'd had no time to ask her, but he knew she must have been ill. Now, after a day walking by the river, there was the beginning of a bloom on her face.

Billy talked.

He answered Cameron's questions about what he knew of the valley. He discussed the sandstone formations with the geologist. Billy knew nothing about them, but he did the best he could. He spoke to the pilot and the guide about landing strips and the prospects for the tourist industry and the new hunting concession areas.

Billy spoke mechanically. Every time he finished a sentence his eyes returned to Violet's face. Every time she seemed to be watching him too.

Eventually he stood up. He would have stayed there all night if it had been possible, just to be close to her, just to see her across the table, but the others were yawning and he knew he had to go.

Cameron held out his hand.

'It's been good to meet you,' he said. 'Keep in touch. If you decide to stop travelling, remember, I'm always interested in legionnaires.'

Billy thanked him. He shook hands with the others. Then he looked at Violet.

She came towards him, smiling.

The fatigue he'd seen in her eyes last night seemed to have dissolved. Whether it was the sun and the exercise of the day, Billy had no idea. All he knew was that she looked bold and confident.

'Boy—'

She was speaking to her husband over her shoulder.

'I've just had an idea. There's no real need for me to leave with you tomorrow, is there?'

Cameron frowned. 'Not really, my dear. Why?'

'I'd forgotten quite how beautiful the valley was. I suddenly thought I might stay on for a while. I felt so well today and I picked up a bit of sun. I think it might do me the world of good. You could leave me the boys and I'm sure Billy would look after me.'

Cameron was still frowning doubtfully. 'When would you want the helicopter to come and collect you?'

'Oh, we don't need to fix that now. When I'm ready to go, Billy can take me back to the Laager in his Landrover. I can telephone Nairobi for it from the lodge. You'll do that, Billy, won't you?'

He stared at her, dazed. 'Of course. I'd be pleased to,' he managed to reply.

'If it's what you want, Violet—'

347

Cameron began but she cut him off. 'That's wonderful! I'll return as your dutiful and ever-loving wife, but this time restored to health and with a tan that'll be the envy of all those glamorous ladies who flock round you.'

Violet laughed. After a moment Cameron indulgently laughed too.

'Take good care of her,' Cameron said, approaching Billy. 'She's the most precious thing I own.'

Chuckling; he clapped Billy round the shoulder.

Billy walked slowly back to his camp. The river's surface was patterned with the reflections of thousands of stars. He stopped and stood for a long time gazing at them.

Early the following morning he heard the helicopter lift from the gorge, and throb away towards the south.

50

'Why?' Billy asked quietly.

Violet was sitting beside him, her cheek resting against his.

His arm was around her shoulders. Tentatively, almost fearfully, he stroked her hair. As he parted it softly between his fingers he saw the roots were even greyer than he'd noticed before.

The grey was unimportant. What he really saw was the tousled gold he remembered from her childhood.

'Why?' she echoed. 'Do you remember what Bobby Kennedy said in his last speech on the day he was killed?'

Billy shook his head.

'He said: "Some people ask why. I ask – why not?" I'm rather like Bobby Kennedy.' She paused and smiled. 'Why not?'

Billy laughed.

It wasn't an answer, it was another of her gestures of defiance. An answer might come later. For the moment it didn't matter. What mattered was that they were together.

They'd been together all day. In the morning they'd walked to the west along the river bank. Once or twice Violet had taken his hand and laced her fingers through his. Mostly, holding each other or stepping apart through the reeds, they'd walked in silence.

All that was needed then was the reassurance of each other's presence, the tactile feeling that they were there side by side. The talking could come afterwards.

It came after they returned to camp at midday.

They ate the meal the boys had prepared. Then they walked, eastwards, this time to Billy's camp. He'd pitched his tent and made his fire beside a deep oxbow pool carved out by the downward press of the river. Violet looked at the water. The sun was at its height and the air trapped in the gorge was brutally hot.

Suddenly she stripped off her clothes. She stood for an instant on the bank, the skirt, the blouse and her underwear in a little heap at her feet. A random gust of wind caught her hair and plucked it back from her face. The light rippled over her shoulders and ran in waves of radiance down her body.

Billy shivered.

Naked, she was the most beautiful, the most desirable woman he had ever seen. Childbirth and the years hadn't touched her. Her legs were slim and strong, her breasts firm and uptilted, her stomach flat. She plunged into the water.

She surfaced laughing.

She turned and struck out for the far bank with slow graceful strokes. She turned again, came back towards him, and splashed for a while in the shallows, cooling herself as she let the river play over her. Then she waded out. She stood on the shore. Water cascaded off her in showers of glittering droplets, and the sun, reflected from the cliff, haloed her in gold.

She raised her arms, lifting her breasts, and laughed again.

'This old lady wants a towel, Billy,' she said. 'Fetch me one, and I'm yours for ever.'

He ran back to his camp. He snatched up the only towel he had and returned to the shore. He wrapped it round Violet and sat her down beside him.

It was then that the talking began.

It came patchily at first.

Neither of them was quite sure where to start. They were, Billy realised, complete strangers who also knew each other better than anyone in the world. A shared experience in their distant childhood had resulted in their lives being haunted by each other's unseen presence more intimately than anyone else who had come into their existence.

They knew each other – and they knew nothing about each other.

The conversation leapt backwards and forwards. Billy spoke hesitantly of Brixton, of Mally Road and Aunt Doris, his cousin Jack and the horses, of Father Geoffrey, the drunken black preacher, and cunning, wheedling Steve. Violet answered with stories of the house in Kensington, the loneliness of school in the Malvern Hills, Mahadur, her visit to India, and then her growing up.

'I came to look for you once,' she said.

Billy looked at her astounded. 'When?'

'Not long after I came back from India,' she answered. 'All I wanted was to come back here, to be with the elephants. My mother thought it was madness. She was determined I should marry. I knew that was hopelessly wrong, but I needed someone to find a way out for me. You were the only person who could. I went to the house where you lived.'

'In Brixton?' Billy blinked in disbelief. 'How did you find it?'

'Through the War Office,' she answered. 'The army keeps records. I got the address where they'd sent you, and I went there. I met an old lady, your Aunt Doris. She was wonderful – tough and funny and lovely. She said you'd got into trouble and had been sent to prison. She wouldn't tell me where. She said looking for you was just a dream and I should forget it.'

Violet paused. 'I didn't forget it, of course, but I suppose I was too young to stand up to anyone. My mother got her way and I was married to James. It turned out to be a nightmare.'

She told Billy about it.

She glossed over the worst parts, Billy guessed, but he realised it had indeed been a nightmare – a nightmare of boredom, carelessness, sadism, and indifference. So, in different ways, was what happened afterwards. The running away, the endless travelling. the second and third marriages, the brief and always illusory glimpses of happiness, the descent through amphetamines, cocaine, and alcohol into the darkness.

'Which is where Boy found me,' she finished. 'I'm not sure I love him, but I do trust him. He's complicated and strange, but he's strong, he's a rock. I've had enough of buying farms for pretty young men. Enough of setting up their businesses and paying for their presents to the fancy ladies they think I don't know about. I want to be looked after.'

She stopped. 'Does it make sense, Billy?'

He didn't answer.

Yes, on one level, the level of conventional logic, of course it made sense. But on another, on the plane where the dark and turbulent tides of people's feelings flowed, it made no sense.

Violet had spoken the truth as she wanted it to be – not as it was. The proof lay in the fact she hadn't left with Cameron. She'd stayed in the valley to be with Billy. That wasn't the action of someone who wanted to be looked after. It came from the person, Billy guessed, Violet had always been and still was – impetuous, romantic, a searcher

For all his wealth and power, for all the security he gave her, Cameron was simply a stop-gap in her life. Violet was looking for something more.

'And you?' she asked. 'Did you ever look for me?'

Billy smiled ruefully. 'I thought about it often. But, no, in truth I didn't. I never quite had the courage.'

'Mary, pity women!' Violet laughed. 'Why is it always us who have to be bold, who have to take the chances? Why am I here now with you?'

'I asked you that,' Billy said. 'You didn't really answer.'

'And I'm not going to now because I'm hungry.'

She tucked the towel round her, gathered her clothes together, and stood up.

'Give me half an hour to change, then come over to the camp. Boy and I flew here via Paris. I bought some odds and ends at Fauchon. We'll have a feast.'

They ate under the stars.

Billy was learning new things about her with every hour they spent together. One of them, he discovered, was Violet's skill for organising the world around her. She didn't allow circumstances to dictate to her, not at least when she was sober, away from drugs, and in control of her life. She grasped them, examined them, and imposed her own will and tastes on what they offered.

There was a white linen cloth and candles on the table. At Fauchon she'd bought champagne, foie gras, asparagus, quails' eggs, and mountain ham from the Alpujarras in Spain. The champagne had been cooled in the river, the asparagus had been steamed in billy-cans, the ham had been sliced into rosy wafers. The head boy had baked bread in an earth oven, and the tiny eggs had been boiled and cracked.

'Santé!' Violet said, raising her glass as they finished eating.

Billy lifted his own glass in return.

Later he leant back. It was one of the best meals he'd ever eaten. He felt content and filled. He looked at Violet across the table.

She'd changed from her safari clothes into a simple flared dress of plain white silk with a plunging neckline. The neckline was hidden by a rich and dark embroidered Kashmiri shawl which she'd thrown round her shoulders against the night chill of the river air. Under the shawl Billy could see the contours of her breasts.

'And now,' she said, 'we're going to walk. I mean walk, Billy, not talk. For the moment we've done enough of that.'

She stood up and smiled. 'Am I being bossy? Or is it just that I always seem to be the one who takes the decisions?'

Billy smiled back. 'Probably both, but mainly the second. But then you always were.'

He got to his feet. He took Violet's arm and they walked in silence along the bank.

She was right.

They'd talked enough. They'd covered every aspect of each other's lives up to the moment where they paced side by side here in the darkness of the valley. There were details to be filled in, of course, endless details. They could take several lifetimes to exchange and explore, but the rough geography of their separate pasts, the twin charts of the faults and fissures, the gains and losses, the pain and laughter, had been placed on the table, studied, and accepted.

In the end none of it counted. They could have done without the talk and the charts. They had each other. That was enough.

'And now I'm going to bed,' Violet said.

They had returned to the camp.

The boys were asleep in a huddle of snoring figures just beyond the reach of the smouldering fire. They had left a kerosene lamp burning in Violet's tent. Its light caught her face.

The glow seemed to shine incandescently through her skin, highlighting her cheek-bones and drawing sparkles of turquoise light from her eyes. There was no grey in her hair now, only the cascading gold he remembered.

'Yes, of course,' Billy said.

His tongue dried in his mouth. He felt awkward and confused. He could not believe that any woman anywhere had ever looked so beautiful. He stepped away from her tent.

'Billy,' her voice stopped him, 'I was rather hoping I was going to go to bed with you.'

He turned and gazed at her.

They lay in each other's arms.

'No,' Violet said. 'I don't want to make love to you. Not yet, anyway. If it happens, it'll happen in its own time. For now I just want to hold you.'

Gently, tentatively, inquiringly, her hands moved over his face. They travelled across his shoulders, and began to explore his back.

Billy relaxed. He lay still. Once again he remembered that she had always been the leader, the initiator. She still was. He felt her fingers touch the welts of scar tissue on his ribs. Her hand hesitated as she probed them, then it glided down and stopped again at the incision on his thigh.

'My goodness, Billy, where have you been playing?' she asked. 'This isn't a body, it's a moonscape.'

He smiled.

'I can give you chapter and verse for each one. Starting at the top, Algeria, a grenade fragment. On the righthand side of the ribs a booby-trap bomb, Algeria again. On the left another grenade, Chad this time. The big cut and rebuilding in the thigh, that was a sniper's bullet in Guyana.'

He ran through all the wounds and their surgical repairs

down to the landmine which had almost taken his foot off.

'Oh, Billy, couldn't you have gone into banking or insurance or something? It's what all my boy friends did.'

'Your boy friends didn't grow up in Brixton. From what you've told me, they didn't become your lovers either.'

'At least they tried.'

'I'm catching up.'

Violet laughed. She clung to him, wrapping her legs round his.

Billy held her tight.

He rocked her softly in his arms until from the slowness of her breathing he knew she slept. For a while he lay awake. He listened to the sounds of the African night. The call of the pearl-spotted owl which had adopted the camp as its food source, the plaintive cry of jackals, the distant roar of a hunting lion.

For the first time in his life he felt strong and confident and fulfilled. Strength had always been with him. It had hardened and tempered him from the Crown and Garter boxing ring to the battles with the legion. Confidence had come with the years. Fulfilment, the deeply satisfying awareness of holding and protecting someone he loved, he had never known.

Until now. Now he did.

It was guarding a stranger with grey-gold hair and needle-marks on her wrists – he'd seen the punctures as she waded out of the river – against the dark.

Billy enclosed her and slept.

They both woke at the same instant.

Billy had no idea why. Perhaps a lion had padded close and roared, perhaps an owl had swooped down and called as it plucked insects from above the smouldering embers of the fire. If there had been a sound, it had ended by the time he opened his eyes.

Billy glanced at the tent's entrance.

Outside the stars were pale and fading. A faint shell of blue-grey light marked the approach of dawn. He could smell the river – damp and mist-strewn and clogged with rotting rafts of reeds. He looked at Violet.

Her head was on the pillow close to his and her eyes were open. Whatever had woken him had woken her too. She looked at him with a curious intense gaze.

'I want you, Billy,' she said simply, 'I want you now.'

She unbuttoned her shirt and kicked off the cotton shorts in which she'd been sleeping. She pulled him towards her.

Billy felt a hardening of desire that he'd never felt before in his entire life. He lifted himself on top of her, sensing her legs parting and splaying sideways, and he slipped into her.

'Billy.' For a moment she stopped him. 'Who've you had before? Prostitutes?'

He found he couldn't speak.

Prostitutes, whores, tarts, of course. Tens or even hundreds of them. It was what legionnaires did, what all men did. A quick relief from the goading tormenting scourge between one's legs.

It had never mattered to him, never been of any interest or consequence. He had taken the women, used them – or more accurately, he thought, been used by them in return for the money he paid – and then cast them aside. After a while he'd even stopped doing that.

Sex was a trade item. He'd given up dealing in it years before. He had better things to spend his money on.

'I'm not a prostitute, Billy,' she said. 'I'm me. I'm a living breathing woman. I'm yours, now and for ever. Just take me and hold me.'

She placed his hands on her breasts. Billy rose and plunged into her and the world seemed to dissolve.

Afterwards he lay beside her. Violet stroked his head. Her fingers found another ridge of scar tissue at the back of his neck, and she propped herself up on her elbow.

'Is there any part of you, Billy, that someone hasn't taken a gun or an axe to?'

'That one's different. It was a hammer.' He smiled. 'I got into a fight in a bar on a Friday night with another legionnaire. He sledged me once, but in the end he finished second. I went to see him in hospital and we made it up. I think it's now called domestic violence.'

'Billy, you're incorrigible,' she said in exasperation. 'Did anyone ever tell you that?'

'No. It wouldn't have made any difference if they had. I don't know what it means.'

'It means you're the same as ever, that you've never changed.'

Violet threw off the unzipped sleeping-bag that covered them and got to her feet. She ducked under the tent's entrance and stood upright outside. She was naked and the moon was full.

Earlier that day in the sun by the river she'd been bathed in gold. Now in the moonlight she was sheathed in silver. The night glow seemed to drench and pour off her, cascading down like water.

'Billy,' the tone of her voice had changed suddenly, 'there's something wrong. Do you remember Uhuru?'

'Of course.'

'Where is she? Where are all the elephants? I haven't seen one since we arrived.'

She glanced back at him. Even in the moonlight Billy could see her face was clouded. He stood up and joined her outside the tent.

'Don't worry.' He put his arm round her. 'I wondered that too when I got here a week ago. But I went out walking, much much further than we've been. I found them. They're grazing about thirty miles to the west. They'll drift back.'

'Was Uhuru with them?'

'They're still being led by a big female,' he answered. 'It won't be Uhuru. She'd be a hundred now if she was still alive. I think much more likely it's her daughter, the calf Ngoro showed us, or even her grand-daughter. I've been watching her. She's edgy and wary, kept chasing the others away except when she took them down to drink. I have a feeling she's pregnant.'

'Are they going to be all right, Billy?'

He frowned.

'Why on earth shouldn't they be? They're protected in

Kenya now. The Somali poachers have been pushed back. There's no reason for anyone to come out here and disturb them. All they need is the river—'

He broke off and stared at her. There was something, he suddenly sensed, that she knew and he didn't.

'What is it, Violet?'

She glanced away from him. For a long time she was silent. When she turned back her eyes were filled with anguish.

'Boy offered me what he called a life-raft,' she said. 'It was safety. I needed it then more than anything, so I took it. I was deeply grateful. Still am. In return I said I could give him a river as a wedding present. I didn't know what he meant until he reminded me—'

She gestured back towards the tent.

She had brought her saddle-stitched leather bag with her when they'd returned to Billy's camp. She was referring to what was inside it. She didn't have to say what she meant. Billy knew. She was indicating the deeds to the valley, her half of the worn and dog-eared papers they'd shared for so long.

'He wants the valley. He intends to dam it and change its flow. When it's dry, he's going to excavate it. He believes the Garden of Eden lies underneath.'

51

'Tell me,' Billy said.

They were sitting out on the river bank.

They had both dressed, putting on clothes against the fading chill of the night air. Morning was close and a rim of light was beginning to lift over the wall of the gorge on the far side of the water.

Behind them a little spiral of smoke rose from the embers of the fire. The open flap of the tent rustled and snapped in the dawn breeze. A black-backed jackal, its coat gleaming russet and bronze, stepped delicately along the sand, sniffing and probing the earth. It caught their scent, froze, and whirled away.

'Please tell me,' Billy repeated urgently.

Violet drew up her knees.

She folded her arms across them, and rested her chin on her hands. Her skirt hung down in folds as if it had been sculpted in the same dark rock that rimmed the river's edge.

'Boy made me promise I wouldn't,' she said. 'I suppose I've been breaking promises, telling secrets I swore I'd never reveal, all my life. Don't we all?'

'Some of us,' Billy said.

'Then I'm one of the some of us. Not the best of the some of us. Just one of the ordinary ones. The ones who hope and pretend and lie.'

She raised her hand to her mouth and chewed on her finger-nail.

'Boy didn't tell you the truth, Billy. He said the valley was just an interesting archaeological site. It's not. If he's right, it's the most extraordinary, the most important site in the world. It may be the birthplace of man. It may even be the Garden of Eden.'

She explained.

She took Billy through it step by step, just as Cameron had explained it to her.

'That's why he wants to dig here,' she finished. 'It'll be a huge operation, it'll take years. But if his guess does turn out to be true, it'll be the most remarkable find ever made. Boy thinks he's found the place where we were born, the cradle where we were rocked, the nursery where we grew up.'

Billy sat in silence. He felt stunned. For a moment his mind couldn't absorb what she'd said.

'But the Garden of Eden,' he struggled to find the words, 'surely that's just a fairy story? I mean, I know it's in the Bible, but it's still just a story. It's not real, it's not like history.'

'Stories have to come from somewhere,' Violet said. 'People used to think Troy and Helen and the Greek gods were just a story too. Then they found Troy and it was a real town with bricks and streets and shops. They thought Noah's Ark was just a story. Now they think they've found the remains of a huge boat high up in the Turkish mountains.'

She paused. 'Stories get changed as they're handed on down the years, but they all start somewhere in truth, in reality. Boy believes Adam and Eve became symbols, but they began as real people. So did Cain and Abel.'

Violet stopped again. 'I'm explaining it very badly. Boy does it much better. He's not religious at all, it's got nothing to do with that. He looks at it like a historian. He believes myths begin in fact. And it's not just him. The scientists working for him, the palaeontologists and biologists, are starting to think he could be right.'

Billy still couldn't take it in.

'Are you telling me he married you to get his hands on the valley?'

Violet smiled quizzically.

'I hope I'm worth more than that. No, in Africa Boy's almost like an emperor. With his wealth and influence he could have acquired it anyway. He'd always known I owned it from his first visit to the Laager when his plane crashed.

When his magnetometers showed what might be underneath it, his people checked the land registry in Nairobi and found the valley was still mine. He traced me through a friend of mine. I think he became intrigued by me, so he asked me to marry him.'

She speculated aloud as she'd several times speculated silently to herself.

'He's never been married before, but there comes a moment for people like him when they need to be to complete something. Boy came from a poor part of Berlin in pre-war Germany. I'm what's known as an "elegant European aristocrat". I'm a wonderful hostess, even if I say it myself. I suppose in a way I make the perfect trophy wife, I round things off.'

She laughed. 'Whatever the reason, I'd like to think it wasn't just for the valley – although perhaps it made it easier for him.'

Billy was silent again. He was still trying to grapple with the implications of what she'd told him.

It was so far-fetched that at first every instinct in him wanted to dismiss it as absurd. Somehow he knew it wasn't, nor were Cameron and his millions. Across his mind flashed images from the television programmes about the origins of man he'd watched over the years. It was a subject of endless fascination to the French, and he must have seen dozens of explorations of it – in the barracks at night there was little else to do except watch television.

Almost every one suggested man had an African genesis. If he did, if there had been an Adam and Eve and a Garden of Eden, then it had to be possible they and the garden lay buried somewhere on the dark continent. Cameron believed it was hidden under the landscape in front of them. He wanted to excavate it to find out.

'If your husband drains the valley,' said Billy, 'the elephants will move away. They need forty gallons of water a day to survive. The trouble is, there's nowhere for them to move to.'

He was speaking very quietly, almost to himself. He examined the implications one by one.

'The headwaters, the drainage off the mountains, might be channelled into an artificial lake. But if your husband's right, if there really was a Garden of Eden and it's here, this is going to become the biggest tourist attraction in the world. It doesn't matter what he does. No one could keep that a secret.'

Billy plucked a dry stem of grass from the earth and shredded it between his fingers.

His face was furrowed and perplexed.

'A lake wouldn't make any difference. Sheer human pressure would drive almost all the wildlife away, it always has done. The elephants would back off. They'd look for somewhere else to drink and they wouldn't find it. Then, slowly, they'd begin to die off. It wouldn't happen quickly, not in my time or yours. Some of them would return for the water. They'd push through to get it. But each year there'd be fewer and fewer of them. They'd be token elephants, ghost elephants.'

He spat the husks of the grass seed from his mouth.

'At the end they wouldn't even be ghosts. They'd be gone.' He turned to look at Violet. 'If your husband takes over this valley, the herd is finished.'

She stood up, her face distraught.

'Boy saved me. I mean, literally saved me. Without him I'd be dead. I promised him the valley. I'm making it over to his foundation, the lawyers are dealing with it now. It means more to him than anything else in the world.'

She turned imploringly towards him. 'What can I do, Billy?'

He rose too.

Dawn was near now.

It was going to be a fresh and shining African dawn, one of the swift, scented changes between night and day Billy had come to love. The constellations of the stars in the Southern Cross still hung in the sky like the jewelled needle-point in a medieval tapestry, but the sun was rising.

There was mist over the river, birds were calling, and he could smell wild thyme on the morning breeze – somewhere buffalo or antelope were trampling the herb underfoot as they approached the water. The light caught the rim of the gorge and flowed over it, pouring down and turning the flecks of quartz into diamonds as it had the morning he and Violet saw it first with Ngoro.

He took her hand.

It was like the first morning of creation must have been, like the beginning of the world as the old monks had imagined it. Cameron and his scientists would have mocked the idea. 'Primal soup' was the phrase they'd have used. No stars, no fragrance, no spilling cascading sunlight, no bird song, no almost unbearable sweetness in the air.

Just a broth of organisms which had multiplied, fragmented and evolved into the encoded DNA material which in its turn had formed building blocks for the bones, flesh, and brain structures of a man called Adam and a woman called Eve.

They were wrong.

They were deeply and fundamentally wrong. Cameron and the rest of them didn't know Adam and Eve had been baked by a lion in a clay oven, and the lion had made an elephant to dig them a garden. Ngoro knew that, and the old Masai with his spear was wiser than all of them put together.

Billy laughed with delight.

Violet glanced at him startled as the sound echoed joyously off the cliffs. Before she could say anything he spoke.

'We're going to go out and find the elephants,' he said. 'We'll find Uhuru's daughter or grand-daughter. Whichever she is, if we're lucky, if she lets us, we'll follow her to the water. Afterwards you can decide what you and your husband want to do with the valley.'

Whatever might have happened, whatever did happen, Billy knew that every successive moment of the time that followed was the most important moment he'd ever spent.

He spent the entire time, all the moments, with Violet. Afterwards he realised he was lucky, immeasurably lucky. He was aware of the importance, of the value and intensity and strangeness of the time even as it passed, trickling through his hands with the swiftness of dry sand. And it was strange.

Although they did very little, in everything they were

inseparable, like mountaineers roped together on the north-west ice face of Everest. They took each breath as if both their lives depended on their closeness.

They breakfasted at her camp – in Billy's eyes it was no longer Cameron's, it was hers. They went back to his small fire and tent. They swam naked in the river. She was a wonderful swimmer, fast and supple and graceful. Compared to her, Billy was clumsy and slow. He struggled, he panted, he had to trudge back on to the bank with his chest heaving.

Violet followed him, arcing through the water like a dolphin.

She stepped out lightly, shaking her head and running her fingers through her hair as the spray cascaded from her. She scooped holes in the sand to hold her breasts and her hips and lay down, toasting herself like a tortoise in the sun.

She'd instructed the boys to make lunch – newly baked bread, pork rillettes from a great glass jar, and a bottle of white wine from her shopping expedition in Paris.

'Isn't it fun?' she said as they walked back. 'I'm starting to think of my camp as the town house and yours as the country cottage. Country cottages, of course, are where people get up to no good.'

She gave him the quick challenging smile he remembered from so long ago.

They lay side by side under the canvas shelter in the midday heat, and then as the hours passed in the dwindling afternoon's warmth. They didn't, as Violet had put it, get up to no good.

'At our age,' she said, 'we probably need a second bottle of wine and the discreet cover of darkness.'

They didn't, Billy thought, need either – and she knew it too. What they did need was each other, and that in their enveloping arms they had.

It was dusky inside the tent.

The sun came through in hot lathes of random sand-scattered light. Flies and spiders tumbled in it. He explored her face and ears and shoulders with his fingers. He reached down and touched the rest of her body. Her skin felt warm and resilient and struggle-hardened. All her life she must have fought to keep a certain private armour round her.

Now she had stepped out of the armour. She was naked and sheathed in gold and the smell of her rose to his nostrils from beneath the protective chainmail she'd cast aside.

It was a blend of sweat from the heat, the bottled scent she used – musky and fragrant and expensive, it must have come from Paris like the foie gras, from Dior or Lacroix – and something indefinable. Her own smell. It underlaid all the others. It was warm and rich like apples drying in the loft of a Normandy farmhouse, or the odour from a Burgundy hay meadow when the summer grass had been scythed.

It was Violet's. Billy let it sift across his face. Then he settled his head in the fold of her neck and slept.

'Billy, they're back!'

He jerked upright at the sound of her voice. He grabbed a towel and scrambled outside, knotting it round him as he ran.

He gazed round.

It was dusk and the last of the light was draining from the sky. On every side under the emerging stars huge grey shapes were appearing from the trees and pacing in columns down to the water. There seemed to be hundreds of them. There were old bulls, groups of young bachelor males, females with calves, and at the head of them what Billy was sure could only be Uhuru's grand-daughter, the new great matriarchal leader of the herd.

'They're wonderful, Billy.' Violet's eyes were shining. 'Even more wonderful than I remembered.'

The sight only lasted a few minutes. The African night closed in, and darkness hid the elephants. For an hour the sounds of trumpeting and splashing echoed through the gorge. Then there was silence.

'They've gone back into the bush to feed,' Billy said. 'They'll be back to drink again at dawn.'

'What time's that?'

'It begins about five. If you really want to see them properly, you should be up half an hour earlier.'

'I don't mind staying up all night not to miss them.'

Billy smiled.

'You don't have to do that. But just make sure I'm awake too. They may be the most beautiful animals in the world. They can also be the most dangerous. God help anyone who gets between a mother and her calf. A cow elephant can weigh six tons. She can run at thirty miles an hour and she's as agile as a dancer. If she thinks her calf's threatened, she becomes a killer – nothing can stop her except a high velocity bullet. That's why I've got a rifle.'

He reached out and ruffled her hair. 'I don't ever want to use it. Except for you, of course, I'd use anything.'

They spent that second night, like the first, in Billy's tent.

Once in the early hours he woke. He glanced across at Violet's head on the pillow beside his, and saw her eyes were open too. She was frowning slightly as if she'd been studying him. She smiled and kissed him softly on the mouth. Then she settled back again and the uncertain troubled expression returned to her face.

'I've been lying here thinking,' she said. 'I don't believe I can let Boy dam the river and dig up the valley. The past's dead, it's gone. The elephants are alive, they're more important even than the Garden of Eden now. There are so few of them left anywhere. I can't let this herd be destroyed.'

Billy opened his mouth, but she silenced him before he could speak.

'No, Billy, don't say anything. You'll just confuse me. I made Boy a promise, I gave him a present. I hate breaking my word, and I've never taken a present back from anyone. I want to think some more.'

She turned firmly away from him. Billy waited for a long time, but she said nothing else. Eventually he slept again. And then he heard the sound.

It was a scream, a human scream.

Drowsily Billy thought it was part of his dreams. He blinked and stared at the roof of the tent. The echoes of the scream still seemed to be hanging in the air. Instinctively he reached out for Violet. There was nothing there. His hand touched only the warm empty hollow where she had been lying.

He frowned. Suddenly he jerked upright. As he did the scream came again, agonised and terrified.

It was Violet.

Billy hurled himself out of the tent. For an instant he stood appalled.

The greyness of the coming morning filled the gorge. A line of bare footprints led away along the bank and turned into the water. He followed them with his eyes. He knew they could only be Violet's. Then he saw her.

A hundred yards away the huge silhouette of the herd's new matriarch reared above the shallows. The elephant was holding Violet in its trunk.

In a few dizzying sickening instants Billy realised what must have happened.

Violet hadn't woken him. She'd slipped out of the tent on her own with her camera and swum down the river, intending to photograph the elephants as they came forward to drink. She'd come too close to the shore, she'd frightened the pregnant female, and the elephant had plunged forward and seized her.

As Billy watched, the great animal tossed Violet down into the water. Billy saw her head rise and her arms beat wildly. The elephant trumpeted in a chilling blend of anger and fear. Then the animal waded forward and dropped to its knees, crushing Violet beneath the surface.

Billy shuddered. He opened his mouth and emptied his lungs in a frantic shout.

'No!'

He began to run towards the elephant. He'd taken fifteen or twenty steps when he halted.

His voice wasn't going to stop the animal. It wasn't strong enough. He whirled round and raced back to the tent. He grabbed his rifle, snapped off the safety catch, and threw himself outside again.

There were a dozen bullets in the magazine. He didn't even lift the weapon to his shoulders, he simply kept his finger on the trigger, worked the bolt action, and fired into the air.

The detonations roared down the gully and reverberated off the sandy walls. The devastating impact of the sound did what he could never have done. It terrified the animal. The elephant shied back. She raised her trunk, flared her nostrils, and searched for the source of the noise. She couldn't find it. She hesitated for a moment. Then she turned and vanished into the bush.

Billy tossed the gun away and frantically ran forward.

Violet was floating on her face when he reached her. He pulled her ashore, lifted her in his arms, and carried her back to the tent. She was still breathing when he laid her down on the truckle bed, but Billy knew even before he examined her that she was dying.

He tried to put it out of his mind. He composed himself and methodically checked her injuries. It was something he'd often done in battle.

Both her legs were broken and so was one of her arms, but the lethal wounds were to her chest and hips. Her entire rib cage had collapsed under the pressure of the elephant's knees, and her pelvic girdle had been shattered. Her internal organs had been squeezed as if they'd been caught in a vice. Blood was leaking from her everywhere, from her ears, from her mouth, from between her legs.

Only her head miraculously had been spared.

As she lay unconscious below him, with small shallow breaths pulsing painfully through her lungs, she looked almost more beautiful than he had ever seen her. The few days in the valley had brought a rose-gold glow to her skin. Her face was serene, her lips warm, the long eye-lashes trailing down from the closed lids were wheat-coloured and shining.

Her body was broken but her beauty was intact.

His eyes filled with helpless tears and he rocked back on his heels.

There was nothing he could do. He might conceivably have tried to ferry her across the river, carry her the ten miles uphill back to the Landrover, drive her to the Laager, and telephone from there for a helicopter to take her to hospital in Nairobi. It would have taken a couple of days at least, it would have been unendurably painful, and it would have been pointless.

Violet would have died long before they got there.

Billy shook his head and stood up. He frowned. He was wrong.

There was something he could do, something very small but even unconscious, in agony and trauma, it would help her. As a senior legionnaire he had always carried morphine. It was standard issue for use in combat. He still had his kit with him, the hypodermics, the sachets of powder, the sterilised solution.

Billy pulled it out and injected Violet in the arm. Within minutes her breathing slowed and stabilised. It would make no difference to the outcome, he knew, but as the end approached, it might at least make her last moments more comfortable.

He settled himself by the bed again and waited.

'Billy.'

His head came up. The voice was very quiet, almost a whisper. He must have been drowsing. He shook his head to clear the sleep away, and leant forward.

'Yes, I'm here,' he answered.

'What happened?'

As gently as he could he told her. Part of it was his own guess, the rest was what he'd seen.

'Oh, Billy, I'm sorry,' she said. 'I promised to wake you and I didn't. You looked so calm and peaceful, I just thought I'd let you sleep. And I got myself into a frightful mess, didn't I?'

Billy had to come closer to the bed to hear her. He smiled.

'You certainly did,' he said. 'I doubt it's the first time.'

'But this time it could be the last. Am I going to die, Billy?'

He hesitated. 'Remember what they say. It's not over until the fat lady sings.'

It was night then and dark in the tent. Even in the darkness Billy thought he saw the faint smile on her face.

'Oh, Billy, I think the fat lady's about to sit down at the piano.' Violet paused. 'I feel very strange. I can't move anything. I feel all sort of broken and wrecked, but there isn't any pain.'

'That's probably the morphine I gave you.'

'It should have been champagne, Billy, much more my style. But thank you, anyway.'

Her head shifted slightly on the pillow.

'It wasn't the elephant's fault, you know that, don't you? It was my bloody fault entirely. She came out of the trees and the mist, and she was so lovely I just wanted to get closer to her. Wasn't I an idiot?'

'Yes.'

'I don't really mind dying, or I don't think I do. I would mind if she and the herd died—'

Violet broke off.

Her voice had been coming in thin hoarse spurts of sound like little coughs. For a time it faded altogether. Then it came back.

'I'm going to do what I always said I'd never do. I'm going to break my word and take my present to Boy back. He can't have the valley, it belongs to the elephants. He can't destroy them. Billy—'

Her head rolled towards him.

'Boy and I signed pre-nuptial agreements before we married. Everyone does these days, it seems. We agreed neither of us would ask anything of the other if it didn't work out. I also made a will at the same time. Boy suggested it, he's so practical. I left everything to my daughter, Rose, except of course the valley. I left that to Boy's foundation if the transfer wasn't completed at the time of my death.'

Billy had lit the kerosene lamp in the tent. In its oily yellow light he could see the pulse in Violet's forehead slowing. At the same time her voice, extraordinarily, became stronger and more urgent.

'The transfer hasn't been completed. I want it cancelled. I can do it through a codicil. Write something out for me and I'll sign it.'

Billy looked at her in amazement. She was dying and all she was considering was the elephants – the elephants who'd killed her. He thought for a moment.

'If you change your will, the valley belongs to Rose,' he said. 'What happens if she's not interested in it?'

Violet barely hesitated. She could have little more than an hour or two left to live, but her mind was suddenly lucid and alert.

'Then put something else in. Make it a condition that she spends a month out here with you before she inherits. If she doesn't understand about the valley, you'll have to convince her. That's up to you. I can't think of anything else.'

Billy had a ring-bound notebook in his travel bag.

He pulled it out. He sat with his face wrinkled as he tried to work out the phrases. Then he wrote them down. They didn't sound very official, they were stilted and awkward, but they seemed to represent what Violet wanted. He read them to her and she nodded in agreement.

'I must sign. Help me . . .'

He cradled her in his arms and lifted her up.

She moaned involuntarily. In spite of the morphine she must have felt one of the splintered bones piercing her flesh. Then she took the pen. Very slowly and carefully she wrote out her name. She lay back.

'Sign your own name as a witness, Billy,' she said. 'You'll need another one, too. There have to be two.'

Billy bit his lip. 'There's no one else here.'

'Then go back to the Laager. There's a woman there, a lovely woman, called Mama Ngina. She's old Ngoro's grand-daughter. Say I asked her to do it for me. Say she has to think I'm standing beside her as she signs. She'll do it.'

Billy sensed the trace of a smile on Violet's face again.

'We're women, Billy, just like the elephant. We're not looking for problems – we're looking for solutions. I was looking for you. I was lucky – I found you.'

She was silent. Then she whispered something so quietly Billy had to place his ear against her mouth and make her repeat it twice before he understood.

'Say I'm sorry to Boy. Say I'm grateful for being allowed to hold Eve's skull, but I remembered elephants were even more important than God. Oh, Christ, Billy, why all my life have I had to be sorry for everything?'

It was the last thing she said to him.

He took her hand, sat by her as the night passed. Sometime

in the darkness of the early morning the kerosene in the lamp burnt out and the flame spluttered and died.

Minutes later Violet died too.

He called the boys in from her camp and told them what had happened. Together they buried her in a deep grave on the river's edge, piling the earth with stones against the jackals and hyenas. The boys had ample provisions and Billy told them to remain where they were.

Then, with the codicil to her will wrapped in an oilskin pouch, he swam across the river, climbed up to his Landrover, and headed for the Laager.

He felt cold and numb, and his eyes were red-rimmed from lack of sleep, but there were no tears. He'd shed all of them during the night. When morning came he'd roughly and brutally made himself stop them. What accompanied him now as the Landrover swayed and bucketed over the track was the shining presence of the person he'd found and loved and seen savagely taken from him.

She had gone, but she'd left him the valley and her daughter Rose.

52

'You were with my daughter when she died?'

Billy nodded. 'Yes.'

Sir Michael Somerset was silent for so long Billy began to think he must have fallen asleep with his eyes half-closed, or that he'd forgotten Billy was there.

In spite of the early-summer sun outside, the log fire burning in the grate and the heavy rug across his knees, which the butler had adjusted when he showed Billy in, Sir Michael kept shivering with the persistent chill of age. He was a very old man, well into his eighties, with a mane of ice-white hair and a face that although almost skeletal now must once have been handsome and commanding.

Billy waited patiently on the other side of the fire. Finally, just as Billy was about to cough to try to attract his attention, Sir Michael spoke again.

'Poor child! She made a hash of everything and at the end she was trampled to death by an elephant. What a melancholy epitaph.'

His voice was a little hoarse but still clear and resonant.

Billy remembered Violet had described her father to him as: 'The personification of the traditional British diplomat – designed, dressed, and voice-coached by Central Casting.' She'd given an affectionate laugh. 'Except, of course, with Daddy it's all real.'

Billy understood now what she meant.

'We've never met before. How well did you know her, Mr Ramsden?' the old man asked suddenly.

Billy hesitated.

There were so many ways he might have answered.

He might even have said that this wasn't their first meeting.

Almost fifty years ago Michael Somerset, long before his career had earned him his knighthood, had given a vague smile to the scruffy little urchin Violet had insisted on dragging along the Liverpool dock to present to her father before the family disappeared in their chauffeur-driven car towards London. Billy had glowered then, hung his head, and shuffled his feet in embarrassment.

Strangely he felt almost as embarrassed now.

'On and off we were friends for many years,' he said awkwardly.

'She had everything,' Sir Michael went on. 'Beauty, intelligence, wit, money, and she blew it all. She simply picked it up and threw it out of the window.'

The old man paused again. He twisted his hands together on top of the blanket across his lap. Billy glanced down. His fingers were stiff and swollen with arthritis.

'Know France, do you?' he asked suddenly.

'Yes,' Billy answered.

'She should have been French, I always said that. In the end her problem was men. In France they handle those matters better.'

He raised his hand to the lapel of his tweed jacket.

Threading the button-hole was the scarlet insignia of a Chevalier of the Légion d'Honneur. As he plucked vaguely at the closely woven silken threads, Billy remembered again that his last posting had been as British Ambassador in Paris.

'According to the actuarial tables, men die first, Mr Ramsden,' Sir Michael went on. 'There is every reason it should be so. Biology, psychology, statistics, so many more. I, sadly, defy the norm. I am the exception which proves – in the proverb, as you know, the word means to challenge – the rule. My wife is dead, my daughter is dead, my granddaughter is dead. Metaphorically, certainly, and quite possibly literally, too. I challenge the rules and so does my granddaughter.'

For an instant, as unexpected to Sir Michael as it was to Billy, a tremor of a smile rippled across the old man's face. His elaborate construction had resulted in a joke.

'Have you heard of "Class Warfare", Mr Ramsden?'

Billy shook his head.

'Or "We are the writing on the wall"?'

Billy shook his head again.

'If you persist in looking for her, you will encounter them both. One is the regiment, the other the regimental motto.'

Sir Michael chuckled. Billy frowned. He hadn't the slightest idea what the old man was referring to.

'Go and see my solicitor. He deals with her. If anyone can help you, he will.'

Billy stood up to go. As he reached the door Sir Michael spoke again.

'I wasn't a good father, Mr Ramsden, although I wonder how many men are. Absorbed by the Office, travelling, away too much. And Violet's mother was, let's say, rather more full of life than most women. I knew, of course, but I accepted it. She was a wonderful support in my career.'

The old man wrinkled the dry paper-white skin on his forehead.

'We weren't appropriate as what I read today are called role models. However, we formed Violet and she no doubt, even in her absence, formed my granddaughter. If you find Rose, Mr Ramsden, I fear you may not altogether like what you find.'

There was a vast sadness in his voice.

Billy couldn't think of anything to say. He nodded and went out.

'Just a moment.'

Billy leant forward. He slid back the glass partition, and spoke to the cab-driver.

'I've just remembered something. This Courtney Terrace, is it a few streets on from Ramillies Crescent?'

'That's right, squire,' the cab-driver pointed ahead. 'In fact Ramillies Place – it does a dog-leg into the crescent – is just over there. In the old days I'd have driven down it to get to Courtney Terrace, but since they put in the one-way system you've got to go round.'

'Along Malplaquet Road and down by the railway arches?'

'That's it,' the driver said. 'Know the manor, do you?'

'I did once, but I haven't been back for bloody years,' Billy answered.

'You'll see a lot of changes, mate.'

The traffic lights in front of them flashed from green to amber and the cab slowed. On a sudden impulse Billy said, 'Pull in and I'll walk from here.'

He paid for the journey and the cab drew away. For an instant Billy stood on the pavement with his eyes closed in disbelief.

He still couldn't understand why it hadn't registered on him before.

The solicitor Sir Michael Somerset had referred him to had given Courtney Terrace as Rose's address. That was where her monthly cheques from one of her mother's trust funds were sent. As far as the solicitor knew she was still living there. Certainly the cheques were still being received and cashed – the bank statements on the account he administered showed that.

Courtney Terrace was only a hundred yards from Malplaquet Road. For ten years of Billy's life it had been almost as familiar to him as Mally itself. Aunt Doris' sister, Gertie, lived there, so did Steve's uncle who owned the flower stall on the corner near the hospital. Billy must have visited it twice a week.

He hesitated.

A strange and confusing feeling of curiosity, a sudden nostalgia for that first bitter winter in Britain and the years that followed, tugged at him. It would mean a detour but he felt an almost irresistible urge to walk along Mally, see the house again, smell its pungent scents of boiled cabbage, damp, and smouldering coal, call back Aunt Doris' boisterous scolding voice, visualize the dark icy nights as he ran to keep up with Jack on their way to the horses, and so much more.

Billy battled against the impulse. The detour might only take him fifteen minutes, but he hadn't even time for that. Sentimental journeys into his past could come later.

What mattered now was to find Rose. Everything else was irrelevant.

*

Number 42 Courtney Terrace was identical to its neighbours on either side of the street.

Taller and later in date than the Malplaquet Road houses, it was a three-storey brick building with a flight of steps leading down to a sunken well that gave access to the basement. The top three storeys were clearly derelict and deserted. The front and back doors had been hacked off, all the window frames were shattered, and the wind blew through the house across empty and rotting floors. If anyone lived there it could only be the occasional drunk or vagrant.

The basement was different.

Judging by the unbroken glass behind the iron bars guarding the lintel-light, it was still inhabited. Billy climbed down. The pitted concrete of the well floor was furred with islands of green moss and running with slime, apparently from a sewerage overflow. Billy wrinkled his nose in disgust. Several empty milk bottles were floating in the slime, and the rank stench of urine and raw faeces was almost over-whelming.

He pressed a bell button set into the wall.

There was no sound of a bell ringing inside and after a while he hammered on the door panel.

'What do you want?'

The voice coming through the slit of a corroded brass letter-box belonged to a woman, a young woman.

'I'm looking for Rose,' Billy said, 'Rose Somerset.'

'There's no Rose here. What do you want?' the voice demanded again.

The accent was South London.

It was almost perfect, but not quite. It had been adopted, acquired, absorbed like camouflage, and the hairs rose on the back of Billy's neck as he listened to it. Not just because he knew the authentic South London accent, but because he knew even more intimately where every one of this young woman's intonations and inflexions came from.

A child could no more throw off the imprint of its mother's speech than it could change its fingerprints. This young woman was speaking 'Brixton' in Violet's voice.

'I'm a friend of Rose's mother,' Billy said. 'I want to talk to Rose. I've got important things to tell her.'

'Fuck off!'

The answer was hurled back at him so venomously an arc of spittle glittered out through the opening into the sunlight and drifted down to melt with the slime.

Billy waited.

He heard movements inside, the mutter of voices, and then grunting and panting from what he realised were dogs. The ventilation panel on the lintel-light was swivelled open, and he sensed he was being inspected.

Then the door opened a crack.

'Okay, anything you want to say to Rose you can say to me.'

It was the same voice. The door was on a chain, and the young woman's face was hidden in darkness.

'I'm quite a patient man,' Billy replied, 'but not very patient. You either open this door right now or I go. If I do, you'll regret it to your dying fucking day. I'm talking money, young lady, your ma's money. It's just about to walk away down the street – and I mean for ever.'

A whispered argument broke out inside.

Billy turned and noisily started to climb the steps. Suddenly he heard the chain being unclipped and the door creaking open. Billy came back down the steps. The foul-smelling ooze lapped round his shoes.

He looked at Violet's daughter.

'Hullo, Rose Somerset.'

She was standing four-square in the centre of the doorway with her legs planted apart and her arms crossed.

The posture was deliberately aggressive and challenging, a way of presenting herself that she must have copied from some feminist magazine. A cigarette was slanted down between her lips – it was a French Gitane, Billy recognized the smell – and a tall gangling black boy was peering over her shoulder.

At her feet were the dogs Billy had heard snuffling, two savage-looking pit bull terriers.

'Right,' she said. 'Just call me Rose. Not Rose Somerset, I don't answer to that crap. Rose X it is, like Malcolm X. I'm doing it through the deed poll.'

Billy began to understand what Sir Michael meant by his references to Class Warfare. Rose Somerset was making an embittered protest against everything in the world including her own family and background.

He shrugged. 'That's fine by me. Some of my friends don't have names at all. You're way ahead of them.'

Billy studied her for a moment.

It was almost impossible to believe she was Violet's daughter. She had her mother's height but her body was gross and puffy, her eyes were narrow and vacant, and her short-cropped spiky hair had been dyed black.

'What the hell do you want with me?'

'I'm afraid your mother's died, Rose.'

He paused and drew in his breath. Then he went on.

Billy had intended to tell her the truth about what had happened to Violet. At the last moment he changed his mind. The whole story of her final marriage and the valley and the elephants and how he'd come to be with her at the end, was too complicated to go into on the doorstep with her boy friend scowling behind her.

The truth would have to wait until later.

Instead Billy said simply that Violet had been killed in a car crash in Africa. Before she died, he added, Violet had made a will which he'd been instructed to execute. Rose was the beneficiary, but there were conditions to be met before she could inherit.

'Your mother loved Africa,' he finished. 'She wanted you to know it too. She decided you should spend a month out there with me. What it means in a nutshell is that you can either come to Africa with me now, in which case you'll shortly end up a very rich young woman, or you can stay here and remain sodding broke. The allowance your ma paid you ended with her death. You've just had the final payment. You can check with her lawyers, but they'll tell you the same.'

The girl was silent for a while.

The news of her mother's death seemed to have left her unmoved. The conditions in Violet's will were different. She took them in and her face became rigid with anger.

'What if I don't?'

Billy glanced at the slime puddling round his feet.

'You go on wading through this shit until you change your mind. By which time, blossom, it may be too late. The will says a month in Africa with me. Like everyone else I've got a sell-by date. When you come round to it, I may not be there.'

Rose opened her mouth and let out a scream of fury.

'The fucking bitch!'

Rose's boy friend had been watching Billy with suspicious hostility over the girl's shoulders.

When she screamed he unleashed the two pit bulls on Billy. He whirled on his feet. He took the first dog in its throat with the toe of his boot, and dropped the second with an axe-blow of his flattened hand across the animal's spine.

The first animal tumbled over and collapsed coughing blood, the other shuddered, fell and lay inert.

Billy glanced at the boy friend. Billy's eyes were bleak and pitiless.

'I eat pit bulls for breakfast,' he said. 'What I do to boys who get up my nose would break your fucking heart. Know what I mean?'

Rose's boy friend knew exactly what Billy meant. He backed away, slammed the door, and ran away down the corridor inside.

Billy waited until the sound of his footsteps had faded. Then he looked back at Rose.

'I've got two tickets on today's flight to Nairobi. You're going to be sitting in one of them. They moved the writing while you weren't looking. It's not on the wall now. It's on the departure board at Heathrow.'

Billy glanced at his watch.

'Pack your bag, Class Warrior. You've got exactly thirty minutes.'

53

'Africa fucking sucks!'

Rose was crouched like a malevolent baboon on the fallen tree-trunk Billy had dragged up to the campsite to serve as a bench.

He glanced at her across the fire.

Her remark embraced her view of the entire five days and nights they'd spent together in the valley.

They'd driven there in his Landrover straight from Nairobi, not even breaking the journey at the Laager. When they'd crossed the river and reached the camp, Billy had pulled his sleeping-bag into the open and turned his tent over to her. For most of the five days she'd barely left the tent, emerging only to eat and light one of the endless cigarettes she smoked before scuttling back into its safety again.

The only other times she came out were for the morning and evening rituals of putting on her make-up before a little mirror she'd propped in a cleft in one of the trees. Twice a day she'd plaster her face with the garish cosmetics she'd brought with her from London – a thick layer of foundation, heavy lines of black smudged round her eyes, a slash of white lipstick across her mouth.

Then she'd plump up her hair with her pudgy fingers, examine herself in the mirror, lick her tongue round her lips, glower at him, and return to the tent.

Billy watched her despairingly.

He didn't know what she did inside the tent – she certainly never read and he guessed she probably lay there on her back dozing in vengeful anger. She was impervious to the valley, to her surroundings, to the life of the river, to everything.

She might never have left Brixton.

Billy had never imagined she could possess patience, but that in a way was what she was demonstrating. As Rose saw it she was living through a bad dream. She would live through it, too. She'd endure and outlast it. She was much stronger, he had begun to realise, than he'd expected. At least she had that in common with her mother.

The realisation made his heart sink all the more.

Normally Billy had to call her from the tent when the evening meal was ready. Tonight for some reason she'd chosen to stay outside after she'd finished layering her skin at the mirror.

'I bet you fucked my mother, didn't you, Billy?' she said suddenly. 'I bet your cock got me into this whole fucking mess.'

Billy said nothing.

He'd assumed – heaven knew what he'd assumed except that as Violet's daughter Rose would be something like her mother: bold and brave and funny and beautiful. It had never occurred to him for an instant she'd be a coarse foul-mouthed monster.

'She was a real slut, my ma,' Rose went on. 'She'd screw anyone. A proper scrubber, she was. Know that? Of course you do. Don't need me to tell you that.'

Billy fought to control himself, fought not to respond.

At that moment he hated Rose more than he'd ever hated anyone in his life. She had the ability to goad him close to violence, and he feared her for it. He'd experienced it the evening before when for some reason she'd suddenly clawed at his face, leaving a long raw scratch down his cheek.

He'd held himself back then. He controlled himself again now. Somehow he forced himself to go on silently stirring the guinea fowl stew he was cooking.

'Say something, for Christ's sake!' she shouted at him.

Rose's voice had the edge of hysteria Billy already recognised as the build-up to a tantrum.

'Food's ready,' he answered calmly.

He lifted the stew off the fire. Carefully he began to ladle the pieces of meat, potato and onion into the two tin plates.

'Crap!' she screamed. 'The food's crap!'

'It's all there is.' He held out the steaming dish.

Rose stared at it. Then, enraged, she swung her foot, still in the thick-soled army boots she was wearing when he found her, and kicked the plate from his hand. The plate soared into the air, showering Billy with its scalding contents.

He flinched as burning liquid ran down his chest. He stood up and circled the fire until he was standing above her

'You little witch!' he said through clenched teeth. His fists were bunched and his eyes were moist with anger and pain.

Rose shrank back and raised her arm to protect her face.

'Shit! What you cook's shit!' she repeated provocatively.

She wet her lips and stared up at him. There was a gleam in her eyes.

Suddenly Billy knew what the gleam meant. It was neither fear nor triumph, but anticipation. She was hoping he would hit her. She enjoyed being hit. It gave her a perverse form of power.

Billy unclenched his hands. Moving slowly and deliberately, he returned to his seat on the other side of the flames. He picked up his own plate and began to eat.

'You eat like a pig!' she spat out at him.

'Well, at least I do eat,' he said quietly. 'You won't until you mend your manners. Unless, of course, you intend to hunt and cook for yourself.'

'How the Christ can I do that?'

'Same as anyone else. You can start by filling the water barrel – it's only five minutes down to the river.' He paused. 'I'll make a deal. A full barrel – that's six jerry-cans – gets you a plate of food.'

'Fuck off!'

'Fine.'

Billy wiped his mouth and stood up.

He walked across the little clearing and reached up into the overhanging branch where he had hitched his sleeping-bag. He brought it back to the fireside, slipped inside, and settled down for the night.

'Sleep well, Rose.'

She swore and spat. She coughed and lit another cigarette.

Then she sat brooding on the trunk with her hands on her knees.

A tiny spotted owl swooped low over the firelight, its pearly wings glimmering as it trawled for the insects drawn to the flames. Somewhere in the distance a hyena howled, a short staccato scream that sounded almost human, and further away still a male lion roared.

Rose started. Then she settled back into angry resentful immobility.

'What the fuck's it for?'

Billy lifted his head. 'The hyena or the lion?'

'I don't mean the noises. Fuck the noises! I mean everything, all this.'

She waved her hand at the shadowy star-strewn darkness, filled with the stirrings and calls of the night which had enveloped the camp.

'Africa. What the hell does it mean? It scares the shit out of me. Why doesn't someone just get out there and flatten it? Make roads and houses, light it up, get a bit of life into it. Shoot all the fucking animals, or put them in zoos. That's where they belong.'

She chewed on her fingernail.

'Tell you what, craphead,' she went on, 'I'll go along with you. You said I could hunt. Fine. Give me a gun and I'll go out tomorrow. I'll come back with dinner. I'll shoot every fucking thing I see. How about that?'

'Go to sleep, Rose,' he said wearily.

'I want to talk. Why won't you talk to me, fuck you!'

Billy turned his back.

'Why won't you even tell me why I'm here? For the good of my soul, is it? Is that what you and my ma cooked up? Thinking I'd change, thinking I'd become a nice neat little aristo like she was, is that it? Christ, if it was, have you got a lesson coming your way, you bastard!'

Billy didn't answer.

He hunched his shoulders and buried himself in his sleeping-bag as the girl's monotonous voice whined on, draining away even the little energy he had salvaged from the day.

Beyond the circle of embers, the flames cast their glow

in flickering pinpoints of light which bounced back from the trimedra grasses as if they were being reflected from the saucer-shaped eyes of the little animals who hunted by night, or the clustering fireflies – or even from the ghosts which haunted the valley.

There were thousands of them, hundreds of thousands, millions of them. The great grey shadowy shapes which had paced down to drink from the river since the beginning of time. Billy sensed their presence round him on every side in the darkness.

Fifty years ago Finlay Hampton had told him and Violet that soon there would be nothing but ghosts left in Africa. It hadn't quite happened yet, although the elephants had dwindled close to extinction almost everywhere on the continent. In the valley one of the last healthy breeding herds was still clinging on.

If Cameron got his way, they would vanish, too.

'I want to eat!'

Rose's voice was shrill with anger – an anger sharpened by hunger.

It was the second evening that Billy had refused to share his meal with the surly young woman. For the past two days she had had nothing but dry mealies – corncobs he'd allowed her to soak and roast in the embers of the fire.

When Billy returned to camp an hour earlier he'd seen her take a bite out of a baobab fruit that a band of vervet monkeys had dropped. The fruit was unripe and bitter and she spat it out.

'Even the fruit's shit!' She hurled the kernel away into the bushes. 'Why didn't you warn me?'

'You didn't ask,' he replied mildly.

'Fuck you!'

Billy didn't feel like smiling but his features relaxed briefly in what could have passed for a wry smile.

There was nothing Rose seemed prepared to do except vent her rage and resentment in a very limited range of swear-words. She could have taken a few lessons from his colleagues in the Legion, particularly the Russians. Their curses were much more imaginative.

'For Christ's sake, at least let me have some of that!'

Billy was ladling out a plate for himself from the stewpot. He glanced at the water barrel. It was still unfilled.

All he said was, 'I see we're still short of water.'

Rose leapt up.

Under the grotesque make-up her face was white with fury and frustration. She started to lunge at him, grabbing for the pot on the ground beside Billy's stool. Billy didn't need to move. Before he'd even started to put down his plate, she stopped herself and drew back.

One thing she knew, they both knew, was that physically Billy was infinitely stronger than her.

'Bastard!' she screamed.

'You're right,' he said. 'I am. But I'm also a clean fucking bastard. I keep that way with water.'

He went on eating. The scent of the stew, venison with kaffir greens, sweet potatoes and scattering of coarse black pepper, rose fragrantly into the evening air.

Rose stared at him.

Her eyes were so narrowed by hatred Billy could barely make out her pupils, but he could see the muscles in her jaw pulsing. For an instant he thought she was going to attack him again.

Then without a word she picked up the jerry-can and headed for the river.

It took her an hour to fill the barrel. When she finished the make-up was sliding in runnels down her cheeks, and the skin below was scarlet and glistening with sweat.

Billy filled a plate from the pot and handed it to her.

'Thanks your Almighty fuck-face!' she said.

The rage, the bitterness, the resentment, were still there. But for a moment it seemed to Billy they were tempered by what could almost have been a fleeting smile – an acceptance that although they'd gone to war, although they were still in battle, although they were evenly matched and the struggle wasn't ended, somewhere far ahead lay the possibility of a truce.

Billy shrugged.

'It's a Thomson gazelle,' he said. 'I shot it out on the plain. It makes good eating.'

'It tastes like shit!' She stabbed her fork towards him. 'Know what? I'm a prole. Give me fish and chips every time. That's what real people eat.'

Billy said nothing.

Leaving Rose eating hungrily, he stood up. He went over to his sleeping-bag, and climbed inside. What had happened today wasn't much, but it was a start. Tomorrow, whether she liked it or not, he'd start to educate her. He'd teach her about the wild.

For the first time that week Billy fell asleep quickly.

54

'Do you want to go fishing?' he asked.

It was very early in the morning. The sun hadn't risen over the gorge and the valley was still sheathed in the misty paling darkness of the night. Billy had knelt down and pulled back the flap of Rose's tent to look inside.

Rose drowsily heaved herself up on her elbow and peered at him. Her first response was predictable. She opened her mouth but before she could even say the words, Billy spoke them for her.

'Fuck off!' he said cheerfully. 'Fine, now we've got that out of the way, do you want to go fishing?'

She scowled at him.

Billy could just make out her face. It was caked with the inevitable make-up but however much she layered it on, however much she hid herself in the tent's shadows, the remorseless African sun was beginning to dry and flake it away. In places her skin was acquiring a warm tanned flush.

'What the hell do you mean?' she demanded suspiciously.

'You said you liked fish,' Billy answered. 'Out here there's only one way to get it – catch it. Now's the time to work the river. Get dressed. Five minutes and we're off.'

He dropped the tent flap back and stood up.

Billy waited by the dull coals of the fire. He hadn't the slightest idea whether she'd respond. Most likely, he thought, not. She'd probably lie sulking in the tent and then drift cursing back into sleep again. On the other hand he had nothing to lose.

He had to gamble. He had to come out towards her. He had to put away everything he felt – his own hostility and contempt – and somehow draw her out into the open, into life. He owed

it to the elephants, he owed it to Violet, he owed it to the past
that had tangled and woven them all together.

Billy shivered and swore in the morning chill.

'What do I have to do?'

To his astonishment she'd emerged from the tent fully
dressed. She yawned and stared at him aggressively. It didn't
matter. At least she was there.

'I'll show you.'

He'd bought a rod in Nairobi and used it several times since
he'd been in the valley. The river teemed with tiger fish and
tilapia, and it was almost impossible to throw out a line for
more than a few minutes without hooking something. Rose,
Billy knew, was unaware of that. To her as an urban child
fishing was a complete mystery.

'Right,' he said. 'This is what you do.'

They were standing on the water's edge.

Billy handed her the rod and started to teach her how to cast
out the silver spinner into the river's centre, and then reel it
slowly back in towards her. She tried. She was clumsy and
awkward. She wrapped the line jerkily several times round
a rock, and twice snared the hook in the bush behind her.

'This is crap!' she snapped. 'I can't fucking do it.'

'Everything's crap,' Billy answered as he patiently unravelled
the line from a mopane branch. 'We both know that. Give it
one more try anyway.'

Rose muttered something and sullenly cast again.

This time the spinner arced out clear of the rock and
dropped cleanly in the water. She began to reel the line in.
Something flashed coppery-gold just beneath the surface, and
the rod's tip jerked down. Billy caught her wrist and plucked
the rod up.

A few moments later he waded into the river, gripped
the transparent leader, and came ashore with a wriggling
three-pound tiger fish dangling from his hand.

'Shit!' Rose looked at the fish astounded. 'I caught
something.'

'It's a tiger,' Billy said, knocking the fish's head on a stone.
'Bony but just about edible. Try again. See if you can get into
a nice fat tilapia.'

'Shit!' Rose repeated in awe.

She threw out the line again. For the first time her face had lost its invariable expression of bored truculence. Her forehead was furrowed in concentration, her eyes were bright, and she looked almost eager.

'You're a natural,' Billy said an hour later when the sun was over the gorge and the dawn rise had ended.

There seven fish lying on the bank, including several good tilapia. Rose had caught them all. He took the rod from her, stripped off the reel, and headed back for camp.

'Crap! Don't fucking think this means anything,' Rose said truculently as she followed him.

'Of course I don't,' Billy replied. He paused. 'Well, it does mean something. At least it means fish for the proles for supper tonight, even if we have to do without the chips.'

He walked on.

That evening as he cooked the fish Billy noticed that without any prompting from him, the water barrel had been refilled again.

'How about exploring down river?' Billy suggested next morning.

Rose shrugged.

'Exploring for what? Sex, drugs, and rock and roll? Any chance of them? Because that's all you think I'm into, isn't it? Well, don't fucking patronise me. Know what? You're a psychological illiterate. You don't know where I'm coming from or where I'm going – and believe me, sergeant fucking major, I'm going to get to where I want to be, not where *you* want me to be. Understand?'

Billy swallowed.

As so often, he had to make a conscious physical effort to control himself. There were so many contradictions in her, so much aggrieved anger, so much bitterness and resentment, so many defiant howls of rage against her past, her mother, society, the entire world she inhabited. And then once or twice, as when she'd caught the fish, a few small flashes of eagerness, of excitement, of optimism.

Billy had thought he was battling solely for the valley and

the elephants. He wasn't. He was caught up in a struggle for what he could only think of as the soul of Violet's daughter.

'Get your boots on and let's go.'

Billy turned.

He had no more idea than yesterday whether she'd follow him. Again, he doubted it, but decided to give her five minutes. He propped himself against the tree beyond the camp-fire, his back deliberately turned to the tent, and glanced at his watch.

He waited.

'All right, you bastard. Where the fuck are we going?'

The voice came from behind him. Billy didn't even turn. He allowed himself the briefest half-smile. Then he set off towards the west.

'Along the bank and on to the plain,' he said. 'We'll see if we can find the herd.'

He listened as he walked. He heard the angry stamp of footsteps behind him. He strode on.

Billy didn't know if it happened then or when Rose caught her first fish.

It was probably the fish, he thought. He sensed it was a catalyst, a tiny catalyst maybe, but still an achievement that had begun to draw her into the landscape. She had caught the tilapia and eaten them and the river would never be the same again. It was no longer a dull coiling channel of water, as grey and sullen as her face.

Suddenly the river was something wild and living, a challenge and a larder.

With skill and care and dexterity you could trawl and gather food from it. The river had its moods. It surged and sparkled at daybreak and in the evening. In the hot hours of the sun it slumbered like a snake, charging itself with warmth for the rhythms of its life to begin again. Then as the insects dropped onto the water's surface, it could be gently hunted once more.

Rose was starting to understand that.

Billy's relationship with her – and her own relationship with the valley – was changing. She would never give in easily, she would never altogether, he guessed, surrender the attitudes and values that surrounded and protected her like the flint-strong carapace of a desert tortoise.

What she had done, like a tortoise which felt itself both hungry and curious, was stretch out her head to test the air. The valley's air, to her surprise, was fresh and sweet.

'Have a look at this.' Billy paused and squatted. 'We had a leopard keeping us company last night. From the size of the pug-marks, it's a female.'

He traced his finger round the indentations in the ground.

'She may have cubs. She probably killed for them and came down here to drink afterwards.'

'How do you know?' Rose demanded.

'I don't. I'm guessing, but it's a reasonable guess. Old Ngoro, he'd have known for sure. Finlay Hampton used to say Ngoro could even have told you the leopard's name.'

'Who the hell were they?'

'Ngoro and Hampton?' Billy stood up. 'Just people I knew once, people who could really read the bush.'

He went on.

Patiently he tried to show her how to understand the landscape.

How to tell from the warning cries of the vervet monkey packs that a predator was close. How to learn from the shrill chattering calls of the weaver birds that a green or black mamba snake was coiling up a tree towards their nests. How to scan the branches for scrambling bush-babies, their eyes gleaming even brighter than the sun.

He showed her lion and antelope spoor, and taught her how to distinguish between the tracks of a cat and an antelope. He made her listen to the calls of lourie birds, with their clamouring 'go-away' song, and the plaintive mews of fish eagles. He picked up dry bone-white hyena droppings, shredded them in his palm, and held them out for her to smell.

Rose winced and drew back. Then she cautiously bent over his hand and sniffed.

'Shit!' she said. 'Smells of fucking herbs, like rosemary.'

'Twenty out of twenty, young lady.' Billy smiled. 'Hyenas

eat everything including bones. When they've finished eating, they nibble rosemary to help them digest.'

She looked at him in disbelief. 'Are you serious?'

Billy nodded.

'Not kidding me, truly?'

'I don't joke about the wild, Rose. Anything else, not that.'

She wrinkled her nose and sniffed again. 'Jesus fucking Christ!'

Rose hesitated. Then she pushed forward.

For the first time she was striding out in front of Billy. Her eyes searched the ground, quartered the bush, and swept over the trees. Billy followed her, hardly daring to believe what he was watching.

Rose was looking at the wilderness, not just with her eyes but with her mind.

Five days later, close to the end of what had become by then one of their daily forays along the valley's floor and down on to the plain, Rose paused. She'd taken to walking ahead and she dropped to her knees in front of Billy. She wiped the sweat from her face and beckoned him forward.

'What the hell's this?'

Billy came up to her shoulder.

Quite involuntarily he checked as he reached her. He stared down at her questioning upturned face.

Over the past week she had changed almost out of all recognition. Without his noticing it, she'd stopped caking herself with make-up. Her skin was clear and tanned and glowing. Her body had shed pounds, too. When he'd dragged her out of the Brixton basement, she'd been gross and puffy. Now she was lithe and slender, and seemed to gleam with health.

Billy shook his head and knelt beside her.

He had no need to kneel. If Rose hadn't been crouching in front of him and obscuring it, he could have seen the huge print from yards back.

'Elephant,' he said.

Billy explored the rim of the print with his fingers.

The crispness of its edges told him it was fresh. He glanced to left and right. A trampled track led away on one side into the bush and on the other down to the water.

The herd had drifted away after Violet's death. Their departure had nothing to do, Billy knew, with the appalling incident by the water's edge. It was simply part of the random dynamic of their feeding habits. They had moved downstream to the west.

Now they were circling back again. Soon they'd begin to throng the banks round the camp to drink.

'I haven't seen any elephants yet, have I?' Rose said.

'No,' Billy smiled. 'You'd hardly have missed them if you had.'

'You never told me there were elephants here.'

'True,' he acknowledged.

'Why not?'

'I just thought we'd wait until they came.'

She gazed at him. Her stare was acute and penetrating. For the first time Billy saw a reflection, an echo of her mother's candid commanding look in Rose's hare-bell blue pupils.

'Does this have anything to do with my ma?'

Billy shifted uncomfortably on his heels. Rose's perceptions, like her mother's, were frightening in their immediate, arrow-piercing accuracy.

'Your mother liked elephants, yes,' he answered lamely.

'Not good enough, Billy, not fucking good enough!'

She had seen the opening, the vulnerability, the uncertainty, and went for it with the ruthlessness of a falcon swooping from the sky on some wounded pigeon.

'I want to know about the elephants. Most of all, I want to know about my ma. Tell me!'

Billy heaved himself to his feet. They walked together in silence back to the camp.

Then he told her.

55

Rose looked at Billy in silence.

For once she didn't even seem able to call up one of the tired worn expletives that prefaced everything she said.

Instead she pushed back her hair from her face and asked softly. 'Why didn't you tell me any of this?'

Billy thought for a moment.

'I'd intended to,' he answered. 'Then when I saw you first in that house in London with your boy friend and the dogs, I changed my mind. I didn't think it would make any sense.'

'So you told me my mum had been killed in a car-crash?'

Billy nodded.

He'd made up the story on the spur of the moment, and he'd barely thought about it since. He'd blocked it out of his mind, while waiting for the right moment to tell Rose the truth. There was no right moment. Rose had simply drawn it from him as if she'd made the choice herself.

'Shit!'

Her favourite word had come back to her, but this time she wasn't using it in anger, Billy sensed, more in bewilderment, as a punctuation mark in the confusion of her thoughts.

'What else is true and what else is lies?'

'There aren't any more lies,' Billy answered. 'Everything else I've told you – your mother's will, Boy Cameron, and what he plans to do to the valley – it's all true.'

'And this Mr Cameron, my mum's new husband, he doesn't know she's dead?'

Billy shook his head.

It was another of the decisions he'd made. Cameron was travelling in the Far East. Once Violet had decided to stay on in the valley, Cameron knew she'd be out of contact and he wouldn't have expected to hear from her. Apart from Billy and Rose, the only people who knew Violet had died were the boys. To them it was no great matter. They were Africans and sudden death was a commonplace in their existence.

'He'll have to be told soon, of course,' Billy said. 'But I wanted you to know first, and I wanted you to come here first.'

Rose frowned. 'If Ma died here, was she buried here too?'

'Yes.'

'Where?'

Billy hesitated. 'Do you want to see?'

'Of course I want to see!' she blazed out at him. 'You only get given one mother, don't you, even if you never really knew her? Show me!'

Billy stood up. He led her along the bank and then into the bush to the cairn of stones he and the boys had piled over Violet's grave.

Rose stood looking down at it.

After a while she turned. She headed for the river and came back with a handful of yellow-white lilies she must have plucked from the vegetation that carpeted the water. She knelt and placed the lilies on the highest point of the cairn.

'Hullo, Mum, it's me, Rose,' her words were so quiet Billy could barely hear them. 'Love you, Mum. Sleep well.'

She stayed on her knees for several minutes.

Then she got to her feet. She shook her head and stared at the bush. The black dye in her hair was being burnt out by the sun, and every day she looked fairer and more tousled.

Billy thought of Violet with her flying skirts making great loops like a swallow on the swing in the gardens of the Laager, and the way her hair had streamed out behind her – golden and rippling in the mountain wind of the Aberdares. Rose was her mother's daughter, she was becoming Violet.

He closed his eyes. Then he heard Rose's voice.

'Why don't you just go and leave me alone?'

He blinked and looked at her.

Rose was glaring at him. There was so much savagery

in her eyes, so much fury and grief and confusion, that he rocked back on his heels as if she'd hit him.

Billy recovered his balance, and turned and walked away.

He went back to the camp. He collected his sleeping-bag and ferreted around for what he'd need in the bush – a few knives, an iron cooking-pot, a box of matches. Then he set off towards the plain.

Rose needed time and space on her own. That was all he knew. Everything else, every decision and choice that followed, was up to her.

As he walked along the bank Billy noticed pug-marks in the sand.

He stopped out of habit and examined them. They belonged to a lioness. It was spring. The plains' grasses were growing, the antelope were drifting back to feed, the lioness probably had cubs. She had, he guessed, come down to the river either to drink or more likely in search of prey.

He considered the possibilities for a moment. Then he walked on.

In the end, Billy reflected long afterwards, it wasn't Rose who made the decision and the choice.

It was made for her either by the lioness whose tracks he'd crossed or by the great female elephant. He would never know which, nor would Rose. All Billy knew was that he'd taught Rose how to use the rifle, just as he'd taught her how to use the rod, and the last thing he did before he walked away was to remind her where he kept it – under the truckle bed in the tent that used to be his and now was hers.

He made his own camp, an outpost or 'fly-camp' as it was known in the language of the bush, a mile away on the edge of the plain. He was prepared to stay there if necessary for several days to give Rose the peace and time she needed.

He was only there for twenty-four hours.

The lioness lay in the long grasses close to the river with her chin resting on her paws.

Her tongue flicked out and across her dry lips as she continued her vigil. She was hungry, desperately hungry, but not for herself although the hunger in her own body gnawed at her. She was hungry for her litter of five cubs in the bush behind, hungry to fill her belly so her udder would swell and discharge enough milk to feed them.

The lioness inhaled deeply.

The breeze lifting up from the river brought a tangled skein of scents to her nostrils, all of them carrying messages from the water and the bush on the banks on either side. She wrinkled the tawny mask of her face and delicately began to unravel what the messages signalled.

The year had been a catastrophe.

The rains had been meagre and most of the plain's grasses had failed in the dry barrenness that followed. The antelope herds the lioness depended on for food had scattered far and wide in search of their own nourishment. Then she had lost the four other younger lionesses who would normally have made up the pride's hunting strength.

Two had been gored to death by a buffalo herd in a misguided attack on a young buffalo cow. One had died from infection after being pierced by porcupine quills after an equally incautious attack. The fourth, slowed by a congenital deformity in her hind leg, had fallen behind as the hunt continued and been pulled down by some of the bravest and most ferocious predators of the African bush, a hyena clan.

All the while the lioness was nurturing the seed implanted in her months earlier by a rogue wandering male lion. The male had long since vanished. Now she was alone without hunting partners – but with her five cubs.

The river was her last resort. Almost every animal, prey or predator, the lioness knew, had to visit it to drink. Without water none of them could survive. The river's banks offered her a final opportunity to kill and save both herself and her litter.

The lioness scanned the scent messages coming back to her on the air.

For minutes and then for hours the breeze was as barren as the dusty floor of the plain. And then towards evening she stiffened and the hairs prickled on her hide. A huge creature, a female like herself, was shouldering its way down to the water. The creature was an elephant.

The lioness knew instantly from the spores of the uterine discharges the elephant was not only pregnant, she was about to give birth.

The wind never lied.

Saliva filled the lioness's mouth. An elephant calf was the most dangerous prey of all to try to seize from its mother. It was also the plumpest and richest, and like every other mammal an elephant was at its most vulnerable in the few moments after birth.

In other circumstances the hunting strategies programmed into the lioness's brain over millions of years would never have allowed her to consider a solitary attack on an elephant calf. Now she had no choice. She could hear her hollow-flanked cubs whining in starving dying anguish behind her, and she herself was not only famished but desperate.

She flicked out her black-tipped tail.

The great cow elephant came closer. The lionness's tail twitched and froze. The wind was in both their faces. It carried no warning. The elephant strode by her and headed for the river.

As quiet and still in the dry grass as one of the gorge's ancient rocks, the lioness waited patiently and ravenously for the moment of the birth.

The elephant was Uhuru's granddaughter and the herd's matriarch for the past ten years.

She pushed her way through the undergrowth, trampling down the thick thorn in her path as if it had been paper. Her trunk swung enquiringly from side to side and her great splayed feet crunched through the papyrus rafts as she reached the marshy edges of the water.

Beneath her swayed a swollen belly as tight and round as a gigantic grey tsama melon. Her time was upon her.

She'd left the herd behind her feeding on the plain. Unusually for an elephant she'd chosen to give birth alone. She'd even dismissed the group of unmated cows and the old barren aunts of her family group who would normally have shielded and supported her when she went into labour – releasing scent spores over them to convey her decision.

She was the matriarch. She feared no one and nothing. The river and the valley belonged to her. Her ancestors had always come there to drink, to give birth, and to die. So had she and because she was the herd's leader, she'd come on her own terms and for her own unfathomable reasons alone.

In the darkness she began to search round for the place where she would drop her calf.

Rose slept little during the night.

Once when the moon was high she'd left the tent and visited her mother's grave again, ignoring all Billy's warnings not to stray from the camp in the darkness. She'd stood for a while listening to the owl calls and the rustling of the water as she gazed down at the desolate little cairn.

For some reason Violet was much more vivid and real to her in death than she'd ever been in life. Then she was a distant but seldom-glimpsed presence, beautiful and romantic to Rose as a child but also puzzlingly cold, careless, and selfish. Rose had longed passionately to be with her, to talk to her, to feel her mother's arms round her so she could pour out her troubles and be comforted by her.

It never happened. All her life she had faced her nightmares and shed her tears alone.

As she grew up she felt at first bewildered, then betrayed, and finally filled with bitter resentment and anger. No other mother treated her child with Violet's callous indifference. Violet could only be a monster. Rose turned violently against everything she believed her mother stood for – her class, her values, her wealth, even her beauty.

It had led Rose to the squalid Brixton squat and the black boy, Sammy, and his pit bulls and his crack-dealing. It had also led her out again. She thought she could reject and forget the past. It was impossible. The past and all the luggage that travelled with it, including the legacy of her mother's fortune, was all she had.

Billy had thrust it back at her on the Brixton street.

Now Rose was utterly confused.

She understood nothing except that Violet wasn't a monster. Violet was simply her mother, a strange, wilful, and unknown woman lying buried in the African earth. She'd been crushed to death, according to Billy, by an elephant. Rose hadn't even seen an elephant. She knew nothing about Billy either except that long ago as children he and Violet had visited the valley, and they wanted to preserve it.

Rose shook her head.

She turned weeping, ran back to the tent, and threw herself down on the truckle bed. Eventually she fell into a tormented sleep.

She woke very early before the sun had lifted over the gorge. Her mind was still numb, and she felt dull and lifeless. Somehow she knew that if she was to get through the day, she had to perform the routine tasks of the camp. The first was to replenish the water supplies. Mechanically she picked up the jerry-cans and headed for the river.

Rose saw the elephant when she was barely fifty yards from the water.

The herd's matriarch had chosen the river's shallows as a birth-bed. She'd picked a place among the reeds and lilies in the shadow under the acacia branches, where the soft rose-coloured mud could buoy up her swollen belly and she could cool her skin with water sucked up by her trunk from the gentle flow of the current.

At first, spotting the dark water-washed bulk lying among the lilies, Rose thought a boulder had tumbled down from the cliff above. Then she saw the bulk's flanks heave and realised the great mass was something alive, and she froze in terror.

She waited, trembling.

Minutes passed. Slowly Rose realised it could only be an elephant – an elephant, she guessed, that must have heaved itself into the water, collapsed, and was dying. She crept forward and crouched on the bank only feet above the creature in the shallows below.

The matriarch was unaware of Rose. The elephant was unaware of anything except that she was in the last stages of labour, and the calf inside her was straining to be born.

Rose inched closer. She could see the elephant's painfully parted legs now, and a gleaming trail of mucus mixed with blood from the torn membranes flowing from the birth channel. With a sudden shock Rose realised the creature wasn't dying – she was about to give birth.

The elephant's flanks heaved again and a great shuddering spasm ran over the animal. Almost instantly Rose saw it – the new-born creature, for a moment no more than a tangle of deeply wrinkled limbs, fragile and formless as they slid out into the silver light of the valley's dawn and floated snuffling on the water. Behind it the mother's pelvic muscles continued to clench and unclench convulsively.

Rose tensed and waited spellbound, her own body aching in sympathy with the sufferings of the mother.

And still the birth wasn't over. The elephant heaved herself upright, her feet sending cascades of spray over the lilies. She lifted the calf with her trunk, plucked away the umbilical cord, and placed her child on the bank. Then she settled back into the shallows to expel the after-birth.

Just beneath Rose the calf staggered and almost fell. It regained its balance, lifted its tiny trunk, and gave out its first call – a thin piteous cry for help to its mother.

Rose's eyes filled with tears.

Her muscles were stiff and chill from the long silent minutes she'd spent on the bank watching the unfolding miracle of the birth. Instinctively she stretched out her hand to touch the calf in a gesture of comfort. Her fingers fondled the damp oily skin on top of its neck. As they did the mother elephant swung her head round.

For an instant Rose and the matriarch locked eyes. They stared at each other.

In some remote chamber of her mind Rose was aware she'd done the most dangerous thing it was possible for her to do – to touch a new-born elephant calf within sight of its mother. It was an invitation to death, an invitation for an instant reflex response from the mother elephant to hurl herself from the water and crush the threat to her child. Rose's own mother had been killed by the same animal for much less.

Rose knew it and she was still unable to stop herself. As if she was in a trance she gently caressed the calf's neck.

The matriarch looked back at her.

She didn't charge as she had at Violet. She seemed to acknowledge Rose. It was almost as if they had both shared the supreme moment of all warm-blooded female creatures – the joy of birth, the triumph of life over death. Rose might have been one of the unmated females from the matriarch's own family. She had left them behind on the plain, but now she was glad to have Rose with her.

The elephant trumpeted quietly and expelled the after-birth. She rinsed herself in the water and began to turn to climb up the bank to suckle her calf. And then it happened. She stopped with her feet still in the shallows and screamed out a warning.

Later Rose didn't know if it was her own instinct or some extraordinary communication between herself and the matriarch. She only knew the scent of fear and danger that invaded her nostrils was so rank and powerful and urgent, it almost overwhelmed her.

The waiting lioness knew no such emotion as fear.

The lioness knew only hunger. Hunger and patience. Moving silently, her belly low to the ground, she had worked her way to within yards of the girl and the labouring matriarch. She too had watched and waited all through the night and then the dawn. She had been disturbed by the presence of the human on the bank, but the birth had taken place, the calf was in front of her, and she could wait no longer.

The big cat gathered herself to spring.

Rose saw no more than the flicker of the black ear tips and the movement of the black-tipped tail. It was enough. She had disobeyed almost all of Billy's instructions, but at least this time she'd brought his rifle with her. It was beside her on the grass. She seized the rifle, snapped off the safety catch, and began to pump the trigger.

She fired with what she realised in bewilderment afterwards was astonishing calmness and control. She barely knew how to use the gun – she'd only fired off a few rounds the day before when Billy taught her how the mechanism worked and how to use the sights. Now she felt fearless and confident, as if she'd been handling weapons all her life.

Later still Rose realised why. In the brief moment their

eyes had locked together, an unbreakable bond had been forged between her and the elephant. For both their sakes she could not let the calf be killed.

Her first, second, and third bullets ricocheted harmlessly off the rocks in the lioness' path, but the detonations were enough to make the animal swerve. The lioness checked for an instant. Then she snarled and bounded on again. She leapt upwards, her sinuous body tracing a tawny arc against the mist as her talons reached out for the calf.

Rose fired again.

She was steadier and more composed than she'd ever been, and she thought she had the lioness in her sights. She would never be sure. It might just have been luck, but it didn't matter. The bullet caught the animal high up in the muscle above her shoulder-blade.

The lioness spun round in mid-air as if she'd been hit by a massive hammer-blow. A roar of anger welled out of her open throat, and she dropped to the earth. She lay for a moment, stunned. Then she stumbled to her feet and limped, still growling furiously, back into the trees.

Rose watched her disappear. Then she dropped the rifle and wept uncontrollably.

56

Ten miles down the valley, at its entrance to the plain, Billy's head jerked up.

He listened.

The distant sound had shattered the stillness of the morning air. The funnel of the river's bed and the steep cliffs of the gorge both magnified and distorted the noise, but he had no doubt what it was.

A rifle-shot.

Billy listened again, straining his ears. He heard more shots in swift succession, then a lion's roar, and then the screaming of an elephant. The sounds followed each other so quickly they almost blended into one. Icy surges of adrenalin began to pump through his stomach. There was only one rifle in the valley. It was his and he'd given it to Rose.

Barely ten days before he'd fired the rifle as Violet was being trampled to death at the same place where the sounds were coming from now. The elephants, he knew, had returned.

With a sickening sense of the past repeating itself in tragedy again, he began to run, his feet pounding frantically along the bank.

He was strong and fit and used to the African bush, but the journey still took him almost three hours. When he reached the camp-site Billy glanced round sweating and heaving for breath.

There was no sign of Rose.

Puzzled and fearful he ran over to the tent and pulled back the flap. He blinked at the dusky interior after the harsh white sunlight outside. Rose was lying asleep on the bed. Her face was pale and there were runnels of what he guessed were tear marks down her cheeks.

Billy closed his eyes for an instant in relief. At least she was safe. He squatted down by the bed and waited for her to wake.

'I saw the calf being born,' Rose said.

It was an hour later.

While Billy had watched her she'd been sleeping so deeply she might have been in a coma. Her chest barely moved and her breathing was almost indetectible. Now she woke instantly. Whatever had forced her to retreat into sleep in the middle of the morning – it could only have been some trauma, Billy guessed – had been exorcised as she lay still.

She was healed. Her eyes were bright and clear, and her voice steady and thoughtful. She looked at him unblinking.

Billy didn't need to ask what calf. Even as he raced towards the camp his trained eye had seen the footprints of the great female elephant leading back into the bush, and the small fragile spoor of her newly dropped calf in her wake.

'What happened?' he said. 'Why did you fire?'

Rose rolled out of bed.

She had taken off her clothes against the heat and stood for a moment naked in front of him. Unselfconsciously she raised her arms, yawned, and shook her head, sending her hair swirling out in a golden fan in the light streaming in through the tent's open flap.

Billy felt his stomach turn over.

Rose had been with him in Africa for less than three weeks. He'd been aware she was changing, but not like this. He remembered the sullen puffy-cheeked girl in the stench of the Brixton basement, with the layers of caked and dirty make-up on her face, her spiky black-dyed hair, her blotchy pallid skin, and the smell that came off her – almost as rank as the garbage swilling round her feet.

It had gone, all of it.

She hadn't so much changed as been transformed. She was tall and slim and lithe. Her breasts stood out firm and strong. Her body was tanned and glowing. There were muscles and sinews in her legs and arms in place of chalk-white padding of fat. Her head was still tinged with black, but the African sun had burnt out most of the dye and the natural tawny-yellow of her hair, growing longer and more tousled every day, gleamed.

Billy had despaired of ever seeing her as Violet's daughter. He was wrong. She wasn't just Violet's daughter – she was Violet. Violet in her early-twenties as Rose was now. The Violet he'd never known but had imagined and yearned for across the years.

He closed his eyes again, and shook his head in wonder.

'Shit!' he heard her say.

Billy opened his eyes and looked at her.

Rose had picked up a towel and was wrapping it round her. She might have become Violet, but she would never stop being Rose. Nothing would ever change that or the language she used.

Billy remembered her mother and the swear-words they'd proudly traded as children. Perhaps that was part of Rose's inheritance, part of her identity and the uniqueness Violet had passed on to her. Neither mother nor daughter cared about the polite conventions of society. They were happier using the language of the streets.

He smiled to himself and followed Rose out of the tent.

They stood side by side together looking down towards the river.

'It's mine, Billy, isn't it?' She swept out her arm towards the gorge, across the valley, and down towards the plain. 'All of it.'

He nodded.

'And my mum gave it to her husband, to Mr Cameron, for his foundation.' She was working through in her mind what Billy had told her. 'Except in the end she didn't. Because when she was dying she cancelled that. She gave it to me instead.'

'Yes,' Billy said. 'We had to bend the rules a little. A will needs two witnesses. I was the only one available. There's a woman at the Laager, the granddaughter of old Ngoro. Your ma had made friends with her and I got her to sign it, too, on my way to collect you. I think it'll stand up.'

'She wanted to keep the valley safe for the elephants and her husband wants to dig it up,' Rose paused. 'Are you a Christian, Billy?'

Billy frowned. 'I believed in Father Geoffrey. I believe in God when I'm under gunfire and when I'm flying. Most soldiers do. Otherwise God and I, we tend to leave each other alone.'

'So you're not. But if you were,' she insisted, 'and if this really was the Garden of Eden, wouldn't it be the holiest place on earth?'

'Yes, if you think life is holy,' he answered after a moment. 'No, if you think religion's holy. There are much more important places than the Garden of Eden. Bethlehem and Jerusalem and Calvary—'

Billy broke off.

He searched his mind for other places in his childhood memories of the Sunday school Bible classes Aunt Doris had made him and the other children in the Mally house attend at St Barnabas in Brixton. Nowhere else came back to him.

'But what do you think?' Rose demanded.

'I just like life and I like elephants.' Billy gave his wry shuttered grin. 'Maybe they're the same. Maybe, like old Ngoro said, when one goes so does the other.'

Rose was silent.

Her face was creased in thought and her expression was impenetrable. Billy hadn't the slightest idea what she was thinking. He knew he'd done his best, he knew she'd changed beyond recognition, but he didn't know whether he'd got through to her. All he knew was that it was up to her now.

'I've had four fucking abortions,' she said eventually. 'Know that?'

Billy shook his head. She'd never mentioned it.

'The last one was a year ago. I left it late and had it done cheapo. A week afterwards I started to bleed. Sammy took me into casualty. They kept me in a week and stitched me up good and tight. Just before they tossed me out, I asked the gynae – a woman, she was – why the fuck they couldn't come up with a reliable contraceptive?'

Rose stared at the water.

Anger had come back into her voice as if she was reliving a still-raw and wounding experience.

'Know what the old bitch said? They would very soon, she said. Except I needn't worry. It wouldn't make any difference to me. My innards had been duffed up so bad, I'd never have a child.'

The towel was beginning to slip down her body and Rose broke off. She gathered it up and tied it round herself again. Then she rounded on Billy. Her eyes were suddenly intense and frighteningly, hauntingly, lonely.

'Think I'm mad, Billy?'

'No,' he said quietly.

'Well, you will now, believe me. Because when I walked out of the hospital, I promised myself I'd prove that old cow of a gynae wrong. I would have a child and I'd give it everything my mum never gave me. That was what I was going to show mum and her. One day I'd go back to both of them with my child and say, "Look, you bitches, look at what I've done in spite of all you've tried to stop me. I've won, not you— "'

Rose broke off. 'Except, of course, I couldn't.'

For an instant tears filled her eyes.

They weren't tears of self-pity or even anger. They were tears of a deep tormented frustration. She wanted to get even with Violet and the gynaecologist. It was in her prickly defiant nature. But more than that, more than anything, Billy realised, she truly wanted a child of her own.

He drew in his breath.

In spite of all the changes in her, she was still to him the sulky foul-mouthed slut he'd found in the Brixton basement. He'd been prepared for almost anything after that. Not this. Not this extraordinary confession of longing and despair.

Rose tossed her head, angrily shaking the tears from her eyes.

'Well, I've got a child now, haven't I? A fucking elephant calf! Not quite mine but the best, the closest, I'll ever get. I was there when she was born. I watched it all. I looked at her mum and she accepted me. And then when that lion tried to kill her, I stopped it. I saved her. She's mine, Billy, she's mine!'

Rose laughed and glanced at him, her hair tangled and wet with the sweat of her sleep.

'Told you I was mad, didn't I?'

'You're not mad, Rose,' Billy said quietly. 'I think you're very sane.'

'Sane or barking, I'll tell you this. No one's going to take that calf from me, nor this valley either.'

She paused and added softly, 'You got what you wanted, Billy.'

For a long time he said nothing. He looked at Rose and then across the river at the cliffs on the far side.

From somewhere up there, more than a lifetime ago it seemed, Ngoro had shown him and Violet the valley and the elephants. Now it all belonged to Rose, even the elephants which were so inextricably woven into the valley's life, and she was committed to their survival. Billy hadn't the slightest doubt about that.

A circle had been completed. The valley and its animals were safe.

It should have been the end.

Promises were the hardest of all things to keep, but he'd kept them. To Violet, to himself, to the elephants, even in a way to Rose. He could walk away and leave the rest to her, so much younger, passionate, growing into maturity, Violet's real daughter – not the lost and lonely grotesque he'd found in London – with all her mother's failings but all her infinitely greater strengths, too.

It was not the end.

Billy's mind wasn't on Rose or Violet or even the elephants. It was on Cameron, and something undefined but dark and troubling was plucking at the back of Billy's brain. The man was powerful, charming, magnetic, and immensely rich. He was also secretive and obsessive. Violet had told him that, and Billy had seen enough of it for himself to know it was true.

Cameron had spent his life on a hunt for the 'bones and stones' that charted humanity's beginnings, on a quest that was almost a personal crusade to find out where man was born. Now he believed he'd finally found the answer and the Garden of Eden.

Would he, Billy wondered suddenly, surrender it to an arbitrary change in the will of his dying wife?

Billy glanced back at Rose.

'I think it's time for Mr Cameron to know what's happened,' he said. 'Your mother was his wife, after all. He'll be somewhere midway through his business trip. I think you should write and tell him everything, including the change Violet made to her will. We can fax your letter to one of his offices from the Laager. He'll have it within hours.'

Rose hesitated. She looked at him uncertainly. 'Is there something behind this, Billy?'

'No,' he answered. 'I'd like to think he'll just accept it, but I doubt that. I think he'll come back to the valley immediately to meet you. I think he'll try to make you change your mind.'

'And let him dam the river and dig all of this up? You think I'll say yes?' She smiled the bright youthful smile of unshakeable confidence. 'Shit, Billy, you still don't know me!'

'Maybe,' he replied sombrely. 'But I do know Mr Cameron.'

They drafted the letter that evening by the light of the camp's kerosene lamps.

Billy wrote most of it. Rose added a few phrases of her own. The letter was short and simple.

'Dear Mr Cameron,' it began, 'My name is Rose Somerset. As you will know, I'm the only daughter of your wife. Three weeks ago my mother was tragically killed by an elephant here in the valley where I write from. She has been buried peacefully on the bank of the river.

'I was brought here from London by my mother's childhood friend, Billy Ramsden. I believe you have met him. Billy has been a great help to me. He thought I should know of the tragedy first, and left it to me to tell you. I do so now very sadly. She was a wonderful person. You will know that as well as me.

'I have now seen my mother's grave and am beginning to gather my thoughts, although I am still deeply shocked.

Before she died my mother made a few changes to her will. I believe she was going to leave the land she owned here to your foundation. She has left it instead to me. She loved the elephants of the valley and wanted to keep them safe. She thought it might be better for me to have the land. I shall do my best to respect her wishes. I hope you approve.

'I hope to meet you soon. I shall be staying on here in Africa for some time. I end in sorrow for a grief I know we both share.'

Rose signed the letter.

The next morning she and Billy crossed the river, climbed up to his Landrover, and headed for the Laager. They sent the letter by fax to the head office of Cameron's corporation in Harare, and set out for the valley again.

'What happens now?' Rose asked as they bumped away down the track.

'We get on with living while we wait for his helicopter.'

'You're sure he'll come?'

Billy nodded.

'I don't see what difference it's going to make.' She shook her head in exasperation. 'Mum's dead, the valley's mine, what on earth can he do to change that?'

Billy didn't answer. He didn't even want to think about it.

Instead he concentrated on guiding the vehicle through the thorn bushes.

57

'Rose!'

Cameron strode forward to greet her.

His arms were stretched wide and his white hair was streaming back from his powerful craggy face in the draught from the still-whirling helicopter blades.

Rose looked pale and hesitant. Cameron ignored her uncertainty. He reached her and caught her up in an embrace that combined warmth, sympathy, and protectiveness.

Billy watched.

Even from where he was standing twenty yards away, the force of the man's presence was almost overwhelming in its vigour and intensity. Cameron held Rose to him for several moments. Then he stepped back and studied her affectionately, his head tilted to one side.

'Violet's daughter,' he said softly. 'How could you be anything else? What sadness to meet you first like this, but also what happiness and support. I may have lost your mother. At least I have you.'

'Thank you,' Rose said in a dry nervous voice.

Cameron turned and looked at Billy.

'Mr Ramsden – or may I call you Billy now? And please call me Boy – how good to see you again even in these tragic circumstances.' He held out his hand. 'Obviously I want to know everything, but there's one thing I don't have to ask. I know you must have done everything in your power for Violet. I'm deeply grateful for that.'

Billy came forward and shook Cameron's hand awkwardly.

It was late in the afternoon three days after they'd sent the letter from the Laager, and the helicopter had just landed. Cameron had alighted alone. Billy had no idea where the letter had found him, but he must instantly have cancelled all his plans, taken the next flight to Nairobi, and flown from there to the valley.

It was exactly what Billy had expected him to do.

'Are my camp and the boys still here?' Cameron went on.

Billy nodded.

'Excellent. I think Rose and I, perhaps all three of us, need some time alone together. I'm sure we all need a little peace. I'm sending the helicopter away. I've arranged for a vehicle to be left for me up on the other side of the river. I'll drive it back to the Lodge myself when we've worked out what to do.'

Cameron called to the pilot who was unloading his luggage. The pilot ran over and Cameron spoke to him briefly. Ten minutes afterwards the helicopter took off and circled away over the gorge to the east.

'My dear,' Cameron took Rose's arm, 'can we tackle the hardest things first? I would like to see your mother's grave. Will you take me there now?'

'Of course,' Rose answered.

Billy saw her cheeks were white now. Cameron's arrival, the impact of his physical presence, and the awakened memories of her mother's death had shaken and unsettled her.

'And, Billy,' Cameron swung round again, 'would you excuse us? This is something I feel Rose and I should do together. Would you get the boys to take my things into camp? I've brought some provisions with me. Tell them to prepare a meal. I think we should all get together properly over supper.'

He turned once more before Billy had a chance to reply, wrapped his arm comfortingly over Rose's shoulder, and led her away.

Billy stared after them as they walked along the bank. Rose was moving stiffly, almost like a marionette. Cameron was towering above her with his head lowered towards hers. He was evidently talking to her, but they were too far away for Billy to hear what he was saying.

All the strength and grace Rose had acquired in the valley, all Violet's energy and determination, seemed to have gone. Beside Cameron she looked like a cowed and frightened child. Billy's heart sank.

He waited until they were out of sight. Then he swore and called for the boys.

'Rose and Billy,' Cameron leant forward, 'I want to talk to both of you. What I'm going to say mainly concerns you, Rose. But perhaps it also involves you, Billy.'

His eyes moved from Rose's face and Billy felt Cameron's steady piercing gaze on his own.

'I want to talk about the valley.'

It was dark now and they were sitting by the fire after dinner in the main camp – Violet's camp as Billy would always think of it.

Cameron and Rose had come back from Violet's grave as dusk fell. Billy didn't know what they'd talked about while they were away and he hadn't had a chance to speak to Rose since, but she seemed even more tense and wary than when she left.

It was only as they sat down and she reached under the table to give his hand a quick squeeze that Billy felt any small sense of relief. Cameron, he guessed, had turned the full power of his personality on her. Whatever he was out to achieve, he hadn't succeeded yet.

'Your mother has gone, Rose,' he went on. 'That's a sorrow you and I will share for the rest of our lives. The best legacy she left is our memories of her alive. They will always be unforgettable. But she left other legacies too. Among them of course is the valley, which at the end she gave to you. Billy was there and he's told me why.'

He glanced over for confirmation. Billy nodded expressionlessly.

While Rose was washing before dinner, the men had spent half an hour alone. Cameron had questioned him courteously but with the incisive insistence of an interrogator about every aspect of Violet's death. Billy told him the truth in every way but one – that he hadn't found Violet missing from her tent, as he said to Cameron, but from his own.

Whether Cameron suspected anything else or even cared, Billy had no idea. The man gave away nothing at all. The rest was exactly as it had happened and Cameron seemed satisfied.

'She was in pain, she was dying,' Cameron was saying to to Rose. 'She was worried about the elephants. She thought they'd be safer with you. I believe she was wrong, Rose, but I understand and respect her decision. However, it's not just the elephants who inhabit the valley.'

He paused. 'I wasn't altogether frank with Billy when I was here before. You know that now. I had good cause and I'm sure Billy accepts that. Your mother told him the real reason and he told you. You know what I thinks buried beneath the river?'

'The Garden of Eden,' Rose said.

'The Garden of Eden,' Cameron repeated musingly. 'The bones of Adam and Eve, of Cain and Abel, and all their descendants. The first apple tree and the first serpent. The cradle, the nursery, from which the first true humans, the scavengers and hunter-gatherers, stepped out and began to colonise the earth. The birth-place of man.'

He stood up and began to pace round the fire as he talked.

Billy listened to him mesmerised. He knew Rose was doing the same. It was impossible not to. It was the most compelling, spell-binding performance either had ever heard.

Cameron spoke of his own past and the start of his lifelong quest among Finlay Hampton's little collection of fossils and rocks at the Laager. And then of an infinitely greater past, the past of all humanity which he'd tracked and searched for across half a century.

He spoke of galaxies and stars and meteors. Of oxygen and water interacting and how, millions upon millions of years ago, some organism might have formed in the primal soup of the world's beginnings and been heaved up on to land. How the organism's constantly multiplying and changing offspring had evolved across the ages into groups of recognisable creatures.

One of the groups, he said, had become the primates – the apes and monkeys. Strain after strain of them withered and died out, but some survived. They clung on, adapting to changes in the climate, the landscape, and the vegetation, until finally one line – the last link in the chain that coiled back into the darkness of the universe's own beginnings – emerged on the plains of Africa as Homo sapiens, conscious, thinking, modern man.

'It happened here,' he finished. 'I showed your mother a skull once, Rose, the skull of a woman. I told her it was the skull of God. I believe it is. I believe She was born within sight of where we are now. I'd like to know. I think we can find out. I want you to share the discovery with me.'

Cameron turned and gazed at them from the other side of the fire.

They were both sitting utterly still and stared back at him. Rose was trembling and Billy felt almost hypnotised. Then somewhere far back on the plain an elephant trumpeted.

Billy shook his head. Somehow the sound, at once plaintive and powerful, broke the spell. Reality, the reality of the living valley, broke back in.

Billy knew exactly what Cameron had been trying to do.

Using all his extraordinary powers of persuasion and eloquence, he'd been trying to seduce them – Rose above all but Billy too. He'd tried to sweep them away with him, to compel them into accepting that what lay beneath the valley was infinitely more important than anything that lived upon it. He'd offered Rose a partnership, a share in the glory and excitement of everything they found there. He'd told her it was her duty and destiny to join him.

Billy had been right. Cameron hadn't given up. Billy didn't know how far he'd go, but he sensed the man would stop at nothing.

Rose sat very still. 'The elephants—' she began.

'The elephants will be protected,' Cameron interrupted her. 'Of course they need water. Well, we'll create a lake for them. You can plan it with me.'

'But the valley will change—'

Again Cameron didn't let her finish. 'My dear, the valley is always changing. It has been since it was formed. It's changing right now as we talk. It'll go on doing so long after you and I have gone.'

417

Rose hesitated. She felt cold and confused and frightened.

'But people will come,' she tried again. 'They will really change everything.'

'Rose, people are spreading everywhere,' he answered. 'They've been doing it since the first ones walked away from here. We can't stop that. At least with me there's a chance of controlling them for a while.'

Rose closed her eyes.

She couldn't fight him. He was too strong, too articulate, too intelligent. Every argument she tried to put forward, he simply countered with another that sounded so much more logical and convincing it made her feel humiliated, a naughty ignorant child called to judgement by an adult.

At her side Billy didn't move.

He felt impotent, powerless, a bystander watching a grossly unequal and unfair struggle. Once he'd thought of himself battling for Rose's soul. Now Cameron was doing the same, but he had infinitely more weapons in his armoury than Billy ever had.

The same coldness that filled Rose enveloped Billy.

'Rose.'

Cameron came round the fire and stopped above her. Rose seemed to shrink back at his approach.

'The valley is the most important archeological site that can be or ever will be found,' he said. 'However it happens, it's going to be excavated. Nothing and no one, not even you, is going to stop that. But I've asked you to be my partner in doing it. I know it's what your mother would want. I know we can look after the elephants. I know you've got the whole of your life ahead of you and whatever you think now, you won't want to spend it on a remote and dusty African plain.'

Cameron bent over her.

'I ask you for the last time, my dear, will you join me?'

Rose slid deeper back into her chair. She felt herself becoming ever smaller, more fragile, more frightened and vulnerable.

Cameron had gathered all his arguments together in one final statement that was both an appeal and a command. His voice was still hypnotic and beguiling, but there was an edge of menace in it now. She gazed up at him. He was smiling but his eyes were chill and brutal.

Rose thought she was going to faint.

She struggled against the waves of dizziness flooding over her, and bit her tongue so hard she knew from the salty taste in her mouth she'd drawn blood.

And then suddenly from nowhere an image of the new-born calf came to her – the wrinkled glistening creature lying among the water lilies and the mother elephant's eyes locking with her own, and the snarl of the leaping lion and the detonation of the rifle-shot.

'No!' Rose shouted.

She threw herself sideways out of the chair.

She tumbled into the embers of the fire and smelled the stench of scorched flesh, her own flesh, she dimly realised. She clambered to her feet and shook the sparks from her clothes and her skin, unaware of the pain.

The terror was fading with every second now, but she had to be away from the overpowering malevolent presence that threatened to suffocate her. She was still trembling and kept backing away, but she gazed at Cameron in implacable clear-eyed defiance.

'No,' she repeated, her voice shaky but stronger every moment. 'No one's going to have this valley. No one at all except the elephants.'

'Is that your last word?' Cameron asked.

Rose couldn't control the tremors running over her, but she managed to nod.

'Very well,' he went on. 'But in times to come, young lady, remember this. Remember I wanted a different solution. Remember I offered you everything and you turned it all down.'

He reached into the inside pocket of his safari jacket and pulled out a bundle of papers. He tossed them down on the table where they'd eaten.

'They're copies of an application for an expropriation order on all the land your mother left you here,' he said. 'They've been filed in Nairobi on grounds of the site's international archeological importance and its national tourist value. There is nothing you can do to contest it. I've many friends in government, Rose. The order, I promise you, will be granted.'

Cameron smiled at her.

'It isn't your valley any longer. What remains is a formality. Within months, or even weeks, it will belong to my foundation in partnership with the nation. Which means, you could say, it belongs to me.' A gust of the night breeze caught the fire and the flames crackled upwards.

It was the only sound in the silence which followed. Billy had jumped up when Rose threw herself out of the chair. All three of them were on their feet and for an instant standing immobile. And then it happened. Something in Cameron snapped.

Billy never knew why.

Cameron had won everything he wanted, he'd made sure of that before he landed in the valley. He could have turned, gone to bed, and waited to cross the river and drive away in the morning. He didn't. Perhaps it was the stubborn defiance in Rose's face. Perhaps it was because he needed not just to conquer but humiliate, and he'd failed. For once all of his skills, all his silver-tongued eloquence, all of his authority, intellect and wealth, had been challenged by a mere child.

Perhaps it ran even deeper than that.

Maybe he'd never possessed Violet and in taking the valley from her daughter, he'd have won control over Rose as he hadn't ever been able to over her mother. He hadn't succeeded. It wasn't Rose who'd been humiliated. It was him.

At that moment the reason didn't matter. Nothing mattered except what Cameron did next.

He took three or four great strides forward, moving so quickly that Rose didn't even have time to step back. He caught her shirt in one of his massive hands, and wrenched her up off the ground. He held her in front of him and shook her like a rag-doll.

'You vain and stupid little whore!' he bellowed. 'I offer you everything and you're too mindless to understand what it means!'

He began to beat her across the face, clubbing her with

the open palm of his other hand so her head jerked dizzily backwards and forwards.

Billy heard the sickening thuds of the first few hammering blows, saw a smear of blood on Rose's lip, then he launched himself forward. He drove into Cameron, swung one arm round his waist, and put up the other to block the blows he was raining down on Rose. Then Billy swivelled. He kicked out and tried to knock Cameron's legs from beneath him.

The man was heavy and immensely strong, far stronger for his age than Billy had believed possible. He must also have been taught to fight ruthlessly at close quarters. He staggered but kept his balance. He hurled Rose away, broke Billy's grip, and kicked at Billy's own leg.

Billy had taken his eyes off Cameron for an instant and glanced at Rose to see if she was all right.

Cameron seized the chance.

He was wearing hard-tipped bush boots. The toe of one of them smashed into the nerve just below Billy's knee. An agonising wave of pain flooded over him. Billy coughed and reeled. As his legs wobbled drunkenly, he realised he was going to fall on his back. Before he could even collapse, he saw Cameron wrench out the ironwood post that tethered the tent's guy-ropes and raise it above his head.

The post crashed down on Billy's shoulders and neck. Afterwards there was only darkness.

He was crawling along a tunnel of utter darkness. A winding claustrophobic tube of blackness like the underground passages the German legionnaires told him threaded the Westphalian coal mines.

Every few moments his head struck one of the rocks protruding from the roof, and a jolt of pain ran down from his skull to his ankles. His head dizzy and aching, he crawled on. His nostrils were clogged with dust. Finally he saw a speck of light. He inched towards it. The light became a flare and then a blaze, so fierce and hot he couldn't stand its incandescence.

Billy moaned and turned on to his stomach.

'Billy!'

Dimly he knew the voice. He lifted his head wearily and glanced back. There was someone behind him holding the source of the blaze. After a while he realized it wasn't a blaze at all, only a candle, and he recognised the face above it. It was Rose.

He battled to remember. Piece by piece at first and then in a gathering wave, everything came back. He struggled to his knees.

'Where am I?'

'By the fire.'

Billy blinked at the circle of glowing embers and the last piece fell into place.

'Where's Cameron?'

'He left about five minutes ago,' Rose answered. 'He packed up his things and called for one of the boys to row him across the river. He's going to walk up to his truck and drive to the Laager.'

'How do you know?'

Billy winced as he spoke. His head was throbbing and he could feel a great bruise swelling up at the base of his neck.

'He came here before he left. He said he was going to have you arrested for attempted murder.' Rose hesitated. 'He said all sorts of other things. Billy, I think he's mad—'

She broke off. 'Are you all right?'

She reached out to touch his neck, but Billy brushed her hand away. He glanced up at the sky.

The moon was high and full but darkened every few seconds by racing bands of cloud. He thought furiously. Five minutes. Cameron would barely have reached the middle of the river. Billy listened. He was right. He could hear the distant splash of a paddle in the water.

'Rose.' He climbed unsteadily to his feet. 'Run to my camp. Get the rifle. Beside it under the bed there's an oilskin gun pouch. Get that too and a box of ammunition from the pack.'

'But Billy—'

'Just run, for Christ's sake!' he snapped furiously.

Rose vanished white-faced into the dark.

Billy walked up and down. He bent and touched his toes.

He rocked from side to side and pivoted slowly on his hips. He picked up the jug of water from the table and emptied it over his head. He spotted the bottle of brandy Cameron had produced after dinner and gulped from the neck, feeling the fierce strong liquor sear through him.

Then he stopped. He breathed in deeply and clinically took stock of himself. He was still giddy, his shoulder was lacerated and stiffening, and his arm muscles kept convulsing with darts of pain. But at least, Billy knew, he was functioning. As a soldier it was what he'd been paid to do in combat all his life. It was no different now.

He heard the sound of running footsteps and glanced round. Rose reappeared with the rifle, the pouch, and the ammunition. She thrust them into his hands.

'What are you going to do, Billy?' she asked, panting. She was frowning and her face was streaked with sweat.

'He'll be on the far bank by now.' Billy slipped the gun into the pouch and pocketed the ammunition. 'He's still got two hours' walk ahead to his truck. I'm going to swim across. I'll be faster. I know the paths and he doesn't.'

Billy was heading for the river as he spoke. He reached the bank and glanced back at Rose as she hurried behind him.

'Men like Cameron,' he said, 'they'll kill everything in their path. He's welcome to try to see me dead, but not the valley and the elephants. I'm going to stop him.'

He plunged into the water.

58

Billy knelt and listened.

He'd only just waded out of the river and tightened his grip on the rifle as the water cascaded off him. He could hear nothing except the rustlings and stirrings, the calls and cries, of the African night.

Billy peered round.

There were half a dozen game-paths leading up from the bank to the plateau on top of the gorge. He'd explored two or three of them on his visits to the Laager over the past month. One, broader and clearer of thorn bush than the others, had obviously been favoured by recent generations of animals as they came down to drink.

It was the one Cameron would almost certainly use. Billy picked another steeper and narrower path that angled up to the south. He checked it first for human footprints. There was no trace of them, only the cloven spoor and pug-marks of animals.

Billy began to climb.

He moved with short rhythmic steps, leaning forward against the angle of the slope and trying to ignore the hammering in his head and the throbbing ache in his shoulder. Occasionally he used the rifle to lever himself upwards. It was something he'd been trained all his life never to do, but now it didn't matter.

If Cameron got away he'd destroy everything. There was only one way to stop him and that was to kill him before he reached the truck.

Billy had taken the decision beside the fire within a few moments of regaining consciousness. Rose was right. Cameron was mad. Mad and vengeful and obsessive. Billy had heard it in the compulsive way he'd talked, he'd seen it in the savage way he'd beaten Rose, he'd felt it in his frenzied attack on himself.

Cameron was possessed by some dark and strange dream, some demon. Maybe the dream had haunted him for years, gnawing at his brain, worming its way into his consciousness, distorting and perverting his thoughts until his mind was gripped by insanity. Now, with the discovery of the valley, he'd let nothing stand in his way until the dream was realised.

Billy went on.

Every ten minutes he stopped and listened. He knew the paths but not well enough to know when they converged on each other and ran together before parting again. Each time he strained his ears, trying to pick up the sound of Cameron's ascent. For an hour and a half there was nothing. Then close to the top of the gorge he heard it – the tramp of footsteps and the grunts for breath.

Billy froze and listened again.

The noise came from just above him and thirty or forty yards to his left. Cameron had climbed even more quickly than Billy had thought possible. He was only a few hundred yards below Finlay Hampton's long-abandoned campsite, the obvious place for his vehicle to have been left.

Billy scrambled on. He was still trying to move as silently as possible but he was climbing more quickly now. He had to get above Cameron before the man reached his truck.

Sweat streamed off him.

He felt the thorns scrape and gouge at his legs. He heard the oilskin of the rifle's pouch rip as a spear-sharp branch jagged and tore through it. He stumbled on an almost vertical bank of sand, slid back, and used the rifle to heave himself up again.

Suddenly he was over the rim of the gorge and on to the gently sloping shelf of the plateau. The clouds had gone and the moon was high. He started to run, weaving between the trees and ducking into the pools of shadow beneath. Then he spotted the truck in front of him, exactly where he guessed it would be.

Billy raced up to it. He pulled the cover off the rifle, threw himself down, and rested the barrel on the fender, trying to still the heaving of his chest.

He looked through the sights and waited.

Cameron appeared eighty yards ahead of him in the moonlight. First his head emerged over the lip of the ground, then his broad heavy shoulders, then his entire body. He was moving steadily and purposefully, showing no sign at all that he'd just made the steep two-hour climb up from the river.

He paused and peered ahead. Cameron too had seen the truck. As he came on again, Billy aimed and fired at the centre of his chest.

Even before he heard the detonation, Billy knew something was wrong.

The trigger grated as he pulled it, and the barrel jerked slightly to the right. Billy looked up. He was just in time to see Cameron stagger slightly and clutch his arm. Then he disappeared.

Billy tried to pump another round into the chamber. The mechanism grated again and then stuck. He fought furiously with it for a second or two, and stopped. He knew what had happened. When he'd ripped the protective cover as he levered himself upwards, sand must have poured in and clogged the breech.

The weapon was useless.

'For Christ's sake, stop! I'm Mr Cameron! Who the hell's up there?'

There was no fear in the voice that roared up the slope, only fury and outrage.

Billy tossed the rifle aside and waited.

A silence followed.

He knew he'd hit Cameron but it could only have been a flesh wound. With the gun slicing to the right, the high velocity bullet had probably gone straight through his arm. It would have made a small and deeply painful puncture in his flesh, but it wouldn't have incapacitated him.

It took only a few moments after Cameron's initial surprise and shock for him to realise what Billy knew he was bound to guess – that it could only have been Billy who'd fired.

'Is that you, Ramsden?'

He didn't answer. All he registered that he was no longer Billy, he was Ramsden now, and Cameron had moved. The shout came from a slightly different direction.

'If it is you, Ramsden, listen to me.' The voice echoed up the slope again. 'I think you're mad, both of you, you and that little slut down there. She's of no interest to me. Nor are you, but for your own sake take this in. I was going to have you arrested for attempted murder. Now you've doubled that.'

Cameron was still moving.

Billy cocked his head and tracked the changing position of Cameron's voice. He was edging to the north, to where the escarpment dipped down towards the plain.

'I'm prepared to let it drop. Go back to the river and take my boat. Collect your things and get out of the country. As soon as I hear you in the water, that'll be the end of it. Nothing's going to happen to the girl either. Understand?'

Billy remained silent.

He felt for his belt and slid his hand along until he found the sheath of his hunting knife. He gripped the knife's handle, pulled it out, and ran the blade lightly across his palm. Billy let his breath out in relief. The knife was razor-sharp and undamaged.

'Can you hear me, Ramsden?' the shout came again. 'They put people in a black prison for life for attempted murder here. For Christ's sake, you know that! Be sensible, man! Answer me!'

Cameron's voice was more distant now. Billy got to his knees. His mind racing, he tried to work out what Cameron was doing.

The man was strong, resourceful, and cunning.

By now he'd be certain who it was who'd fired. He'd also know there was no chance of a response to his offer – he wouldn't believe Billy would trust him any more than he'd trust Billy.

Billy glanced at the gun. He could strip and clean it but it needed light to work by, oil, and time. He had none of them. Cameron didn't know that. Billy thought again, trying to put himself inside Cameron's mind.

Cameron had been buying time. He'd assumed Billy would come after him with the rifle. Meanwhile he was placing as much distance as possible between them. When he calculated he was far enough away, he'd brush out his tracks and hide up in the bush.

The Laager was Cameron's sanctuary – his only sanctuary.

As dawn approached he'd drop down to the plain. Cameron had lived in Africa all his life. He'd know on the plain he'd be impossible to follow. The scrub would hide him and the thick bed of dry grass would absorb his footprints like a sponge. He'd circle round and choose his own way back to the lodge.

If Billy followed his spoor now – and in spite of the moon it would be immensely difficult to trace the prints under the deep shadows beneath the thorn bushes overhanging the paths – Cameron would hear him long before he found him. Billy was virtually certain he didn't have a gun, but he'd seen a heavy hunting knife like his own hanging from Cameron's belt.

Billy shook his head grimly.

To try to track Cameron in the dark would be walking into a death-trap. Cats, not humans, were programmed and equipped to hunt by night.

All he could do was exactly what he guessed Cameron was doing.

Billy crawled away from the truck. He stood up in the bush and made his way along a game-path in the direction from which he'd last heard Cameron shout. He found a hollow under a close-growing mopane copse which a family of warthogs had hollowed out as a shelter against the winter rains.

Billy cut a branch from one of the mopane saplings and returned to the clearing. Walking backwards, he swept away his footprints. Then he slipped into the hollow and curled up with his knees close to his chest.

The bruise on his neck had risen into a great dark and swollen lump. Each time he moved, plagued by the fleas the warthogs had scattered in the hollow, small shivers of pain shot through him. He tossed restlessly and coiled his arms across his face.

Somewhere close to him – probably less than half a mile

away – Billy knew that Cameron, also wounded, would be doing the same. They were linked by more than pain and discomfort. They were bound together, Billy thought, by a common purpose: to kill each other.

Hovering between sleep and wakefulness, Billy tried to rest.

As soon as the first thin shell of dawn light began to seep into the sky, Billy crawled out of the hollow and stood up.

In all he'd managed to doze for about an hour. His eyes were raw and bloodshot, and his shoulder had stiffened up so much in the chill and dew of the night he found he could only swing his arm a few inches. It needed ten minutes of massage and exercises before he'd pumped enough blood into the muscles to be able to move.

Then he set off towards the north.

Billy picked up Cameron's tracks an hour later. He squatted and studied the footprints. They'd been made while there was still enough of the night's moisture in the air to glue together the earth round the outside rims and the criss-crossed sole marks. Now, as the sun and the temperature rose, the impressions were beginning to crumble and break down.

Billy calculated.

Cameron was doing exactly what he'd expected. He'd left with the first glimmerings of light and was heading down for the plain. He was an hour ahead which in the bush meant about two miles.

Billy got to his feet.

He still had one immense advantage. Cameron believed he was carrying a rifle. Cameron might have tried to ambush him in the dark. By day it was far too risky. All he could do now was run.

Billy's lips were drying as the air warmed. He licked them. For once in Cameron's long life, it occurred to Billy, he wasn't the predator and hunter. He was the hunted.

Billy pressed on.

Another hour later, with Cameron's tracks still leading him, Billy reached the northern edge of the escarpment. He looked down. The ground fell gently towards the plain. In the distance the sluggish metallic coil of the river meandered its way out of the valley and vanished towards the west. Until then he'd been moving along game-paths of bare earth through the rim of the mountain forest.

Now the trees stopped. In their place waves of pale matted grass flowed up towards him, rippling under the morning breeze as if they were being pushed forward by a tide that lapped and surged round the islands of thorn. From now on there would be no spoor to follow. The tangled layer of dead vegetation would swallow up any print.

Billy would be tracking Cameron blind.

Sand and dead pollen rose in plumes from the grass and spun in tiny dust devils towards his face. A fit of choking coughing convulsed him as the dust seeped into his mouth. Billy retched. He managed to swallow and spit it away, but his throat felt so dry and parched that for a moment he could hardly breathe.

He recovered and stood there heaving.

All he wanted in the world was water. He wanted it to drink, to swill round his mouth, to gulp down, and lubricate the desiccated shrunken channels of his body, to pour over his limbs and cool himself, to immerse himself in it, bathe his neck and his shoulder, and come out invigorated and healed.

Water was the one thing thing Billy had overlooked.

Now as the sweltering African sun rose he knew the discarded rifle barely mattered. Ahead of both of them were hours of dehydrating dryness. Like the elephants, he and Cameron needed the river. Without it they would first become incapable of moving and then they would die.

Cameron couldn't head for the Laager. Like Billy he had to go back to the river.

Billy set off after him.

He was two-thirds of the way down the slope when he spotted Cameron. He dropped to his knees and narrowed his eyes as he peered intently ahead. The man wasn't as far in front of him as he'd guessed. He was less than a mile away. Perhaps the gathering heat or his wound had slowed him, but he was walking steadily and was heading, as Billy knew he had to do, for the river.

Billy frowned and his mind raced again.

He was hunting.

Every hunt required constant reassessment, sometimes hour by hour, sometimes minute by minute. Last night Billy had assumed Cameron would circle across the plain and head back up into the Aberdares for the Laager. Lack of water had stopped him. Before he could try to reach the lodge, Cameron had to go to the river and drink.

Cameron, Billy guessed, would lie up by the river until darkness came again. When it did, when night fell, he'd head for the lodge. By day he would reckon Billy and his rifle held the mastery. At night it was different. Then he'd either be able to escape, or if not, he'd at least have an even chance of killing Billy in the darkness.

He had to kill Cameron before darkness fell.

If he didn't, by next morning either Cameron would be gone or it was possible Billy himself would be dead.

The sun lifted, the last of the mist cleared from the plain, the heat and humidity intensified.

For hour after hour as the morning passed and then the furnace-like temperatures of the early afternoon rose, Billy followed him. The occasional vulture or battaleur eagle patrolled the sky. A bush lark sang, a grey lourie, the 'go-away' bird, called mournfully, once a jackal barked in anxiety, once a sleeping in the shadows lion, its rest disturbed, growled in anger before lowering its head on its paws again.

Otherwise there was nothing – only Africa, arid and golden and lonely.

As the hours went by Billy didn't know whether Cameron had glanced back and glimpsed him – he tried to hide himself by slipping from one island of thorn to the next. It wasn't important. Whether they could see each other or not, they both knew each other was there.

It was a war of attrition, physically and mentally. Physically they were both wounded and tiring, and both desperately needed to drink. Mentally the battle was one of strategy and ultimately of survival. Cameron wanted darkness. Billy needed light.

As the sun began to lower Billy suddenly wrinkled his nose and stood up.

He had followed Cameron all day, lurking in the shadow of thorn bushes, weaving and darting from one copse to the next. All the while, from his occasional glimpses of his quarry, he had been closing on Cameron. Now they were close to the river and although Cameron was out of his sight once again, Billy guessed he was within a hundred yards of the man.

Billy sniffed the air.

A warm rank smell filled his nostrils. He recognised it immediately. Buffalo. He didn't even need to scan the ground to find them. He licked his cracked and swollen lips, wiped the sweat from his eyes, and saw them in front of him.

It was a herd of two or three hundred animals, gathered shoulder to shoulder.

They were about a hundred yards away, the distance he thought separated him from Cameron. They stood facing him in a menacing dark grey crescent like one of the Zulu warriors' fearsome battle impis. They'd come from the river and their bodies were shining with water. Billy could see steam rising from their hides and their sweeping horns tossing angrily and their small eyes gleaming as they grunted and stamped the earth.

He stood utterly still. Individually a hippo or a cow elephant might be more unpredictable, but a herd of buffalo was the most dangerous concentration of animals in Africa. If they charged they would scythe down everything in front of them like a raging hurricane.

Billy waited.

He'd expected to see Cameron too. For a moment there was no sign of him. Then a figure rose from the grass midway between Billy and the herd. Across Billy's mind flashed the realisation Cameron had been doing just what he'd been doing – moving and hiding.

Cameron's left arm was thrust out awkwardly from his body and Billy could see it was coated with dried blood. Cameron seemed to ignore it. He didn't look back. He stood gazing at the herd, his white hair ruffled by the breeze. Then slowly and deliberately he walked towards the buffalo.

Billy stiffened and stared at the man.

A ripple ran over the herd. Horns heaved and flashed ironwood-brown and bone-white against the sky. The animals at either end of the crescent surged forward, hesitated, and stopped. Cameron walked unhesitatingly on. On the evening breeze the herd's smell, heightened by discharges of fear and confusion, was ranker and more pungent by the second.

Billy watched disbelievingly.

Cameron was almost enclosed by animals now. Calfs moaned, cows bellowed, bull buffalo roared. Dust rose in clouds from the grass under the pawing feet. Still Cameron strode on towards them. And then it snapped. A final great pulse quivered through the herd and the animals launched themselves forward in a wave of blind murderous destruction.

Billy didn't know what happened.

He heard the drumming of the stampeding hooves, he saw the surging grey and mud-black tide sweeping towards him, he hurled himself to the ground. He was lucky. In front of where he took cover was the thick stump of an old lightning-blasted acacia. The herd parted round it like an ocean breaker shorn in two by an ancient rock, and galloped away.

Minutes later Billy stood up.

He was dizzy and his mouth was full of sand. He spat the sand out. His nostrils were so dry and his mouth so parched it was difficult to breathe. He gulped and sucked at the air, and drew some oxygen into his lungs. When he fell a sharp root or perhaps even a blow from a buffalo's hoof had sliced through the bruise on his neck.

His shoulder was sheeted with blood. Billy tried to staunch the flow. Then he walked forward.

When he found Cameron he thought at first that the man was a buffalo calf that had been crushed to death in the herd's charge. Then Billy saw his boots and the ragged tatters of his safari jacket. Cameron lay half-buried in the grass and trampled earth, broken and shattered by the passage of the herd's feet.

Billy stopped and knelt beside him. He pulled one of

Cameron's wrists from the furrow where it had been battered into the ground and felt for his pulse. There was still a faint movement under the torn skin.

Billy lifted up his lacerated head and held it cradled in his hands.

'Can you hear me, Cameron?' he asked.

For several moments there was no reply. Eventually a voice whispered back at him.

'Yes.'

There was a terrible choking cough and silence. After a long while the voice whispered again.

'Is there water?'

'I'll go to the river.'

Billy laid his head back on the ground.

He ran down to the river, waded into it and and submerged himself, cooling his body and gulping the water greedily at the same time. Billy shivered with relief. Then he took off his shirt, dipped it again, and returned to Cameron. He propped up his head and squeezed water from the cloth over the man's face and into his mouth.

The water briefly revived him. His eyes flickered open and he managed to focus on Billy.

'Had to drink,' Cameron muttered. 'Thought they'd let me.'

Billy said nothing.

He was still wringing out the shirt over Cameron's skin. The man must either already have been delirious from lack of water when he walked forward, or so arrogant and confident that he really believed the herd would part in front of him.

'You tried to kill me.'

Billy remained silent.

'No need now,' the gurgling cough rasped out again and a spasm ran through him. 'They did it for you.'

Billy knew Cameron was only moments away from death. He hesitated. He felt that in spite of everything Cameron had done, he should say something. Billy remembered some of the last words Violet had spoken to him.

'Before she died,' Billy said, 'your wife asked me to tell you

434

that you'd saved her. She was grateful and she loved you for it. Can you understand what I'm saying?'

Cameron's chest heaved and he gave a small grunt of acknowledgement. Billy waited but he didn't say anything.

'Is there any more I can do?' Billy asked after a while.

He waited again, his head lowered towards Cameron's mouth. This time he thought Cameron had died. Then as Billy reached out to pick up his mangled wrist and see if the pulse had stopped, a final convulsive tremor quivered over the wreckage of Cameron's body.

'More water,' the thin husky voice croaked up at him. 'Water like your elephants need.'

The words were disconnected and wandering.

Billy looked down at him and frowned. For an instant Billy almost imagined the shadow of a wry ironic smile had crossed Cameron's face.

Billy rose.

The last surge of the day's heat was so intense his shirt was already dry and stiffening with grey salty rims from the sweat with which his own body had saturated the cloth. He went back to the river and soaked it in the shallows.

When he returned Cameron was dead.

59

Exhausted and wasted by dehydration, Billy slept for most of the night out on the plain.

Every hour he woke and went back to the river to drink. Once in the darkest part of the night he heard the calls of hyenas and the barking of jackals. The scavengers had found Cameron's body. He lay down in the grass and slept fitfully again.

He got back to camp just before dawn.

Billy didn't go down to the river. He stopped and waited on the low ridge above one of the river's bends, looking down over the tent and the still-smouldering fire as the stars dimmed and the sky began to pale. For some reason he was sure Rose would appear to meet him. He was right. He'd been there barely ten minutes and the sun was still below the horizon when the tent flap opened and she stepped outside.

She was barefoot and wearing a long loose sweater against the early-morning chill. She glanced round, not sleepily but keenly as if she'd already been awake for some time. Then she lifted her head towards the ridge. She saw his silhouette instantly, almost as if she'd been expecting him to be there.

Billy saw her stiffen.

He didn't know what he was going to do, whether he was going to call up to him, but he made an urgent movement with his hands, gesturing for her to be silent. Rose understood. Her safari boots were beside the tent door. She put them on and ran up to him.

'Billy, what happened?'

She was gazing at his arm, her face taut with anxiety.

He glanced down.

He'd forgotten the bruise had been sliced through when

the herd charged. The wound had opened again as he walked back and the whole right-hand side of his body was covered in blood. Blood was still pumping out now.

'Don't worry,' he said. 'I'm fine. Just go back and fetch my medical box and the small bag I keep by my bed. Meet me by the big rock on the pool below the tent. And for Christ's sake don't wake the boys.'

She opened her mouth and hesitated. Then without speaking she nodded. As she turned and ran back, Billy headed down towards the pool.

'Give the dry side of the melomine pads a good sprinkling of powder, put them on running longways along the cut, and tie them fairly loosely with the bandage.'

It was five minutes later.

Billy was lying on the sand propped up against the rock above the pool with Rose kneeling beside him. She had a safety-pin between her lips. She pinned the last length of bandage into place and leant back.

'Will that do?'

His face was still strained and tense.

Billy lifted his shoulder and winced. The bruised flesh was swollen and throbbing, but he'd injected himself with antibiotics and knew he should be safe from infection. It would take time but the wound would heal.

He managed a grin. 'People have tried to hammer me more often than you've had hot dinners, young lady. They haven't succeeded yet. These are just scratches.'

'What happened, Billy?' Rose repeated the question.

He thought for a moment. Then he shrugged and told her.

'It's over,' he finished. 'That's all.'

'Does it mean—?'

He didn't give her a chance to finish. 'It means whatever you want it to mean,' he interrupted. 'Cameron's dead. That's all that matters. The rest is up to you and the valley.'

She looked at him steadily for a long time. Then she asked, 'Do you think he loved my mother?'

Billy thought for an equally long time before replying.

'I'd like to think he did. It would have made it better both for him and for Violet. But in truth, no, I doubt it. I think he was only concerned about himself and what he was looking for.'

She frowned. 'Did anyone love my mother?'

'Are you asking me?' Billy smiled.

Rose smiled back, a quick heartwarming smile. 'Apart from you, of course.'

He thought again. 'It's better to ask what she loved. You know what that was. This place and the elephants. Look after them both for her. That's probably the only answer you need.

'It's going to be hard. But you're young, you're strong, you're rich. If the Kenyan government's got any sense, it'll work with you. I think you'll manage. I think the valley's in safe hands.'

Billy stood up and touched her cheek. Then he limped down the bank and gazed across the river.

The sun had just risen and the water glittered in the early light. On the sand below was the print of the night's spoor. A leopard had come down to drink, lily-trotters had patterned its pugmarks with the delicate leaf-like marks of their claws, a hippo had lumbered back from its grazing pastures and scored the ground with the great scoops of its feet.

He closed his eyes and inhaled deeply.

The dawn air was bright and sharp and clean. A fish eagle called and somewhere an elephant trumpeted. His skin tingled and the hairs rose on the back of his neck. It was like the first morning not just of his life, when he'd stood in almost the same place as a child with Violet and old Ngoro, the first morning of the world.

This was an African morning. This was what it had been like in the Garden of Eden. This was what Adam and Eve had woken to. This was what he'd been ready to kill to save.

Billy turned. Rose had come down the bank too and was standing just behind him.

'I'm going,' he said.

'Going?' She stared at him, startled. 'Where are you going? Why?'

The questions tumbled out of her in confusion. He cut them off.

'Sooner or later, and it won't be very long, people are going to start looking for Cameron. They won't find him, but there's no point in either of us answering needless questions. You didn't see Cameron or me from the moment we left camp. Nor did the boys. Understand?'

Frantically Rose tried to take in what he was saying. She nodded.

'Cameron and I walked out and didn't come back. That's all you know. None of this ever happened.'

He pointed to the medical box.

'What's really going to happen is you're going to take me across the river. I'll pick up my truck on the other side, and drive south. I'll ditch the truck near the Tanzanian border. Once I'm in Tanzania, I'll fly to Europe.'

Rose fought to assemble her thoughts. Almost incoherently she started to argue.

Billy ignored her.

He headed for the mooring post where the inflatable craft Cameron had brought with him in the helicopter and used to cross the river was swinging in the stream. Five minutes afterwards he and Rose were standing on the far bank.

'Take the boat straight back,' he instructed. 'The boys don't know much about spoor, but trample out my prints just in case. Then go back to camp. With any luck they'll only just be getting up.'

'But Billy—'

Rose caught his arm. She looked at him, distraught and imploring.

'You can't leave like this. You can't just disappear.'

'I can,' he said curtly. 'For you, for your ma, for myself, for the valley and the elephants, of course I can.'

Rose shook her head. Her eyes filled with tears.

'Where can I find you again?'

Billy paused.

He'd been about to suggest Le P'tit Canard in Marseille. After Zimbabwe he wasn't sure he wanted to go back there. Somewhere else would be better.

'Paris,' he answered. 'There's a bar in the Rue Maubert on the left bank of the Seine. It's called La Vieille Rose, the old rose. Every year in October the Legion marches down the Champs-Elysées to commemorate Cameroun. Afterwards we go and drink.'

Billy thought of Paris.

The grey waters of the river in autumn. The leaves tumbling from the trees. The faded-green bookstalls above the quays. The couples strolling in the misty air with their arms round each other's shoulders. Lovers, most of them young lovers, students from the Sorbonne or the left bank art schools like the Académie de la Grande Chaumière.

He'd never done that.

If things had been different, if the world and life and class and crime and wars and money had been different, long ago it might have happened. The sweet-smelling hair brushing his face might have been Violet's, the breast touching his arm might have been hers, the laughter carried away on the wind hers too.

The world wasn't like that. The world was brutal and simple. It had its system. It divided people and kept them apart. It had kept him and Violet apart until it was too late. Except – perhaps – it wasn't ever too late.

He looked at Rose. Blurred with tears as they were, they were still her mother's eyes.

The people might be different, but the Seine still flowed, in the old-fashioned hotels the sheets still smelled of lavender, the coffee still tasted gritty and strong, and the children still played with balloons and marbles in the Tuileries gardens.

'I'll see you in Paris,' he said.

He reached out and brushed her cheek again, then turned and walked up the bank.

'Billy!' Rose called after him. 'What happens if you're not there?'

He paused and glanced back.

'I'm a soldier,' he said. 'Soldiers go to war. If I'm not there this October, that'll be the reason. Maybe not next October either, perhaps not even the one after that. But one of these days I'll be there. Soldiers always keep a rendezvous.'

As he spoke an elephant trumpeted again.

He raised his eyes and looked across the river. Slowly the

great grey shapes of the herd, the dew still glistening on their backs, began to emerge from the trees and move down to the water to drink.

As always the matriarch with her calf beside her led them.

Billy turned and walked on.